Praise for *Song of Miriam* by Pearl Wolf:

"The book rings with truth—emotionally, psychologically and politically. There are moments of sheer lyric poetry and emotion. I was completely moved to another time and place. The scenes of intimacy are unforgettably enticing as well as dignified. An excellent 'read' which drew me into the lives of the people and their story."—Rabbi Harvey M. Tattelbaum, Rabbi Emeritus—Temple Shaaray Tefila New York

"The book captures the essence of Jewish life during the reign of Catherine The great and Alexander I. I found it to be exhilarating, sad, happy, lustful, plus filled with the tragedies which befell the Jewish community."—Dr. Sidney Sherter, Professor of Russian History, Southampton College, Southampton, New York

"Kudos to Pearl Wolf whose sweeping narrative weaves history and romance together in a book you simply can't put down."—Randye Lordon, award-winning author of the Sydney Sloane series, including *BROTHERLY LOVE, EAST OF NIECE and FATHER FORGIVE ME.*

Song of Miriam

Pearl Wolf

HILLIARD HARRIS
PUBLISHERS

Published by

HILLIARD  HARRIS
PUBLISHERS

P.O. Box 3358
Frederick, Maryland 21705-3358

Song of Miriam Copyright © 2003 by Pearl Wolf

First Edition

ISBN 1-59133-025-4

Designed by HILLIARD HARRIS

Cover design by S. A. Reilly
Cover art: Konstantin Flavitsky (1830-1866),
(detail from) *Princess Tarakanova, 1864*
The State Tretyakov Gallery, Moscow, Russia

Manufactured/Printed in the United States of America
2003

Dedication

To my grandchildren:

Benjamin Ross Wolf

Michael Robert Wolf

Aidan Lance Okamoto-Wolf

Acknowledgements

It is my pleasure to acknowledge the expert help I received in the writing of this work. My editor, Carol Edwards, helped shape the final manuscript. Rabbi Harvey Tattelbaum, Rabbi Emeritus of Temple Shaaray Tefila in New York City, made sure the religious rituals of Judaism in the eighteenth century were correct. Dr. Sidney Sherter, Professor of Russian History at Southampton College in Southampton, New York, made invaluable suggestions on the history of the period. G. Miki Hayden helped with my synopsis. I am also grateful for the excellent advice on medical issues in the eighteenth century that I received from Dr. Brian Goldstein, Melville, New York and Dr. Rick Nedelman, Cincinnati, Ohio. The staff of *A La Vieille Russie* in New York City, a museum-like establishment that sells eighteenth century Russian jewelry and artifacts, taught me a great deal about the jewelry Russian Royalty favored.

In addition, I want to thank Dr. Jeri Fink, Shelley Freydont, Stephen Hausler, Randye Lordon, Marilyn Newman, and Alice Orr all of whom enriched my life and encouraged me along the way. A special thanks to Joe Silver, who is the perfect model for Josef Brodsky.

Permission for the quotation from *Catherine the Great*, a biography by Joan Hazlip was granted by ICM for Macmillan.

If errors have found their way into these pages, I offer sincere apologies to the reader. The errors are all mine.

Pearl Wolf

"No event was ever more publicized and dramatized than the empress of Russia's voyage to the Crimea...decried by Potemkin's enemies as a gigantic hoax of cardboard villages. The empress' journey...cost the country nearly ten million rubles. It was made with the double purpose of impressing Europe and terrifying the Turks. Her guests included the ambassadors of Austria, France, and England...The empress spent three months at Kiev to await the breaking of the ice on the Dniepr."

"On January 18, 1787, fourteen coaches mounted on sled, one hundred and twenty-four sleighs, with forty more held in reserve, and five hundred and sixty horses set out from Tsarskoye-Selo...on a journey of nearly 4000 miles."

CATHERINE THE GREAT, Joan Haslip. G. P. Putnam's Sons. New York. C197 pp.303-309

Book One
Kiev 1787

ONE

"Where are the Jews?" Prince Potemkin demanded upon his entrance into the Grand Ballroom. His booming voice caused heads to turn.

Fashioned after St. Nicholas Hall at the Winter Palace in St. Petersburg, the immense room was two hundred feet long and sixty-one feet wide. The walls were lined with pale, ivory colored silk and hung with enormous mirrors framed in gold. The floors were inlaid with marble and rare woods in intricate designs. Ornate candle-lit chandeliers cast a lovely glow over the guests and caused their jewelry to glitter and sparkle. Servants who wore elaborate surcoats emblazoned with the royal crest, red shoes and white stockings, stood like statuesque sentinels at every door. Tall lackeys in red turbans and black pantaloons silently opened doors. The Grand Staircase, flanked by huge marble columns and steps, was lined with Cossack Life Guards in scarlet tunics.

Tonight's Grand Ball celebrated Czarina Catherine's departure from St. Petersburg. Her Majesty would arrive in Kiev within three weeks and remain until the ice on the Dniepr River melted, at which time she and her entourage would set sail for the southern provinces. The ballroom was filled with Nobles, Caucasians, Hussars and Uhlans, some who had come from as far as the frontiers of China. Fountains overflowed with wine, barrels spouted vodka and champagne corks exploded as guests gorged on caviar and roasted meats.

The tempestuous love affair between Catherine and Potemkin was long over, yet rumors of a secret morganatic marriage persisted. The powerful prince, meticulous in the beribboned uniform of Field Marshall of the Army, waited impatiently for his young guests to be presented.

"Reb Dov Zeklinski and Madame Miriam Zeklinski, Sire," murmured his aide-de-camp.

"Charming." Potemkin appraised the young woman. She wore a pale ivory gown etched with seed pearls, a fetching contrast to her olive complexion and almond-shaped eyes.

"Arrange to see me, Zeklinski," Potemkin said to Dov, dismissing him with a wave of his hand. "The sooner the better. Shall we dance, Madame?"

Rumors flew through the air like wisps of smoke from a candle. Who was the mysterious woman led by Prince Potemkin? From which part of the empire had this exotic princess emerged? Persia? Byzantium? Her sultry eyes certainly suggested the orient. The ballroom buzzed with speculation, except for the few who knew who she was.

"Potemkin courts the Jews in public," Count Petrov said as he observed the prince's flagrant display. "He has the czarina's blessings, no doubt." The count was stout, his face bloated from years of excess food and drink. He had all to do to keep from scratching his head for relief from the irritating wig on his head.

"Beware, Petrov. You court treason with such talk."

"Nonsense. He taunts the nobility with this act. Is it not our duty to save Mother Russia from Jewish infidels?"

"But what can we do? Potemkin is powerful."

Petrov ignored the comment. "That blackguard has depleted the royal treasury for this unnecessary journey. He sees to it that the czarina's eyes will fall only on clean, whitewashed cottages, freshly gilded church spires and well-dressed serfs. Mark me, sirs. The day will come when the czar-killer of Ivan and Peter, and her lover will be called to account."

⌘

"Your beauty soothes our weary eyes, Madame Zeklinski."

"You flatter me, Sire," Miriam said. She curtsied as he bowed, and took the hand he offered as they reached the dance floor.

"Can you not see that all eyes are upon you tonight?"

"On the contrary, it is Your Majesty who draws all eyes."

The prince smiled. "Perhaps. Your French is flawless, you possess wit and you dance with grace. This bespeaks a superior education. Is this so with all Jewish women of your station?"

"My father's doing, sire. He will be honored to hear that you admire my tutoring since he insists on the finest education for his children."

"Please convey our compliments to your father, Madame. Did you know that the czarina is committed to the education of women? Her Majesty established the first school for Christian girls twenty years ago. There are many such schools now."

"A noble idea, Sire. Perhaps Jewish women might also be allowed to attend Her Majesty's schools one day." He raised an eyebrow, causing Miriam to wonder whether she'd been too bold. When the music ended, she curtsied.

"Our pleasure, Madame." Potemkin gave her hand to the tall officer who had presented her and her husband to the prince. His uniform of dark green jacket

2

and gold-braided cape, white pants and black boots marked him as an officer of the Preobrazhansky Guards, the czarina's battalion. He had fine blonde hair, a beard that barely concealed the scar on his right cheek, and seductive blue eyes that seemed to tease.

"Count Razovsky at your service, Madame."

"You can serve me best by returning me to my husband, then."

"At the moment, gentlemen who wish to take advantage of your husband's financial words of wisdom surround him. May I claim this dance? I prefer to be first before you are besieged by eager admirers."

"What do you mean, sir?"

"No need to pretend coyness, Madame. My meaning is clear. Now that the prince has favored you with the first dance of the evening, you can have any man here, but perhaps you already have a lover."

Miriam reddened. "What right have you to pose such an insolent question?"

His eyes widened in amused surprise. "Have I offended you? I meant only to flatter."

"You are wide of the mark, sir."

"My apologies, then. Please, Madame. Don't abandon me on such poor terms. My sister and Countess Gorov will be furious with me for having driven you off before an introduction."

She began to turn away, but he placed a restraining hand on her arm and added, "May I present my sister, Countess Anya Razovsky."

Miriam noted the young woman's handsome Slavic features; hair the color of fine wheat, pale blue eyes, fair skin very like delicate porcelain. The family resemblance was remarkable.

"And this is our dear friend, Countess Gorov," Razovsky continued, indicating the older woman at his sister's side.

"You're the Jewess? Where is your husband?" The older woman's lined face suggested a lively intelligence in spite of her startling questions.

"He is otherwise engaged at the moment."

"I wish to meet him. There were few Jewish subjects in Russia before the Polish Partition, you see. We must come to know one another better, my dear. Invite me to tea."

"My pleasure, Countess. Would Wednesday at three be suitable?"

"Of course. Anya shall escort me." The feisty old woman turned to the count. "Dance with me, Alexei, before I grow too old for such pleasures."

The count's sister smiled. "Take no offense, Madame Zeklinski. Natasha loves to shock, but she means no harm."

"No doubt," Miriam replied, flustered by the dowager, yet oddly not offended.

"Are you visiting our city?"

"No. My husband and I reside in Kiev."

"Forgive my ignorance. My brother and I have been abroad." The countess spoke with the breathless voice of youth, her smile friendly. "A fortunate journey for me since I met my betrothed, Prince Peter Bedorov, in Paris." The young countess liked the look of Miriam, sensing in her a kindred spirit. Perhaps she wants a friend as much as I do, she thought. For her part, Miriam was warmed by the woman's easy manner. She was also struck by the marked contrast to her insolent brother.

A young officer claimed the countess for a promised dance, but Miriam was not alone for long.

Count Razovsky asked, "May I have this dance?" Unable to invent a dignified way to refuse him, Miriam allowed the offensive officer to lead her to the floor.

"You dance well, Madame."

"Does that surprise you?"

"I see that I am not yet forgiven for my *faux pas*. I am determined that, in due time you shall." Miriam fled when the music ended, but the count had no time for reflection.

"Who was that mysterious woman you were dancing with, Alexei? Everyone's dying to know." Hannelore von Hals' impish green eyes shone like burnished emeralds. Her powdered wig, ringed in curls, was piled on top of her head in the current French fashion.

"She is Madame Zeklinski. Her husband's a financier."

"The Jewish tycoon whose name is on everyone's lips?"

"Yes. It is good to see you, Dunya."

"Dunya is no longer my name darling, an unpleasant reminder of my humble serf origins. I've discarded it for Hannelore."

"I never thought of you as a serf. Hannelore, eh? Suits you well."

"Madame Hannelore von Hals."

"So you married old von Hals. Congratulations, then."

"Offer me your condolences. Hermann died six months ago."

"Oh? Sorry."

"You needn't be. I saw to it that we had a good life together."

"I would not have expected any less of you."

"And how are you faring?"

"Alas, this day is one of the worst of my life."

"Are you in need of a sympathetic ear?"

"Badly."

"Do tell, then. Why so glum?"

"Potemkin gave me distressing news this morning. To make matters worse, I seem to have offended Madame Zeklinski."

"Whatever did you say to offend her?"

"I said she could have her choice of lovers."

Hannelore laughed. "Poor Alexei! You're unused to women who scorn your advances."

"I only meant to compliment her desirability."

"I wonder why she took such offense. Every woman at court would swoon for your attentions. What of the bad news from Potemkin?"

"I'm not to be allowed to join my regiment and take part in Empress Catherine's journey. My orders are to return to St. Petersburg following the czarina's departure in the spring."

"He hasn't forgiven you for disobeying him and taking your sister abroad, I take it. Are you no longer his aide?"

"I remain in that post, but only because my uncle has influence at court. The dear man has advised me to accept my punishment without further complaint."

"That's wise. Was the grand tour of Europe worth all the trouble it has caused you?"

"Not a question of worth. It was necessary for my sister's sake, with fortuitous results, I might add. Prince Bedorov met Anya in Paris and they fell in love. They plan to be wed next year. Potemkin's displeasure is a small price to pay for having done my duty. She'll marry well, which is what my parents would have wanted for her." A flicker of pain at the thought of his dead parents crossed his face, and he changed the subject. "What brings you to Kiev?"

"The empress requested that my husband join her for this journey. Hermann built several frigates and battleships for the Royal Navy, you see. The czarina intended to honor him for his services to the empire, but by the time the news reached Berlin, he was dead. I am here to represent him."

"Excellent," he said, admiring her audacity at accepting an invitation meant for her husband. "Will you live here when you return?"

"No. I shall continue to live in Berlin in our palace. I've many friends there."

"Your husband left you well provided for?"

"Yes. I'm enormously wealthy."

On her hasty retreat from the irritating count, a young officer who begged for the next dance accosted Miriam. The pink-faced cherub seemed barely old enough for the military uniform he wore. His words tumbled out in a rush.

"Lieutenant Petrov at your service, but you would honor me if you would call me Ilya. I must confess that your beauty and your wit have bewitched me. Truth be known, Madame, I am madly in love with you."

"Then you are indeed mad, sir, for you do not know me."

"Don't mock me, Madame. I know my heart well enough to know when I'm in love."

"She suppressed the desire to laugh at the absurdity for she had no wish to offend such a child. "Forgive me, then. Apparently you possess a romantic soul, but I am already spoken for."

"Your husband is of little consequence to me."

"He is of great consequence to me, though I am flattered by your attentions."

"Can we at least be friends?"

"Of course, Ilya is it?"

"Then you must dance with me. It will make me the envy of all the men in my company."

At the end of the evening, Miriam and Dov sped home under the warmth of sable throws. Dov's blue eyes blazed with the triumph of the evening. He was a handsome man, short of stature, yet comely in spite of it. He longed to share his successful evening with his wife, yet his anger prevented him. They rode in uneasy silence, both still simmering over Borschov, their overseer.

"He steals from us, Dov," Miriam protested earlier in the day. "Our serfs hate him."

"All overseers steal. Borschov must deal with four thousand serfs and he turns a profit for us. If you treated him with the dignity his position demands, we wouldn't be arguing."

"I manage our estate. Why didn't you order him to speak to me directly?"

"I'm far too busy with Zeklinski Enterprises to be burdened with petty disputes. Learn to carry out your duties properly."

"How can you expect me to accomplish that when you interfere?"

"Carry on you must, my dear, but do it without upsetting Borschov's operations."

She clenched her fists. "Do not encourage that detestable man to disobey my orders. It's the least you can do when he disagrees with me."

"All right, then. Tell Borschov that he is to order supplies from my office henceforth. My clerk Hershl will see to his needs. In return, you are to treat him with respect. Agreed?"

"Agreed." She heard anger in his voice in spite of his words, but experience had taught her that there was nothing further to be gained.

⌘

The Zeklinski mansion, a handsome pillared structure, was three stories tall. It occupied the highest promontory on the estate. On a clear day, smoke from its many chimneys could be seen from as far away as the wharf on the Dniepr River.

The entrance led to a circular marble hall that rose to the height of the second and third floors. A huge crystal chandelier hung from the dome of a sky-blue ceiling decorated with painted cherubs lounging atop swollen white clouds.

The ground floor held a drawing room, dining room, library, Dov's study, Miriam's morning room, a piano conservatory, ballroom, and a synagogue, which had once been a chapel. The circular staircase led to the second story balcony where the master suite and guest rooms opened onto the balustrade.

The servants' quarters were on the third story, reached by a back staircase connecting all three levels. Below stairs were two kitchens, one for meat meals and one for dairy meals, both designed to meet the strict Judaic dietary requirements of *kashruth*. In addition, there was a fine wine cellar and many storage rooms as well as a specially constructed bath, or *mikveh*, a religious ritual.

Dov had employed an Italian architect to renovate their new home, for it had fallen into neglect. In spite of falling plaster, fresh paint and dangerous scaffolding, the two were content to be free from the constraints of childhood in their new home. The work was finished by the time they celebrated their first year of marriage.

Miriam broke the silence as they readied for bed. "How was your evening?"

"Very dull. Men of noble birth begged me to tell them how to increase their wealth. And you? What did the prince have to say?"

"He was most flattering. Jealous?"

"Have I reason to be?"

She smiled. "No. He did ask me to be sure to thank you for agreeing to billet the Israelovsky Battalion when they arrive with the czarina."

"It's a great honor to host the first Jewish battalion in the history of the Russian army.

"I also met a young lieutenant who vowed his undying love for me. Ilya something or other."

"Shall I challenge him to a duel?"

"A duel? How silly! You've never held a sword in your life."

He laughed. "Nor would I know what to do with a sword. Besides, it would interfere with my audience with Potemkin on Wednesday."

"That is such good news. Wednesday, did you say? I've invited Countess Gorov and Countess Razovsky to tea then." She hesitated. "Actually, Countess Gorov ordered me to do so. Remarkable woman. She apologized in advance for the bigotry we shall have to endure from her ignorant countrymen."

"Were you offended?"

"Not at all." Miriam described her encounter, to Dov's amusement.

"Countess Razovsky must be the wife of Potemkin's aide."

"No. The countess is his sister."

"Then he's not married?"

"I don't know, but if he is, he's very presumptuous."

"What did he presume?"

"Asked me if I had a lover."

"That was bold, but you do have a lover. Let me show you." Dov took her in his arms and brushed his tongue over her lips, an erotic act that roused a fire within her. In spite of such a promising beginning, Dov's passion swiftly reached its peak as usual.

7

"Goodnight, dear," he said, disengaging. He stroked her flushed cheek and in an instant he was asleep.

Miriam lay awake feeling restless, like a mountain climber at the summit unable to descend. She had come to believe that her lustful cravings were a shameful affliction, an aberration of character.

Once she'd asked Dov to hold her in his arms afterward. He fell asleep holding her, only to wake and complain of a stiff arm. Did lovers hold their sweethearts and whisper tender phrases of love only in romantic novels, she wondered? She'd even tried to hint that he might be more adventurous in bed.

"Making love isn't like a business contract," she had said once. Dov reacted with annoyance at the suggestion that he was somehow remiss and she never dared suggest it again.

Seventeen and not yet pregnant, she thought in misery. Miriam's eyes filled with tears.

TWO

"I will not tolerate these delays, Vassily. The Israelovsky Battalion arrives in less than two weeks, yet when I inspected the camp site yesterday, precious little work had been done." Scoundrel, Miriam thought, angry with her overseer's resistance.

Vassily Borschov wore trousers tucked inside black boots and an embroidered belted blouse. His face had been scarred by some childhood ailment, marking him with a malevolent air, much suited to his dour disposition. The serfs had good reason to be terrified of him, for he was a cruel taskmaster. He was overseer when she and Dov took up residence, yet Miriam disliked him from the first.

"I repeat. Build platforms for the men so they need not sleep on icy ground, a cabin for the sergeant, two well-equipped kitchens, and a synagogue. The soldiers require a corral for their horses, as near to the stream as possible for water. See to it that they have a daily supply of kosher beef and poultry as well as grain and fresh produce from the Zeklinski storehouses."

The overseer replied as if Miriam were a child. "One kitchen is sufficient, Madame."

"Your insubordination exceeds your intelligence, sir. Two fully equipped kitchens are necessary to meet the requirements of our religious dietary laws. One is used only for meals that contain meat, and the other is used only for meals that contain products from our dairy. Prince Potemkin has asked for a report on the comfort of the Israelovsky Battalion, in which he takes great pride," Miriam lied.

Borschov seethed with fury over this unexpected development. So, Madame will not trust me to order on my own, Borschov thought. They say Jews trust no one. The tradesmen I deal with will be angry over losing so much business. Puts an end to my commissions from them.

"Draw up a list of what you need for my husband's clerk."

The overseer coughed.

"What is it?"

"I shall need more lumber."

"I've already told you to see my husband's clerk for your needs. My carriage is waiting."

"Allow me, Madame," he said, holding the door for her. He bowed with deliberate insolence, but the performance was lost on her. She was on her way to visit the salon of Madame Henriette. The French seamstress had gained a reputation as the finest in Kiev and Dov had insisted she patronize her.

⌘

The Israelovsky Cavalry traveled to Kiev with Her Majesty's entourage. Every evening, Sergeant Josef Brodsky recorded the day's events in the company log. He appeared older than his twenty years. Some said he was homely, yet his deep-set brown eyes spoke of compassion. He paid scant attention to the bitter cold inside his tent as he wrote.

His parents had died of pneumonia in the severe epidemic of 1767, when he was an infant. Local authorities set fire to his small village to prevent the epidemic from spreading to nearby hamlets. The few survivors took refuge with relatives, but no place could be found for the infant. Too many mouths to feed and far too little food burdened the countryside. Josef was placed in the care of the orphanage in Shklov where he remained until his conscription into the army.

By the time he was old enough to inquire about his parents, no one knew anything about them. Even the records at the orphanage were meager. A little card stated that his father, who died on May 15, 1770, was a tailor named Yitzhak. His mother's name was Mollie, deceased two days earlier.

Josef had come to expect little from life, but his fortunes improved when he turned thirteen. The caretaker at the orphanage died and Josef took his place, receiving a small stipend and a room of his own. On his free evenings, he took to patronizing the local tavern. He would nurse one drink and watch the men compete in arm-wrestling, a favorite local sport. He couldn't remember when he found the courage to challenge the winner. He just knew for a certainty that he would win and he did. When his reputation reached the ears of the Christians in the village, they flocked to the Jewish tavern solely to pit their skill against his. Taken in by his frail appearance, his competitors and their friends bet against him, but his supporters always won, paying for the lad's drink and pressing upon him a few coins to prove their generosity of spirit.

When he became sergeant of the Israelovsky Battalion, he took to caring for the men of his battalion, a hapless group of Jewish soldiers who had the misfortune to be conscripted either because they had been orphans like him, or because their widowed mothers were too poor to pay the recruit levy. He warned his men that they had to be a better cavalry than the other horse regiments, for they represented their people. He needn't have worried, for his soldiers were willing to do anything he asked. To his surprise, he found in them a family of his own.

⌘

Potemkin's headquarters in the Petcherskaya Lavra Monastery loomed like a fortress against the vast landscape of spires and mosques and minarets in Kiev.

"Welcome, Reb Zeklinski," said Count Razovsky. "Follow me, sir." He led Dov past hordes of men hopeful for an audience with the prince. The count knocked once, opened the door for him, and withdrew.

"*Shalom*," the prince said. "How is your grandfather?"

"In good health, Sire. He arrives next week."

"The *Shtadlan* is a fine man," the prince said. "Do you call him that?"

"I call him *Zayde*, Sire."

"He has written to tell us that you are brilliant."

"Isn't that the way with doting grandfathers, Sire?"

Potemkin laughed. "Quite so. He has chosen you to head Zeklinski Enterprises, a great burden for one so young. We trust you are equal to the task."

"I shall do my best, Your Majesty."

"Let us add that your wife's beauty is striking. Outspoken, but charming. Take care you treat her well."

"Most certainly, Sire. I am devoted to my wife." Dov wondered what Miriam might have said to the prince to warrant such a comment.

"We compliment you on your choice."

"Thank you, Sire, but the choice was not ours to make. We were betrothed at birth."

"That so?"

"An ancient Jewish custom."

"You build barges?" the prince asked, abruptly changing the subject.

"Yes, Your Highness. Forgive my impertinence. Might I inquire how you learned of our newest venture?"

"Our business to know what is of advantage to the Crown. Her Highness needs barges, but we suspect you knew that when you contracted to build them. How many are you prepared to deliver ready to sail by the first of May?"

"Fifty, Your Majesty,"

"One hundred."

"Forgive me, Sire. My small shipyard can only produce fifty, perhaps sixty at the most."

"Get another. We shall also require seven large galleys for Her Imperial Highness and her entourage."

I'm being tested, Dov thought. "Of course, Sire."

11

"We intend to hold you to your word."

"Your Majesty flatters my humble abilities," Dov began boldly. "Yet lumber is scarce in winter."

"Precisely. We are prepared to help as a special favor to your grandfather. We had the foresight to ship enough lumber from our forests in the north last fall, before the Dniepr froze. You may purchase all you need from our stock."

"Thank you, Your Majesty. My grandfather will be so pleased," he said, understanding that there was no point in dissent. "And the price?"

Potemkin named an outrageous sum.

"That is a great deal of money, Sire. Fairly takes my breath away. Might I inquire whether this sum includes the deed to your forests?" Dov wondered whether he'd gone too far.

Potemkin laughed good-naturedly. "We like your spirit, young man, but the price is firm. Surely, you've wit enough to know that you can make up the cost of the lumber on the sale of the barges to the Crown, just as your grandfather has always done when he fulfills our exclusive army contracts. Let us discuss what we have in mind."

Dov mentally computed costs as he listened to Potemkin. Both men would realize a handsome profit.

"Agreed, Your Excellency. One more question?"

"What is it?"

"When the vessels are no longer of any use to the Crown, Sire, may we repurchase them for one third of their cost?"

"One half."

"Done, Your Highness."

"See Razovsky about the lumber, and inform your grandfather we look forward to his visit. We want to hear more about the academy he is establishing for the advancement of your people."

⌘

"Countess." Madame Henriette said. She curtsied, believing she faced a titled lady. The dressmaker's spirits soared with the anticipation of huge profits.

"Why don't you examine these sketches? The latest Paris fashions, I assure you, whilst I arrange for tea, Princess...?"

"Madame Zeklinski," Miriam corrected, absorbed in the sketches.

"Forgive me, Madame." The disappointed dressmaker hurried off to assist a more important patron in her busy salon.

"That gown is lovely. Just right for you, countess. Follow me and we'll pin out the hem."

"This won't do, Henriette," the angry countess said.

"Is there something wrong with the gown, countess?"

12

"Nothing to do with the gown. It's that woman."

"Do you know her?"

"Henriette, you will rue the day your clientele learns that a Jewess trades here. Cancel my order, for I refuse to patronize the same salon with the likes of her. My friends will do the same when they hear of this."

"Mon *Dieu*! I had no idea. You are perfectly right, countess. I can't have a Jewess ruining my trade. What nerve, to presume she would be welcome here. Excuse me while I correct the situation. Come here, Lisette. Pin the countess' hem at once."

⌘

Dov closed the door behind him, needing time to digest the full import of his interview. Instead, Count Razovsky led him to a small cell that served as his own office.

"Brandy? The monks here make it themselves. By the way, I understand that my sister and Countess Gorov are having tea with your wife today."

"Yes, my wife needs friends. We know so few people in Kiev."

"Then my sister and I shall introduce you at a dinner in your honor. Does three weeks from this evening suit you?"

"Most kind," Dov said, amused. The man had to know they had been ignored because they were Jewish.

Razovsky said, "Our pleasure, sir. Shall we review the Crown's requirements?" He spread out the drawings. "These are the specifications for the czarina's galleys."

Each one was designed with room to hold doctors, hairdressers, master chefs, engineers, a large staff of servants and a full orchestra. Seven palaces on water for only one journey, Dov thought, awed by the excess. He wondered how Potemkin had learned about the shipyards, since he'd only signed the agreement two days earlier. Misha Golanov, his barge builder, would have apoplexy when he saw the drawings, most likely, but Dov was sure that Misha would find a way.

"More brandy?" Dov declined as the count poured himself another. Now for my own business, the officer thought grimly. "I wonder," he began, "Might there be an opportunity for me to invest my capital in your business?"

Dov raised an eyebrow. "What have you in mind?"

"My funds are tied up in other ventures at the moment. Perhaps there is a way for me to use the fall harvest from my estate as collateral for a loan. Is that feasible?"

Bastard's scratching for a bribe, Dov thought. Let him squirm a bit while I think it out. Does he really think I can be fooled by the offer of his harvest as collateral? What would I do with a few measly stalks of wheat? Use them for oars for the barges? He's offering to introduce us to society in return. Not such a bad exchange. Miriam will be delighted and it suits my purposes.

"Of course," Dov said at last. "But there's no need to trouble yourself with collateral. Allow me to advance you the capital from my personal funds. Interest free, of course. No, no. I wouldn't think of charging interest to a friend. How much will you need to tide you over?"

⌘

"Countess Gorov and Countess Razovsky, Madame," announced Boris as he ushered the women into the drawing room. Miriam noted her butler's obvious pride with some amusement. Jewish guests never received the same warm welcome.

"You've excellent taste in furnishings, Madame Zeklinski. The Cherssovs used to live here, you see. They were friends of my parents," said Anya. "They all died in the influenza epidemic of 1768."

"How terrible for you." A servant entered the drawing room with tea and cakes. Miriam poured tea for her guests.

"How did you meet your husband?" asked Anya with the interest of a woman whose mind was taken with her own future.

"Our parents broke the plate when I was two months old. It is traditional to hold a family betrothal celebration at which a plate is literally smashed to symbolize that the agreement cannot be broken."

"You grew up with your husband?"

"That would have been improper. When I was ten, our families moved to St. Petersburg, but my husband remained behind with his grandfather to complete his education. By the time we married, I had forgotten what he looked like. I have to confess that I was terrified. I didn't sleep well for weeks before my wedding."

"You needn't have worried," said Countess Razovsky with a smile, "He was pointed out to me at the ball, though I've yet to be introduced. He's quite handsome."

Time flew by for Miriam as the afternoon advanced. She reveled in the easy familiarity, for the women behaved as though they'd known her all their lives. This blending of two cultures was not as difficult as she had imagined. Yet not without its thorns, she thought, recalling the humiliating scene in the dressmaker's salon. She was sorry to see the afternoon come to an end.

⌘

Dov's spirits were so high as he related the triumph of his audience with Potemkin, Miriam hadn't the heart to describe of her own humiliation at the hands of the dressmaker. Instead, she recounted the afternoon spent with her two new friends.

"I'm to pay a visit to Countess Razovsky tomorrow afternoon, and she and I have both been invited to tea with Countess Gorov next Wednesday."

"Razovsky and his sister are arranging a dinner in our honor three weeks from tonight. Madame Henriette should have one of your new gowns ready by then."

Miriam's face turned a flaming red.

"What is it?"

"I was humiliated by that horrid dressmaker."

"What do you mean?"

Miriam related the painful story. "She snatched the sketches from my hands, and demanded I leave at once. `Jews are not welcome here,' she said in front of all her patrons."

Dov scowled. "It won't happen again, I promise you."

"Of course not, for I shall never again step foot in that woman's salon."

"Yes you will."

"No, I won't."

"We'll see about that."

"Are you angry with me? Why would you want to force me to repeat such a vile experience?"

"Refusing to go back is not the answer to anti-Semitism."

"I mean it, Dov. I won't be humiliated again. Let's drop the subject."

"All right," he agreed, vowing to have his way in spite of her protests.

"I've had a letter from my father today," he said. "He and *Zayde* and my uncles will be here within the week."

THREE

Tears of joy sprang to Miriam's eyes at the sight of her father. "What a wonderful surprise, Poppa. What brings you to Kiev?"

Chaim Jacobs was a tall vigorous man grown portly through the years. Bristled black hair peppered with gray crowned his ruddy face. "How could I resist the opportunity to see my sweet daughter? I was about to leave for Amsterdam, but your father-in-law persuaded me to detour, so I accompanied him."

"How long can you stay?"

"Only the night, I'm afraid. Tomorrow I must continue on to Amsterdam. My brother has purchased a huge consignment of raw diamonds from South Africa for me."

"How are Momma and the twins? Are they well?"

"Your sisters keep busy irritating their tutors while your mother admonishes them to improve their minds. Hopeless, but they're darling girls anyway. They all send their love."

"Does Momma still suffer those awful headaches?"

"They don't seem to be so bad anymore," he lied, unwilling to burden her. "Let me look at you. How are you?"

"I'm well," She answered a bit too quickly, yet her eyes told him otherwise.

"There's something troubling you. What is it?"

"Just homesickness at the sight of you, that's all." Tears flooded her face. "Oh, Poppa! I want so much to have a child."

"There, there," he soothed. Her pain invaded him, becoming his pain, for he loved his oldest daughter dearly. "Surely you will be with child in time." Each of her shuddering sighs stabbed at his heart.

"We've been wed nearly two years."

"Have you shared this...unhappiness with Dov?"

"I'm sure that he doesn't want to hurt me, so he says nothing. I'm proud to be his wife and that makes me feel even worse, do you see?"

Her father paused for thought. "Dov's grandfather is planning to dedicate his academy in Shklov in June. If you're not with child by then, you can discuss this with your Uncle Leon. He's a fine physician. Put it out of your mind until then. All right?"

She attempted a smile, ashamed of her childish outburst. Her father set out to cheer her with amusing anecdotes about her eight-year-old twin sisters, Bela and Bluma. She laughed at his tales, grateful for deliverance from the pain weighing on her heart.

⌘

Dov's private office was on the second story overlooking the wharf, for he relished the view of the busy Dniepr waterfront. His clerk Hershl sat outside his door facing the visitors' anteroom. A large meeting room for conferences, a kitchen and a water closet completed the second floor.

His clerks, most of whom were related to the family, worked at writing desks on the ground floor, but they had more than mere family ties in common, for they had grown up with Dov and they were intensely loyal to him. Three in particular, were invaluable to him. One was an expert in contract law who had a special aptitude for Russian statutes. No easy task, for the labyrinth of fiats and decrees and ukases were often contradictory. No one ever thought to rescind the old before implementing the new. Another was a brilliant mathematician who could deliver complex cost estimates with astonishing accuracy. The third man was Hershl, Dov's dependable head clerk who paid meticulous attention to the smallest detail. In addition to serving as his private aide, he supervised the growing army of scribes, assistant clerks and messengers.

From the first, the anteroom burst at the seams with optimistic hopefuls pleading for an audience. Some petitioners begged for work, some were there to solicit a loan, and some were unscrupulous adventurers hoping to convince the new tycoon to invest in one outlandish scheme or another.

Dov had had the foresight to envision future expansion, and carefully acquired a five-year option to buy the two buildings on either side. The imposing sign, **ZEKLINSKI ENTERPRISES**, never failed to thrill him when he came upon it early each morning.

"I'm glad we've had time to talk." Dov said as they waited for *Zayde* to return from his audience with Prince Potemkin. "What do you think, father? Will Uncle Moses cause difficulty?" Dov resembled his father Avram, dressed in tasteful western fashion. Both had blue eyes a Grecian nose and a square-cut chin.

His father smiled. "He wants your position, Dov. I'm sure he wonders why I turned it down in your favor."

"I often wonder the same thing."

"You have a special aptitude for business that I lack, son. Your grandfather and I both agree that you are better suited to the machinations and difficult maneuvers involved in our vast holdings. Quite frankly, I haven't the stomach for it. I am content to support my only son's efforts."

"Thank you, father." They sat in comfortable silence as they waited.

⌘

"How was your visit, *Zayde?*"

The *shtadlan* wore the traditional garb of the orthodox Jew; black caftan, wide-brimmed fur shtremel over a skullcap. Kalman Zeklinski towered over his son and grandson, an attribute that might have caused envy in Dov had he not idolized the patriarch. The imposing patriarch's features were handsome— white hair, alert blue eyes and dense eyebrows.

"The prince said I have reason to be proud of you, Dov."

"I'm relieved to hear it. Did he discuss the nature of our negotiations?"

"No. He preferred to discuss religion, a topic of great interest to him. He spent two years in a monastery as a young man and his interest lingers. He's promised to visit the academy so he can debate the meaning of God with our Talmudic scholars." The older man paused. "By the way, he spoke favorably of your wife. Said she was spirited. What could he have meant by that?"

Dov told him what Miriam had said concerning Jewish girls attending Her Majesty's Christian schools for women. The three men laughed indulgently at Miriam's boldness.

"Potemkin's aide-de-camp had kind things to say about you as well."

"I shouldn't wonder," Dov's father commented. "Tell your grandfather about your meeting with him."

Dov recounted his dealings with Razovsky. "What do you think, *Zayde?* Was forty thousand rubles too steep a bribe?"

"Not in the least. If he's anything like Potemkin, he's up to his ears in gambling debts. We've built Zeklinski Enterprises with the Crown's exclusive contracts as a result and you will continue to do the same. Cultivate your new friend, Dov. His patronage shall open doors for you and your wife. That alone is well worth the price."

"Forty thousand rubles for Judaism."

"I can assure you it won't compromise Judaism but it will show Russia how capable we Jews are of making major contributions to the empire."

FOUR

"We'll have coffee and brandy in the drawing room," said Dov to his uncles after dinner.

"How is the progress of the academy, *Zayde*?" asked Uncle Moses. Tall and slim, his intense brown eyes peered out from under dark, bushy brows, though his hair had turned prematurely gray.

The *shtadlan* paused to sip his brandy. "The study of science, philosophy and literature is the mark of a truly civilized society, isn't that so?" His eyes shone with the fervor of a prophet. "As you know, the academy will house a synagogue, study rooms, library, laboratories, printing presses. All designed with the most modern equipment.

"I grow old, my sons. Only God knows how much time He will allow me to remain on this earth. Written in the book of life, no? If the city of Shklov gains a reputation as the home of Jewish culture and enlightenment in Eastern Europe, my small contribution will not have been in vain. We shall all celebrate the opening with dedication ceremonies in June."

"Wonderful idea."

"The whole family will be delighted."

"You can count on our being there."

There was an uneasy pause in the conversation, for the patriarch's academy was not foremost in the minds of Dov's uncles.

Uncle Asher was in charge of producing army uniforms, a cottage industry ranging in homes and factories all over the country. He was the handsomest of the *shtadlan's* sons-in-law. "The academy's progress is welcome news, father-in-law, but frankly, we'd like to hear about your new plans, Dov."

"Yes. Tell us," urged portly Uncle Isaac in charge of leather goods for the army. He always made a display of refusing second helpings at family dinners, but he fooled no one, for he was a prodigious eater.

"It's no secret that we're growing as rapidly as is the Russian Empire itself, Uncle Isaac. Zeklinski Enterprises intends to keep pace with that growth."

"What are your plans?" asked Uncle Moses, the family banker.

"There is untapped territory out there, gentlemen. I'm talking about the Southern Provinces where Potemkin plans to lead the czarina in the spring. Kherson, Ekaterinoslav, the Crimea. In a word, Byzantium. The Crown waives the usual travel restrictions in order to encourage its subjects—Jews as well—to migrate to the southern provinces. They've been promised free land, freedom to worship and no taxation. In keeping with this, Zeklinski Enterprises is about to enter a new era."

"What's that?" prodded Uncle Isaac.

"We are going into a new business. Barge building." Stunned silence greeted Dov's news.

"Why? Aren't we doing well enough as things stand?"

"That isn't the point, Uncle Asher. We lower our margin of profit when we're forced to pay others to transport our goods. Misha Golanov, an excellent builder with a small shipyard, will build for us. Our capital will finance his expansion in return for the exclusive right to purchase the barges he builds. We stand to gain on all fronts. Our builder takes all the risks inherent in operating a shipyard and we buy his product for a price well below market." Dov saw no need to reveal his promise to Potemkin.

"Why a reduced rate of interest when we earn a safe return on the open market?"

"I knew you'd ask me that question Uncle Moses." The others laughed at Dov's sly reference to Moses' tight rein on funds.

"Answer the question," Moses demanded, more sharply than he'd intended. "Why is the man selling his product for less than the going price?"

"Golanov is having trouble collecting money owed to him for completed work. You know how lax the Russians are about paying their bills. He has a reputation as one of the finest of shipbuilders in all of Kiev in spite of the fact that he's on the brink of bankruptcy. We plan to purchase one hundred barges."

"One hundred did you say?" Arrogant young bastard, Moses thought. Dov's remarks confirmed his worst fears. "That's far too many."

"Not at all. The Crown needs them for the Czarina's journey. We'll sell them at a profit when the journey is over. Isn't that so, Zayde?"

His grandfather nodded in approval. "Dov has my full support. He is your leader now and he needs yours as well."

"You have mine, Dov," said Moses, hiding his skepticism.

"Mine, too," added Isaac.

Dov was drunk with power as he outlined the details of his plan to his uncles.

Miriam was grateful for the monotonous task of weaving the needle in and out of her tapestry as she listened. It added an air of serenity she did not really feel. She was fascinated by the passion in Dov's eyes and the excitement in his voice. Something deep inside nagged at her. An echo. A whisper. An ache. A startling thought raced across her mind like a bracing wind.

Dov's voice was full of a lover's passion. She yearned for him to pursue her with such ardor.

FIVE

"You should not have done such a childish thing, Miriam." Dov did not bother to disguise his anger.

"I don't see any wrong in it."

"How dare you reveal our most intimate affairs to your father?"

"Dov, please. I'm upset because I'm not pregnant."

"You ought to be ashamed of yourself."

"But he's my father."

"This is no one else's concern but ours. Do you understand me? You've humiliated me. You owe me an apology."

"I've already said I was sorry."

"Promise never to discuss our personal affairs with anyone but me, do you hear?" He went on lecturing her until she could bear it no longer.

"You've made your point. It won't happen again though I meant no disrespect. Why can't you understand how I feel about not becoming pregnant? I suspect you are worried too, though we never discuss it, do we?"

Dov bit off every word through clenched teeth. "Pregnancy happens when it happens! You couldn't have chosen a worse time for this petty nonsense. It is you who fail to understand how much my work consumes me. My enemies, and that includes my own dear uncles, would love to see me fail. I certainly don't expect my wife to be disloyal."

"As you wish," she answered, yet it was she who felt the more betrayed.

"What are you wearing to Razovsky's dinner party tonight?"

"My rose gown. Does that suit you?"

"It will have to, I suppose." He took a deep breath. "It's time you went back to Madame Henriette's salon."

"Never."

"Madame Henriette will welcome you this time."

"I mean it, Dov."

"It's important to me that you return."

"Why?" she persisted stubbornly.

22

"I have my reasons. Need I remind you that a dutiful wife should not question her husband, or are you intent on betraying me over this as well?"

"Enlighten me, Dov. Why must I return to such a hostile establishment?"

He ignored her question. "Be sure to choose the best designs, the finest silks and satins and velvets and any finery that takes your fancy. I don't care whether you need it or not. When other women admire your clothing, you can also say they were made by that fine French dressmaker, Madame Henriette. I'm going to change for dinner and I suggest you do the same or we'll be late."

⌘

Count Alexei Razovsky owned more than twenty five hundred serfs. Among them were skilled shoemakers, carpenters, grooms, stable boys, dairymaids, farmers, cooks, bakers, dish-washers, laundresses, foot-men, butlers, house maids and valets, as well as musicians, actors, poets and painters, to name but a few.

He had gone to considerable expense to ensure the success of the dinner in honor of the Zeklinskis, extending his credit well beyond his means. It was not the first time he incurred debt, nor would it be the last.

His first guest, however, did not applaud his efforts. "I fail to understand why a dinner for Jews is so necessary. They're anti-Christ, you know."

"Come, come Petrov. Reb Zeklinski performs essential services for the Crown. It is your duty to be here tonight. Think how pleased Prince Potemkin will be when I inform him that Count Petrov, one of Kiev's most prominent noblemen, was among my guests."

"Delighted to see you, Countess." Alexei turned to kiss the tall woman's hand. Petrov's wife was a beak-nosed matron whose lips seemed permanently frozen in disapproval. "Where is your dear daughter Marya?"

"She's home. Not well."

"Sorry to hear it. Send her my wishes for a speedy recovery. And how are you, Ilya?"

"Where's Madame Zeklinski? It's her I came to see," the young officer pouted. His father glared at him, for they had had a nasty row that morning.

"Ah, here they are now. Allow me to introduce you to Reb Zeklinski and Madame Zeklinski. This is Count and Countess Petrov."

"Welcome to Kiev," Petrov mumbled,

"Darling," Ilya said. He bowed with a flourish and kissed her hand. "I've missed you."

"Hello, Lieutenant. Allow me to present my husband. This is Lieutenant Petrov, the young man I met at the ball, dear."

"My wife informs me you are an admirer of hers."

23

"Your wife is very beautiful. Be on your guard, sir." Petrov's father turned away in disgust, but the exchange of silent scorn between father and son did not escape Dov.

"I'll heed your warning, lieutenant," Dov answered, amused, "But I trust you to behave as a gentleman, for I am forced to leave my wife in your care. Will you both excuse me? Our host beckons."

"May I have a word, Dov?"

"Now?"

"No, but soon."

"Nine o'clock tomorrow morning? In my office."

"Excellent. Now come and meet Countess Gorov. She's insisting upon it."

"Come closer." The dowager raised her lorgnette to study Dov. "Your wife is the first Jew I've ever met and you are the second. Never had the opportunity before, you see."

"I've never met anyone like you before, either." What a beauty she must have been in her day, Dov thought, noting the faded color of her lively eyes and the fine structure of her age-lined face.

"Are you as wealthy as they say?"

"Yes," he answered, startled by the rude question.

"Beware, then. You'll be much envied, and envy always leads to trouble." The old woman turned her attention to General Brezhnovin's wife and ignored Dov as though he were no longer there. "Ah, Elizabeth. How is your rheumatism?"

⌘

Miriam and Ilya had become friends since they met the night of Potemkin's ball. He called on her frequently, often taking her riding out in public at which time he would fill her with amusing court gossip. "I've had the worst row with my father today." He couldn't bring himself to add that his friendship with Miriam was the major cause of contention.

"What could have made your father so angry?"

"The usual. He thinks I gamble and drink too much. But he has no right to interfere with my life. I'm a man, aren't I?" Miriam stifled a smile, for Ilya was a child in her view.

"Fathers do tend to worry, I suppose. I know mine does." As soon as the words were out of her mouth, she recalled the anguish of her argument with Dov.

"Yes, but you are free to do whatever you like because you are a married woman."

24

Dov was relieved to hear the butler's announcement, for he'd been trapped by General Brezhnovin, who had insisted upon reciting the tale of his role in a battle long since played.

A liveried serf stood at attention behind every chair, to see to each guest's comfort. As each course was served, the servant promptly filled the proper wine glass with another rare vintage.

After the first course, Razovsky stood and tapped his glass for attention. "Our guest of honor, Reb Zeklinski, supplies the army with uniforms, leather, horses and provisions. He's engaged in building the barges and galleys for the czarina's journey as well. Isn't that so?"

"Your guests will think me immodest, Count Razovsky," Dov protested, pleased nevertheless be the center of attention.

"What a coincidence," said Hannelore von Hals. At her request, Razovsky had seated her on Dov's right. "I happen to own shipyards in Sebastopol."

"Really?"

"My late husband left them to me, but my solicitors are advising me to sell. Do you think that's wise?"

"Are you requesting advice, Madame?"

"Would you be willing to offer it if I were?"

He laughed, understanding that she was toying with him. "Would you be inclined to accept my advice?"

"I'm prepared to listen, after which I would decide whether or not to accept it." Her sly smile intrigued him.

"You show excellent judgment, Madame von Hals, and a great deal of wit. Feel free to call on me for advice and do with it what you will."

Dov turned to Countess Gorov, who sat on his left. "Would you do us the honor of joining us for dinner some evening?"

"Did you think I would refuse because you and your wife are Jewish?" All eyes turned her way, for she had spoken in a loud voice. Countess Petrov and Countess Brezhnovin who had been deep in conversation, were shocked into embarrassed silence.

The dowager glared at the two women seated opposite her. "We've all heard the most shameful tales about your people. Wrongly, we've been led to believe that Jews are all greedy profiteers who sell false papers, kill Christian babies at Easter and drink their blood." Countess Brezhnovin choked on her champagne.

"Don't make such a fuss, Elizabeth. You know it's true." The silence that followed was thunderous, but the countess was not to be denied. "The Zeklinskis know what we've been taught to think. Isn't that so, Reb Zeklinski?"

"You speak truth Countess Gorov. *L'chayim*, which means, `To your health,' in the language of my people. Your honesty is refreshing and I salute you for it." His toast woke General Brezhnovin who had sipped too much champagne.

25

"Yes, yes, of course," he sputtered, raising his glass. "To our charming host and hostess. *Nazdrov'ya!*" he toasted in Russian, smiling in the direction of his wife, unable to focus his bleary eyes on her glowering face.

At the end of dinner, Razovsky announced to his guests, "Gentlemen, please stay and enjoy your brandy and cigars while the ladies retire to the drawing room. When you are ready, join us in the conservatory where Madame Zeklinski and my sister will perform a piano duet."

The two young women played well, except for an occasional wrong note that was invariably Anya's error, yet she recovered in time to keep up with Miriam's flawless performance. Dov glanced at his host who seemed absorbed by the music.

In truth, Count Razovsky barely heard the music. He found himself immersed in a private fantasy in which he was the successful financier and Miriam was his wife, playing for his ears alone. In a fleeting vision, he made love to her right there in the conservatory. When the applause jolted him out of his reverie, he joined in as if he had heard every note.

Anya said graciously, "Thank you, but it is Madame Zeklinski to whom you should be most grateful. Her patient tutelage inspires me to perform far better than I've ever done before."

After the last guest departed, Anya said to her brother, "What a lovely evening! I do wish Peter had been here. He's bound to grow as fond of the Zeklinskis as we are, I'm sure." She stifled a yawn. "I'm off to bed, dear. Coming?"

"I'll have a nightcap first."

He retired to the library and poured himself a brandy. He removed a pearl-handled pistol from the gun case, one of a pair on display, and took aim at nothing in particular. Damn near killed myself with this after my parents died, he recalled as he returned it to its place. Should start hunting again. Rusty. Mustn't lose my touch. Last brandy. Zeklinski might turn me down tomorrow. Wouldn't blame him if he did.

He moved unsteadily toward a chair and sank down. His scar began to twitch and the glass slid to the floor, its contents staining the Aubusson rug.

SIX

"I'm in need of an additional loan."

He's been gambling again, Dov thought. *Zayde* warned me. Not much substance to my new friend. "How much?"

"Ten thousand rubles."

So last evening's dinner party cost ten thousand rubles. Was it worth the price? We'll have to see. "The amount is entirely within reason, Alexei." But you'll have to work for it, he decided, shaping a plan as he spoke.

Razovsky suppressed a sigh of relief. "Decent of you old man."

"Matter of fact, I was about to offer you a position in Zeklinski Enterprises, with ample compensation for your work, Of course. What do you say?"

"I'd like to help you, but I know so little about commerce."

"Do you happen to know a shipbuilder by the name of Igor Potowski?"

"I'm afraid not."

"My own builder has already begun to build the first fifty barges but he can't handle more than that. Potowski has the means to deliver fifty more by the first of May."

"What's the problem?"

"Man's a bigot. 'I don't do business with Jews,' he scrawled on the first letter we sent. When we sent a second request, I used Potemkin's name. He wouldn't mind, would he?"

"The prince would mind if you didn't deliver what you promise."

"Potowski responded by asking ten times the amount we're paying our man Golanov. 'Take it or leave it, Jew,' he scrawled across the second letter.

"What an outrage. He ought to be flogged with a knout for treating you so shabbily. How can I help?"

"Here's what I have in mind." Dov's eyes registered concern when he finished. "I'm not being too hard on the man, am I?"

"I wouldn't worry, Dov. It's a brilliant plan. Even Potemkin would laugh at the mischief, but he'll never know."

"I'll have my clerk fetch your draft."

Imagine Zeklinski asking for my help. Means he thinks highly of me. If I deliver, it will give purpose to my life. I'll give up gambling. And drinking. Resign my commission. Become a magnate. Marry. Have children. Put my life straight. My father hated men with no purpose.

"Here you are," Dov said when Hershl returned with the bank draft. "Shall we celebrate?" Dov poured two glasses of brandy.

"*L'chayim*, Alexei."

"*Nazdrov'ya*, Dov."

⌘

"My brother Alexei is pleased we've become good friends, Miriam."

"Is he?"

"Oh yes. If it weren't for him, I'd still be living in the dark ages, so to speak."

"What do you mean?"

"I was educated at the convent where we were taught the most outrageous lies about Jews. The sisters weren't really cruel. They just didn't know anything other than what they themselves had been taught. If not for Alexei, I might have believed all that nonsense and there might have been no chance for us to become friends, do you see? Alexei insisted on our grand tour of Europe in order to broaden my education. He's such a good influence."

"Then I'm indebted to him, for my life has changed for the better since we met."

"I can't wait for you to meet Peter. He's such a wonderful man. He's tall and big-boned, with blue eyes that lend an air of melancholy, but he's really very sweet. We both want a large family. He loves children, you see. Doesn't that tell you what kind of man he is?"

A dart of pain stabbed Miriam. "Yes, it does."

"I wanted to go with Peter when he sails with Her Highness on the first of May, but he thinks it improper to travel together before our wedding."

"Where will you live when you marry?"

"In Moscow, in the family palace. My good fortune that he loves me."

"His good fortune, too, for he's going to be blessed with a lovely bride."

"I'm the more blessed. He might have chosen a princess, but it's me he wants. When we met at that Paris ball, he filled my dance card, leaving no room for anyone else. He's masterful like that. Always knows exactly what he wants. Even his letters are concise and to the point."

"Love letters?"

Anya laughed. "Peter write love letters? Dear me, no. He wouldn't know how. He writes about his hopes and his dreams for our future and about our obligations to the Crown, to his family, to the church. Am I making him sound too stuffy? I don't mean to. It's just that I admire his strong sense of honor. Mother Russia and God come first."

"I can't wait to meet him, Anya. I've already fallen a little bit in love with him."

"You mustn't, because I'm outrageously jealous. Good heavens! Here we chat like two noisy blue jays and three hours disappear as if they were three seconds."

A servant appeared at the door of the drawing room. "Forgive me, Your Grace. Madame's driver wishes to inform you there is a blizzard brewing."

"In that case I must be off."

As Miriam was helped with her fur, the huge front doors flew open, bringing in a blast of arctic air.

"Oh, it's you, Alexei. Madame Zeklinski was just leaving."

"My good fortune, then, for I have a request to make of her." His teasing laugh rang out before Miriam could find her tongue. "May I beg your pardon for my rudeness on the night of Prince Potemkin's ball? I tried to apologize to you last night at dinner, but young Petrov never left your side. Will you forgive me for my impertinence?" His eyes sparkled with mischief as he took her hand in his and raised it to his lips. "I've nothing but sincere admiration for your loyalty to your husband, Madame Zeklinski. Had I known you better, I would have held my impudent tongue."

"Alexei, you mustn't detain our guest." Anya turned to her friend and said with indulgent good humor, "My brother's an insufferable rake, Miriam. He means no harm by it, but there it is. Do say you'll forgive him."

Miriam's mouth was as dry as if she had been caught in a windstorm. "You're forgiven," she said stiffly, "If you'll excuse me, I must hurry before the blizzard turns treacherous."

"*Au revoir*, Miriam," said Anya. "Until next week."

"*Au revoir*, Madame Zeklinski," added her brother, a look of roguish triumph on his face. "Allow me escort you to your carriage. Here. Give me your hand."

⌘

"I saw the dressmaker this morning, Dov."

"And?"

"And she behaved herself this time, but her eye was swollen. She said she tripped over some fabric on the floor of the workroom. Does her husband beat her, do you suppose?"

"If he doesn't, he ought to. What did you order?"

"A dozen gowns in all, and a scandalous amount of new lingerie. The most intricate designs I could find among her sketches. I chose a sleeve from this one, a bodice from that, a skirt from another. I was next to impossible to please. And properly haughty."

Dov laughed. "That's the spirit. Serves her right."

"I have some other news."

"Good news, I trust?"

"I'm menstruating." She turned away, unable to bear the scowl falling across his face.

"Perhaps next month."

"Can we discuss this with Uncle Leon? He may know of a cure."

"You know I don't like anyone in the family to know our personal business."

"We can count on his discretion."

"Are you sure?"

"Absolutely. Besides, it may be some minor condition, something easily corrected."

"All right. I see you have your heart set on it." Dov's casual tone belied his distress, for he wanted children, yet his stubborn pride and a mistaken sense that it was somehow unmanly to admit his vulnerability kept him from sharing his anguish with his wife. "We leave for Shklov as soon as the czarina sails in May. We'll discuss this with your uncle then."

"That's fine."

"By the way, I've some news about Benjamin Moskowitz, my cousin Sophie's husband. When he was here, Uncle Moses asked me to offer his son-in-law a position in Kiev."

"That's good news. Sophie hates living with her mother-in-law. It will be good to have my childhood friend here. What kind of work do you have in mind for Benjamin? He is devoted to studying the Talmud."

"His ability to concentrate on the intricacies of the Talmud tells me he's smart and he's ethical. I've already sent him a proposal."

"I'm glad. For Sophie's sake I hope he accepts."

"Zayde's agreed to talk to his mother. If anyone can persuade her to listen to reason, it's my grandfather. Don't mention it when you write to Sophie. Why raise her hopes? That old woman has an iron grip on Benjamin and there's always the chance that she may not let go no matter how good an opportunity this is."

Dov yawned. "Good night, dear. I must be up early." He blew her a kiss and retired to his own chambers, for it was ritually forbidden for him to share his wife's bed when she menstruated.

SEVEN

Church bells pealed and cannons pierced the wintry air to signal the arrival of Empress Catherine II. A riotous rainbow of troops in turbans and caps and flying cloaks preceded the royal sleigh. Behind the royal party, Hussars in high cylindrical hats and dolman sleeves flying loosely from their shoulders marched proudly into Kiev.

Dov observed the spectacle from his office window for a time, after which he sped home to prepare for the Sabbath. The Israelovsky Battalion had been part of Catherine's triumphal march into the city. Miriam had invited Sergeant Brodsky and eight of his soldiers to dinner.

"*Shalom*, gentlemen. Which of you is Sergeant Brodsky?"

"Begging your pardon, Madame Zeklinski. My name is Moshe. Sergeant Brodsky sends regrets. He is tending one of our comrades who is ill. He's asked me to extend his thanks for the excellent quarters you've provided for us."

The men were dressed in the new uniforms of the Russian army, designed by Potemkin himself, which included tunics, wide breeches and lower boots that did not pinch their feet. The prince had done a great deal to alleviate the harsh treatment of the common soldier.

"*Shabbat shalom*, gentlemen," Dov said. "Won't you join us while my wife lights the Sabbath candles?"

The men dutifully trooped after their hosts into the dining room, and listened respectfully as Miriam lit the candles and chanted the Hebrew prayer to welcome the Sabbath.

"*Boruch ato Adonoi elohenu melech ha-olom Asher kidhsonu b'mitzvosov v'tzivonu l'hadlik ner shel shabbos.*"

Miriam and Dov exchanged delighted glances as the soldiers fell to the task of devouring dinner with hearty appetites. Miriam had ordered chicken soup with matzo balls, gefilte fish, potted beef with gravy, roasted potatoes, kasha, vegetables, *challah*, wine and *blinis* with apricots for dessert, food she knew would remind the soldiers of home. Boris raised an eyebrow when Dov demanded more bread and beef for the hungry lads. The haughty butler complied at once with his customary efficiency, though with a disapproving posture.

"I've heard that you men form one of the finest battalions in Russia."

"Thank you, sir, but we would have been disbanded years ago if it weren't for our sergeant," said Moshe.

"What do you mean?"

"Army life is difficult, but our sergeant is not."

"We would do anything he asks."

"Sergeant Brodsky's devotion to us is the only thing that gives us the courage to go on," Moshe said, eliciting a sympathetic murmur from the others.

"While it's true that one of our men is ill with a fever tonight, he's not in danger. The sergeant chose me to take his place so I could dine with you in comfort. It's his way."

The men chatted easily, each one eager to add tales of their sergeant's compassion for them.

At the end of dinner, Miriam said, "It's time now for services, but afterwards, you must all join me for tea and cake."

⌘

Dov smiled seductively and pulled her close to him. "It's a blessing to make love on the Sabbath, darling." His hands played their familiar strain on her body as she responded to his touch. When his passion reached its peak, he did not turn over and fall asleep as usual.

"I'd like to meet Brodsky. Arrange it, will you? Let's hope for the sake of the Israelovsky Battalion that rumors of war with Turkey prove to be false."

"I hope so, too, but if war does break out, I'll feel much safer knowing we're being protected by our own people."

EIGHT

"The chancery clerk who works in the Office of Permits for Ships and Wharves agreed to inspect Potowski's facilities after I hinted at suspected violations."

"He knows he's not to interfere with Golanov's shipyards?"

"Of course. Two more clerks came to see me when they heard of their colleague's good fortune," Alexei continued, an oblique reference to bribery. One works in the Office of Taxation and Finance and the other in the Office of Labor Permits. They are examining Potowski's records as we speak. You were right, Dov. Potowski does have an outstanding note on his shipyard."

"Good work, Alexei. See if the lender will sell the note."

"I wouldn't advise you to use your name. Potowski's a nasty troublemaker with friends who are also hot-tempered."

"Zeklinski Enterprises will never appear in any legal documents."

"They say Potowski is short of the men to build the barges he's promised. Golanov's hired most of them."

"What are you driving at?"

"I can help with my serfs to complete the work once Potowski is out of the way. I have skilled carpenters, painters and blacksmiths. The women can plant the spring wheat and free my men to work in the shipyards."

"You're to be congratulated on your fine business sense." Dov didn't add that he would have asked for the manpower had Razovsky neglected to offer it. He calculated that the serf labor from the Razovsky estate would cost him nothing, since he'd already advanced Razovsky funds he never expected to see again.

⌘

Alexei visited the Austrian ambassador's castle that evening. The Diplomatic Corps called it the Cafe de l'Europe for its nightly diversions of wit and gaiety.

"You haven't been here for ages, Alexei. I've missed you," said a young woman of his acquaintance. Alexei kissed her hand.

"Won't you join me at the gaming table? I've lost a fortune this week. If I confess it to my husband when he returns next month, he'll pack me off to a convent."

"Next month?"

"Yes. He'll be gone for one whole month. Isn't that nice?" She took his arm and led him to the gaming room. "I know you'll bring me luck tonight."

"And if I do?"

"And if you do, you'll want a reward, I suppose."

Razovsky watched her play, proud of his self-control, for he had vowed never to gamble again. He reached for the woman's chips.

"Cash in, Yelena dear."

"Yelena? My name's Svetlana!"

"Forgive me. You remind me of my beautiful mother Yelena, may she rest in peace," he lied. "My passion for you is driving me mad. Save your dear husband some rubles and I'll change your luck elsewhere."

"You wicked man," she said, but her eyes denied it.

The first time he took her, the vision of Miriam replaced the witless woman beneath him. He slept for a time, but she woke him and roused him once more. This time his passion was quick and indifferent.

NINE

The overseer peered into their carriage. "Reb Zeklinski. Madame. And Countess Razovsky is it? Good day to Your Highness." Borschov turned to Dov. "I trust everything's in order, sir. I've seen to it that the battalion has every luxury."

"The sergeant informs me his men are comfortable in their quarters. Keep up the good work, Borschov."

When the overseer withdrew, Miriam seethed at the man's nerve.

The sergeant had invited them to watch the battalion rehearse cavalry maneuvers. His soldiers had dressed in their new dark green winter cloaks, white breeches tucked into gleaming black boots. It amused Miriam to think of the unseen skullcap under each soldier's black fur headdress. When they visited for dinner on Friday nights, the white fringes of their *tsitsis*—prayer vests—were often visible under their tunics.

The men on horseback paced and stepped with precision at each command. Such a nice man, Miriam thought as she watched Brodsky bark out orders. Not at all shy on the field. Not handsome, yet there's something appealing about him just the same.

"Wonderful performance," said Anya at the end of maneuvers.

"They're well trained," agreed Dov, whose mind was already on the day's work ahead. "I'll take you both home and then I'm off to my office."

Vassily Borschov sat astride his horse and watched the sledge ride off in the direction of the mansion. Jews in Kiev? What's the world coming to? His eyes narrowed as he focused on his hatred for Miriam. *Parshchivi Zhid!* He cursed the 'dirty Jew.' Thinks she can order me about like a lowly serf. I could teach her to heel. Turn her knees to jelly, I would. Crush her big breasts and make her beg for more. Aroused, he stripped her clothing off none too gently and ravished her in his mind's eye.

⌘

Igor Potowski's bellows reverberated throughout the Zeklinski offices.

"Sorry, sir," Hershl said, pushing his spectacles back in place. "We informed that man that you were too busy to see him just as you ordered, but he refuses to leave."

"Tell him I'll see him in five minutes." Dov kept the builder waiting for half an hour.

Dov faced a bear of a man. His hands were callused, his dark eyes small. "Good day, sir. How may I serve you?"

"You know why I'm here."

"Some tea, perhaps, Master Potowski? Or vodka? Yes, of course. A man like you prefers vodka." Dov rang.

"Vodka," he said, noting his terrified staff peering over Hershl's shoulder. "Make sure you take it from our private stock," he added, knowing there was no such thing. "Nothing like good vodka to conclude a deal, eh?"

"More like it," Potowski said. "Where's my money? You begged me for those barges."

Dov's clerk tripped over the rug in his haste to set the tray down.

"Business is business, my grandfather always says, so let's drink to our deal. Let bygones be bygones, eh? *L'chayim*! No, no. That's a Jewish toast. I meant *Nazdrov'ya*, a good Russian toast." Potowski drained his glass while Dov pretended to drink.

"I need my money."

"Patience, Master Potowski. The future is his who knows how to wait, they say. My staff must make sure the papers are in order." Dov refilled his glass. Bastard's a bottomless pit, he thought in grim amusement. "You'll have the barges ready by the first of May as promised? Isn't that why I'm paying you so much?"

Potowski scowled. "Problems. Why I came today."

"Would you mind speaking up?" he asked, having heard every word.

"I'm a builder, damn it. Don't know 'bout plots and schemes and conniving *Zhids*."

"Is there something wrong?"

"Where's my goddam money? Lumber's paid for, men and materials have to be paid."

"I see your point, Master Potowski." Dov stroked his chin. "My accountant can't believe I was foolish enough to pay such an outrageous price for your barges."

"Deal's a deal," Potowski muttered.

Dov rose from his desk and began circling, hands clasped behind his back. "You have me there, sir. A deal's a deal and I'm a man of my word." The builder tried to keep Dov in focus.

36

"Even Jews have a sense of honor, though you may not think so. It's my staff. They're not men of the world, like you and me. We understand business, don't we? Get the best price. Make the best deal."

Potowski's words slurred like shards of shattered glass. "So?"

"My staff has made some changes in our contract, to tie up all the loose ends. You can read, can't you?" Dov paused as the besotted man filled his glass.

"If your solicitor says that everything's in proper order, send them back and we'll each sign two copies, one for you and one for me. In front of witnesses if you like."

"How long will this take?" Potowski's head swayed like a wounded bull in a ring.

"A week or two at the most."

"To hell with the contract. Need money now, d'ya hear? Or else."

Dov affected shock. "You wouldn't think of calling the deal off?"

"Take care Zeklinski." He grabbed the sheaf of papers and rose unsteadily to his feet. "I have rights, protection from my Craftsmen's Guild. Contract better be right. Won't stand for nonsense. Wait and see what I can do, just wait and see."

"I'm so glad we've had this friendly chat," Dov said to the man's back.

"Alexei," Dov dictated to his scribe when Potowski was gone.

"Call in the loan at once."

TEN

"How can you ask me to give up my friend, Peter? How can I hurt her like that?"

"You needn't give her up as a friend. I'd never ask you to make such a sacrifice."

"But if I can't invite her to our wedding in Moscow?"

"Do stop weeping. I can't bear it." Jews at my wedding? Out of the question! How can I bring dishonor upon my parents? Father despises them and mother would be mortified. Better to tell her now.

"Dry your tears, my precious. You've not been out of my thoughts since we met, and the first thing I do when I see your lovely face is to make you weep. I'm so clumsy with words, but I love you just the same." He cupped Anya's face in his hands and kissed each tearful eye.

"It's so unfair, Peter."

"Now is not the right time to fly in the face of custom. Moscow just isn't ready for such a bold move. Perhaps in time."

"Oh, do you think so? It would ease my heart to think that we can invite the Zeklinskis to our home some day."

"You must consider their feelings. Suppose someone made a rude remark? You wouldn't want them slighted."

"No, I couldn't bear it. That would be too awful. It's so kind of you to think of their feelings."

"How did you meet these Jews?"

"My brother introduced them to me."

Alexei. I might have known. Gambles heavily. Yes, that's it. His gambling. Probably needed to borrow money to pay his debts so he went to the Jew. Uses his innocent sister for his dirty business. It's a wonder she's so good-hearted. Knew she was the woman for me when we first met. God's grand design, else why would I love her so?

"You'll be kind to them tonight, won't you? For my sake?" Her voice quavered.

"Of course. There's a dear. So brave. And such compassion. For the Jews, I mean. It's your tender heart, and I love you all the more for it. What have I said now, my love?" he asked, alarmed at the fresh outbreak of sobs.

"What shall I tell Miriam? How can I explain this to her?"

"I'll tell her, to spare you."

"No, Peter. Kind of you to offer, but it just wouldn't be right. You'll understand when you meet her tonight. I'm sure she'll bewitch you just as she's bewitched me."

Bewitched? Odd word. Is it possible? The cheerful expression on his face belied his dark imaginings.

⌘

"Is everything in order, Boris?"

"Yes, Madame. It will be an honor for the staff to serve you and your distinguished guests this evening."

"I rely on all of you then, to be at your best." Never says such things about Jewish guests, she thought, feeling more amused than insulted.

"Will that be all, Madame?" Who would have thought these Jews would come so far, the butler mused. Impressive guest list. Prince Bedorov from Moscow. Madame has style. Manners of a countess. Such bad luck to be born a Jew.

"Order my carriage. I've an appointment with Madame Henriette."

⌘

There were no other clients in the dressmaker's salon at that hour for it was very early in the day, a time Miriam had chosen for precisely that reason.

"Have you come for a fitting?" The dressmaker's voice dripped with spite as if it were poisoned sap from some malevolent tree.

Miriam reddened. "A fitting? Surely you don't mean that. I intended to wear the gown this evening."

"We'll do our best to have it finished."

"Don't bother. Consider my entire order canceled and I shall instruct my husband to disregard your bill." Miriam stormed toward the door.

"Madame, please," the dressmaker pleaded. "You mistake my intentions. We're so busy. My staff is overworked. We'll try to finish your gown this afternoon."

Miriam unlatched the door.

"Please! We'll have it for you in one hour."

Miriam yanked the door open.

The dressmaker clutched Miriam's cloak in desperation.

"It's ready. Colette! Bring Madame's gown this instant." She pushed the door shut. "Let me help you off with your wraps." The dressmaker frantically fought the furs in her haste to make amends.

"How many gowns have I on order? How much lingerie? You've one week to deliver them, for I'll not set foot in here again. I shall pay only for what suits my fancy. Is that clear?"

The young seamstress appeared, gown in hand. The fitted blue velvet bodice was shaped like a laced vest. Puffed ivory sild sleeves tied with blue velvet bows flowed into an ivory silk full-length skirt covered with pale Belgian lace.

"So it was ready after all." She swept past the terrified dressmaker and followed the seamstress to the fitting room.

My God, we won't be able to repay the loan to Zeklinski. Rene will be furious. Our ticket home to Paris and I've ruined it. No, not me. That bitch of a Jew. Rene will beat me, but I deserve it this time. She hurried into the dressing room.

"You are a vision of loveliness in that gown, Madame." Miriam ignored her.

"Allow me to examine the hem." She dropped to her knees and measured. "Take this up a fraction, so Madame doesn't stumble, Colette. No need to move. She'll do it this instant. You wear clothes so well, it's a pleasure to fit you." she continued to babble to the hollow echo of her own wretched voice.

⌘

"I threatened to cancel the gown as well as all the others. I told her I'd advise you not to pay for them, which upset her, perhaps because the fabrics are so costly. The woman's a fool, but why spoil our evening? I'd much rather show you how splendid the dining room looks. Boris is so impressed with our guest list, *sans Juifs*, he and his staff have surpassed themselves."

"You'll not have further trouble with the dressmaker. I'll see to it."

"You needn't bother. I tried on all the other gowns this morning for final alterations. She's going to send them here with Colette, her seamstress. It won't be necessary to return to her salon."

"All right." He hesitated. "You look lovely in your new gown."

"Thank you, dear." She led him into the dining room.

"What do you think of Boris' handiwork?" The crystal glittered like diamonds and the dinner plates glistened like mirrors.

"You deserve all the credit, darling, not Boris or the staff. You've earned their respect as well as their devotion." Dov reached into his waistcoat pocket and drew out a velvet box.

"What's this?"

"A gift."

40

"A sapphire and diamond brooch and earrings to match!" What a wonderful surprise. A gift from Dov? So unlike him, she thought in puzzlement. The diamond-shaped brooch held a huge diamond set in silver in the middle, surrounded by sapphires. She fastened the dangling earrings, a cascade of diamonds flowing down from large sapphires at each lobe. Dov's hands brushed across her breasts after he fastened the brooch on her gown.

"Do you like them?"

"I love them. What's the occasion?"

"You know me only too well." He grinned, thinking of his clerk Hershl, whose task it was to remind him of birthdays and anniversaries. "Alexei introduced me to a jeweler and that gave me the idea." He saw no need to add that he had advanced the grateful jeweler a large sum to start his business. The jewelry was purchased at cost.

"I'm delighted darling. Perhaps I might repay you later."

⌘

"Blue velvet and pale ivory suit you, Miriam. Madame Henriette?" Anya asked. Miriam nodded.

"Excellent choice. She's the best couturier in Kiev. Peter darling, this is my friend Miriam."

Miriam sensed something amiss, but Anya averted her eyes. "Pleasure to meet you at last, Sire. Anya speaks of little else but you."

A nervous Anya changed the subject. "Where did you get that brooch? It's lovely."

"A gift from my husband."

"I'd like you to meet my fiancé, Dov. Prince Bedorov."

"Welcome, Sire." Dov extended his hand.

"Pleasure," Bedorov said. Dov was stunned by the coldness of the man's reluctant handshake. Bastard doesn't want to be here. Without another word, Dov stalked off, but Alexei followed him.

"A moment, Dov. Potowski's been turned down by every money-lender in Kiev. There's a bankruptcy notice nailed to the door of his yard."

"Think he'll make trouble?"

"No. He's disappeared. You're well rid of him."

"We're well rid of him," Dov corrected, drawing an appreciative smile from Alexei. "See to it that all the violations on his yard are removed. After that, his creditors will settle for ten percent."

"Only ten percent?"

"Yes. They're probably crying into their vodka right now, thinking they won't see so much as a kopek. They'll be overjoyed when they hear our offer."

"How will you go about it?"

"Golanov will let it be known around the wharf that he's interested in buying the shipyard. They'll come sniffing around like hungry dogs when they hear the news. They'll demand fifty percent of what they're owed, but Golanov will offer them two percent."

"Two? I thought you said ten."

"Just part of the game. The creditors will counter with an offer of twenty-five percent, perhaps. Golanov will raise his offer to five percent. They'll put their heads together and agree to fifteen percent, along with threats to keep him from reopening the yard if he doesn't meet their terms. Ten percent is his final offer, he'll insist. Golanov will complain that he doesn't need the headache of owning two yards. He'll withdraw his offer.

His friends in the Guild will tell the creditors they think Golanov's crazy. Who but a fool would make an offer for a shipyard with so many violations?

"Then they'll ply Golanov with drinks at his favorite tavern and plead with him to change his mind. They'll agree that ten percent is fair. They'll get down on their knees if they have to, but Misha can't hold that much liquor, so he'll consent after a few drinks."

"I have a lot to learn about business, Dov."

"You're a willing student which is all to the good. Shall we rejoin my guests?"

⌘

Miriam's diamond and sapphire brooch shimmered in the candle-lit dining room as she watched Boris supervise the servants.

"You're lovelier than those sapphires you wear," Alexei said. He sat on her left at dinner.

Miriam felt the beginnings of a flush at his words. "My husband said that you introduced him to the jeweler who designed it, Count Razovsky."

He raised his glass. You might repay me."

"How?"

"Call me Alexei. Your husband does."

"If it pleases you."

"Say it, then," he prodded.

"Alexei."

Razovsky's heart soared at the music of his name on her lips. We can be friends, can't we, he reasoned to himself when she turned her attention to General Brezhnovin on her right. Why not? Just don't forget, old man, she's Dov's wife.

"I was lonely without your company," he said lightly when Miriam turned his way again.

"Your future brother-in-law's very handsome," Miriam said, ignoring his banter.

"Frankly, my future brother-in-law's so dull, I envy the general's talent to sleep during dinner." Miriam smothered her laugh with her napkin.

"Would you like some water?"

"Yes, thanks." She took a sip, feeling more at ease. "Your sister keeps warning me of your reputation with women," she said, surprised at her audacity.

"I seem to have earned that reputation, yet I make no excuse for it. You laughed and that broke a barrier between us. Now, perhaps we can be friends."

"Of course, Count...Alexei.

"Will you permit me to call you Miriam?"

"If you like."

⌘

Dov announced that the men would remain for brandy and coffee after the ladies retired.

"Can we expect another concert this evening?" Countess Gorov asked before the men departed.

"Anya and I cannot perform a duet since our music room has only one piano," answered Miriam.

"Pity. Perhaps one of you, then?"

"I've a suggestion," offered Razovsky. "Will you sing for us tonight, Peter?"

Anya's face lit up. "Do say yes, Peter darling. I'll play for you." Bedorov agreed with a nod, for singing was his passion.

Anya played as though borne aloft by the beauty of Bedorov's elegant baritone. He sang tender folk ballads about unrequited love and livelier airs, but he sang the sad lyrical poems best.

Perhaps he's just shy, Miriam speculated as she listened to his haunting voice. Have I misjudged him? He seemed so surly when we were introduced. It's clear that he adores Anya.

⌘

"Where's my reward?" Dov let his hands rest on her shoulders after he unfastened the brooch. He released the hooks of her gown, letting it slide to the floor. He led her to bed. Why isn't she with child? The thought drained him of all passion. "No good, Miriam."

"Please. Don't stop now." Her hands continued to caress him frantically.

"Can't. Sorry."

43

ELEVEN

The fabric of their life suffered, for Dov hadn't made love to his wife since the night of their dinner party. In fact, he avoided all intimate conversation, embarrassed by that evening's disastrous ending.

He entered the drawing room. "What's that you're reading?"

"A letter from your cousin Sophie. Why didn't you tell me that Benjamin accepted your offer?"

"Didn't seem important."

Which means I'm not important, but Miriam chose not to challenge him. "She writes that your grandfather's visit to her mother-in-law helped them." What could he have said to change the old woman's mind?

Dov smiled. "*Zayde* can charm a snake. He might begin with small talk. 'How are you feeling, Sadie dearest? It is hard for you since your saintly husband passed on. Only God knows how much time we have on earth, eh?'"

"I didn't know that your grandfather knew Benjamin's parents."

"*Zayde* knows every Jew in Shklov. A woman with a heart as pure as yours cannot deny your only son the chance to carry out a father's dream, a golden opportunity for his son. There for the taking, as they say, like a ripe olive from a tree in Jerusalem."

"And if poor Sadie Moskowitz hasn't burst into tears by this time, *Zayde's* capable of demanding that she behave like a good Jew. But with *Zayde*, that's rarely necessary. That's why they call him *shtadlan*. No doubt he suggested ways in which the bereaved widow could enrich her life. He might suggest she visit the sick and the needy and the children at the orphanage. Don't be surprised to hear she's been named head of the sisterhood when the Zeklinski Academy opens. That's as close to the truth as we're likely to come, because my grandfather would never agree to break a confidence between him and his good friend Sadie."

Her laughter broke the icy coldness between them.

"I've had a letter from my mother as well."

"What news there?"

"She complains of her headaches. They're so frequent now, she can't even eat." Dov suppressed a smile.

"I know she eats more than she should, but what if it's more serious this time?"

"Not much sense in worrying. We'll see for ourselves in June." He yawned. "I'm going to bed. 'Night, dear."

"No, Dov. Not just yet. Please?"

"Can't it wait till morning? I'm weary."

She took a deep breath. "I love you. And I'm sorry."

"Sorry? For what?" he asked uneasily.

"For not giving you the child we both want so badly. This thing hanging over our heads is like a sword ready to fall and tear us apart. I want a child as much as you do." She covered her face and began to weep.

"I don't like to see you so unhappy." He held her as she sobbed, searching in his mind for a solution the way he would search to solve a dilemma in business. Weigh this fact. Weigh that. There had to be a way. He could not accept defeat.

"Dov?"

"What is it?"

"Lie down. On your back."

"Why?"

"Do it," she urged as she removed her dressing gown. "Close your eyes and lie still." She raised his nightshirt and stroked him, sensuous, rhythmic strokes. When her nails raked his skin, he cried out in pain, yet felt sheer pleasure. Her tongue reached his navel and hesitated for a split second before spiraling down between his legs. He shuddered and made a feeble attempt to stop her, but she pressed him down with her body.

"Lie still," she ordered, running her hands down to his buttocks. Her feverish lips soothed the angry red welts her nails had made. She raised herself over him, pinning his arms and lowering her body to meet his. Her hips swayed as Dov strained to meet her rhythm.

"Now, Dov. Move. Faster."

TWELVE

"Anya needs to spend all her time with her fiancé."

"She might have included you in some of her plans. I suspect, had it been the other way around, you would not have overlooked her."

"It's all right, Natasha. We'll see lots of one another when the czarina sails in May, and there's always her wedding in Moscow to look forward to, isn't there?"

Countess Gorov scowled, for she knew the ways of the Muscovites. She resolved to force Anya to tell Miriam the truth. "Don't delude yourself into thinking that her abrupt withdrawal from your life is accidental. Bedorov has surely had a hand in it."

"I suspected as much. He doesn't like Jews, does he? Perhaps when he comes to know me better." As she spoke to the older woman, Miriam was startled by a fleeting vision of Countess Gorov as her mother. Rational. Humane. Warm. Witty. Christian.

"So long as I have you for a friend, I shan't be unhappy. My mother would be terribly jealous if she knew about you."

"Why?"

"Thinks I ought to save all my loyalties for her, I suppose. She's always been quick to take offense even where none is meant."

"Your mother's fortunate to have a daughter like you. How old are you?"

"I shall be eighteen on the twenty-seventh of April."

Natasha sensed her young friend's discomfort.

"Something is distressing you, isn't it?"

"Yes, I'm dreadfully unhappy because I haven't conceived. So is Dov. It hangs like a stone wall between us. Just admitting it to you makes me feel better somehow. Isn't that odd?"

"You mustn't allow this to become the tragedy of your life, dear."

"It matters a great deal to us both. Children are a great blessing, a biblical commandment. `Thy wife shall be as a fruitful vine.'"

"Why not adopt?"

"Dov won't hear of it, but I wouldn't mind."

"We Russians are a peculiar people, born of rock and misery in the wilderness of winter as it were, while you and Dov are fighting to be heard, bright stars awash in the mire of our country. That's what's important. Don't waste your time on something over which you have no control."

"I admire you for your intelligence, Natasha."

"We women don't have many choices in life. We're property in the eyes of society. A man may murder his wife for her infidelity and go unpunished, yet a woman would be hanged for such a deed."

"The czarina's a free woman."

"Not true. She has many enemies. Her preference for young lovers gives them cause to ridicule her even as they indulge in their own illicit *affaires de'coeur.* If she were a man, no one would think the less of her for her carnal appetites. I've had my share of amorous liaisons, but I've grown too old for the game."

"I don't think of you as old. You think young thoughts. Wise thoughts. You're a tonic for me. When I came to see you this afternoon, my heart was heavy with the weight of my childlessness. You help me see things clearly, and for that I thank you. Your husband was fortunate to have had so rare a wife as you."

She laughed. "What makes you think he appreciated me? I embarrassed him when I said what I pleased. In spite of it, I must say he was a kind soul. A bit too taciturn for my taste, but an honorable man nevertheless. He was content to leave me to my diversions—and I had many—so long as I didn't interfere with his."

Natasha fanned the flames of her mind with a fire Miriam sometimes forgot she possessed. It made her feel alive and vibrant and human and it fortified her against life's indignities.

⌘

"The architect left the sketches you requested. He wants to know when he can begin."

"I leave for Shklov in June. He can begin then."

"Your mail." Hershl said. Dov frowned at the sight of his Uncle Moses' hand.

"The jeweler left these for you to choose from. And Monsieur DuBois is waiting to see you."

"Tell DuBois I'm busy. Tell him to pay his installment to you. If he doesn't have it, he'll have to pay additional interest. I'm expecting Golanov. Arrange lunch for us." Dov read his uncle's letter when Hershl withdrew.

Dear Dov,

Thank you for offering my son-in-law Benjamin a position with Zeklinski Enterprises in Kiev. My daughter Sophie is delighted.

I received your request for additional funds for this barge business. These are huge sums you request. I have only the best interests of Zeklinski Enterprises at heart. Why take foolish risks that may have dire consequences?

Let us continue to maintain our sound financial position as we always have under the leadership of our founder, the revered shtadlan.

Uncle Moses

Damn, he's stubborn. Can't let him interfere with my plans. Still, I'll have to try to save his damned pride because he's my uncle. Tell Hershl to transfer the bulk of our funds here, but leave a small sum in Petersburg for him to manage.

Dov made notes on the architect's sketches, pleased with planned expansion.

He opened the jeweler's case and studied the selection, finally choosing a set with a five-strand seed pearl piece clasped together by a diamond-studded brooch, in the center of which was a huge pearl. It was to be worn fastened over the bodice, draped from shoulder to shoulder. A bracelet—a diamond covered cuff with a matching pearl in the center, and earrings that began at the lobe with a huge pearl from which a loose spray of alternating diamonds and pearls flowed downward.

"Master Golanov is here, sir."

"Have the jeweler wrap these for me, a birthday gift for my wife, and return the rest to him. Send Misha in."

Dov rose to greet the man who had become his good friend and was immediately enveloped in a bear hug and kisses on both cheeks. "Haven't seen much of you lately. You used visit me more often."

"No time these days, but I'm not complaining. Two shipyards keep me busy, which is better than spending my time at the tavern drowning in vodka. You want a progress report?"

"How goes it?"

"I have enough labor and the chancery people stay away from my yards, thanks to you, though it's a mystery to me how you manage to bribe such a hungry army. They ruined Potowski, but I'm fine."

"Potowski ruined himself."

"I don't feel sorry for that cheat. When business was slow, he'd undercut my price. Then he'd build some sucker a leaky tub. I can't count the times his customers crawled back to me to fix his botched job. It cost them more than if I'd built it right for them in the first place. He cheated his suppliers, too, they say, by refusing to pay the final few kopeks. 'Settle for the rubles. That's all I can spare. What's a few kopeks to you, anyway?' he'd tell them. So each sucker lost a few kopeks. He's a mean son of a whoring troublemaker, that one. Glad to be rid of him. Besides. Times are good. No one thinks of him since everyone's making money these days."

"Glad to hear it."

"What's on your mind, Dov?"

"Let's eat first." His clerks waited on them in silence.

"Food for a peasant like me, eh? *Kasha. Blinis. Borscht.* I have a feeling it's going to cost me, even though it's free. Never mind. I'm a happy man, a wealthy merchant instead of a starving merchant."

"Glad to hear you're happy."

"Why shouldn't I be happy?" He paused to belch, a lion's growl.

Dov strolled to his window and beckoned Golanov to join him. "I love that sight. It churns my blood to see men busy building and doing. What do you think will happen to them when the czarina sails on May First?"

Golanov shrugged. "The men will get drunk on vodka and talk about the good old days when the czarina was here and they made a fortune. These men take life as it comes. Besides, it's the will of the Lord."

"Why rest when there's more work out there waiting for us?"

"What are you driving at?"

"Can you build frigates?"

Misha Golanov threw back his head and roared with laughter.

"What's so funny?"

"In Kiev? The Dniepr's just a shallow, muddy river. Have you any idea how big those monsters are? You can't transport huge frigates over land to the Black Sea."

"I hadn't thought of that. But then, you're the builder, not me. Suppose I were to tell you that we can get the commission to build not just one, but a great many frigates for the Imperial Navy."

"Potemkin?" Dov nodded. "You can't build frigates here."

"What do you suggest?"

"Buy an existing shipyard somewhere on a large body of water. Building a new one is costly."

"All right. Then I want you to take a little holiday, Misha. When the czarina sails, I want you to go to Sebastopol. See what you can see. Then come back and we'll talk."

"I've never built a frigate before."

"I wouldn't think of forcing you to build something if you don't know how."

"Who says I don't know how? There isn't a ship on this earth I couldn't build better than any man alive."

"Well, then. Don't do it for my sake. Do it for the glory of Mother Russia."

⌘

Dov's scribe took the chair opposite him, quill and writing board ready. Dov dictated several notes in quick succession, to be dispatched by private messenger, a system he'd long ago created since the Russian mail system was far too slow to suit him.

His final note contained a brief message to Potemkin:

Imperial Majesty,
As per your wishes, work has begun work on the new project.
Your humble servant,
Reb Dov Zeklinski

THIRTEEN

On the appointed day, Miriam, Dov and Natasha Gorov observed the pomp and pageantry on the parade grounds.

They witnessed Empress Catherine II enter on horseback, Prince Potemkin at her side. All cheered the two leaders, except for Catherine's current favorite, twenty-two-year old Count Mamonov, who wore a look of boredom as he lounged in the Royal Box.

The czarina waved to acknowledge shouts of "Long live Little Mother!" and "God bless our czarina."

The Preobrazhensky Guards, Catherine's personal regiment, were first to present colors to Her Highness. The Ismailovsky Regiment followed and the empress stood in acknowledgment, for the Ismailovsky was the first to recognize her as their sovereign when Czar Peter was overthrown twenty-five years earlier.

Loud huzzahs of appreciation greeted the next battalion of Ukrainian Cossacks who raced fiercely onto the field as if ready for war. Ribbons of black leather studded with ammunition lay crisscrossed over blazing red jackets trimmed with curled black fur. Their tall black hats stood guard over faces extended by long beards. Tatars and Georgians and Armenians followed, a mélange that encompassed the immense diversity of the empire.

Miriam's uneasiness grew. She wondered if perhaps the Jewish battalion had been ordered not to perform after all, for the hour was late and viewers were already quitting the grounds.

"Where is the Israelovsky? When will they present their colors?"

Dov scanned the field with his opera glasses. "There they are now."

Sergeant Brodsky paused before the czarina and raised his sword in salute. When he turned to his regiment and gave the command to present arms. he could not observe the czarina rising to leave. Potemkin lingered another moment before he followed.

Regimental Sergeant Josef Brodsky and the men of the Israelovsky Battalion performed their flawless maneuvers to empty stands and hollow cheers.

The czarina's hasty departure was a stinging rebuff to the Israelovsky. Potemkin's token gesture amounted to the same thing.

Because the men were Jewish, Miriam thought. She took no notice of the crowds that gave way as they made their way toward the reception at the Razovsky estate. Weary citizens, many of them drunk from the long afternoon's celebration, waved as the carriage passed, displaying that camaraderie of good will invoked by such festive occasions. Kiev had not seen such pageantry since the days of Prince Vladimir.

"Don't take it so to heart," Natasha said, aware of Miriam's distress.

"Brodsky and his men worked so hard."

"If it's any comfort to you dear, I think they performed exceedingly well."

"Even so, my heart aches for them."

Dov stared out the window and said nothing.

⌘

"I want a word with you, Alexei."

"What is it, Petrov?"

"It's that Jew."

"You know as well as I do that Dov Zeklinski is favored by the Crown."

"Well and good, but this is Kiev and the Crown's patronage will soon go up in smoke."

"Come to the point."

"All right. Man name of Potowski used to build barges on the wharf. Says the Jew forced him into bankruptcy, though he can't prove it. Is it true?"

"I don't know what he's talking about. The man must be lying to gain your sympathy."

"No. Potowski's a devout Christian. He's living on my estate. Can't let the poor man and his family starve."

"Decent of you, old man. Excuse me." He hurried to welcome his guests, having caught sight of the Zeklinskis.

"What took you so long? Everyone from the parade grounds arrived at least an hour ago. Good to see you, Natasha." Alexei kissed the dowager's hand, but she brushed him aside. She grasped Anya by the arm and led her out of earshot.

"Miriam thinks she's to be invited to your wedding. I insist you tell her the truth at once."

"How can I hurt her so?"

"Don't be a fool! The truth won't hurt her."

Anya sighed. "It isn't Peter's fault, you know. He thinks it's so unjust."

"Never mind Peter. Tell her now and be done with it." She dragged Anya back toward Miriam.

"May I have a word, Miriam? Let's go into the conservatory, shall we?"

Natasha's eyes never left the two as they made their way through the crush of guests.

"Confess, Natasha," Alexei interrupted. "Have you a secret lover? A gentleman has been asking after you ever since his arrival. Do you see him? Over there."

"At my age? What nonsense," she said, yet she laughed in delight. "Ah, I do see him, though my eyesight's not what it used to be. He's far too old for any assignation, but at our age, no longer necessary. Still, he once was a handsome cavalier and I fancied him." The countess swept past him to greet the man.

"What a rare woman," said Dov.

"The best. Here comes Madame von Hals. Hannelore's a childhood friend of mine, Dov."

"We've met before." She smiled at Dov as though they shared some private secret.

"You promised to call on me for advice. Do you find it no longer necessary?" She laughed, the sound like a carillon to Dov's ears.

"I find it more necessary than ever, though there's no need to spoil a perfectly lovely party to discuss business. When shall we meet?"

"Will tomorrow at my office be convenient?"

"Fine. But now I fancy a stroll in the garden. Care to join me?" She took his arm. Her beauty seared his senses like hot ashes on bare flesh as they made their way out to the garden.

"You've an unusual name. Austrian, isn't it? Yet you speak French like a Russian."

"I am Russian-born, but I married an Austrian. And your name? Polish?"

"I was born there, but I'm Jewish." He wondered why he felt compelled to tell her something she already knew. "You're astonishingly beautiful."

"My greatest asset, for I wasn't born to wealth. Beauty is the price of admission to a pleasurable life. I don't hold with those who think that life's a random accident. We make of it whatever we choose."

"I feel the same way," Dov blurted, furious with himself for sounding like a nervous schoolboy.

"They say that you're brilliant."

"Rumors." He shrugged.

"You needn't be modest. You know you have an enviable reputation as a barge builder for the Crown. You do recall my telling you I own a rather large shipyard in Sebastopol, don't you?"

⌘

Nightfall hovered in the shadows at dusk. All was dark below the treetops, yet the sky was streaked with pale pink and blue hues lit by the lingering sun.

53

Miriam could not help but feel despondent. Out in the open at last, she thought. Can it ever be the same between Anya and me?

Dov is so determined for us to become part of this life. Is it worth the effort? We're like battering rams, yet the wall's impenetrable. Wouldn't we be better off living in Shklov among our own people where we'd know our place? My mother was right when she objected to moving to St. Petersburg. Jews don't belong here.

She turned her head at the sound of footsteps crackling on the harsh tile floor.

"What are you doing here by yourself? Is something troubling you?" Asked Alexei who had been searching for her.

"Anya had unhappy news for me."

"What news?" He took her hand in his, relieved that she didn't recoil from his touch.

"We're not to be invited to her wedding in Moscow. Because we're Jewish."

"How cruel of her."

"No. Anya was really brave to tell me. It's just the way things are, that's all."

"You're the brave one, not Anya. She doesn't have to bear the trials that you face every day of your life." He took her face in his hands. "It's you who has courage. Anya's still a child. But you are willing to sacrifice yourself to break down barriers. God knows how much bigotry you put up with, yet you bear it with dignity, with grace, with honor. I've never met anyone like you. And I don't mean merely your beauty, though you're one of the loveliest women on this earth." Miriam's eyes glistened with tears. He brushed them away with his fingers.

"Such a burden to be a Jew, isn't it? Yet you have a quality that transcends all the ugliness and the suspicion and the mistrust. I wish I could accept the trials of life as well as you. Your husband's a very fortunate man. I hope he knows that. On my honor I hope he knows that. There isn't a woman who equals you in intelligence and in sensitivity."

She touched her head to his shoulder as he held her to him in the shadowy dusk. "It's kind of you to say such lovely things, but I'm not as wonderful as you make me out to be."

"In my eyes you are." They fell into a silence that somehow becalmed her.

"Odd," she said at last.

"What is?"

"You cannot know how much of a comfort you are to me today."

"I'm glad."

She smiled at him through her tears and his heart soared.

⌘

"It was a lovely party."

"I wouldn't call the insult to Brodsky and his men lovely."

"Cheer up. That's bound to change some day."

"I wonder, Dov. Can't you see the hate, the suspicious glances?"

"I'm not immune to it. I'm also not about to let a few bigots spoil my life. I happen to think we're making progress." He changed the subject. "I met an interesting woman. I wanted you to meet her, but I couldn't find you."

"Who is she?"

"She's asked me for help with her late husband's estate."

"Decent of you to help an old widow." She reached for him, needing him to soothe the bruises in her soul.

Dov had no trouble this time. He thought of Hannelore von Hals as he made love to his wife.

FOURTEEN

Serfdom was the foundation of the Russian economy. Serfs tended the land, made clothing during the bitter winter months when there were no fields to tend, labored in factories that produced china, pottery and furniture as well as the sundry artifacts so essential to life. The number of serfs owned calculated the wealth of the nobility. Serfs could be bought and sold at will.

In addition, Noblemen sought opportunities to invest with Zeklinski Enterprises since State banks paid little interest. A few had doubts about the motherland's need for Jewish finance, yet they put aside their misgivings for profit. Others petitioned to borrow for business purposes.

One such petitioner had the effrontery to request a loan to finance the purchase of a printing press. There was no profit in a printing press, Dov told the man in indignation, since more than ninety percent of the populace could not read.

⌘

Madame von Hals is late, Dov thought, impatient for her arrival. Remarkable woman. At least she's honest. Admits that she married that old von Hals for his money.

Does she want more than just business advice from me? He let his thoughts fly. Her lying beneath me. God, I'm aroused.

"Madame von Hals," said Hershl at last.

Dov rose to greet her. "Please, sit here, Madame von Hals."

"My friends call me Hanne."

"Hannah? My mother's name is Hannah, though you aren't old enough to be anyone's mother, let alone mine."

She laughed. "I like humor in a man."

"You say the most unexpected things."

"The unexpected adds spice to life. Since Hanne reminds you of your mother, call me Lori. My late husband did."

"My name is Dov."

"Hebrew for David?"

"No, Dov means 'Bear' in Hebrew."

She laughed. "Well, I can't call you bear, so I shall call you David."

"Why? Is Dov too Jewish?"

"Actually, your being Jewish puts us on equal footing." She spoke with amusement in her voice.

"How so?"

"I'm an outsider, like you. I was born illegitimate, the result of a brief liaison between a prince and a serf. My mother died when I was a child and my father placed me in a convent for my education. The year before I was to complete my studies, father sold off his estate to pay his enormous gambling debts and died of syphilis soon after. I owe the rest of my education to the largess of Alexei Razovsky's uncle, my father's good friend. He needed a companion for his elderly mother, but I had no intention of using my assets so ill for the rest of my life."

"I should think not, with your good looks and your charm."

"Ugly women command excellent husbands if they're well born, while beautiful but destitute women must settle for the lame or the blind or the idiot hiding in the family closet if they marry at all."

"Yet you succeeded."

"Yes. I met Hermann at a ball in St. Petersburg. I was eighteen then and he was seventy-one. He was unable to resist my beauty and I was unable to resist his wealth. He offered me a mansion and a generous allowance if I became his mistress, but I refused. I chose to risk losing him for the chance to become his wife. What are assets for if you can't use them properly?

"We lived in St. Petersburg for six months at the request of the Crown. Hermann spent his days in the Admiralty building and his nights with me before he went south to Sebastopol to see to his shipyard. I wrote to him every day. When he died, he left me the Sebastopol shipyard and a generous stipend. His children received the bulk of his estate."

Dov asked, "What advice do you seek from me?"

"I don't wish to sell, because war is good business and the profits are enormous, but I want to decide how to proceed. I've heard that men fawn over your words of advice."

He smiled. "Men three times my age treat me as though I'd inherited the wisdom of Solomon."

"People believe that wealth and wisdom are one and the same. Where's the harm in that? Part of life's game."

"I agree. Life is a game."

"Well, there you are." She paused for thought. "They say your business empire stretches across Russia. Is that true?" Dov nodded. "In that case, I'd like you to arrange for the von Hals Shipyards in Sebastopol to carry on as before."

"Have you some idea of how to proceed?"

"None, but I'm not here to solicit free counsel. Alexei Razovsky assures me that you are an honorable man. Alexei's judgment about people is excellent, though his conduct's another matter. I've often cautioned him not to drink and gamble so much, for fear he'll end up like my father, but he's too busy bedding down other men's wives. It's the royal sport, you see."

"So I've noticed."

"How old are you, David?"

"Nineteen. Does that lower your good opinion of me?"

"Quite the opposite. Your financial prowess amounts to genius in one so young. I'm twenty, by the way."

"What sort of arrangement do you have in mind?"

"A full partnership. As my partner, you'd be concerned with my own interests as well as yours, isn't that so?"

"You've no fear that I might take advantage of you?"

"None at all."

"I accept with pleasure. Allow me to suggest a way to proceed." Dov explained that solicitors in his office in St. Petersburg would meet with her solicitors to review her current position. Once the net worth of von Hals Shipyards was determined, they would form a partnership. His staff would prepare correspondence for her representatives. "In fact, I'm sending someone to Sebastopol. Would you consent to allowing him to inspect your yard?"

"Of course."

"Perhaps we can meet before you return to Berlin, to finalize our partnership."

"Precisely the result I expected. You play the game of business well. You should learn to play other games."

"I haven't the time."

"Too bad. Games add spice to life. One needs them to tease the palate."

"What do you suggest?"

"For a start, the night life at the diplomatic palaces is most diverting."

"Perhaps Jews aren't welcome."

"On the contrary. Count Cobenzl, the Austrian envoy, would be delighted to meet you. Would you care to join me tonight?"

"I'll have to ask my wife."

Hannelore von Hals' amused laughter filled the office. "What for?"

Dov turned red, furious with himself for misunderstanding. "Sorry. I've had so little experience in these matters."

"I can see that. I'm perfectly willing to be your tutor. I'm also willing to leave you to your wife if that is what you wish. I'm shocking you, I see."

"Perhaps you are shocking me."

"You're a charming innocent, David. I find that appealing, somehow. I'd love to be your tutor in the ways of the world. If you change your mind and decide to escort me to Count Cobenzl's palace tonight, you would be lionized by the men, and the women would cling to you like shards to a magnet."

"You're turning my head."

"I am trying to. You must know that you're a leader. You know what they say about horses, don't you?"

"Horses? The connection escapes me."

She rose to leave. "They say that lead horses have the best view."

FIFTEEN

Dov observed his sleeping wife. Lips too thick. Breasts too large. Stubborn. Persists in harping on the incident on the parade grounds. Sees insults where none are meant.

Madame von Hals knows what she wants. Does she want me?

He toyed with the breakfast Boris placed before him, a vision of Hannelore von Hals asleep in her bed tantalizing him. Serene.

"Will that be all, sir?"

"Yes, thank you. I shall be back late this afternoon. Inform Madame and be sure my evening clothes are ready, won't you?"

"Yes, sir."

"You're a good man, Boris."

"Your carriage is waiting, sir." Boris watched his master depart. Jew doesn't appreciate my work, he thought.

⌘

A feeling of apprehension plunged Miriam's emotions to the depths of her soul. Dov working on the Sabbath? How could he do such a thing?

"The overseer is here to see you, Madame," Boris added.

"Send him in."

"You sent for me?"

"It has come to my attention that you beat one of my serfs with a knout. Twenty lashes, enough to kill. Do you deny it, sir?"

"Of course not."

"I shall dismiss you if you ever repeat such punishment to any of my serfs again."

"What's that you say?" Uneven circles of red stained his cheeks. "I'll not have you meddling in the proper conduct of my affairs, Madame."

"I am mistress here."

"It is well known that all serfs are lazy by nature and shirk their chores when they can."

His arrogance infuriated her, but she held her tongue until she'd had an opportunity to tell Dov. *He'll surely agree to dismiss him, but I won't tell him tonight. Why let this insolent fellow spoil my birthday?*

She ordered him to return Monday morning to hear his fate, which she implied might be dismissal. *Thinks he can patronize me. We'll see who wins this battle.*

It was a perfect sunny April day, without a hint of chill in the air. She tried not to dwell on Dov's failure to observe the Sabbath and on her fight with Borschov, but her heart was heavy just the same. She examined the swollen buds on the branches, a hint of splendor by summer. With each passing hour, Miriam's feelings toward Dov began to soften.

I'm being too hard on the poor dear. Everything will be fine once the czarina sails on Wednesday. She settled down to read a romantic French novel Anya had given her months ago. She became engrossed in the familiar tale of love between a beautiful countess cruelly imprisoned by an evil count and a swashbuckler who spent chapter after chapter attempting to rescue her.

⌘

"Where on earth have you been?"

"Unavoidable. Business."

"Are you angry with me?"

"No."

"That can't be, Dov. First you break the Sabbath, then you come home without a moment to spare on the night of the czarina's final ball and then you act as though I'd done something wrong."

Dov took a deep breath. "Is it too much to ask you to be more considerate?"

"What are you talking about?"

"I'm sick of your complaints. And since I think you have little reason to warrant such an occupation, I've good reason to be furious." His words assaulted her as though he'd slapped her.

"I couldn't wait for you to come home tonight to tell you that I forgive you for breaking the Sabbath today."

"I should think, after what I learned today, that it is you who should beg my forgiveness."

She felt hot tears rising as she spoke. "What are you driving at?"

"Let well enough alone tonight."

"No. Tell me now. I don't deserve your scorn." She couldn't take her eyes from his angry face as he sat down to eat the cold supper waiting for him. He

61

wiped his mouth and pushed the chair away from the table. When he spoke, his voice was so low, Miriam had to strain to hear.

"Borschov came to see me today. I think you know why."

"And?"

"When I heard him out, I told him he is to deal with my office, where men understand these things. I apologized for you, my dear, and explained how unfamiliar you are with worldly affairs."

"You didn't!"

"I did and I meant every word. I can no longer rely on you to supervise the management of our home. As if I didn't have enough to do as head of one of the largest industries in Russia." His words pierced like falling icicles.

"Borschov nearly killed that poor man over the loss of three measly hens."

"A serf, Miriam. Property. Can't you understand it's the way things are? Did it ever occur to you that there might be some consequences if Borschov weren't allowed to assert the necessary authority? You can't tie a man's hands behind his back and order him to do his job at the same time."

"You're being terribly unfair."

"What has unfairness to do with proper management? Man's doing what he's paid for. No more no less."

"He nearly killed the poor man. Sergeant Brodsky said to warn you that there might be an uprising from our serfs over this."

"What do I care what that damned orphan said? Serfs are property, not people. I can buy and sell them but I can't always find an experienced overseer. So what if he's a tyrant? It's his business to be a tyrant."

"That man's also the most prejudiced..."

"So what? The whole damned country hates Jews. Who cares? We don't need their love, just their respect."

"You certainly were on my side about the dressmaker."

"Every well-born woman in Kiev visits the dressmaker without complaining, but not you. I wish, just once, you could hear yourself complain about all the Jew-haters. Borschov. The dressmaker. Our butler Boris doesn't behave as well toward Jewish guests as he does toward Christian guests. Yet I've never noticed anyone lack appetite over the insult. Your list is so long, my dear." He ignored the tears streaking her face.

"I don't deserve your cruelty."

"Yes you do, dear wife. You've earned it. Any other woman might thank God for a husband who is as good to her as I am to you. Yet you persist in rewarding me with your petty grievances." Miriam began to sob, yet Dov went on, his voice dripping with sarcasm.

"Fortunes rise and fall when I so much as cough. But why should you concern yourself with such bourgeois matters? More important that I come home to you at night, to suffer news of the real concerns of the world, isn't that so?" Miriam stifled her sobs, for there was something menacing in the tone of his voice.

"I made the error of thinking you were clever enough to manage our estate, but you weren't even able to do that properly. You're just as witless as your mother, aren't you? But then, they say the apple doesn't fall far from the tree."

"That's cruel, Dov."

He shrugged, "It's true just the same. I've seen your mother carp at your father. You've said so yourself, haven't you?"

"I'm not like my mother."

"And I'm not like your father. I'm damned good to you and look how you repay me. You aren't even woman enough to give me children."

Miriam drew in her breath at the sting of his words. "Why are you hurting me like this? I wish I were dead."

"Don't be so damned dramatic," he said. "Wash the tears off your face. It's time to go. Here." He drew a velvet jewel box from his waistcoat and threw it on the bed. The box flew open and revealed an elaborate hair ornament. An oval gemstone hairpiece encrusted with rubies, sapphires, emeralds and diamonds embedded in gold.

"Happy birthday. These are for you, dear wife. Wear them tonight so you can show all your enemies at the ball the kind of man you married."

SIXTEEN

Miriam had no one to share the wonder of a ballroom full of hundreds of people, all dressed in dazzling finery, for she and Dov had not spoken since they'd left home. We're like two strangers now, she thought.

"Champagne?" Dov handed her a goblet from the servant's proffered tray. In defiance, she drained the glass, an act that earned her a look of scorn. She retaliated by tapping a passing servant with her fan and taking a second, which she drank as quickly as the first.

"Careful. You're not used to champagne."

"Afraid I'll embarrass you?"

"Suit yourself."

When the trumpets sounded, they found a place at the side of the grand staircase from which to catch a glimpse of the arrival of Czarina Catherine and Prince Potemkin.

The imperial pair stopped to acknowledge those to whom they were being introduced, but she and Dov had not been so favored this time. The czarina wore a richly embroidered white silk gown adorned with ribbons and medals resting on her ample bosom. Potemkin was equally resplendent in full dress white uniform trimmed with gold braid. Miriam's sidelong glance at Dov revealed boredom as his eyes swept the room.

"There you are," said Anya. She clutched Peter Bedorov's hand, seeming to drag his lumbering frame behind her. "We've been looking for you." She kissed Miriam's cheek. "You look exquisite in the gown Madame Henriette designed for you. The simple empire waist flatters you. And that hairpiece is stunning. I've never seen it before."

"Today's my birthday. It's from my husband."

"Happy birthday, darling. Aren't they lovely, Peter?" But she didn't wait for an answer. "We've a present for you as well, don't we Peter? Go ahead, dear. Ask her."

"May I have the next dance, Madame?"

"My pleasure," Miriam curtsied and swore undying devotion to Anya for rescuing her from her anguish.

"Miriam's the dearest woman. She dances so well, doesn't she?" Dov nodded, barely attending to Anya's chatter.

"Hello, little sister. Where's Peter? Nice to see you, Dov."

"Miriam is dancing the minuet with Peter. Do you see them?"

Alexei leaned over to whisper in his sister's ear. "How did you manage to get Peter to dance with Miriam?"

"His idea. To soften her disappointment. Isn't he wonderful?" She took his arm as they watched the dancers.

When the music ended, Dov caught sight of the object of his search. "There's someone I'd like to talk to for a moment. Be a good friend Alexei, and look after my wife for me, won't you?"

"Considering how dazzling she looks," Razovsky answered with wry good humor, "And considering my reputation, it's a wonder you dare ask me that."

Dov hurried off, much to the count's amusement, for he, too, had caught sight of Hannelore von Hals. He watched Dov hurry to her side. *If Hanne wants him, he's done for. She won't let go until she gets what she's after. Bad luck for Miriam, poor thing. She's so devoted to him.*

"We're friends now, just as you wish, Anya." Bedorov, magnanimous in victory, smiled at her. *One dance with the Jew's wife was worth the adoring look in Anya's sweet face.*

"I promise to look after her when you're gone, Peter."

"Happy birthday, Miriam. Many happy returns."

"Thank you, Alexei." She glanced around her. "Where is Dov?"

"Your husband had some urgent business. He's asked me to be your escort until he returns. I confess, I hope he'll remain away long enough for this next dance."

He bowed with such mock formality that Miriam blushed, heightening the color already wrought by two glasses of champagne. He led her to the floor, where she glided effortlessly in his arms. She followed his graceful movements as if in a trance, yet she could not focus.

Alexei stopped to steady her, for she had stumbled. "Are you all right?"

"I need some air," she gasped, feeling queasy.

He led her out to the terrace. "Sit here a moment."

"The champagne went to my head. Sorry to spoil your evening."

"Nonsense. I've attended enough Balls to last a lifetime. Rest your head on my shoulder until you feel better."

As he waited for her dizziness to subside, his glance fell on her cleavage. Her full breasts aroused him. *Dov's a fool to leave this treasure for the likes of Hanne. I wouldn't trade her for one hundred Hannes. Not Dov's fault, I* suppose. It's Hanne. She makes the choices. Just like she chose the old bastard she married.

"A stroll might help to clear your head."

She stumbled on the steps to the path below and he grasped her arm to steady her. Flaming torches held by servants lighted their path, illuminating the brilliant red and gold and orange Holland bulbs.

"It's as if this palace has been here for centuries."

"Precisely the effect Prince Potemkin meant to achieve. At the moment, I don't think well of him."

"Why not?"

"He's sending me back to St. Petersburg. Won't honor my repeated requests to accompany him and the Czarina on what is likely to be the most memorable event of the century. I'm less than happy as you can see, but there's nothing I can do about it."

"Life is full of disappointments."

"Surely not for you. You and Dov have an ideal life together, but I must be a good soldier whether I like it or not. It's a bitter pill to swallow." Miriam stumbled again, but he caught her. "Let's rest here, shall we?" He led her to a secluded garden settee within a small gazebo.

"You're nice to stay with me when you ought to be dancing."

"I'm quite content being here with you. In fact, I hope your husband is heartbroken without you. As for me, I'm trying hard to forget he exists."

So am I, she thought, full of misery. "You're such a good friend. Your sister and Natasha, too. I'm sorry she refused tonight's invitation. Said all this pomp tires her. I like it, though. Such beauty. The palace. The czarina. The prince." Miriam shivered, feeling chilled despite the warmth of the evening.

"You're cold. Here. Take my cape." He unhooked the chain that linked his dress cape and placed it around her shoulders. "Better?"

She nodded, grateful for the warmth. "I don't belong here. Dov and I will always be outsiders."

"I feel like an outsider, too."

"You, Alexei? How can that be?"

"I've always felt that way, though I didn't think much about it when my parents were alive. All this pomp signifies emptiness. The ball, the dinners, the parties." He waved his hand. "Potemkin flies in the face of convention in a way that I admire, because he has power, but I don't dare imitate him or I'd be sent to Siberia to count the birches, as they say. I dance, but the tune isn't mine. I wish I were more like Anya's fiancé Peter. He's at home in his exalted position in the Table of Ranks. Fine for him and for my sister, I suppose. But it makes me restless."

"Anya says you're a free spirit."

"I'm certain she sees me that way, but that's only because she's led a sheltered life. She does have a good heart, doesn't she? I'm proud of her for that, though I had very little to do with her virtues."

"You saw to her upbringing after your parents died. And you live a useful life."

"Useful? No. I live the high life, as they say. Say clever things. Gamble. Drink. Talk of honor. Honor's very important, you see. If a man's insulted, the only course is to challenge the offender to a duel. You can't imagine the high death rate this causes among us."

"Is that why you have a scar?" She ran her finger along the jagged furrow on his cheek.

"No, but it makes a much better tale to say so. I fell off a horse when I was ten years old. I tried to jump the hedges, but I misjudged. I can still recall the sting of the wound and the blood pouring down my clothing. My father was furious at my recklessness. He forced me to watch as he shot the poor colt whose leg was broken from the fall."

"How awful." They sat in silence for a bit. "Why have you never married?"

"I cannot bear the eligible young ladies of my station. There's a sameness about them that stifles me." Yet if it were you, he thought, and his heart quickened at the idea. "I might have married had I met someone like you."

"You're teasing me."

"I mean it. You're not like anyone I've ever known, but you belong to Dov."

She laughed for the first time that evening. "You're a wonderful person, Alexei. I'm fortunate to count you for a friend."

"You didn't like me when we first met."

"That's true, but I no longer remember why." She placed her hand on his. "You'll never know how much you've lifted my spirits tonight."

"I'm glad if I've done something to please you, because I think I've fallen a little bit in love with you." It startled him to hear the words escape his lips. "Does that offend you?"

"No. I feel close to you tonight. As a friend, I mean."

Such dignity, he thought as he searched her eyes. Imagine facing a woman like her every night, an impossible dream. Is that why I ache for her? Because I know I can't have her? She's courageous in spite of adversity, yet she doesn't give ground. Stands firm, yet she isn't malicious.

"If you were anyone else's wife, Miriam, I might not behave properly," he said aloud. "I might plead to be your lover. That's what I said that offended you the first time we met. I told you that you could have any lover you choose." He held her hand and examined her palm before he raised it to his lips. "I'd give anything if it were me."

Miriam felt a deep, uncomfortable regret within. Regret for being tied to Dov. Regret for being childless. She wanted, all at once, to belong to this

67

sweet, sensitive man who brushed his lips across the palm of her hand with such compassion.

Dov no longer cares for me, she thought. Why not Alexei? No. Foolish thought. He's just being kind. Still, he's uncanny. Does he feel the depths of my misery?

A roar of trumpets pierced the quiet peace of the garden.

"What's that?"

"The signal that Her Majesty and Prince Potemkin are departing," Razovsky explained. "The ball is coming to an end." They rose from their seats and he turned her to him. "Have I offended you?"

"No."

"If you were mine," he heard himself say, "If only you were mine." He kissed her lightly on the lips, but Miriam strained to meet his mouth and he drew her closer.

Their embrace was born of the desperation of two lost souls battered by the winds of a stormy sea, an embrace full of hope somehow, tainted only by hopeless despair on this balmy April night. They could not stop, had no thought of stopping.

He pulled her to him roughly, yet she felt only gentleness in his arms. His hands tugged at her clothing, deftly removing her gown and what lay beneath. She clung to him, hungry for his touch. His mouth fed on each breast, on her body, below her navel. Wild with desire, she wrapped her legs around him as he took her.

⌘

"My wife," Dov said, pointing Miriam out to Hannelore von Hals. Miriam was with Count Razovsky in the center of the ballroom, her face glowing with pleasure as they danced.

"You've excellent taste in jewelry." Her smile was enchanting. "I'll be waiting for you at Count Cobenzl's salon tomorrow evening." She turned and walked away without looking back, but Dov could not tear his eyes off her receding form.

⌘

His stony silence on the way home oppressed Miriam even more that his words had earlier in the evening. She chose instead to think of Alexei. She tried to recapture their passion. It filled her with wonder, yet it frightened her. How could something so beautiful be so sinful? Yet she knew it was.

"Where are you going?" Miriam asked as Dov gathered his nightclothes.

"To my chambers," he answered, cutting off each word as if with a knife. He slammed the door behind him.

It was nearly dawn by the time she fell into a troubled sleep, her thoughts wavering between the wonder of Alexei and the misery of Dov. When she woke, Dov was gone.

In the days that followed, Miriam felt as though she were trapped in a living nightmare. Dov rose well before dawn each morning and returned late only to retire to the bedchamber he used when she was menstruating.

She waited up for him one night, determined to confront him. "How long shall you go on punishing me with your silence?"

"Be at my office tomorrow morning at nine," he said. "Catherine sails then. I've invited guests to observe her departure."

"I demand an answer."

"We'll have our discussion after the sailing. Now if you'll excuse me, I must get some sleep. Boris has orders to wake me in three hours, which might give you some idea of how difficult my life has been all week."

SEVENTEEN

"Join us for tea tomorrow," Alexei said to Natasha and to Miriam.

"Tell Anya we'd be delighted. I'll fetch you at two, Natasha," Miriam said, but further conversation proved impossible, for the clamor of trumpets and drums signaled the approach of the czarina.

Seven red and gold galleys stood ready to depart on the Dniepr River below, their gleaming white canopies flapping in the breezes of this first day of May. On the open deck of each one, a full orchestra waited for the signal to play the royal march.

Henriette DuBois glanced at her husband as they waited among the hordes of people who lined the waterfront for a final glimpse of Czarina Catherine. Rene was such a handsome devil, she thought, and so good in bed. Especially after a beating, when he was full of remorse for having lost his temper.

She well knew Zeklinski could ruin them. Her insolence had already cost them additional interest, money they had counted on for their return to France. She'd directed her seamstresses to take great care in finishing Madame Zeklinski's gowns, for it was impossible for her to sew after Rene broke her arm.

"That's Zeklinski Enterprises," Rene said, pointing to the sign above Dov's office windows, since his wife had never learned to read.

She bristled with fury when she caught sight of Miriam at the window. *Cocotte!* Some day I'll pay her back, she thought, her right arm throbbing with pain.

Vassily Borschov also trained his wrathful glance at Miriam. Hope her husband beat her, after what I told him. In his mind's eye, the overseer covered Miriam's body with welts and bruises.

A third pair of eyes peered out from the immense multitude and fixed themselves on Dov's office windows. Igor Potowski no longer wore the prosperous attire that marked him as a merchant and respected member of the Guild. He glowered at the offices of the man who had destroyed him, as he lusted for revenge.

At the sight of the czarina, the shouts and cheers of the pushing, shoving multitude below exploded into a mighty roar. Fireworks, drums, bugles, and all seven orchestras burst into a joyous symphony of resounding consonance.

Miriam had to cover her ears as she watched the priests bless the Royal Fleet. When Catherine II boarded her galley, she turned to face the crowded shore and waved. Her subjects screamed in a frenzied rhythm that threatened to rival all seven orchestras.

At last, the flagship galley began its slow journey down river, to more whoops of jubilation from the crowd. By the time the first few barges departed, the cheering subsided but the crowd remained until dusk began to settle on the waterfront. Under torchlight, the slow process of the spectacular launch of one hundred barges would continue far into the night.

"Congratulations, Misha. You've done a fine job," Dov said.

"I've come to say farewell."

"What time are you leaving?"

"Late tonight, on one of the last barges. Captain's an old friend."

"Try to get some rest, will you?"

"Don't worry, I plan to sleep all the way to the Black Sea. Be back as soon as I can." He hugged Dov and kissed both his cheeks.

"God be with you, my friend. Take all the time you need in Sebastopol."

"Till tomorrow, Miriam." Alexei's eyes searched hers with acute longing. His hands twitched, yearning to touch her.

"Till tomorrow," They held one another's gaze for what seemed an eternity, though barely a moment had passed. But the spark between them did not go unnoticed.

"Beware, Miriam," Natasha Gorov said. "You two are playing a dangerous game."

Miriam reddened. "I can't help it, Natasha. I love him."

"From the look of things you're treading on dangerous waters and no good can come of it. No good at all, I can assure you."

The older woman saw consternation in Miriam's face. "It's not my purpose to meddle in what is clearly none of my business. My warning is only meant to spare you grief, for I've no wish to hurt you. You mean too much to me."

EIGHTEEN

The summer heat hung heavy as Miriam and Dov sped silently across the steppes of the Ukraine toward Shklov, the Polish city where they were born. Their estrangement haunted her.

Her life had gone wrong, somehow. Dov was angry with her and she had returned Alexei's passion. How had she let that happen? It was better for them both that Alexei had been dispatched to St. Petersburg, far from temptation.

Natasha had been right to warn her, but it was too late. The deed was done. Guilt weighed heavy on her heart. She indulged in daydreams to relieve the dreariness of her days. She'd begin by stroking the scar on Alexei's cheek until he took her in his arms and crushed her to him, just as he did on the night of the ball. She wondered about the strangeness of him...uncircumcised. Her thoughts took their toll, for on the only night Dov indicated a desire for her, it wasn't the weight of his body she felt crushing hers. It wasn't his hands that fondled. It wasn't his tongue that probed.

⌘

"There's Uncle Leon's house," she said with joy in her heart.

"Be brief. *Zayde* is expecting us."

"Go on without me then. Send the coach back for me later."

"I'll wait. My grandfather might suspect there's something wrong between us."

As the coach drew up, the door burst open and her sisters flew into her arms. The sight of them brought tears to her eyes, like the welcome of a warming sun. Uncle Leon, Aunt Yetta and their daughter Malke surrounded them at once.

"Where's my mother?"

An uneasy silence pervaded until Uncle Leon said, "She's resting." His was a kindly face, with warm brown eyes, but he wasn't smiling.

"Is there something wrong?"

"She has a headache."

"Has my father arrived?"

"On his way." Uncle Leon turned to his wife. "Yetta dear, why don't you see to refreshments?" His wife was plump, with a round face that exuded warmth. As a child, Miriam admired her Aunt Yetta's devotion to her uncle, a contrast to her own mother whose sharp tongue caused her father such grief.

"Malke, take the children into the garden." Miriam's cousin bore a faint family resemblance. Her lips were as full as Miriam's, but she seemed to compress them in perpetual disapproval.

Miriam felt apprehension grow as her uncle ordered his family about, but she held her tongue until they were alone in the drawing room. "What's wrong, Uncle?" Dov tried to take her hand as if to lend support, but she yanked it away.

"Your mother has a tumor pressing on her brain. Two physicians have already confirmed my diagnosis."

"Will she recover?"

"That's in God's hands."

"Is she in pain?"

"I give her opium for the pain. I must warn you that her appearance may shock you. She's lost weight and she's often irrational. Sometimes she's lucid, but we never know what to expect. Don't take notice if she calls you by another name. She becomes agitated if you try to tell her she's mistaken."

"My sisters? Do they know?"

"The twins know there's something wrong. She pleads to see them, but then she scolds them until she reduces them to tears. Your mother's so like a child herself in her illness."

"Can't you reason with her?" Dov asked, as though reason could solve her illness.

"My sister's reactions have nothing to do with reason." Uncle Leon said.

"Does my father know?"

"I wrote to him in Amsterdam, to prepare him."

"May I see her?"

"Of course. We've hired a nurse to care for her. It's best." He rose and led them up to his sister Clara's room. He signaled to the nurse to leave the room.

Her mother's wizened face belied her thirty-four years. Damp matted hair clung to her forehead over sunken eyes. Her skin lay in wrinkles, as though it had been ill fitted clothing.

Miriam grasped the chair next to Clara's bed when her knees threatened to give way.

"That you, Momma?" Clara Jacobs asked the question in the plaintive voice of a child.

"Yes, dearest." Miriam wrung out the cloth resting in a bowl on the bed stand and wiped her mother's brow. "Would you like a sip of water?" She held her mother and let her sip the liquid.

"You aren't mad at me any more?"

Miriam flinched. "Of course not, dear."

"I didn't mean for baby Leon to hurt himself. He fell when I wasn't looking. Please don't hit me again."

"How could I hit such a sweet child? I love you." Miriam kissed her mother's feverish forehead.

"Is Poppa mad at me?"

"No. He loves you, too."

"Where is he?"

"He's praying in the synagogue."

"Is it *Shabbos*?"

"Hello big sister." Leon said.

"I am not your sister!"

"How are you feeling?" her brother asked, ignoring her anger.

"My head hurts. You promised to take the pain away."

"Miriam and Dov have come see you."

"Hello, Momma." Miriam kissed her on the forehead.

"Hello Mother Jacobs."

"I'm mad at you, Miriam. You don't write to me, you don't visit me, and you haven't given me a grandchild. You make promises and you don't keep them. Go away." Clara turned her face to the wall, prompting Uncle Leon to motion them to leave.

In the drawing room, Miriam collapsed into her Aunt Yetta's arms and sobbed. Dov stared out into the garden, embarrassed that his wife had turned to her aunt for comfort.

"Go on without me, Dov. I'll stay here," she said at last.

"I suppose that's best. I'm sorry, Miriam."

"Thank you."

"I mean it. Forgive me. Our misunderstanding seems trivial now."

"All right."

"You don't sound as though you mean it."

"For God's sake, Dov, leave off." She paused. "I want a child, do you understand. We need to talk to Uncle Leon."

"Can't it wait?"

She glared at him.

"I'll go and find him." He was back a moment later and lead Miriam into her uncle's book-lined study, a room she remembered well from her childhood when she would try to read the titles of the strange-sounding Latin books on his shelves.

"There are several things we can do," said Uncle Leon when he had heard them out.

"You should be examined, Miriam. Sometimes the position of the womb can prevent conception. I know an excellent midwife I'd like you to see. You ought to wait a few days, though. You still have your father to deal with."

"No. The sooner the better. What about Dov?" She spoke of him as if he were not sitting next to her.

"I'll examine you, Dov."

"Of course, sir. We have great confidence in you."

"I'll arrange for the midwife to see you tomorrow. You can see me at your convenience, Dov."

After Dov departed, Miriam sought out the twins. "Momma says things she doesn't mean because of her sickness. She loves you both very much. I do too, my angels."

"Will she die?" Bluma asked.

"If God decides to take her from us, it's because he doesn't want her to suffer any more."

"She yells at us," Bela said.

"You mustn't pay her any mind. She doesn't mean it."

NINETEEN

"How is she?" Chaim Jacobs asked when he arrived early the next morning.

Miriam shook her head in response.

"God help us." Chaim began to sob.

"Shhh, Poppa," Miriam murmured, searching for words to ease his pain. "Uncle Leon thinks her headaches were a symptom."

"I want to see her now."

"You mustn't betray your feelings because she becomes agitated and that's harmful for her."

When Clara opened her eyes, he said, "Hello, dearest." He leaned to kiss her cheek.

"Don't touch me, you lecher."

"Don't say such things, Momma."

"Take his side, Miriam. You always do, don't you? Your father hates me. He can't wait to go to his mistress." Clara rambled on and on, piercing them with the poisonous sting of her words.

"You'd better leave now," said the nurse. "I'll see she quiets down."

When they were alone in the drawing room, her father asked, "How long does she have?"

"Uncle Leon says it could be months, weeks, days, hours."

"The twins?"

"They're terrified. You'll have to be strong for them."

"May God grant me the strength, then." He rose.

"Where are you going?"

"To the synagogue to pray. What else can I do?"

The aura of death hung like a pall over the household, as if mourning had already begun. Dov and his family came every evening. He sat by Miriam's side while his parents tried to comfort their friend Chaim. Sophie and Malke came by every day with their children, which helped to distract the twins.

As for the dying woman, she alternated between the child she had become and the wife and mother she was. She screamed accusations at Chaim and vacillated between scolding the twins for giving her bad headaches and pleading for a kiss from her darling girls.

As Clara grew weaker, her accusations increased. It was as if her words were a weapon to stave off death. She cursed Chaim for his infidelity. She cursed the twins for her headaches. She cursed her brother for not releasing her from pain. She cursed Miriam for her barrenness.

⌘

Uncle Leon paused to shuffle some papers on his desk. "Miriam ought to be here, Dov. She asked to be present when we discussed this, didn't she?"

"I'm trying to spare her. I'll tell her everything you say, Uncle Leon. You have my word."

"The midwife found nothing that would prevent your wife from becoming pregnant. As for you, my examination reveals nothing that would prevent you from impregnating your wife.

"Can you suggest solutions, sir?"

"None whose effectiveness has been proven. Still, they can't do any harm, so you've nothing to lose."

"What are they?"

"I've read papers in professional journals that suggest certain times of the month may be more favorable than others for ovulation. Coitus must take place every other day for a week beginning ten days after the inception of the female cycle, a conflict with Judaic law, which says relations cannot resume for twelve days."

"Anything else?"

"Ask the midwife. She favors old wives' tales."

"Any I might take seriously?"

"Just one, though I'm not convinced. Adopt an orphan."

"I don't see the connection."

"There isn't much of a one in my view, but there are reports of barren couples having borne a natural child after adoption. Why not adopt?"

"No. We're still young. There's plenty of time before we consider that course." Damn, he thought. I won't legitimize somebody else's bastard. I want an heir, and I want it to be mine.

"How does Miriam feel about adoption?"

"What difference does it make? I'm firmly against it. Are there any other solutions?"

"This is not as businesslike as you make it sound. I'd hardly call this a 'solution,' but if you believe in miracles, you might seek out the nearest Jewish mystic and pay

77

him a fortune for some absurd 'cure,' a special oil, perhaps, or a powder to add to your food. There are hundreds of them right here in Shklov."

⌘

Mirele?"

Miriam started at the unfamiliar clarity in her mother's tone. "What is it, Momma?"

"Where's your father?"

"He's saying his morning prayers."

"That's nice. Would you ask him to come here when he's finished? There's a sweet girl." A gentle smile lingered on her wasted face.

Miriam flew down the stairs. "Momma's asking for you."

He tore the leather strips of his phylacteries from his arms and his forehead and took the stairs two at a time.

"Wake my uncle," Miriam whispered to the nurse.

"How are you, Chaim?"

"How are you, my sweet wife?"

"Maybe if I eat a little something, I'll get my strength back."

"Of course, my love." He pressed her frail hand to his cheek as tears rolled down his own.

"Chaim dear," Clara began, "...did you remember? You know. What I asked you to do?"

"What was that?"

"About our darling babies?"

"What? Yes! Oh yes. Of course I remembered," he said in sudden understanding. Miriam was mystified by their cryptic conversation.

"I almost forgot to tell you." Chaim nodded to his brother-in-law, who held Clara's wrist to count her pulse. "We'll celebrate with Leon and Yetta and all our friends just as soon as you feel better, because it's all settled." His tears fell as his brother-in-law listened to the erratic beating of her heart.

"Fine young lads, Clara darling, from the best Jewish families in Amsterdam. One is ten and the other is eleven years old. They're first cousins, so our babies will have the same family name. It's Teitelbaum. Does that make you happy, my love? I told them that my generous wife insisted upon a huge dowry for her daughters. We'll have a double ceremony just as you've always wanted." Clara's eyes closed, yet her smile lingered as he continued.

"Moses is the older, so he's betrothed to Bela, and Aaron's betrothed to Bluma."

Dov caught the last few words as he entered the room.

"Find my sisters."

Clara turned to her daughter. "Are you pregnant yet?"

"Yes, Momma."

"Mazeltov, Mirele. You shouldn't have made such a long trip in your delicate condition."

"Uncle Leon says I'm fine."

"If it's a girl, name her after my dear mother, may she rest in peace. All right?"

"Of course. The twins have come to see you." Miriam urged the frightened children forward.

Clara smiled. "Are you going to the fair today? Come give your momma a big kiss before you go. Hold your big sister's hand so you don't get lost, eh? Try not to eat too many sweets. We can't let you become fat now that Poppa has found you such fine husbands. Be good, my darlings, and practice the piano every day, so you'll play well, just like your sister. Chaim, give them each a few extra kopeks to spend, won't you? Go, darlings. Momma wants to rest."

Miriam, her father, and her brother Leon refused to leave her bedside.

"What is it, Momma?" Miriam asked as she observed her mother raise one arm and wave to some unseen phantom in her imagination. She shook her father awake.

"Clara darling? It's me, Chaim. Clara?"

Clara Jacobs shuddered in answer, a death rattle.

Her loved ones shed tears of grief tempered by relief. She had been released from the prison of her painful illness at last.

TWENTY

Clara Levinski Jacobs was interred on the day following her death, as is prescribed by Judaic law. The undertakers prepared her in a shroud, covered her eyes with broken shards, and covered her thinned out hair with a wig.

Miriam viewed her mother as though she were a stranger. Such a ravaged face, she thought. Not the face I've known all my life. She bent to kiss her forehead, startled by its icy coldness.

Clara's pallbearers were Dov, his father, his three uncles, and Malke's husband Samuel. They bore the coffin from Uncle Leon's home to the waiting hearse that wended its way through the streets to the synagogue where Dov and Miriam had been wed.

The principal mourners—Miriam, her father, the twins and Uncle Leon—walked behind the hearse. Once inside, the rabbi chanted the prayer for the dead and tore a piece of each mourner's clothing, an ancient ritual.

Mirrors in Uncle Leon's home were covered with sheets while Clara's mourners padded around in stockinged feet and sat on hard wooden stools to signify the pain of their grief. Relatives and friends flowed through the house during *shiva*, the seven days of intense mourning, to pay their respects to Chaim, his children, and Clara's brother. In addition, the men came to Uncle Leon's house to say *kaddish*, the prayer for the dead, with Chaim and Uncle Leon every day. Miriam prayed in silence for children of her own, as she listened to the men chant the ancient prayer with her father and her uncle.

Her mother's death had brought to Miriam a clearness of vision that cut through her like a sharp knife. Dov's devotion to her was a game he played, to show others what a good husband he was, but it left her unmoved.

⌘

"Why couldn't you have had the decency to wait for me to finish mourning my mother's death? You knew I wanted to hear Uncle Leon's explanation." Her eyes were lit with hate.

80

"I'll repeat what he said word for word. I promise."

She wasn't in the least surprised when Dov implied that the problem was hers. Still, she had no time to dwell on his version of the truth, vowing to ask Uncle Leon herself. Not just now. Not when the loss of her mother lay so heavy on her heart.

The realization of how much she'd loved her mother began to plague her. She felt twisted with grief, berating herself for not having revealed the depth of that love to Clara when she was alive. Why hadn't she told her before it was too late?

On the day of her mother's funeral, another cruel twist of fate assailed her even though she was a week early. She began to menstruate. She told Dov to plan a calculated course of action, according to Uncle Leon's prescription.

Miriam cooperated, agreeing to return to their bed in *Zayde's* home every night after the proscribed week of mourning ended. But each morning she hurried back to Uncle Leon's house to console her father and her sisters.

The death of Clara Jacobs caused the postponement of the dedication of Kalman Zeklinski's Hebrew Academy till the end of August. Dov took the extra time to tend to business affairs. He spent his days closeted with his father and his uncles, as well as with Benjamin Moskowitz. His cousin Sophie's husband was quick to learn, Dov was pleased to discover.

He met with Uncle Moses early in June, while Clara still lay dying. The banker was destined to relive that stinging confrontation over and over again.

⌘

"You're putting obstacles in my way, Uncle."

"It's my duty to point out to you that prudence is the wiser course."

"I know how you feel," Dov interrupted in a harsh tone, "but we can't run our business on your prudence. I'm transferring ninety percent of all the firm's financial assets to our banks in Kiev. You can control the rest. You have sole discretion over your funds. You have my word on it." Dov took note of the fiery flush of anger on the older man's face, yet chose to ignore it.

"How dare you," the older man mumbled, the stench of defeat pervading his nostrils.

"We're family aren't we? Didn't I just hire your son-in-law? Perhaps you can teach him the intricacies of banking. He's a quick study, that one. He and your daughter Sophie will live very well in Kiev." The banker glowered at his nephew.

"Here's a letter for you to sign, arranging for the transfer. I've a messenger waiting to leave for St. Petersburg right away."

"And if I refuse? If I insist that a family council be convened to discuss this? Are you prepared for a fight? Because I think I can win, you see. Asher and Isaac..."

"Why refuse? It can only cause unpleasantness."

"What do you call this? A celebration?"

"Call it whatever you like, but I'm head of Zeklinski Enterprises." Dov raised his voice. "I make the decisions now."

"Really? I don't agree."

"Don't force me to do something I don't want to do."

"And what, may I ask, is that?"

"I've prepared a second letter for you to sign. Choose whichever you like." He passed the document across the desk.

The banker read it through. "My resignation?"

"No family member ever resigns. How would that look? How old are you? Forty or so? You and Aunt Gittel can continue to live well, as a result of a handsome lifetime pension for your faithful years of service."

"Give me the blasted quill," his uncle snapped as he tore the second letter to shreds. "Your grandfather made a mistake when he chose you to head the firm. You're no gentleman."

"No, uncle. Gentlemen make poor businessmen."

⌘

"Dov?"

"What is it?"

"I want to stay in St. Petersburg with my father and the children when they return, until they can manage without me." Her tone hinted at defiance, as if she expected an argument from him, but he agreed without hesitation.

"Of course. You must do what's right. You're irritable because you're tired. Come to bed, dear. It's perfectly all right with me." He thought for a moment. "In fact, I need to attend to some business there, so it's fine for both of us."

Miriam arranged for their departure on the first day of September, the warmth of summer still lingering in the air.

"You're a fine woman, Miriam," said Uncle Leon. "I'm proud of you. My sister lives on, you know. Through her three lovely daughters." Their farewell was interrupted by the clatter of horse's hooves as Sophie's *droshki* came careening into view.

"I'm so glad I didn't miss saying good-bye to you," she said. Dov's cousin Sophie was a tall young woman, usually slender, but not in her ninth month of pregnancy. Her hazel eyes seemed to flash with fire, for she was an opinionated woman accustomed to speaking her mind.

"You need the midwife with you, Sophie," Uncle Leon grinned, patting her huge stomach. "Your baby might decide to enter this world at any moment."

"From your mouth to God's ears as they say," she rolled her eyes. "I can't wait to be relieved of this tiny burden. Maybe then I'll be able to sleep again."

"Take care of yourself, Sophie. I'll see you in Kiev," said Miriam.

"I'm counting the days. But where's your father? And where's Dov?"

82

"Dov plans to leave tomorrow with his parents and my father is resting."

When Sophie departed, Miriam went to seek her father. She found him sitting in Uncle Leon's study staring at nothing, an open prayer book on his lap.

"Time to go, Poppa," Miriam said.

"I've said my goodbyes to her a thousand times, Mirele. What will I do without her? I loved her, you know." He began to weep.

"She knew you loved her, but you mustn't cry so. You'll frighten the twins. Be brave, Poppa." She led him to the waiting carriage.

As their carriage rode past the cemetery, Miriam said silently, "Good-bye, Momma. I love you. Forgive me for not telling you that often enough. Rest in peace, my dearest."

TWENTY-ONE

Turkey declared war on Russia in September, the second such conflict in less than ten years. During Czarina Catherine's journey, the Porte feigned humiliation at her presence in the Crimea. He insisted upon its return to the once proud, crumbling Ottoman Empire.

"'...and Louie still snores and Leib still stutters, but only when he's excited, which seems to be most of the time. Sammy mislays his spectacles at least twice a week, and we have to find them, for he's blind as a bat without them.'" Miriam read aloud.

"Noah's letters are amusing." Dov said.

"There's a note from Brodsky, too. Just two brief sentences. 'How are you both? All is well here.'"

"I'm not surprised. He hates to write. By the way, I met Alexei Razovsky this morning."

"Really? Where?"

"In the Admiralty Building. He's coming here after dinner. Wants to pay his condolences to you."

"Tonight? You might have asked me first."

"I thought you'd be pleased."

"It's common courtesy to ask first."

"Courtesy has nothing to do with your anger, and you know it," Dov said. "God knows how patient I've been these last three months. Can't you let bygones be bygones?"

"Whatever you like," she answered.

"Damn, Miriam."

The door burst open and the twins tumbled into their chambers. "Can't you two learn to knock before you enter? You might try teaching your sisters some manners!"

"Don't you dare berate my sisters." The twins stood frozen at the door.

"Take care, I warn you. Take care or I'll..."

"Or you'll what?"

Dov glared at her. "I'll not be here for dinner after all," he yelled, and stormed out, nearly knocking the children down.

"We're..."

"...sorry, Mirele."

"Never mind, dears. You didn't do anything wrong."

"But we forgot to knock."

"And now Dov's mad at us."

"Dov's right about that. It is polite to knock before you enter a room. Try to remember next time. Come. I'll help you wash up."

⌘

"Where's Dov?" her father asked at dinner.

"He had to go out. Business."

"Mirele and Dov," Bela began.

"Yelled at each other," finished Bluma.

Chaim raised an eyebrow.

"Nothing serious, Poppa. Oh, by the way, I'm expecting a visitor tonight. Count Razovsky, a friend of ours from Kiev. Dov met him today and told him about Momma. He wants to pay his respects. Do you mind?"

"Why should I mind?"

Miriam was sorry the twins had spoken up. Chaim's malaise since his wife's death was painful to witness. Miriam worried about the time when she'd have to return home to Kiev. It occurred to her that the thought of leaving her family had been troubling her all day. Perhaps that was why she'd snapped at Dov. She promised herself she'd apologize to Dov later.

⌘

"Poppa, I want you to meet Count Razovsky."

"Sorry to hear of your wife's death, Reb Jacobs." Razovsky added some more words of condolence, but his concern was for Miriam. She looked so pale in her black gown of mourning, like a sparrow in winter.

Chaim eyed the soldier with suspicion and asked himself, what kind of friend looks at Miriam that way? What can Dov be thinking, to allow this?

"My daughter tells me you work at the Admiralty Building."

"Yes, sir. I'd have preferred active service, especially since we're at war, but Field Marshall Potemkin insists upon my remaining here."

"What do you do?"

"I am in charge of the recruit levy. We lost a great many soldiers in the war. Two of our ships were sunk off the coast of Sebastopol in a terrible storm. To replace the soldiers, we've had to raise the levy from two in five hundred souls to three.   Unfortunately, I'm besieged daily by an army of wealthy merchants and peasants who buy their way out of service for five hundred rubles."

Her father smiled. "It's a wonder you manage to recruit as many as you do."

Alexei turned to Miriam. "I met your husband this morning. He was seeing to some naval contracts. I didn't know he was building frigates for our navy."

"Neither did I. He rarely discusses his business activities with me. What news of your sister? I'm afraid I've neglected to write."

"Anya's fine. Had your mother been ill long?"

"She'd complained of severe headaches for years, but we never realized how serious they were. Her brother is a physician and he believes it was likely she had a tumor on the brain." She wondered why she felt such a compulsion to recount the grisly details of her mother's illness.

Miriam's father listened to their every word, though he appeared to be reading a copy of the *St. Petersburg Gazette.*

The twins appeared to say goodnight.

"These are my twin sisters, Bela and Bluma."

He bowed and kissed each child's chubby hand. "I'm honored, but I'll never be able to tell two such beautiful young ladies apart." The shy twins scurried to their father's side.

"You're doubly blessed, Reb Jacobs, with two such beautiful children."

"Say goodnight to our guest, darlings, and kiss Poppa goodnight. I'll be up soon to tuck you in."

She touched Alexei's elbow. "Let me show you our garden." Chaim kept his silence against his better judgment.

⌘

"It was horrid," Miriam confessed when they were alone. My mother was in such pain, poor thing." To her surprise, she began to weep.

"I wish I might have been there for you to offer what little comfort I could." He handed her his handkerchief. To hold you in my arms, he thought, to make love to you once more. "My parents were also young, like your mother. I was eighteen and Anya was ten. The grief was dreadful. I can still recall it."

"Does the pain ever go away?"

"Time does heal."

"Thank heaven for that."

"Where's your husband? He said he'd be here tonight."

"Some unexpected business came up."

"I hear he's been asked by the Crown to finance the war."

"That so? A whole war? Imagine." Her laugh lacked mirth. "You're a tonic for me, my friend. I hadn't realized till I saw you how much I miss our life in Kiev. Perhaps it's time we returned home. My father and the twins will have to learn to do without me sooner or later, won't they?"

"I suppose that's true. What a pity."

"Why?"

"You leave me to suffer here alone." Miriam laughed and his heart was glad.

"I've thought about you often, Alexei. No, don't interrupt. I wanted you as much as you wanted me. I'll never forget that night. I must live with my sin, but it must not happen again. We must remain only friends. You do understand, don't you?"

"We were like Romeo and Juliet, weren't we?"

"Star-crossed lovers?"

"I meant the Capulets and the Montagues."

"Christian and Jew. A good parallel, but we shan't end so tragically, shall we?"

"I accept your friendship, if that's all I can have of you." He kissed her hand, thinking that he'd agree to any terms at all, if only to be near her. "You've a beautiful soul, Miriam. I've never met anyone as wise or as wonderful."

"Promise me that your admiration will never again take the turn that it did that night."

"So long as you promise not to banish me from your life."

She linked her arm through his and propelled him toward the house. "Let's return before my father charges out here and challenges you to a duel."

⌘

When he left, Alexei's thoughts wavered between his love for Miriam and his hopelessness. He wished he were with Potemkin facing the Turks in the Ochakov Fortress. To hell with Potemkin, he fumed. To hell with St. Petersburg. Stuck here for good, at least for the duration of the war. Better make the best of it. Take my mind off her with some diversion.

He leaned forward and barked an order to his driver.

"The Millionaya. You know the house."

⌘

"My apologies, Dov," Miriam said that night. "You were right to be cross. I've been edgy and out of sorts. I've been thinking."

"That's an improvement."

She ignored his anger. "It's time we went home. Poppa and the girls will have to get along without me sooner or later, won't they? Besides, he can always leave the twins with us when he travels. That is, if you don't mind. May I tell him that?"

"Just so long as you teach them some manners."

"You're right about that, too. Momma indulged them a little too much, maybe. It was just her way. She never meant any harm by it, you know." She smiled at the recollection of her mother fussing over them all.

"What's so funny?"

"I was thinking about my mother. The twins' betrothals were the last thing on her mind. Unfinished business, so to speak."

"When can you be ready to leave?" he asked, his mind racing ahead to Kiev and to business.

"Is the end of the week too soon? If that suits you, I'll tell Poppa first thing in the morning. He's such a dear man, Dov. My heart breaks for him."

"Yes, he's decent, but you're right about his having to face life without you sooner or later." He paused in thought. "The end of the week did you say?"

"If that's all right with you."

"Matter of fact, I've been meaning to talk to you about business."

"Have you really been asked to finance the war with Turkey? Alexei said so."

"Man has a loose tongue," he said, yet he was pleased at the hint of respect in her voice. "It's true, but it was meant to be a State secret. Anyway, there's another matter I need to discuss. I shall be away from home a great deal from now on."

"What do you mean?"

"We're starting a new business venture in Sebastopol, building frigates for the navy. After the war, we'll build merchant ships."

"Does this have something to do with that old widow you mentioned?"

"I've bought half an interest in her shipyards. I'll try to be ready to leave by the end of the week, but I may need a few more days."

"Take all the time you need. And really, I'm terribly sorry about the way I behaved."

"Forget it."

"Friends?"

"Friends."

"Do you mean it?"

"Of course. Come here and I'll show you."

TWENTY-TWO

The journey home was tiresome. Dov kept busy with sheaves of papers while Miriam stared unseeing at the undulating wheat in the fields. She couldn't help but wonder why her father chose to give her such an odd gift the day before she left.

⌘

"These belonged to your mother. She would have wanted you to have them. I gave them to her when we first married." He poured five diamonds from a small leather pouch into the palm of her hand. "They are two carats each. Worth a great deal," he added, with the consummate pride of a master jeweler.

"Why only me? What about the twins?"

"They each have a substantial dowry."

She smiled. "I had a substantial dowry, too, and what's more, I'm married to the wealthiest Jew in Eastern Europe."

"No need to mention this gift to Dov, dear. It might embarrass him into thinking I suspect he's not a good provider. Not at all true, is it? Besides, you can pass them on to my granddaughters. Momma always hid these on her person."

"Really? Where?"

He smiled at the thought. "She sewed them into a long roll of strong muslin. Every morning she threaded the roll through the hem of her petticoat."

⌘

The staff lined the driveway in greeting when they reached home. "Welcome home, sir. Madame."

"Thank you, Boris. You're doing a superb job. But then, we've come to expect it of you." A look of pleasure stole across the butler's face at Dov's words.

"Will there be anything else, sir?"

"Yes. We'll take tea in the drawing room."

"A royal welcome? Fancy that," said Dov when they were alone.

"Did you notice how pleased he was at your compliment? He takes such pride in his work."

Boris returned with tea. "Excuse me, sir," the butler said as he set the tea tray down.

"What is it?"

"The overseer is here to see you."

"I'll see him in my study." Dov left Miriam alone to struggle with her anger toward Borschov. She busied herself by writing notes to Anya and Natasha.

When Dov returned, he said, "Sorry, dear. Borschov's arrogant, just as you've always warned. I'll keep an eye out for someone else, but it may take time to replace him. All right?"

"I'd like that," she answered. "I am inviting Natasha and Anya to tea tomorrow. Will you join us?"

"Afraid not. Ask them to dinner soon. Invite the Brezhnovins and the Petrovs, too. I must be off now. Do you mind?"

"No, of course not. I'll have a bath and then rest for awhile."

"Good idea. Tell Boris we'll dine at eight. I'll take your notes and have them delivered for you."

⌘

The last leaves of autumn clung stubbornly to the branches as the air turned chill. Life seemed back to normal except for one jarring note. Count Petrov and his wife did not attend the Zeklinski's first dinner party. They never bothered to send regrets.

⌘

"Have you heard the terrible news?" asked Countess Brezhnovin at dinner one evening. As usual, her husband the General drank enough to put him to dozing before the main course.

"What news?"

"About Petrov's son. Poor Ilya is dead."

"Ilya's only a child! How did it happen?"

"They say that his gun went off while he was cleaning it. The truth is he killed himself for love of a woman. His father refused to allow the marriage. Now they'll never have an heir."

"Don't they have a daughter?" asked Miriam.

"Marya? Not likely she'll ever marry."

"Why not?"

"She wants to live in the convent and devote her life to God."

"But the Petrovs refuse to allow it, I suppose."

"How did you guess, Natasha?"

"It isn't difficult, knowing the Petrovs."

"Who was the woman Ilya Petrov wanted for a wife?" asked Anya.

"He met her on the czarina's journey to the southern provinces. A young widow."

"Petrov's a fool. Look at the price he's paid. His only son."

Miriam listened to the tale, astonished at the loss of a young man's life. "He was a nice young man. It's a sad thing to lose one's child, Natasha, no matter the reason. I'll write a note of condolence to them in the morning."

"Perhaps we can pay the Petrovs a call when they are up to receiving visitors."

"Yes, Anya. That would be kind," said Miriam.

⌘

When Sophie and Benjamin Moskowitz arrived in November, Miriam's days became fully occupied. Oddly enough, she was reluctant to introduce Sophie to Anya and to the countess. She chose instead to keep them in ignorance of one another's existence and divided her time between them.

By late November, Dov informed Miriam he'd need at least two more months to wind up his affairs. Miriam took dinner with Sophie on nights when Dov and Benjamin worked late, for Sophie knew no one else in Kiev.

TWENTY-THREE

What rotten luck, Alexei thought. Lost thirty thousand rubles. How can I repay it? Curse those tables. Sadorov's wife has an eye for me. Rich. Beautiful. Wants me. Why not? Sadorov's lucky enough to be fighting at the front instead of me. Tell her, 'Natalia darling, so sad for you to be all alone in St. Petersburg'.

Razovsky's luck improved after his new mistress paid his debts and insisted he stop drinking. He was quick to oblige, mindful of his embarrassing predicament. The caveat did not include gambling, since the countess shared his inordinate love for the heady dangers of chance. To his astonishment, he proceeded to win huge sums at the gaming table, allowing him to repay the countess within a month.

"You're good luck for me, Natalia," he said late one night. The fair-skinned beauty had long golden hair and spirited green eyes.

"And you are my savior. I wonder how I'll be able to bear grumpy old Gregory when he returns after the war. I'll have to think of you when I'm in this bed with him, to keep from dying of boredom. Do you suppose we can find a way to continue to meet secretly? You're so good in bed." Her hands played idly upon his naked frame.

"Maybe it will be a long war."

"Let's hope so. Ah, how easy it is to arouse you."

"A skill I have."

"But I forgive you your sinful past, because you've made me happy."

"You've made me happy, too. I'm on the biggest winning streak I've ever had, and our nights in bed are perfect. He responded to her touch by proceeding to display his prowess as a lover once again.

One night he asked, "Mightn't your husband look the other way if he found out about us? He's much older, isn't he? Some husbands don't mind."

"I think Gregory would mind terribly. He's not like other men. From my point of view, he's a fine husband. I like his wealth and I like his exalted position at court. The czarina relies on his devotion to the Crown and so does Potemkin. He's sixty; thirty-five years my senior. After his first wife died, he was lonely and I fancied myself in love with him when we met. He can be witty and gallant and virile in bed."

"You don't love him anymore?"

"I'm fond of him, of course, but the difference in our ages precludes love, and he has his eccentricities. He has an uncontrollable temper, though he's always been gentle with me. He pampers me almost as though I were his pet. Still, his pets must behave, or else."

"Or else what?"

She laughed. "It's too delicious a tale to keep to myself, though I've never told anyone before. When we first married, Gregory had a pet, a darling bear cub he'd chosen to rear after shooting its mother on a hunt. He loved the clever creature almost as much as he loved me.

"When we married, you can imagine how startled I was to find the beast at our dinner table when we dined alone. I grew fond of Ivan, for that was his name. He learned to use the proper utensil in spite of his long claws. He learned to nod yes or no, though I never saw him nod 'no' to food of any kind. He even learned to drink from a goblet. Then he'd wipe his mouth with a napkin.

"One night, Ivan had an accident at dinner. He wet himself even though Gregory had trained him to leave the table when he had to...you know."

Razovsky laughed. "What happened to the cub?"

"My husband yanked Ivan's chain and knocked him to the floor. The awful odor gave the poor beast away at once, you see. Then he dragged him off. I can still hear the animal's pathetic screams to this day."

"What did Sadorov do?"

"He beat him to death with a knout."

"A knout? My bad fortune."

"Oh, but Gregory would never beat you."

"I might have chosen a mistress with a less hot-tempered husband. Is he a good marksman?"

"Excellent."

"Let's hope it never comes to that."

But the general learned of his wife's affair from an anonymous note dispatched to his headquarters at Kherson. Sadorov traveled four weeks to reach St. Petersburg, during which time he managed to forgive his errant child bride. Such an innocent could not be expected to ward off the insidious charms of a notorious womanizer.

When the general burst into his wife's boudoir, he witnessed his beloved entwined in the arms of Razovsky. Forthwith, he challenged the blackguard to a duel despite the river of tears Natalia shed on her lover's behalf.

Alexei found two friends to accompany him, cursing his ill luck all the while. He toyed with the idea of hesitating at the count of ten and be done with the business of living once and for all, but decided against it, for the old general might miss his mark and cripple him, a fate far worse than death.

His worries would end were he to die; yet he knew that if he won the duel, he'd have to flee the country, for neither the czarina nor Potemkin would forgive him for the death of a loyal general. The thought chilled him as he composed four hasty letters.

In the first, he begged Anya to forgive him. In the second, he instructed his solicitors to deed his estates to his dear sister Anya and to her new husband on the occasion of their wedding. And in the third, he informed Prince Bedorov of the news, adding a hope that the man would do the honorable thing and marry his sister, despite his own fall from grace.

He congratulated himself on having the good sense to destroy the fourth, for it was a foolish attempt to express to Miriam his undying love.

That week, *The St. Petersburg Gazette* reported that Russia's most valued war hero, General Gregory Sadorov, lost his life at the hand of Count Alexei Razovsky who was nowhere to be found.

⌘

Miriam found her friend Anya sobbing in Natasha's arms.

"Alexei's gone into exile," she wailed.

Natasha fumed. "Alexei might as well be dead, for he'll never set foot on Russian soil again."

Miriam's heart sunk.

"With all the women at court who would gladly bed him down, why did he have to choose Sadorov's wife? He had to know the danger, for Alexei isn't witless." Natasha continued her tirade, yet Miriam only heard part of it. Her mind was fixed on the idea that she'd never see him again and the thought depressed her.

Toward evening, Natasha insisted Miriam return home, promising she would remain with Anya. As soon as Dov came home, Miriam told him the news.

"Too bad. I'd heard gossip about his womanizing and his gambling. Don't look so surprised. I lent him money to pay his debts more than once. In fact, he needed another loan the last time I saw him in St. Petersburg, but I refused him."

When the news reached Moscow, Prince Bedorov sent word that Anya was to join him where they would marry at once. Natasha agreed to chaperon Anya on her long journey.

"Good-bye, dear friend," Anya hugged Miriam. "I'll miss you."

"Goodbye, Anya. Goodbye, Natasha. Take care of Anya."

"I'll not stay in Moscow a moment longer than necessary, I assure you. "

"Lord knows when we shall meet again, Miriam."

"Be happy with your prince. Your brother would have wanted that."

TWENTY-FOUR

"Why can't I go with you? I'm your wife, or have you forgotten that?"

"I'm not cruel enough to subject you to dusty roads and dirty inns in towns where you know no one, while I spend my days with merchants. Why can't you understand?"

"I wouldn't mind. Besides, it might be worth it to have me waiting for you at night."

"Your mother never accompanied your father."

"Only because she preferred to be home with her children."

"Let me remind you that you're my wife and you have an obligation to obey me."

"Let me remind you that you're my husband and you have an obligation as well."

"What is that?"

She bit her lip. "How can I become pregnant without you?"

So that's it, he thought, and he softened his tone. "Does that mean you'll miss me?"

"It means what it means," she answered stubbornly.

"Let's stop arguing. I don't want to leave with bad feelings between us." He took her in his arms and felt her tension. "We still have some time left together to keep on trying for a child, and I promise I won't stay away a moment longer than necessary."

⌘

By the end of March Dov was ready to leave.

"I'll stop to see your father and the twins when I pass through St. Petersburg."

"St. Petersburg? But that's north of here. I thought you said you were going south to Sebastopol."

"I've had to change my plans. I'm on my way to Berlin."

"You never told me you were going to Berlin."

"Didn't I? Sorry. I have to go to Berlin to open up a new munitions factory there."

"You never told me."

"It slipped my mind."

"Berlin is far away." She felt as if she were discussing the weather with a stranger. "How long do you plan to stay in St. Petersburg?"

"A day or two, at the most. Only long enough to go over some business with my father and my uncles. Then I'm going to visit *Zayde* in Shklov. Would you like me to see your Uncle Leon and his wife when I'm there?"

"Yes, thank you. Say hello to Malke and to Samuel, too. I'll I write to tell them to expect you." An uncomfortable premonition began to fester within her like a sore that threatened to linger, a sore refusing to heal. "I'll miss you."

"Well, there's Sophie," he said, looking away.

"Yes. There's Sophie. Will you be gone long?"

"Hard to say. Six months. Perhaps longer."

Her heart sank. "That is a long time. Have you everything you need?" He nodded. "Find time to write, won't you?" He nodded again.

"My carriage is waiting."

"Well," she said, her smile a bit too bright. "Shall we kiss and make up? We oughtn't to part with bad feelings."

He embraced her. "Take care of yourself."

"I will."

"I have to go."

"God keep you safe, Dov."

She shivered as she watched his carriage disappear over the horizon.

Book Two
St. Petersburg 1803

TWENTY-FIVE

"Czar Alexander has convened a committee to resolve the Jewish problem. He has appointed me a member."

"I hadn't been aware that we Jews are the problem, Dov."

"My appointment's a great honor. You see that, don't you?"

"Really?" She folded her arms and glared at him.

Dov ignored her disapproval as though she were an irritating gnat buzzing around him. "The czar believes this to be an historic undertaking. Rabbis from *kahals* all over the empire are being invited to attend. This is the first time Jews have been invited to draft decrees designed to create a better life for our people."

"I doubt these new decrees will be any better than the ones preceding it. The Pale of Settlement certainly didn't help Jews."

"The committee will correct that, I assure you." At thirty-five, Dov retained his youthful good looks. He glanced into the mirror on the mantle and straightened his cuffs, though the cut of his stylish Western dress needed no adjustment.

"The czar has also appointed me his financial advisor."

"How nice for you."

"You never acknowledge my accomplishments."

"What can you expect after two lonely years?"

"I came to St. Petersburg to offer my condolences as soon as I heard of your father's death."

"You came here because the czar summoned you."

"I never know in advance how long I'll be gone. At any rate, I'm here now." He moved to kiss her cheek, but she turned her head. "What on earth is wrong with you?"

"If I were to accompany you on your long journeys, there would be no conflict between us."

"You're just like your mother, always complaining."

"Keep my dead mother out of this."

"The thought of returning home to you fills me with dread, knowing I must face your anger."

Her guilt assaulted her in spite of her efforts to banish the shame from her memory. She turned away to hide her reddened face from his prying eyes. "My anger is tiresome for me as well." She rang for tea.

Dov settled into a comfortable chair near the fireplace and glanced around at her father's well-appointed drawing room. "This is a handsome home. It's only a short walk to the Neva River, and close to the Millionaya. I suppose we can remain here until your stepmother returns. When do you expect her?"

"Kaaren isn't returning. She prefers to remain in Amsterdam where her children live. She's invited us to visit her there."

"Perhaps when I'm not so busy."

That means never, she thought unhappily. "They were making plans to travel together to the Alps the night before he died."

"Let it go, Miriam."

"You needn't bother to protest because I hadn't intended a comparison."

Miriam poured tea for them both when the servant departed.

"What does Kaaren plan to do with this house?"

"She's deeded it to the twins and me, to do whatever we like with it. My father left her a great deal of money including this house, but you know Kaaren, generous to a fault. Insists she doesn't need it."

"You've all agreed to sell, I take it."

"Yes. That's why I'm here. We'll keep some mementoes and sell the rest of the furnishings but we're planning to send Kaaren the proceeds in spite of her objections. Moses and Aaron want it that way. Matter of pride, you see. They're well able to support their families and we certainly don't need the money."

"Your sisters and their families are well?"

"Yes. Bela is with child again. When she gives birth, she'll have three children, like Bluma."

"Do they still prattle at the same time? Always drove me to distraction."

"No. They've learned to let the rest of the world in, but they're still close. My cousin Malke lives near them in Odessa, too. Bela says that Samuel's business thrives."

"Does Malke still begin every sentence with, 'my husband, the apothecary says...'" Miriam laughed at Dov's mimicry of her cousin.

"Some people never change, do they?" he said, relieved at her laughter. How would you like to buy this house from Kaaren, at fair value, of course."

"Buy it? Why?"

"My new appointment requires us to spend a good deal of time here. You've always loved this house, haven't you? Why bother to look elsewhere?"

"I'm flattered to think you've included me in your plans, but I had thought to return home to Kiev. I've so much to do there. The estate, the orphanage…"

"We have serfs to see to the estate and my office can handle anything unforeseen that arises. I need you here with me. They say St. Petersburg is the Paris of the East. We can attend the opera and the ballet and the theatre."

"Opera? Ballet? Theatre? Think you can stand so much of me?"

"Don't mock me. You're very beautiful, and…"

"And we make such a handsome pair, don't we? So good for business."

"Why must you persist in twisting my words? You say you're lonely when I'm gone. Well? His eyes bored into her as if willing her to agree. "You've changed, Miriam. You have more confidence and poise. I've not seen this side of you before, and frankly, it pleases me."

"I suppose I'm not the frightened child you married nineteen years ago."

"Our families were the first Jews allowed to live here in St. Petersburg, pioneers in the new Russian Empire. You left this very house for our wedding, when you were fifteen and I was sixteen."

"Nothing's changed, Dov. We're still outsiders."

"We succeeded in Kiev for a time, didn't we? When you danced with Prince Potemkin at our first ball in Kiev, you were the envy of every woman there. What greater tribute to your father's memory than to pursue his dream. Our dream?"

"You mean *haskalah*."

"Yes. Jewish enlightenment. It will ease the plight of the poorest Jews. Perhaps the new committee can even persuade the czar to abolish the Pale of Settlement. We'll make a difference this time."

He drew her into his arms, knowing she would be unable to resist, for she was a passionate woman. "Two years is a long time for a man to be without his wife. I need you, Miriam. I want you." He kissed her hard, probing her mouth with his tongue at the same time as his hands caressed her breasts.

"Now," he demanded, his voice hoarse with passion. "I want you now."

TWENTY-SIX

Alexei embraced his childhood friend. "Hello Hanne. The years have been kind to you, as your beauty attests."

"And you remain a handsome rogue. The nobles at court had better look to their wives when you return to Russia. How long have you been gone?"

"An unhappy fifteen years."

"Put it behind you, dear. Start a new life."

"That is my intention. Your home is splendid," he said as his eyes swept the drawing room. "Have you remarried?"

"No. Marriage is of little consequence in Berlin. Wealth and position count for much more."

"Have you anyone special in your life?"

"I've many friends. We shared such dreams of glory when we were young. Do you recall?" Hannelore asked, changing the subject.

"I recall that you fretted over the uncertainty of your future a great deal."

"Yes I did. I certainly didn't fancy my bleak prospects. Serfs are not given many choices, are they? My husband Hermann saved me, thank heaven. If it weren't for my marriage to that kind gentleman, I might have become a lifelong companion to some elderly dowager, a horrible fate."

"Your good fortune to have wed such a wealthy man. Look at what we've become, Hanne. I'm the expatriate and you are mistress of this lovely mansion."

"There are worse situations. Besides, you'll be home where you belong soon."

"Odd. The role of outcast never suited me. Like being a bear in a circus, always having to perform. Yet you seem content."

"Yes, I'm content." She hesitated. "Life takes such odd turns. Do you recall Count Petrov's son? We had a brief affair years ago, during Catherine's journey to Constantinople. He was only fifteen, but he fell in love with me and begged me to marry him. The sound of 'Countess Petrov' was lovely to the ears of one born in illegitimacy, but it wasn't meant to be. His father threatened to disown him if he married me."

"Why was that an obstacle? Your husband left you well provided for."

"It had nothing to do with money and all to do with what was expected of him. Ilya lacked the backbone to stand up to his father. He went home to announce his intentions and I never saw him again."

"What happened to him?"

"He shot himself."

"Pity."

"I thought so, too. Ilya hated his father but he couldn't face disinheritance and he couldn't face me, so he took what must have seemed to him the only way out."

"Petrov always was a hard man." He lapsed into silence for a moment.

"Do you miss Russia, Hanne?"

"It doesn't matter, dear. I can't ever return, you see. After Ilya's death, Count Petrov took pains to see to it that I would be most unwelcome if I remained. He has powerful friends at court, so I returned to Berlin at once."

"Did you love Ilya?

"I would have made him happy, for I believe in keeping my vows, but love is a fiction, too often confused with sexual stirrings. I simply gambled and I lost. Life's a game for people like me, Alexei. Since you had the good fortune to be well born, you have no need of games. I've had to make sure to win."

He laughed. "What a rare woman you are."

"You had your chance with me once, you know." She smiled at the recollection.

"Did I really? The more fool I for not taking advantage of such an opportunity, yet I don't recall."

"I never let on, but I was mad for you when we were young. No matter now. I forgive you the error of your youth."

"I seem to be cursed with this penchant for taking the wrong turn in life."

"You lack the love of a good woman, Alexei. It would give your life purpose. Have you never loved?"

"Once, but she wouldn't have me."

Hanne laughed. "That's why you loved her, I suppose. It's your nature to desire what you cannot possess."

"I've often suspected the same thing."

"What are your plans when you return to Russia?"

"First, I must visit my sister Anya and her family in Moscow, then I plan to return to St. Petersburg to live."

"Good choice. You don't want to retire to a stifling existence in Moscow for the rest of your life."

"No, but I might be better off. Along with the pardon, I've reason to expect I must face a long list of instructions for my proper conduct from my brother-in-law Peter. It may well be a life sentence to boredom."

"Even so, you're fortunate. Catherine and her son Czar Paul never forgave you for winning the duel with General Sadorov."

"True, but my sister never gave up on me."

"How is Anya?"

"She's fine. Her love for me is selfless, if undeserved. She never gave up hope for my repatriation. I look forward to my return, if only to play the eccentric uncle to my nieces and nephews. Anya is the mother of five children."

"You might marry and have children of your own one day."

"Not likely. I'm too old to change my ways. Ah, but why do you let me go on so about myself? You haven't said one word about your life. Is it such a mystery?"

"Actually, three mysteries. Would you like to meet them?" She rose to ring for a servant who returned at once with three young children.

"Darlings, I want you to meet *maman*'s dear friend, Count Razovsky," she said, amused by the astonished look on his face. "May I present my son Hans?"

The oldest of the three clicked his heels and bowed. About eleven years old, Alexei guessed. His hair was a fine, silky blonde like his mother's, but the eyes were an appealing blue. I know that face, he thought, but whom does he resemble? Razovsky puzzled over it, but the answer was out of reach.

"I am honored to meet you, Count Razovsky. *Maman* informs me that you are well-traveled."

"Yes Hans," Razovsky replied, amused by the lad's formal manners.

"I look forward to travel when I am of age. Perhaps I shall have the pleasure of hearing about some of the countries you have visited."

"Perhaps."

"And this is Maria."

"*Bon jour*, Count Razovsky." The child blushed as she spoke.

"*Bon jour*. You are every bit as beautiful as your mother. In fact, you look remarkably like her when she was your age. How old are you, mademoiselle?"

"I shall be ten on my next birthday, sir."

Hannelore laughed. "You've only just turned nine, darling." The child had the same green eyes and the same fair color as her mother. "You mustn't be in such a hurry to grow up."

The third child—a toddler—hid behind his mother's skirts. "I haven't forgotten you, my pet. This is Johann. He'll be four soon. Say hello to Count Razovsky, darling."

"*Bon thour*," the youngster lisped. He clicked his heels, but his feet failed to connect and he fell instead.

"Clumsy oaf." Hans said.

The hapless tot burst into tears, while Hannelore glared at Hans. She scooped Johann into her arms. "There, there my angel. Don't cry. Let *maman* wipe your tears. A man doesn't cry, does he? All right children, off you go. You may each take a treat from the cake tray," she added, handing the quieted baby to the governess.

"But you said I might stay and converse with our guest." Hans' cheeks were a mottled red. His mother's stony glance silenced him. He'd ruined his opportunity when he scolded his little brother.

He's arrogant, Razovsky thought as he observed the exchange.

"You've handsome children, Hanne. Maria's the image of you, and so is little Johann. Hans must resemble his father."

"Yes, he does look a bit like his father. He's even embraced his mannerisms. Incredible how children mirror us."

The light in the drawing room dimmed as the day turned to dusk. "I never thought you'd want children. Still, it suits you."

"I love them dearly."

"I'm not like you, Hanne. You've always known what you want, yet here I am at the age of thirty-eight, still searching, while you have three children."

"I'm satisfied with my life."

"Dare I ask who is father to your children?"

"What makes you think they have the same father," she countered with sly humor. "I happen to be involved with someone who prefers anonymity. Still, he's devoted to me and to our children. What difference do marriage vows make, anyway? For some, marriage is an invitation to misery. I won't deceive you, old friend, for I wouldn't mind marrying to legitimize the children. It is not in the stars for the time being, but we cannot know what the future will bring. At any rate, life is a game, Alexei. Play it well and you will reap its rewards."

TWENTY-SEVEN

"Dov?"

"What is it?"

"I want you to know that these past few weeks have been like a tonic. I'm glad we purchased my father's house. And I feel much closer to you."

"Glad to hear it." He turned his attention back to the papers in hand.

"I suppose I ought to be grateful to the czar for forming the committee. It's brought us together again. I'm busy enough at home when you are away, what with my charity work at the new Jewish orphanage and Sophie and Natasha, but it's not the same without you."

Dov removed his spectacles and looked at his wife. "Are you trying to tell me that you're pleased?"

"Yes, but it's not only that. This really is a new beginning for us."

"I told you so." He put his spectacles back on and once again returned to his papers.

"Dov?" She hesitated.

"Now what?"

"Do you love me?"

"You're my wife aren't you?" The irritation in his voice belied his uneasiness at the question.

"That isn't what I mean."

"What are you driving at? We've been married nineteen years, haven't we?" He shuffled the papers. "Now you've made me lose my place with your silly nonsense. Listen to these ideas from the draft of the committee's preamble. We are suggesting that fewer restrictions and many more liberties for Jews will lead to improvement for the betterment of Russia."

"Such noble ambitions. Does Czar Alexander agree?"

"You're missing the point. I thought you'd be pleased by the czar's new initiative for our people but I see you haven't changed. Why can't you keep an open mind?"

"Why indeed? Betrayal's always been our lot, hasn't it? I'll believe it when the czar signs the decree. Look at history, Dov. Look at history."

"You're just too stubborn to see the change that's in the air. Universities in Kharkov, Kazan and St. Petersburg are finally open to Jews, thanks to the czar. He's a forward looking, honorable man, in spite of what you think."

"I hear the Hasidic Jews refuse to recognize the State universities."

"Fanatic Jews battle progress. It can only lead enlightened Jews back in time." He paused. "Where do you stand, anyway?"

"The committee's a good beginning, I suppose. At least the government is listening to the deputies from the *kahals*, and those men have the approval of each of their councils. By the way, how many committee members are we expecting tonight?"

"Ten for dinner. A few more may join us later, the most orthodox. They suspect we're not kosher enough."

Miriam laughed. "They may be right. I can't swear for the servants no matter how hard I try to train them. I'll inform the staff and then I'm going up to change, all right?"

He could have divorced me ten years ago because I'm barren, she thought as she prepared for the evening. Hates to hear me contradict him. Must I agree to think the way he thinks? Poppa loved a good argument. I ought to try harder to please him. How?

⌘

Dov said, "We'll never change the nay-sayers, Rabbi Cohen." The *shtadlan* represented a *kahal* near Warsaw. "Why try?"

"Our people are no better off than serfs as things stand. Use your influence with Czar Alexander, Dov. Get him to withdraw the *ukase* of 1791 and eliminate the Pale of Settlement."

"That's what this committee intends to do," replied Dov.

"Can you be sure the committee will succeed? The authorities continue to support double taxation within the Pale and Christian merchants continue to resist Jewish competition."

"The Christians don't trust us, and why should they when most of our people speak in a language they don't understand, keep to themselves and make no effort to assimilate. That's no way to convince the Russians that we're loyal subjects. We need to send more of our children to their schools, we need to elect Jewish officials to public office, and we need to show a sincere commitment to working with the authorities for the betterment of our country."

"You know, Cohen," chided Rabbi Levy from the *kahal* in L'vov, "This is the first time in history that the Crown has asked us what we want instead of telling us what they think we need. Maybe Zeklinski's right. We ought to urge our people to cooperate."

"Consider the Jews in Berlin," Dov persisted, "They have grown wealthy thanks to their cooperation with the Prussian government. They command the respect and the admiration of everyone and they do not suffer discrimination. I'm in a position to know, since I'm there on business so often. German Jews speak French as well as their Christian friends and Jewish daughters are as well educated as Jewish sons. Isn't that a sign of progress?"

"Depends on your point of view," answered Rabbi Cohen. In his view, Prussian Jews were far too assimilated.

"My wife speaks French and she's well educated, I'm proud to say," Dov said. "She's every bit as clever as Madame Herz, one of the great Jewish leaders of Berlin society." He nodded across the table to Miriam, pleased to note the look of astonishment on her face.

"In fact, my wife plans to follow the example set by Madame Herz and the other fine Jewish women active in Berlin society."

Miriam raised an eyebrow. Follow what example?

"Jew and Christian alike consider it an honor to receive an invitation to visit the salon of Madame Herz. It is in the finest tradition of salons in Paris and London where intellectual ideas flourish."

Miriam was intrigued by Dov's words. A salon? Is it possible? She couldn't wait to question Dov after their guests departed.

"A salon? Why haven't you mentioned it before?"

"What do you think of the idea?"

"It's intriguing, but why didn't you discuss it with me?"

"I've been considering it for a long time," he answered, though the idea had just occurred to him during dinner.

"And our guests? Who will you invite?"

"I've many friends at court."

"This Madame Herz, the woman you mentioned? Perhaps there's something unique about her."

"She isn't the only one, though her salon is the best in Berlin. As good as any in Paris, they say. Mendelssohn's daughter has a salon as well."

"The same Mendelssohn who founded *haskalah*?"

Dov nodded, pleased with himself. He went on to tell her that, by and large, wealthy Berlin Jews were more cosmopolitan, which led to their assimilation into society.

"We can begin next Sunday evening. Does that suit you?"

TWENTY-EIGHT

"You've been avoiding me, Alexei," said Prince Bedorov, distaste in his voice.

"I've only been in Moscow less than a week," Alexei answered.

"We need to talk, sir."

"Why so formal, Peter? If it's thanks for your part in persuading the czar to grant my pardon, then you have it old man." A note of resentment crept into his voice. How is it my sister Anya loves this pretentious bastard?

"Had it not been for your sister's plea, you wouldn't be here. I worship my wife. My role in achieving your pardon is proof of that. Czar Alexander is known for his forgiving nature, which makes you a lucky man. No, no. Don't interrupt me. I'm sure it's for the purpose of making some witty retort meant to wound me. You've yet to discover I am not that easily wounded. Let it be understood that neither one of us much cares for the other, having in common only the love of a very fine woman. At your sister's urging, I continued to send you revenue from the Razovsky estate when you were in exile. Have you used it in pursuit of gambling and drinking and whoring?"

"None of your damned business. It's my life to do with what I choose."

We'll see about that, Bedorov thought. "Your estate belongs to your sister and me now."

Razovsky's eyes narrowed as he listened to the danger in his brother-in-law's menacing tone.

"You are welcome to their use as your country residence. I am told you have found quarters with your old regiment as well. More than you deserve, in my view, yet I've no wish to see my wife's brother live in poverty."

Alexei could not resist. "You mean, what would people think?"

Bedorov glared at him. "I expect you to behave in a decorous manner as befits a noble of the realm. The estate's revenue has been invested for you in Siberian mining ventures. It could be yours under certain conditions."

"And what are those conditions?"

"The conditions are that you lead a useful life, a moral one. Eschew gambling. Marry a decent woman of title. Cease to be a disgrace to your dear sister, to our children, and to me."

"How I live my life is my own affair, Peter."

"I've arranged some useful employment for you in our Petersburg offices. You'll undertake to study mining and various operations with a view toward managing your own affairs one day. If you agree, your stipend increases."

"And if I don't?" Man's dangerous, he thought. There's a trap hidden here somewhere.

"You have little choice. But if you persist in thwarting me, I shall destroy you in spite of my dear wife's love for you." He eyed him with disgust, not failing to note Razovsky's skepticism.

"So I'm to be manipulated like a puppet at your will."

Bedorov shifted to a more affable tone. "Come, come, dear fellow. I'm not proposing a hangman's noose. You might find useful occupation rewarding. Why not take a wife? Find a loving woman who will bear you children. Give your life purpose."

"And if I'm not interested?"

"Nonsense. Your sister is more than willing to help you find the right match and as a wedding gift from us, perhaps part of...no. All of your former estates."

TWENTY-NINE

The nobility attended Miriam's salon in great numbers. Not only princes and counts, but also artists, writers, musicians and women whose curiosity to meet the Jewish matron was strong. Her notoriety spread rapidly, so much so that an invitation to Madame Zeklinski's new salon became prized. It meant the difference between social fortune and ignominy. Miriam was enthralled by all the excitement. She thrived on the weekly preparations for Sunday evening.

She ordered new gowns. She instructed the servants in their roles. She made sure that the food and the drink met her standards and that their home was in perfect order.

Timid at first, and shy in the presence of the lights of the land, Miriam resolved to succeed. She read during the week, to be ready to discuss Voltaire or Diderot or Jewish philosophers such as Moses Mendelssohn. She reread the poetry of Racine, the plays of Moliere. She pored over her father's volumes of Shakespeare's plays and sonnets. Her life took on more meaning. She felt more alive, more full of energy.

Dov marveled at the unanticipated admiration his wife showered him with when he invited Count Mikhail Speransky, the czar's closest advisor, or Prince Kurakin, or Count Czartoryski, the Christian leader of the committee creating the current Jewish legislation.

He basked in the light of the envy he saw in other men's eyes each Sunday evening when Miriam held court at her salon. In a few short weeks, she had become the talk of St. Petersburg. More than one man let Madame Zeklinski know that he desired her. She learned to handle such delicacies with grace. But she favored most the men who admired her intelligence.

Was the subject Voltaire? Miriam spoke of the irony of Voltaire's championship of western enlightenment as opposed to his anti-Semitism.

One evening, she recounted his scandalous lawsuit in Berlin to Count Speransky, the czar's personal advisor.

"Sheer treachery, Sire. In 1750, Voltaire employed a Jewish banker to buy stock certificates in Dresden at less than half their face value. King Frederick had pledged that the state would redeem the bonds when they matured at full value, but only to foreign owners of the bonds."

"Hirsch, the banker, warned him of this, but Voltaire gave him letters of credit and promised him protection. As security, Hirsch left Voltaire some diamonds appraised at the same value as the letters of credit, but Voltaire stopped payment on the letters."

"When Hirsch returned, Voltaire agreed to buy some of the diamonds in exchange for Hirsch's silence. When they fought over the value of the gems, Voltaire knocked the poor man down and had him arrested."

"An old tale, yet you make it seem as though it were a fresh scandal," said Speransky.

"Treachery and deceit are evident even today, isn't that so?" The men surrounding her laughed in agreement, none harder than Speransky who dealt with treachery and deceit every day.

"Please go on," urged the minister.

"Voltaire demanded a public trial. He lied and said that Hirsch was to have purchased furs for him, but the journals of the day found him out and accused him of lying. Even so, the case was resolved in Voltaire's favor. My father was infuriated when he read the account."

"A man who hated injustice, no doubt."

"Yes. I believe I've inherited that affliction from him. Voltaire went free, but the result was far less favorable for poor Hirsch." Speransky led the laughter at the conclusion of her tale, which pleased her.

Count Speransky led her aside and proceeded to question Miriam as to the meaning of Jewish reform and its significance for Russia.

"*Haskalah* is akin to European enlightenment, Sire." She went on to illustrate that such a program in Russia would encourage Jewish youngsters to study the Russian language and secular subjects as well as the customary Hebrew of the Old Testament.

"My father insisted upon a proper education for me and it did me no harm, so far as I can tell."

"Your father must have known what a superior intellect his daughter had. Czar Alexander would be pleased to meet someone as knowledgeable as you."

⌘

"Speransky wants to arrange an audience with the czar for me."

"Good news. Be careful, though. His Majesty tends to be seductive in the presence of a beautiful woman like you."

"You haven't flattered me with such a compliment in years, Dov. I like it. I'm glad you persuaded me to stay, for I feel so much more fulfilled. I mean that."

"Yes, I can see you do. I like seeing you this way. So do our distinguished guests, if one can judge by their lust for you." He said it slyly enough to make her laugh.

"Count Speransky is intelligent."

"The czar thinks highly of him. He's sympathetic to our cause as well. By the way, I met an old friend today."

"Who is it?"

"Alexei Razovsky. The czar has pardoned him."

THIRTY

He stood before her like a cruel gift. The old yearning for him rose to mock her as empty words tumbled out of her mouth. Her tongue was coated with dust, as the words rushed downhill like an avalanche of tiny pebbles.

"Nice to see you again, Count Razovsky. Welcome back. You look well. How is your sister Anya? And her family? You must be pleased. To be back in Russia, I mean. What are your plans? Have you been to Kiev?"

She could not stem the insipid phrases that stumbled from her lips. Can he hear my heart beating like claps of thunder? Stop acting like a fool, she told herself, engulfed in panic.

His warm smile brought sun into her chilled heart.

"How disappointing to hear you address me so formally. 'Count Razovsky' indeed. Have you forgotten our pact of friendship?" His eyes flickered with mischief as he bent to kiss her hand. "My sister's fine, and yes, I'm pleased to be home. Will you allow me the privilege of resuming our friendship? You used to call me Alexei," he reminded her.

She had reached the summit of her beauty, fulfilling the rich promise merely hinted at in her youth. He thought her more regal, yet there was also a subtle hint of sadness about her that smote his heart.

"I'd like that." She listened to the music of his voice in her ears, very like some long forgotten ballad. He stands before me, giving the lie once more to my foolish fancy that I had never loved him.

"Can you not you bear to say my name?"

"Alexei," she murmured. "I thought I'd never see you again."

"Say my name again. I long to hear it from your lips."

"Welcome home, Alexei."

The sound was sweet to his ears. "You're a soothing balm for these old eyes, Miriam. Yet, perhaps that's a lie, for I think your face exceeds my paltry power to recollect. There's a richness the years have added, a rare fullness."

"You've changed as well. That old air of insouciance is gone. You seem more restrained. It suits you."

"Does it?" I've never stopped loving her, he thought, awed by the force of his passion. He feasted his eyes on her like a love-starved schoolboy smitten by the sting of his first romance.

"I see you've found one another," Dov said. "Congratulations on your pardon, Alexei. So Bedorov finally pulled it off, did he? Alexei looks fit, doesn't he dear?"

"You never mentioned you invited Count Razovsky here tonight," Miriam said, with a hint of anger. Alexei raised an eyebrow, but Dov ignored the remark.

Dov swept his hand over the crowded drawing room. "My wife's salon's a great success, don't you think? My idea of course, but she enjoys it, don't you, dear?" Miriam glared at him, but he took no notice.

"Mikhail Toglov is here to entertain tonight. He is the finest Ukrainian balladeer in all of Russia, they say. You'll agree when you hear him, but we'll wait a bit longer to begin. I'm expecting a few more important guests. Why don't you see to our old friend, Miriam? Perhaps he'd like a drink. Ah, there's Count Polikov. I must talk to him. Business." Dov hurried off.

Razovsky's eyes followed Dov, all the while wondering about that spark of anger from Miriam. Can it be she doesn't love him any more? The thought exhilarated him. "You have guests every Sunday?"

"Yes. It's Dov's wish for us to entertain like this."

"I see. Do you enjoy it?"

She hesitated. "I suppose."

"What's troubling you, friend?" he asked. "I see sadness in your eyes."

"I'd forgotten how observant you are, Alexei. Let's walk out in the garden, shall we?" She linked her arm in his.

"This used to be your father's house," he said.

"You remembered, then."

"Yes. The last time I saw you before I left Russia, we strolled in this very garden. I came to pay my respects after the death of your mother. Do you recall?"

"Yes, I do." They didn't speak for a time, each lost in the memory of that night so long ago.

"You told me then you'd never forget the night of Czarina Catherine's final ball in Kiev. I told you we were a bit like Romeo and Juliet."

"We're destined to remain friends, not lovers. You gave me your word." She heard pleading in her voice.

"I had to accept your offer of friendship or lose you. Do you still feel the same way?"

"I'm still Dov's wife."

"I wish there could be more for us."

She put her hand to his lips. "Please don't say that. I want your friendship and nothing more. You see how important that is to me, don't you?"

"Once again you force me to accept your terms." But only for the time being, he thought, with a joy he hadn't felt in years.

"Let's go back inside. I can hear the musicians tuning up. Dov is sure to be looking for me."

THIRTY-ONE

When Czar Alexander appointed Dov to head the Jewish delegation, it turned his head. The work of the committee took up much of his time though it was not the legislation that interested him so much as the power of his new office.

He took great pains to discuss each new detail with Miriam or rather, to have her listen to his account of the tedious daily proceedings. He wanted her admiration. He needed it as an endorsement of his role in history. The new Moses. *Shtadlan* Dov Zeklinski.

She yearned to ask about the new restrictions that would hurt the poorest of Jews living within the expanded Pale of Settlement. She ached to question what this would mean to the thousands of Jewish families barely eking out a living in small *shtetls* across the nation. Why were they being excluded from keeping taverns and inns, or from selling liquor, occupations they had held for years?

At the same time, she detected a subtle change in the quality of their guests, as if, after the first flush of novelty had worn off, the royal court found no need to continue to attend what had merely been an amusing diversion. What if their remaining guests were less than noble, less than royal? Dov managed to elevate them to eminence by their mere appearance at his wife's salon. The only bright moments for Miriam occurred when Alexei appeared each Sunday evening.

In May, the Rabbis from the *kahals* requested a six-month recess in the proceedings in order to report to their local councils. The czar granted the request, hoping for more progress and less bickering when they reconvened.

Dov told Miriam he would use the time to attend to business interests outside the city, but he insisted that she continue her salon in his absence.

"I've asked Alexei to look after you while I'm gone. He'll see to inviting important guests in my absence. He knows everyone worth knowing."

"You might have asked me first."

"Why are you so angry? I thought you liked him."

"Don't you think it an impropriety?"

"Nonsense. He's our good friend."

"People love to gossip, you know."

"He wouldn't dare overstep his bounds, and he's already told me he's more than delighted to be of service. Doesn't seem to do much of anything else, if you ask me. Besides, he admires you. I can't see what you're making such a big fuss about. You've no one else to look after you."

"Isn't that your job? Take me with you."

"No. I need you to carry on here, don't you see? It's critical for eminent people to know how much we contribute to the life of this city. The salon's very well known. What's more, our name is on everyone's lips. Isn't that the way it should be? What we've always wanted? Why not press our advantage? Besides, you wouldn't like Berlin."

⌘

"My apologies, Alexei."

"What for?" he asked in surprise.

"Dov has embarrassed me by asking you to look after me while he's gone. I am a burden to you."

"On the contrary, it's an honor for me. Besides, it would be cruel of you to deprive me of your company. In fact, dear friend, I wondered if you were free tomorrow afternoon?"

"What do you have in mind?" And where will all this lead, she wondered, but she pushed it from her thoughts.

"Ride out with me tomorrow, Miriam. Shall I call for you at one?"

THIRTY-TWO

"Welcome home, dear."

"How are the children, my love?" Dov asked.

"Hans and Maria are fine, but Johann's running a fever, poor baby. Would you like to see them?"

"Not just yet. I want you first."

"Show me just how much you've missed me." She took his hand and led him to their chambers where she was at her seductive best. He lay in bed sipping champagne and watched her remove her clothing. It aroused a fire within him, but through the years she had taught him to wait, to enhance their lovemaking.

Her cool hands caressed him, not with fire but with art. She brushed his lips with hers, a velvet sensation. She pretended to resist his advances, giving in to his superior force at just the right moment. She made him feel powerful in bed, a man in charge. Nor did she ever find fault with him. Not ever.

"Tell me what devilish amusements you've been up to while I've been gone," he asked afterwards.

Her smile was full of mystery. "We're having guests tonight, but you'll have time to rest before dinner."

"Anyone I know?"

"A few old friends and some surprises. We have a guest of honor tonight. Prince Wilhelm. He is monarch of a small German principality near the Russian border. I hear it's full of picturesque little villages in charming valleys surrounded by lovely mountains."

"And I suppose you are scheming for a *dacha* for you and the children in summer."

"For you, too, darling. A place to relax whenever you can."

"Perhaps he'll recommend something. What does he call his picturesque little German State?"

"Wilhelmstadt."

He laughed heartily. "Prince Wilhelm of Wilhelmstadt? What else?"

Pearl Wolf

"You're so clever to think of a summer villa for us, David. We think alike, don't we? Wouldn't you love a villa high on a mountain where it's cool in summer, with a lake where the children could swim and sail?" She paused. "There's something I should warn you about."

"What's that?"

"The prince is far from wealthy. Happens to be one of the reasons he's anxious to meet you. I hinted that you might recommend some kind of industry for his people."

"You could say the same for every petty monarch in Europe. Well, we'll see what we can do for your new friend. You haven't already made any promises?"

"You know me better than that."

"Yes I do. Sorry, darling. You're perfect. Everything I need in a woman."

She smiled and pecked him on the cheek. "Oh, by the way, Alexei Razovsky stopped to see me on his way home. Czar Alexander finally granted him the pardon he'd been pleading for all these years."

He frowned at the news. "Does he know about us?"

"Of course not. I never mentioned you."

"I ought to stop underestimating you. You would never do such a thing. I know he's been pardoned, by the way. I met him in St. Petersburg."

"Would you like to hear another intriguing fancy, my darling," she asked, changing the subject.

"Your intrigues always fascinate me."

"Why not purchase land in Wilhelmstadt in the name you use here?"

"May I remind you, dear heart, that I still have a Russian passport that reads Dov Zeklinski?"

"If you're generous enough, he might grant you citizenship."

"You've some hidden purpose, Lori. I can tell when you're hatching one of your pretty schemes. What is it this time?"

"Just another game, darling. For the sake of the children, if you like. Do you think we might persuade our impoverished prince to bestow a title upon you once you succeed in making him wealthy?"

"My grandfather is probably spinning in his grave at the mere thought. Do your plans happen to include our marriage by any chance?"

"Baroness von Secklin would suit me very well. Don't be coy, darling. You'd love a distinguished title."

The two spent the afternoon building a castle on a mountain and toying with the enchantment of carving a royal life for themselves and their children.

"Don't commit yourself to anything tonight David, all right? I think it's wiser to whet the prince's appetite this first time. We'll invite him to be our house guest the next time he visits Berlin."

"As usual, I have the utmost faith in the soundness of your plan. Come, darling. Let's get dressed. I want to see the children."

120

Dov rose from their bed and extended his hand to her. "One more question occurs to me, my pet. Would Prince Wilhelm be inclined to bestow a baronetcy on a Jew?"

"I doubt it. Would you consider converting in exchange for a title?" Dov laughed as he pulled her into his arms and hugged her.

"Save your artful intrigues for the prince. I was born a Jew and I'll die a Jew. I'm afraid you'll have to think of some other plan."

"Well, then. Since you've thrown down the gauntlet, so to speak, I accept your challenge."

"Challenge? Did I offer a challenge?"

"I'll just have to dream up another way to persuade our prince to bestow a title upon you in spite of your terms."

THIRTY-THREE

"How are you, Anya?" Miriam was appalled at her old friend's appearance. She's only thirty-four. Where's the shapely young girl I once knew?

"You look splendid, Miriam," said Anya. "And I've grown too fat, but I don't mind. It's the children, you see. I grew larger with each birth. My five children are the joy of my life. Peter's too."

"I'd love to meet them. Are they here in St. Petersburg with you?"

"Oh, no! Peter wouldn't hear of it. He thinks this city is a bad influence on young people. Peter believes it's wiser for them to wait until they're old enough to understand the ways of the world. Our children are innocent of such cosmopolitan ways. They have their studies and their friends to keep them occupied at home."

"Alexei tells me the Bedorov castle is handsome."

"Moscow's a friendly city. I love my life there. Our doors are open to one and all."

But not to Jews and certainly not to me, Miriam thought. "Your brother is quite taken by his nieces and nephews."

Anya nodded in agreement, yet something nagged at her. Peter would be furious if he knew of this visit to Miriam, but she couldn't refuse Alexei. What could she do? He was her brother and she loved him. Perhaps it had been a mistake to come here today. Perhaps she should have remained loyal to her husband and not indulged her charming, irresponsible brother.

She pushed the unpleasant thought out of her mind and proceeded to sing the praises of each of her children to Miriam, an activity that took her most of the morning. She left out few details of their intelligence and their bright futures.

"The children are precious to us, you see. Peter insists that the Good Lord meant me for motherhood. We would have had more children if I were able."

"Five children are a fine brood, Anya. Much to be admired."

Anya didn't touch on Miriam's inability to have children. She vowed to pray for her friend. "Tell me about yourself, Miriam."

"There isn't much to tell. At home in Kiev I keep busy with the new orphanage and my relatives. I also see our friend Natasha often." Miriam laughed at the recollection of the feisty countess. "I suspect she's peeved with me for deserting her for life in St. Petersburg. I write, of course, but she complains that she misses me."

Anya frowned. "When Natasha chaperoned me to Moscow, she behaved terribly."

"What did she do?"

"Peter's mother took offense and I was mortified. Peter couldn't wait for her to leave."

"Natasha meant no harm, I'm sure. It's just her way."

"I know that, but Peter and his parents weren't used to her frankness. She persisted in ridiculing Moscow's conventions."

"I see." Miriam disliked the implication in Anya's tone that Natasha was somehow remiss. Anya's changed. Better talk about something else. "Tell me about your life in Moscow."

"We entertain frequently. Dinners, balls, masquerades. We have our own theater as well. Our talented serfs entertain us. After church every Sunday we open our home for a musicale."

"Does Peter sing then? He has such a beautiful voice."

"Kind of you to remember. Yes. Occasionally, we invite our own singers and musicians to accompany him. We're particularly proud of one of our serfs, a talented pianist. We sent him to study at the Berlin Conservatory."

"Do you still play piano?"

"No. You were a much better pianist than I could ever hope to be. Do you still play?"

"Only for my own amusement."

"We've both come such a long way, haven't we?"

"I'm glad to hear that you're content, Anya."

"Peter and I have everything we need. Sleigh rides in winter on the Moskva River and we spend every summer at our country *dacha* on a beautiful lake."

It began to be obvious to Miriam that her old friend was not any more comfortable than she was, and their conversation grew strained. Anya kept glancing at the clock.

Where is Alexei? I wish he'd hurry back, Miriam thought. Time to end this clumsy charade.

⌘

Attendance on Sundays was reduced to those doubtful members of society who were not always welcome in the best of homes. It was plain to Miriam that St. Petersburg had no need of Jews. She wished she had the fortitude to stop the pretense on her own, but she couldn't face the thought of another major battle when Dov returned home.

THIRTY-FOUR

"You're here early today, Alexei."

"Perfect day for a ride in the countryside, don't you think?"

She knew she shouldn't go out riding with him every day. The impropriety nagged at her, yet she hungered for him just the same. Send him away. Tell him you can't go riding today because you're expecting a visit from your cousin.

"Won't you join me?"

"Yes," she said.

"How did your visit with Anya go yesterday?" he asked when they were under way.

"Not well, I'm afraid. We were both uncomfortable."

"What was wrong?"

"I had the strangest sensation. It wasn't so much that she didn't want to be with me. Not that at all. But something was worrying her. Did her husband know that she came to see me?"

He shrugged. "What difference would that make?"

"None, I suppose. It's just that I felt she was uneasy." Miriam searched his eyes. "It's true, isn't it? Peter would never have permitted her to visit me, would he?"

"I thought it would please you both to renew your friendship. Perhaps it was a mistake."

"Don't blame yourself. I have to admit that I was curious to see her again. But there's no longer anything there for us, do you see? It's difficult to go back to the past. That was another time, wasn't it? Another life." They fell silent, each wrapped in their own thoughts as the carriage wended its way into the countryside.

Alexei yearned to hold her in his arms. He ached to tell her what was in his heart. What can I offer her? There can be no life for us, yet I want her so.

"What are you thinking about?" he asked at last.

"I don't know. Nothing. Everything. I feel wonderful here with you. Yet, part of me feels sad."

"Sad? On such a beautiful day?"

"I should have refused to ride out with you. I even tried to lie about another engagement. But I couldn't do that either. God knows I've tried. Do you understand?"

"I love you, Miriam."

"I know and it frightens me to hear you say it, my darling."

They had reached the outskirts of the city when the driver halted the open *droshki* in front of a small cottage.

"Why are we stopping here?"

Alexei stepped down and extended his arms for her. He led her into the small parlor where he drew her to him in a gentle embrace. So peaceful to be held in his arms, she thought, yet inside of me a storm. Is this love? Why does it hurt so much? "Don't, Alexei."

"You want me to stop? Say it, then. Tell me you don't want me to go on loving you." He looked around in despair. The little cottage seemed all wrong, somehow.

"But not like this, my dearest. I hadn't intended a tawdry seduction." His eyes welled up.

"Don't, my darling. I love you. No one has ever made me feel as you do." She kissed his eyes, his mouth, his scar.

"I'm so ashamed for weeping."

"I love you, Alexei. How good it feels to say it at last."

"Before God, Miriam, you're mine. For always, come what may." His tears washed her cheeks. He clung to her as though he were awash in a stormy sea and she a lifeline.

"Don't weep, my love," she whispered, yielding to his touch, needing him as much as he needed her. His lips bruised hers as their urgency grew. Breath quickened to gasps. Hands groped to free clothing. He undid the hasps on her gown and turned her to him. Desire inflamed him, yet he forced himself to slow the pace.

"Don't move, sweet Juliet," he murmured with hoarse intensity. He leaned to brush his lips where his hands had been, mumbling sounds that had meaning only for her. His eyes consumed her breasts with such thirst, such hunger. Had he never known breasts before? The whirlwind of his craving unleashed itself on her and a moan of yearning escaped her lips. He pressed her trembling body to the rug on the floor.

Her mouth was everywhere at once; on his lips, on his face, on his neck, on his chest, on his taut nipples. Her lips lingered there, but only a moment. Urgency forced feverish lips to journey to his navel, to the hardness between his legs. Her tongue circled his swollen member. She gave herself to him, exulting in the wonder of him.

Inside of her, he found a blistering grotto. She rose to meet him, thrusting toward him. Their sighs and moans escaped like thunder. And when his loins

125

trembled near to bursting, and when her depths were swollen, they became one voice, a swelling crescendo of carnal savagery.

At last they lay depleted, exhausted by love. Alexei entwined his fingers in hers and squeezed her hand. She shuddered involuntarily.

"Are you cold, my precious?" He reached for the throw on the settee behind them and covered her with it. He wrapped his arms around her. "Feel better?" She hugged him to her in response.

"I love you, Miriam. That's all that matters."

"Is it, Alexei? Is it all that matters? Does love make it right? What have we done? I'm weak and I've sinned. My heart is heavy. How is it possible to soar to heaven one minute and sink to hell the next?"

"Don't punish yourself so. Don't we deserve joy? I can't give you up. Not now. Let's take what we can."

"I have a husband, Alexei."

"Do you love him?"

"This morning I might have said yes, but I can't fool myself any longer. It's you I love. It's almost a relief to admit it. My heart tells me it's right to be here in your arms, yet my head tells me it's terribly wrong."

"Love isn't a question of right or wrong, my own dear soul."

"When you fled Russia, I was sad but I was also relieved. How is it I never allowed myself to admit how much I loved you till now? We wouldn't have remained friends had you stayed, would we? No, of course not. What a foolish notion. I used to wish Dov would look at me the way you did."

"Let's take our moment, my darling. I'm not a lovesick schoolboy and you're not a child. When Dov invited me to your salon I came to see you that first time in the hope that the love I felt for you was over and done with, part of the past. Loneliness in exile does strange things to the mind, you see."

"Did you think about me?"

"I thought of you often, first in Paris and then when I fled to London when the revolution began. I told myself it was mere homesickness for my country, yet the first time I saw you again, I knew that I still loved you and what I pined for was not Mother Russia, but you. Had I seen indifference in your eyes, I would never have continued to visit but I saw something else, and it gave me hope."

His hands sought her body and their passion renewed itself once more. They filled their need for one another in a poignant desire to appease their starved cravings. She marveled at the pleasure he gave her. He delighted in what she took so freely in return.

"Was I alive before today? I think not. But I warn you. I've a weak spirit, Alexei."

"No, my darling. You're brave and soft and sweet and full of honor."

"Ah, but bravery and honor are precisely what I lack. Will you help this fallen woman learn to live with her wickedness?"

Alexei said, "`Did my heart love till now? Forswear it, sight!
For I ne'er saw true beauty till this night.'"

She laughed. "Well spoken, my sweet Romeo. It strikes me though, that we're both a lot older than those two young lovers." She rose to her feet and began to dress.

"Why are you dressing? Have I satisfied your carnal appetite so easily?"

"Not at all. The exertion of loving you has robbed me of my strength. Is there anything to eat in this charming little love nest, or must I starve to death as retribution for my sins?"

THIRTY-FIVE

Dawn began with his arrival. The blackness of night descended with his departure, a dizzying descent into hell for her. "Thou shalt not commit adultery," she told herself, as though the words were a *knout* mercilessly punishing her for violating God's holy commandment.

The pain of her love for him hurt like the stinging brambles of a thorny vine. Yet she lived for the pleasure of being in his arms. His body was Mount Olympus. She could not fill herself enough with the sweet pleasures of his flesh.

"I need more than these few paltry hours we manage to steal each day. It isn't enough for me. I want to wake in the morning with you at my side. I want to fall asleep holding you, Miriam."

"What can we do? I don't dare stay in this cottage with you overnight. It's hopeless."

"Perhaps not. When is Dov due back from Berlin?"

"He may not be home before the end of the year, but I can't always count on what he writes. The czar may reconvene the committee sooner," she shrugged.

"Write to Dov and tell him you're spending the summer elsewhere."

"What do you mean?"

"Natasha owns a *dacha* on Krestovski Island. She hasn't used it for years."

"And I can write to Dov and tell him I am staying with Natasha?"

"The cottage is secluded on the island in one of those little forks of the Neva River."

"Do you think Natasha will object?"

"Not in the least." He hesitated.

"What is it?"

"Will you hate me if I reveal something of my sinful past?"

"How can I hate you?"

"I've used her cottage before."

She laughed. "I can't erase your wayward past, my love, but I'll certainly make sure you never find a reason to repeat such scandalous behavior."

"We'll go there right after Czar Alexander's Ball. Write to her today."

"Natasha's such a dear, Alexei. I hate to abuse her trust."

"She won't think the less of you. She's had many *affairs d'amour* in her lifetime."

"Yes, that's true. She's never kept them a secret from me."

"What's troubling you, then? Is it Dov? Are you concerned that he'll find us out?"

"He'd certainly be shocked. I already think the whole world knows about our love. Isn't it written all over me? Surely the men who visit my salon know that I'm your mistress."

"That's heartless. It reduces our love to mere indulgence. I worship you. Doesn't that make all the difference?"

⌘

Bedorov listened intently to the man's report of his brother-in-law's movements. "Are you sure he hasn't been to his office for weeks? Where does he go each day?"

"Early every morning, Sire, he drives to Madame Zeklinski's home. She appears to be waiting for him, because they're under way within moments of his arrival. They ride for almost an hour to a secluded cottage north of the city. They don't come out again till well into the evening."

"Servants?"

"Two. An old gardener and his wife. They live in a separate cottage in the back. The old woman prepares food for them, but she's never in the house when they're there. My men have observed the woman enter early in the morning, well before their arrival, with trays of food. Then she returns to her own cottage."

"And they never emerge till late once they enter?"

"Sometimes they sit in the garden. They talk, they hold hands." He hesitated.

"And?"

"And they kiss. Then they go inside."

"Who owns the cottage?"

"I don't know Your Highness."

"Find out. You may go," he said, but the man seemed reluctant to leave.

"Is there something else?"

"Yes Sire."

"What is it?"

"It's Princess Bedorov. No offense, Sire."

Bedorov's face darkened. "I don't recall ordering you to spy on my wife."

The man's knees began to shake. "Begging your pardon, Sire. I wasn't spying on her."

He noted the man's discomfort and added more kindly, "I know you are just doing your duty and I commend you for it. You may speak freely."

"Princess Bedorov paid a visit to Madame Zeklinski at her home."

"When?"

"Two weeks ago. Spent the afternoon. I thought I should report it, just in case you didn't know."

THIRTY-SIX

"I do hope Count Speransky forgets to present me to the czar at the ball tonight." The Grand Ball marked the end of the social season.

Alexei laughed. "I'm the one who has something to fear. Czar Alexander might charm you away from me."

"Never." The intensity in her voice delighted him.

He led her through the crush of guests, stopping here and there to introduce her to acquaintances. He amused her with witty anecdotes about each one's mistress or lover once they were out of earshot.

They glided to the music amid the crush of other dancers, but her gaze was fixed only on Alexei. When the music ended, she detected a frown on his face when his sister and her husband greeted them.

"How are you Miriam?" asked Anya. Her eyes searched in puzzlement. "Where is your husband?"

"Dov is away on business. Your brother was kind enough to escort me tonight."

"I want a word with you, Alexei," Bedorov said, but before Alexei could respond, Count Speransky interrupted them.

"His Majesty grants you an audience, Madame."

Bedorov witnessed the exchange in astonishment. His face revealed nothing as he thought, why does the czar wish to meet the Jewess? It's due to Speransky's power with the czar. Alexei and his Jewish whore can wait. I'll delay my discussion with Alexei until I discover His Majesty's purpose. They say if you chase two hares you'll not catch either.

"What is it you wish to discuss, Peter?"

"Nothing important, Alexei. Some other time, eh?"

"Then I shall dance with your wife. May I have the honor, dear sister?"

"I'm afraid I contradicted the czar," said Miriam when she returned to Alexei. "Will he forgive me, do you think?"

"The czar has no trouble forgiving beautiful women. What did you say?"

"When he asked my opinion on the Jewish question of conversion, I replied that the question was of great interest to Christians, but of no interest to Jews."

Miriam and Alexei were unaware that disapproving eyes followed their movements as the evening progressed. They prepared to take their leave shortly after the czar's departure, but not before they had encountered Anya and her husband once more.

"How are you getting on at the office, Alexei? Beginning to absorb the principles of mining?"

"Matter of fact, I'm taking a holiday, Peter. It's just for the summer, so you can put your mind at ease. I plan to take some books with me to study the subject."

"Good idea, Alexei. Shows initiative."

⌘

"Stop here," Alexei ordered the driver on their way home. The night was bathed in the white light of the summer solstice, the air awash with music and laughter.

"Let's walk a bit," he said. He helped her down and led her to the embankment along the Neva River where young lads clad in their embroidered blouses celebrated the rites of manhood. They strolled hand in hand with willing maidens in colorful costume, stealing kisses in the shadows.

"Reminds me of St. Mark's Square in Venice. Some day I'd like to take you there." Alexei led her into the shadow of a doorway and kissed her.

"Venice is anywhere I'm with you, my love."

⌘

"Keep watch day and night."

"I need more men to do that, Sire."

"Caution them to be discreet."

"Anything else, Sire?"

"No." He busied himself with papers, his mind on his audience with the czar on Kamenny Island.

⌘

"It's a fine thing you propose, Your Majesty. You serve Mother Russia and God with this act."

"Do you think so, Bedorov? A student of Swedenborg predicted greatness for us, you know."

"Your good work shall most certainly be recorded in history, Sire."

132

"As to serfdom, it is a complexity. Surely the nobility understands that we cannot continue to enslave nine tenths of the population. All of Western Europe is against it."

"The nobility believes that serfdom continues to serve our empire well. Serfs constitute Russia's wealth."

"You're suggesting, then, that we take the nobility into our confidence in this matter?"

"The consequences of haste may well be anarchy. Freeing the serfs, while a noble idea, may lead to chaos."

"Surely, the nobility does not plan to rebel?"

"I have heard that said, Sire."

"Speransky disagrees with your views."

"I respect his loyalty to the Crown, Sire, though I question his loyalty to the traditions of our country. Please understand. I am only reporting to you what I hear, as is my bounden duty. My own view is closer to yours. Russia should be ashamed of serfdom, but it may be wiser to slow the process of liberation for the time being."

"You are a true patriot to have brought this to my attention. Perhaps liberation of the serfs can wait a bit longer. We haven't finished dealing with the Jewish question yet, have we?"

"No, Majesty, though I have heard it said that the committee has made some excellent suggestions."

"What does the nobility have to say about the committee?"

"It is said that if our government allows Jewish mercantile competition to continue without hindrance, they might injure local trade."

"You have their pulse, Bedorov. Perhaps the nobility would feel less apprehensive if their interests are protected. Would you accept a seat on the committee?"

"I shall be happy to assist Your Highness in any way I can, for the sake of our beloved Mother Russia. God grant me the wisdom to do it with honor."

"Come to see us more often, good friend. Perhaps we can arrange a government appointment for you. We find ourselves surrounded by too many idealists. A few practical men would temper their enthusiasm for radical change."

"What do you have in mind, Sire?"

"Arrange to see me next week. We shall have an answer for you then. The weather's lovely in July. Why not bring your family here for a holiday?"

"My wife and children are already at our *dacha* near Moscow, Sire. Perhaps next summer."

THIRTY-SEVEN

Each morning she forced herself to think only of the moment. His muscles and veins stood out, even as he slept. Michelangelo's David, peaceful, eternally ready to wake. She studied him as if committing every small blue vein, like the rippling forks of the Neva, to memory.

When Alexei woke, they would make love, for it thrilled him to see her worshipping eyes. He taught her to exult in her sensuality even as he held his own passion in check the more to heighten hers. He led her on voyages she never dreamed possible.

"We've a letter from Natasha. Let me read it to you."

Dear Miriam and Alexei, So. The inevitable has happened, as I knew it must. I had my doubts at first, but you certainly didn't need my consent. It pleases me to know that my little dacha is privy to such passion, for I am too old to provide that sweet cottage with the diversions I enjoyed in my youth. The joy of love is fleeting, my children. Seize what you can of it before it disappears into the wind. Take your precious moment, my dears. Bravo for your courage. God be with you, Natasha

"She gives me much to think about, Alexei."

"You promised you wouldn't spoil our holiday with sad thoughts until September when we return to St. Petersburg."

"I've certainly tried, haven't I? Still, I'm troubled."

He changed the subject, determined to cheer her. "What would you say to the idea of taking the boat out this morning? I'd like to revisit a certain secluded cove." His laughter creased the corners of his eyes.

"Why? Do you want to explore it?"

"No, silly wench. I want to make love to you there."

"Wait. I'll fetch my parasol."

⌘

"Minister of Information? I am deeply honored, Your Majesty." Bedorov was triumphant. Good, he thought. His Majesty is reviving the secret service and I'm to be its minister. Here's a challenge worthy of me.

"We've need of more discipline in our country. More loyalty to the Crown."

"I understand, Sire. There are those who want to change our Russian heritage, yet I am of the opinion that we must preserve them, Sire. Forgive me if I offend you."

"Continue to speak the truth. We have come to trust you because you are a man of honor."

"My humble thanks, Your Highness, for giving me leave to speak so freely. Others who seek your favor for their own purposes surround you, I fear. I accept your appointment not for personal gain, but for Mother Russia."

"You and Speransky are opposites, yet both loyal servants to the Crown. Our duty must be to examine both sides of the coin before choosing the course of empire."

"Your wisdom shall prevail, Sire." But I shall steer you in the right direction, for you waver far too often, Bedorov thought.

⌘

On the last day of summer, they lay on a grass-laden embankment well hidden from view, though it did not matter, for few people ventured near the private enclave.

"I can't bear leaving all this, darling. No more love under the skies? No more walks along the river? No more boating? Is this the end of our paradise?"

"We'll come back next summer, God willing. For now, we'll go on as before in our cottage in the city."

"Dov will return to St. Petersburg soon. What shall we do then?"

He laughed at her. "You're such a novice at assignations, darling. We'll find a way."

"I dread to think he might find out."

"Are you afraid he'll challenge me to a duel?"

She smiled at the absurdity. "Dov doesn't know the first thing about dueling contests, unless of course, he could challenge you to a financial contest."

"He'd certainly win then, for I'm no good at all as a financier, though I fancied it once when he enlisted my aid. You might better worry about how to deceive the rest of the world, for you wear your love openly for everyone to see."

"I'm not accustomed to a life of deception."

"Every Royal practices deception of one sort or another. It's the national sport. Czar Alexander has had a mistress for years. Her *dacha* is on Krestovski Island, not far from here. He finds his way into her arms after a short stroll over a little bridge he's had especially constructed."

"Really?"

"I delight in your innocence, darling." He hesitated. "Don't you wonder what kind of life Dov leads when he's away from you?" As the words escaped his lips, he was startled by a vision of Hannelore's son Hans, a younger version of Dov. So that's it, he thought. She's his mistress and he is father to her children.

"Dov's business is the most important thing in his life, not me. I loved him once, you know."

He vowed never to reveal Dov's secret to Miriam. "What went wrong?"

"He thinks I've failed him and Dov cannot tolerate failure. I couldn't bear him children. Judaic law decrees that a man may divorce his wife after ten years if she hasn't given him children. I've often wondered why he hasn't."

He drew her close. "One can always adopt a child."

"I wanted to, but he's opposed to the idea. Refuses to raise someone else's child, he says."

"If it were me, I'd want to adopt if only to share the wealth of our love. Dov's a fool for not appreciating your wit and your grace as I do."

She laughed. "What a gift you are. I no longer believe I'm afflicted with that dangerous illness called passion, thanks to you. Dov has always made me feel as though I am another business transaction in bed."

"I take it that I'm better in bed, then?" His lazy smile revealed delight.

"No contest, darling. When you make love to me, it's as though we set fire to the universe. The skies ring with the sounds of thunder and lightning though the sun shines. I'm simply driven to love you back, to give you all of me, to be one with you, Alexei Nicholayevich Razovsky."

Alexei kissed her. Her breath quickened as his hands played its symphony upon her. *Andante. Accelerando. Crescendo.* He was orchestra and conductor. She was instrument and audience.

THIRTY-EIGHT

Miriam and Alexei attended balls and danced in drawing rooms of his friends. They went to the theater, to the ballet, to concerts, to the opera. When she protested its unseemly appearance, Alexei insisted that appearing in public was the only way they could keep up the fiction that he was escorting her at her husband's request.

Even so, it made her uneasy. Barely discernible breaches, like some shifting shoreline invaded their love in subtle ways. They seemed so innocent at first. Mere happenstance. A look. A glance. A raised eyebrow. Miriam pretended not to notice.

They rode through the city on a quiet Sunday, when business ceased. They passed Falconet's magnificent statue of Peter the Great, the monarch's horse, front legs proudly raised as if in flight, Miriam read the words on its base.

Petrus Primus, Caterina Secunda

"Tell the driver to hurry, darling. You know I'm expecting guests tonight."
"I haven't forgotten your salon."

⌘

"Sold? Our cottage? How strange," Miriam said when Alexei reported the news. "Have you located another?"

"We'll find something soon." Yet as he spoke, his thoughts wavered. Who had purchased their cottage? Why was he having such difficulty finding another?

"My head aches over this news. You won't leave me while I rest?"

"No. I'll be here when you wake."

When she retired, he poured himself a brandy and thought about the news. He had his own suspicions over the loss of the cottage. That man. Strange. I've seen him more than once. Is he following me? Perhaps it's my imagination.

He dozed and dreamed of his mother in a bridal dress kneeling at his side. No. It was not his mother, it was Miriam, her face glowing in an exquisite light. He glanced at the crucifix around her neck, pleased that his bride was a Christian.

He woke as if from a nightmare. Alexei's hands shook at the revelation and he drained his glass.

⌘

"Agreed, Your Majesty," said Dov. My solicitors will draw up the necessary legal documents. May I say that Madame von Hals and I are very pleased? We look forward to spending summers in Wilhelmstadt."

"It was not my intention to relinquish such a large tract of land to you, but you do drive a hard bargain, eh? I am told that Jews are well known for their craftiness."

Dov frowned. "I was under the impression that I was doing you and your country a service. However, if I have mistaken your need for funds to help your people, we can cancel our contract. Unfortunately, I must leave Berlin tomorrow, since I have urgent business at my shipyards in Sebastopol. Feel free to change your mind about our agreement at any time." Man's a fool, Dov thought. Thinks his title gives him leave to insult me.

"No, no Herr von Secklin," the prince said. "You take offense where none was meant. Of course we shall proceed with this business as planned."

"As you wish, Sire. Shall we join my guests in celebration of the New Year?

THIRTY-NINE

While bitter winds chilled the streets, the fire in Miriam's drawing room blazed as Miriam began reading Natasha Gorov's letter aloud to Alexei.

"My darlings, this morning I received some puzzling correspondence. Peter Bedorov has requisitioned my Krestovski Island cottage for the summer. Urgent affairs of State require the Minister of Information to be available to Czar Alexander when he summers here. Surely you can see that I have no choice but to acquiesce. God be with you, Natasha"

"What's the date on the letter?"

"She posted it on the first of February."

The frown on Alexei's face did little to quell her uneasiness. "We'll find something else," he said.

"So long as I have you, I don't care where we are," but she was disheartened by the news just the same. "Will you excuse me, Alexei? Our guests are due soon and I must change."

"Of course, dear," he said, but his thoughts were not on the evening's visitors to the salon. Why does Peter want Natasha's little *dacha*? It's too small for him and Anya and the children. How did he insinuate himself into the czar's good graces? My friends avoided us at the opera last night. No greetings, no visits to my box. Thank heaven Miriam was too entranced by the music to notice. Last week there were so few guests, too. Will it be the same tonight?

"What's the matter, dear heart? Why so glum? Was it Natasha's letter?" Miriam asked when the last guest departed.

"We had such a wonderful summer last year, didn't we?"

"Yes, my love. Besides, we have this summer no matter where we are, since Dov has delayed his return."

"That's good news."

She paused. "Stay the night, my sweet."

"Here? What about the servants?"

"Let's not spoil our love by fretting about the servants." She led him upstairs to her chambers.

⌘

The man positioned himself across the way, enshrouded by the darkness of night. He saw them kissing, framed in the window. He made a note of the time in his book. When the count emerged, he would note the time again. He pulled his cloak tighter, preparing to wait. Perhaps Minister will reward me for my services, above and beyond the call of duty on such a freezing night.

Did the count notice me the other day? Can't afford to be caught. Bastard's giving it to her in a warm bed. Like to give it to my wife when I go home. Maybe Minister will name me head of the secret police. He uncorked his flask and warmed himself with vodka to celebrate his new title.

FORTY

Czar Alexander offered his hand to the elegant Maria Naryshkina for the polonaise, thus commencing the April ball. With as much dignity as she could manage, Empress Elizabeth witnessed the czar and his mistress leading the dance, while from afar, Maria Naryshkina's husband, whom the czar had appointed 'Master of the Royal Hunt,' stood by.

As the royal drama unfolded, Court gossips recorded every treachery, every betrayal and every deception. There would be ample time to debate the finer points of the Czar's open infidelity in the morning.

"They say Razovsky lives with his Jewish whore openly now."

"Does her husband know?"

"Does it matter? He's one of those dirty little Jews, I hear. All they care about is cheating and conniving to make money. Razovsky's sister is here as well. How nobly she bears the cross of having such a wastrel for a brother."

"He's handsome enough to have any number of women at court, isn't he? Too bad he's chosen a Jew for a mistress."

"No one of any consequence attends her salon any more. It's one thing to have one's little bit of pleasure, but Razovsky has gone too far. Their affair has already lasted more than a year."

"Even so, they were invited to the ball tonight, weren't they?"

"This may be his last invitation to a royal ball. Rumor has it that he's no longer welcome at court."

"They are coming this way."

"Pretend you don't see them."

⌘

"How goes it, Misha?" Dov asked his old friend, now supervisor of the von Hals Shipyards in Sebastopol. The two embraced.

"I don't mind telling you that I'm relieved you're here." "Vodka?" Dov nodded. "How is your wife?"

"I didn't take the time to stop in St. Petersburg to see her when I got your message. I came directly from Berlin."

"She's a fine woman Dov. Send her my good wishes, will you?"

"Of course, Misha. Now tell me what's troubling you."

"We've had thefts of materials and mysterious fires. They're small, to be sure, but they're costly just the same."

"These things don't happen without a reason."

"I can think of a dozen reasons. Sebastopol is flooded with runaway serfs, thieves and disgruntled peasants. A murderous lot, believe me. The rumor is spreading that the Jews are taking over. It's foolish I know, but there it is."

"How did the trouble start?"

"We discovered the first fire after word got out that von Hals shipyards was planning to dismiss fifty workers. There wasn't a bit of truth to it, but you know how rumors are. Take a look at this note. It was shoved under my door last November, the morning after the first blaze."

Dov read the crudely lettered note aloud.

"'This is what you get for sacking good Christians and hiring dirty *Zhids*!'"

"Is this true, Misha?"

"No. We've never hired any Jews."

"How much damage has there been?"

"About one hundred thousand rubles, I'd say."

"Have you contacted the local authorities?"

"They investigate, but they never find any evidence."

"Typical. Have you tried bribery?"

"No. I wanted to wait for you."

"All right. Here's what we'll do. Spread the word around among the men that there's a reward for information leading to the arrest of the troublemakers. How much should we offer?"

"Twenty-five thousand rubles."

"No. That's too much. Offer five. That should do it."

"What if that doesn't work?"

"This is a patriotic enterprise, isn't it? We're building frigates for the Russian Empire. I'll get a *ukase* from the czar and we'll have the governor keep order in the yards with military troops, if necessary."

"Do you want to hear my objections to both plans?"

Dov laughed, but his heart was heavy. "If I said no, you'd speak your piece anyway. Go ahead. Get it off your chest."

FORTY-ONE

The icy reception they had suffered at the April ball was far too blatant to be ignored. So were Miriam's sparsely attended Sunday salons at home. She tried her best to console Alexei. She knew he was not happy even though he put on a brave front. She bought him gifts. She planned intimate evening dinners in front of the fireplace. She sought to smooth the furrows on his brow in a million different ways, to no avail.

"We don't have many friends left, do we?" he asked glumly.

"We have Natasha, dearest. And we have each other. Perhaps if we try to be patient..."

"No, darling. There's only one Natasha. She's always been special, hasn't she? Anyway, she lives too far from St. Petersburg to be of any help to us in this matter."

"Do you mind so terribly?"

"Not as long as I have you, my love. That's all I need."

Yet when he held her that night, it was with a despairing urgency. He sought solace, not passion. They clung to one another and embraced with a voracious hunger that did not satisfy. Instead, it signaled a terrifying dissonance, for they could no longer deny their disquiet. Nor were they able to quell their worry that something was terribly wrong. What was happening out there? Would they be left with only emptiness and desperation? They took to riding out only in the evenings in a closed carriage, unwilling to face the hostile stares and the haughty censure of former friends who turned their heads rather than nod recognition. Alexei slept fitfully. Miriam tried to console him, for she felt him slipping away from her even as he clung to her. He insisted their love was timeless. Antony and Cleopatra. Pelleas and Melisande. Romeo and Juliet. Miriam and Alexei. He swore his eternal love.

In desperation, he began to gamble again late at night, whenever he couldn't sleep. He hadn't meant to begin again. He just wanted to avoid the torment of yet another sleepless night. He eased out of bed that first time, after he heard

Miriam's deep, even breathing. At first, it was easy to slip out and to return before she woke. Or so he thought.

The games of chance masked his pain, as though they were an opiate meant to help him forget. He promised himself that the first few nights would also be the last when he stole back into her bed. Absolutely. He gazed tenderly at his beautiful Miriam then, before he found release in troubled sleep. At first, his luck was good and he won.

⌘

"How often does he go there?"

The man consulted his notebook. "Been there every night this week, Sire. Last night he left at dawn."

"Did he win?"

"No, Sire. He lost. Fourth night in a row."

"How much this time?"

"Manager says he owes thirty thousand all together. I had to bribe him fifty rubles for the information."

"You did the right thing. Go back tonight and inform the manager that he's to extend unlimited credit to my brother-in-law for the time being. You've done well. Report to me next week." Prince Bedorov rang for his aide.

"Have the clerk reimburse this agent fifty rubles and send a message to Count Razovsky. Tell him I seek an audience with him at this office one week from tomorrow at precisely five in the evening."

FORTY-TWO

"Well done, Hans." Dov hugged his twelve-year-old son. "You're quite an expert horseman."

"Thank you, father," he answered, his blue eyes flashing in delight.

"You're welcome. Now be off with you. We're having guests tonight, or have you forgotten? Prince Wilhelm and his family are dining with us. Go and get ready, and remind the governess to dress Maria and Johann in their best." He watched admiringly as the boy ran off.

"Happy, David?"

"Extremely. You've made life perfect here, Lori. How you've managed to build so exquisite a French chateau in such a short a time is beyond me. Must be your special magic. You dazzle them with your beauty and your charm, and architects and builders are suddenly bewitched, just as I am."

"Just a simple country cottage, David," she said slyly.

"How did you arrange to make it look like something out of the thirteenth century? That's indeed a miracle."

"Easy, my sweet. The architect and I merely used a great deal of your money to import the finest materials in Europe."

He laughed. "You're a brazen woman, darling. I'm glad you're on my side and not conspiring against me like some people I know."

"What do you mean?"

"I'm having business...difficulties."

"Here in Wilhelmstadt? I thought you said the new munitions factories are going well...?"

"Not here. In Sebastopol."

"The von Hals Shipyards? My late husband's business?"

"Don't be alarmed. They still show a profit, but we're having labor difficulties there. Too many idle hands in Sebastopol because of the recession. Misha Golanov thinks it will blow over once the job market eases. He's advised me not to take any action for the time being."

"What did you have in mind?"

"Massive bribes to the authorities to stop the vandalism, and if that doesn't work, call on the local *Guberniya* to send in troops."

"Those are desperate solutions and desperate solutions sometimes backfire. Golanov's right to advise caution. But that's not all, is it? I sense something else is troubling you."

"You know me so well, don't you? You're right. It's not only the shipyards. I'm planning to invest in Siberian mining. It's risky, but the opportunity to make a fortune is irresistible. Shares on the 'change are extremely low at the moment. Shall I invest some of your money, too?"

"Go ahead. You know I trust your business judgment. How did you hear of it?"

"Czar Alexander mentioned it."

"What's the problem, then?"

"My Uncle Moses. I know he'll balk at providing the funds."

"The family banker?"

Dov nodded. "Perhaps it's time I put him out to pasture."

"Then do it, darling, and get on with your...with our...business. You always know best."

FORTY-THREE

"Shall we ride out tonight, dearest? It's the first night of the summer solstice. You know how I love the white nights. Please?" Alexei sounded like a young child begging for sweets.

"Of course, darling. Send for the driver while I get my shawl." He's more...alive tonight, she thought. Not so despondent, thank heaven. Haven't seen him this happy in weeks, since the night of the ball. Frightens me when he stays out all night. Where does he go? Is it...another woman? Will he leave me? What would I do without him?

"You're so cheerful tonight. It does my heart good to see you this way," she began once they were under way. "Where are we going?"

"Nowhere special. We'll ride along the banks of the river. Would you like that?"

She smiled. "We're like an old married pair, darling, taking the air, as it were."

"I wish we were married, Miriam. Wouldn't it be wonderful? Domestic bliss!" A note of bitterness crept into his voice.

"I'd go anywhere with you, my love. Anywhere."

"Where is anywhere?" Despair crept into his tone. "Doors are closing for us, Miriam. Doors are closing! You see it, too, don't you?"

"Yes, darling. I see it. But it needn't be...the end of the world." She hesitated. "What if we were to...to live somewhere else?"

"Leave Russia once more? No. You don't know what it's like to be on the outside looking in, to be an alien. A foreigner."

"Yes I do."

"Oh, of course. As a Jew you mean. I forgot. At any rate, there are too many obstacles."

"Too many...? Why won't you tell me what's troubling you, Alexei? I know something terrible is preying on your mind."

"Is it that apparent?"

"I love you, my darling. Remember? If you prick your finger, I bleed. Can't you see that? When I see you frown, I want to smooth your brow with kisses. I want to hold you in my arms and soothe your aches and your pains. You sneak away from our bed every night when I'm asleep. Don't look so surprised. I'm asleep when you leave, but I wake only because I sense you're not there beside me. I turn and my arm falls on empty space and then I can't go back to sleep. Shall I tell you a secret? I'm always awake when you return, though I pretend to be asleep."

"I hadn't meant to disturb you, but why must you pretend? Why have you never asked me where...?"

"I'm so afraid you'll tell me there's another woman in your life."

"Another woman? Have no fear, Miriam. There will never be anyone else for me. I love you and only you."

"We're outcasts, aren't we? I know that you're unhappy since we've become such pariahs. Is it worth it to live here in this cold, cruel country? You waver from delight to despair. I can't bear to see you so miserable, my Alexei. Let me inside. Don't shut the door. They say that two heads are better than one, don't they? Tell me what's troubling you."

"Perhaps you're right, my angel." He took her hand in his, but his tortured thoughts continued to nag at him. How can she possibly help? She doesn't have such sums of money. Go easy. Be cautious, old man. "It would take a fortune to find someplace else to live, even if we wanted to leave."

"How much is a fortune, darling? Name the amount."

"Why?"

"You're evading my question, Alexei. How much?"

"Stop the carriage," he ordered the driver. "Let's walk along the quay, shall we?"

They strolled in silence along the Neva River, lost in the crowds of other lovers though it was well past midnight.

"Do you remember when you asked me where I disappear to in the middle of the night?" He took a deep breath. "Well, I've been gambling, and I haven't been winning." He laughed harshly. "My other passion. Besides you that is."

"I'm relieved to hear that it's merely gambling and not another woman, my love."

"There will never be another woman for me. I'll swear to it on a bible, if you like."

"Oh dear," she sighed. "That won't be necessary. Besides, which bible would you use? Mine or yours?"

They bantered on a bit longer and it lifted Razovsky's spirits. He pulled her to him and kissed her long and hard. Miriam returned his unexpected passion and clung to him, murmuring her love all the while. He held her hand as they walked on, but they stopped again. and melted into a crowd who had gathered to hear a balladeer playing his balalaika and singing a mournful, sentimental verse.

"What is he singing? I can't hear the words. Do you know it, Alexei?"

"Yes. It begins, `As soon as I beheld thee, I thought of thee alone;'" He strained to listen.

"`Cruel Gods! Why have you given her such charms? Why did you destine me to love her, and her alone?'" The applause drowned out the rest of the singer's words before he'd had a chance to end his musical tale of woe.

"The words seem written just for us, don't they? I'll never love anyone else, Miriam. How can I, after you? But it all seems so useless now."

"Stop it, Alexei! Look at me. I have money. Or something equally valuable, which is the same thing, isn't it? My love for you is all I have and everything I own belongs to you. Dov doesn't love me. He hasn't for years. He rarely comes home to see me, isn't that so?" Razovsky nodded in agreement.

"I've no one but you, my beloved. Let's take our chances and find a place for us. Anywhere. I know you didn't like Europe, but I also know we can't stay here much longer. It's destroying our love, isn't it? This...this terrible isolation."

"Where can we go, Miriam? What can we do?"

"What about...Venice? Didn't you say it was a city for lovers? Or...or...America? People call it the new world, don't they? We could start a new life together, couldn't we?"

He sighed a sigh of resignation. "I'm afraid. It's too late. I'm hopelessly in debt, my darling. When you hear how much I owe, your lovely dream will evaporate into the white night."

"How much, then?"

"One hundred thousand rubles."

"How much would five perfect, two karat diamonds bring, do you think?"

"I can't take your..."

"Oh yes you can. If you love me, that is. Take the diamonds and choose a place for us."

"Where did you get them? Did Dov give them to you?"

"No, my father did. Dov doesn't know they exist. We'll use them, darling to buy our way to freedom and a life together."

Is there really hope for us he wondered as his spirits soared. Perhaps. "Venice is too...close. America you say? Why not? We can make a fresh start in a country full of people who all come from somewhere else. Let's hope your diamonds bring enough to get us to America." He hesitated. "Are you sure that that's where we ought to go? Aren't you afraid of the tales of murderous Indians?"

She laughed at the thought. "Why should I be? I've heard tell that you're a superb marksman. It's true, isn't it? Surely there's no need for us to worry about wild Indians skulking about."

They plotted and schemed like two children planning an excursion to the fair. Thus the dream grew larger as their lust for a new life unfolded. He'd heard tell of a place called Pennsylvania, he said. She'd read of a city named New York.

The *St. Petersburg Gazette* reported recently that land in America was free for the taking, he recalled. They could work together to build a new life. Make friends. Have a child, perhaps more than one. Pioneers. Together. Always.

Each part of the dream raised their spirits higher. He vowed to work his fingers to the bone for her. Yes. They would find their own piece of land in the new world. They might raise horses. Or they might farm. They would learn how in America. They would marry. Count Alexei Razovsky's eyes blazed with visionary fervor. Their dreams were clouds in the air, full of glory, full of hope.

"You've given me new life, my sweet. Now I know what love means. I am newborn because of your love and your faith in me." He stopped to hug her to him. "I've reached a height I never believed possible because of you. Happiness? No, that's too paltry a word. Pure bliss. Yes, that's it. Pure bliss. Can you believe it? Just hours ago, I seriously contemplated taking my life…"

"My God, Alexei! Don't ever say such a terrible thing again," She cried out in alarm, holding her finger to his lips.

"Oh yes. It's true. How long do you think I can go on hurting you? Destroying our love? No. I can't bear to see you unhappy. I'd rather die. But God sent you to me. I'm convinced of it. And I don't care which God. Take your choice. They say religion's not so important in America anyway. There may not be any prejudice against Jews in America."

"Am I still Jewish? Somehow, it doesn't matter so much any more. Funny, isn't it? I never thought it possible. Now I know that I'd give up Judaism before I'd give you up. Sinful, perhaps, but there it is."

"Would you? Yes you would, wouldn't you? You'd do it for me. I see it in your eyes, but perhaps that won't be necessary. Why didn't we think of this wonderful idea before? We'll go to America. We'll marry. The ship's captain can marry us when we're under sail. Will Dov give you that divorce now? Never mind. We'll buy false papers and then we'll marry. I want you for my wife. There it is, then. Let's settle it quickly. Matter of fact, I have an appointment tomorrow, with someone who may be able to help us."

"Who, dear?"

"My brother-in-law Peter. He sent for me and now I have reason to see him as much as he wants to see me. Don't worry. He won't be sorry when he hears that I'm quitting Russia forever. He doesn't like me, you know. Thinks I'm a wastrel. An embarrassment to him and his family now that he's become advisor to the czar. Maybe he can recommend someone who'll purchase your diamonds. Let's go home now, darling. I can hardly wait to make love to you, but I give you fair warning, sweet angel; I'll bruise you tonight. With all this energy, I'll make love to you like a carefree boy of sixteen."

Her thoughts turned to more practical matters. "How soon do you think we might leave, Alexei? Shall I write to Dov and tell him? I owe him that much, don't you think?"

"There may not be enough time for a letter to reach him, darling. You can leave him a note instead. Besides, I have a strong suspicion that he won't stop you from leaving," he added, as a picture of Dov's son Hans floated to the surface of his senses.

"What an odd thing to say! Has he ever said anything to make you think so?"

"No, my angel. Nothing...important. Put it out of your mind for now, but remind me to tell you a story some day when we're in America. It's a tale for a long winter's evening in front of a warm fire in our home. After we've put all the children to bed. What a wonderful life we're going to have in America!"

FORTY-FOUR

"You're in rare high spirits, Alexei." Prince Peter Bedorov smiled affably. "Would you like a drink?"

"I certainly am, Peter. I most certainly am in high spirits today. And yes, I would like a drink, thank you. Do you have some brandy? Won't you join me? To celebrate?"

"To celebrate? Have you something to celebrate? You've had some good news? It would certainly please me to hear it. What is it, old chap?" Bedorov dismissed his aide with a nod once drinks were served.

"I'm sure my good news will please you very much, Peter. You are looking at a man who has at last found the right direction in life. Not here in Russia, I'm afraid, for reasons that I intend to make clear to you. No. Not possible. Not here. I had high hopes when I returned, but now it's out of the question. I've tried, but I haven't been able to find contentment here, brother-in-law. At any rate, when I leave my homeland this time, it will be for good."

"Leave Russia for good? Really? That is a surprise, considering how you pleaded to return to your native soil. Your sister will be heartbroken, of course. Well, no matter. She'll get over it in time. So. You're leaving. Not for the same reasons as the last time, I hope. No offense, just a small jest, Alexei. However, I do feel it my duty to ask you some questions, since your sister Anya will surely demand to know why you are leaving this time, to be sure. You wouldn't object to enlightening me on a few minor points, would you?" Bedorov sat back and sipped his brandy.

"The least I can do, Peter. I don't want to quit Russia and have my sister and you retain a bad opinion of me. Believe me when I say I do appreciate what you both have tried to do for me. Yet I would be less than a man if I didn't pursue my own course, isn't that so?"

"How do you propose to settle your debts?"

Alexei was stunned by the question. "My...debts? How do you know about my debts? And what business is it of yours? Never mind about my debts, Peter. I won't embarrass you or my sister, because I plan to settle them all before I leave. Besides, that's my own affair, though I must admit to some curiosity as to how you know about the money I owe."

"Come, come Alexei. Everyone knows that you're in debt. These things are hard to hide. Perhaps I can help. Are we not related? How much do you owe?"

"Help? You'd be willing to help me? That's decent of you, old man. Well, I'll admit it then. I owe an impressive sum. Streak of bad luck, losing like that, but I have a way to pay it back now." Alexei hesitated. Why not tell him? He's Anya's husband even though he doesn't like me. He'd help me for her sake, wouldn't he? Couldn't stand a scandal. Not his way. "I owe one hundred thousand rubles."

"Rather a large sum, isn't it, for a man with precious few resources? To whom do you owe this sum, may I ask?"

"What difference does that make? I told you. I have the means to pay it back."

"Answer my question!" Bedorov demanded.

Something in his brother-in-law's harsh manner alerted Razovsky to...to what? Alexei was deeply puzzled at the sharp change in his brother-in-law's bearing. Bedorov continued to glare at him.

"Why this sudden interest in my personal affairs? I hadn't realized that you knew so much about me. Never mind. Soon it won't make the least bit of difference, and I'd much rather we parted friends. Come to the point. What's on your mind?"

"What's on my mind? Well, brother-in-law, I'm not nearly as good at inventing games and fashioning deceits as you are. So! You propose to renounce your birthright once more. Being a decent Russian of royal blood doesn't mean much to you, does it? What I'd expect from a man with no character. It's a wonder that you and Anya come from the same parents!" Bedorov paused, his condemning eyes bearing heavily down on his prey.

"Go on. Enlighten me, Peter," Alexei said uncomfortably.

"I bought your note."

"You...what?"

"You owe me the sum of one hundred thousand rubles."

"But why?"

"I warned you when you returned last year that I would brook no further nonsense, yet you took no heed of my admonition, did you? Even refused to attend to business in the mining office, a grave error on your part. That was your last chance, you see. I did everything in my power to mold you into a decent, law-abiding Russian noble, one high in the Table of Ranks, I might add. You even said it was what you yourself wanted, correct?

"Your sister was overjoyed at the prospect. How she dreamed of your wedding, and of your children to come! How she dreamed of seeing you carry on the proud name of Razovsky. And when you had the gall to flaunt your Jewish whore..."

Alexei began to rise from his seat. "Whore? How dare you! Watch what you say, Peter! Leave that fine woman out of this."

"Why? Are you planning to challenge me to a duel? Well, let me point out that I am not senile like General Sadorov whom you murdered, poor soul! Let me remind you that I trained at Gatchina with the czar and I'm an excellent swordsman! Sit down! You'd do better to hear me out first!." He waited till Alexei sat back, noting his brother-in-law's clenched fists.

"Your sister was so mortified when she heard of your outrageous behavior, she nearly refused to attend Czar Alexander's April Ball for fear of having to confront you and your..."

"Watch it, Peter! I'm warning you. I'm in love with Miriam Zeklinski. It's given me the only true meaning I've ever had in life. Can't you see that?"

"If gambling and whoring with that Jewess is what you call `true meaning'..."

"The gambling's over. I'll never gamble again so long as I live."

"Remains to be seen. You've already caused a scandal with your debts and that...woman. Your sister's devastated by your callous disregard of her feelings. She can't bear to face her friends. How can you be so heartless?"

"But...I hadn't meant to hurt Anya. You know I love her dearly. I am deeply offended by your insinuations. Don't worry. I'll pay my debt to back you and I'll write to explain things to my sister. I know she'll understand. She wants to see me happy, doesn't she?"

"Not at her family's expense."

"But I have a solution now! Didn't you ask me if you could help? Why not let bygones be bygones? Let's face facts, old man. You've never liked me. You know that and I know that. I know you are devoted to my sister, which pleases me no end. She leads a good life because of you and I'm grateful to you. Really I am." Razovsky took a deep breath. Might as well tell him the truth, he decided. Besides, we need his help. Papers, permission to leave the country...

"Let me take you into my confidence, Peter, if only for Anya's sake, eh? Neither of us want to hurt her, do we?"

"No, of course not. What is it you want to tell me?" Alexei took no notice of his dangerous tone.

"Miriam and I are planning to begin a new life. We're going to America. We love each other and it's impossible for a Christian and a Jew to make a life here. She's a fine woman, in spite of what you think. Anya knows that as well as I do."

"I assume she's given you the necessary money? Or is it her husband's funds you propose to abscond with? That's stealing, isn't it? Even a Jew has legal rights here."

"No need to be sarcastic. She has her own...assets. As soon as I can convert them..."

"Assets? What assets?"

"She has some diamonds. They're very valuable. I just have to..."

"How can you know for such a certainty that a few mere baubles are worth more than you owe? Suppose you're wrong and they're worthless. Then what?"

"I'd send you the difference, Peter. Just as soon..."

"Really? What makes you think I would accept your terms?"

"You're...you're...we're...family, aren't we?"

Bedorov ignored the question. "Have you had the gems appraised?"

"Miriam, Madame Zeklinski says they're worth about twenty to twenty-five thousand rubles each. There are five of them."

"So. Even under the most favorable conditions you can only come up with at most one hundred and twenty-five thousand rubles?" Alexei nodded, his mouth suddenly dry. Damn! Shouldn't have told him. Why did he buy my note? What on earth for?

"That leaves you...let me see. You'd have enough to pay your debt to me, assuming you get top price, with twenty-five thousand rubles left over to carry out your plans. Papers to travel are costly and so is the journey. What with bribes, you have only enough to get you to the border. Then what will you do? Where's the rest of the money to come from? Zeklinski? Is the Jew such a willing cuckold? It won't come from your estate, I assure you, since I still own it."

"Surely, you'd advance me enough to...?"

"Out of the question. I'm afraid you're not going anywhere until you satisfy your debt to me. Unless, of course, you choose Siberia."

"Siberia? You'd do that to me? To your...your own brother-in-law? No. Anya wouldn't let you. I'm sure of it. What can you be thinking, Peter? We can't...Miriam and I, that is...continue to live here. We're outcasts in Russia. But in America, I know things will be different. Let me owe you the money and I'll repay every last ruble with interest. That should satisfy you. I'll be out of your hair once and for all, won't I? Siberia? I thought you said I had a choice. What kind of choice is Siberia?"

"The choice is entirely up to you, one in which your sister and I are in full agreement. It needn't be Siberia, but it certainly won't be America, and it certainly won't be with the Jewess. But if you spurn the offer I propose to make to you, your sister is prepared to renounce you once and for all, for the sake of our dear children. She's promised me that. Make no mistake!"

"Come, Peter. You're destroying my last chance for happiness! What harm have I ever done to you to deserve this?"

"On the other hand," Bedorov continued, ignoring his question, "I'm prepared to tear up your note for one hundred thousand rubles, if you accede. On your wedding day."

"I don't understand. What offer? What...wedding day?"

"Count Petrov has agreed to give you his daughter Marya's hand in marriage."

"Marya? You can't mean Marya Petrov? She's wanted to spend her life in a nunnery ever since we were children! Didn't she take her vows? Besides, she was a spinster when I was a mere boy. Unthinkable! You can't be serious!"

"I've never been more serious. You'll inherit Petrov's considerable estate when he dies, and Anya and I will return yours to you as a wedding gift. That combination will make you the richest man in Kiev. You can have your sordid little affairs, so long as you're discreet, but not with the Jewess. This solution will put an end to the humiliating embarrassment you have subjected us to."

"No!" Alexei thundered.

"Suit yourself," he shrugged. "If you try to leave this office, I'm prepared to begin legal proceedings at once."

"I'll...I'll borrow the difference! I...I have friends..."

"Do you? That's not what I've heard. Your friends have all deserted you, but they'll come back just as soon..."

"I won't do it!"

"All right. Then pay me. Now."

"Just give me a few more days..."

"No. Your time is up. I've only to ring and you're on your way to Siberia."

"I can't believe my sister would be so cruel," Alexei shouted in desperation. "I demand to see her."

"Not possible. She's in Moscow at the moment, but I had a feeling you might refuse. She's written you a note, giving me her full support. Would you care to read it? I see that you don't believe me. You underestimate me, Alexei. More's the pity." Bedorov shoved the note on his desk towards him.

"So you've convinced her to disown me," he said, after he read Anya's brief note. Bastard! He thought, crushing the paper in his hand. He flung it to the floor in defiance. The sweat poured down his face as he tried to control his rage.

"Your sister knows as well as I do that I'm doing this for your own good. You lack discipline, Alexei. Too bad your parents died when they did. I'm sure they would never have tolerated your dissolute behavior. It's my good fortune that your sister turned out so well. Make your choice!"

"How can you do this to me, Peter? Siberia? Am I to be treated like a...a common thief? What will you tell your children? No, no. I cannot believe..."

"I wouldn't have chosen such an extreme course if you hadn't forced it on me. What shall I tell my children? That their uncle is the black sheep? That he's dishonored his good name and their heritage and run off with a Jewish harlot? That he didn't even have the good sense to bed down a decent Russian mistress? That he's a skeleton in the family closet? That he's to be a lesson to them? And that they should pray for the redemption of his lost soul? Oh, yes, I'll tell them the truth, I assure you, unless you choose the proper course."

"Redemption...? Lost soul? Pray? I'd be better off dead than accepting either of your damned choices! Go to hell, Peter!"

An uneasy silence invaded the tense air between them until at last Bedorov spoke. He chose his words carefully, deliberately. He spoke them so softly, Alexei had to strain to hear him.

"Come, come brother-in-law. It's not as bad as all that. Marya Petrov's a decent woman. Her parents are prepared to welcome you with open arms. She's their only child, Alexei. You know that their son Ilya died years ago. Killed himself over a foolish love affair. Frankly, they hope you'll provide them with an heir, but whether you do or not is of no consequence to me. Would you like another drink? Here. Let me fill your glass," Bedorov said, subduing his tone. He rose from his desk to fetch the brandy from the sideboard.

"Your affair with that...Jewess is mere infatuation. I know you can't see it now, but in time, you'll forget all about her, believe me. I'll leave the decanter right here for you, old man. Help yourself."

Prince Bedorov patted Alexei on the back before returning to his seat, all the while murmuring the advantages of marriage to Countess Marya Petrov. He watched his brother-in-law refill the glass and drain it three times in rapid succession.

Alexei felt trapped. Is this a bad dream? He asked himself. Get up and walk out, you fool! Before it's too late, he cautioned himself, draining his glass yet again.

"I've taken the liberty of making all the arrangements for you. We leave tonight for Kiev. Anya and the children will join us. Your wedding to Marya takes place in six weeks."

"Six weeks?"

"It's best that way."

"What are you saying? This is impossible. This is a...a nightmare. Tell me it's not true, Peter. Please. I can never love anyone but Miriam. How can I marry someone I don't love? Marya Petrov must be at least...is she fifty or sixty? Let me do the right thing and leave Russia with the woman I love and then you'll be rid of me once and for all, don't you see? I cannot live a lie, Peter. You see that, don't you? It would be dishonorable to consign me to a life of...but surely, you must be joking. Of course! It's all a joke, isn't it? Capital, Peter. Capital! I had no idea you had such a good sense of..."

"Enough! Love? Honor? What do you know of love and honor? Your idea of love and honor is determined only by the stirring between your legs. Your sniveling ways don't move me in the least, Alexei. You're a scoundrel, but I mean to redeem you in spite of yourself. I do it only for the sake of my wife and my children. Well? Which is it to be, Siberia or a wedding? There are guards outside my door. I need only to sign the order..."

"I...I...I have to...to think. Give me some time..."

"Five minutes."

"Five...? I'll need to...let me go and see Miriam...Madame Zeklinski. I must...explain...to...to...you must let me do the honorable thing. Please, Peter. You're a man of honor, aren't you? I owe it to her, don't you see? And then I'll..."

The snare so carefully set by Prince Bedorov encircled him and tightened. It grasped him as he barked in anguish, like a helpless bear caught in a steel trap. He pleaded, he cried, he begged on his hands and knees, but Bedorov was unmoved. He wept like a child. He banged his fists on the desk savagely. He thrashed about, wild-eyed, in hopeless derangement. Count Alexei Razovsky. Was it he? No. Some other. Not him. And he drank to ease the sting of his agony. His dreams unraveled, one by one, like the stitches in some poorly woven needlepoint.

At seven o'clock, his captor ordered dinner served, but his captive refused to eat. The hours passed and Alexei's rage grew. He screamed. He yelled until he was hoarse. He smashed the empty decanter against the wall. He rose unsteadily and lunged at Bedorov, who merely deflected his weak attempt with a sharp warning. His red-rimmed eyes could barely focus. His nose ran and the circles under his eyes darkened.

By midnight there was nothing left of the man inside Alexei Razovsky. By midnight he was haggard and worn. Something had given way by then, for in his mind's eye, Prince Peter Bedorov ceased to be his jailor.

In a strange metamorphosis, Bedorov was transformed from jailer to father to Christ the Savior. Alexei glanced at the blood on the palms of his hands. The crown of thorns upon his head pressed into his temple. He could feel the warm viscous substance trickling down his face. His body ached as if he'd been nailed to the cross for days. The barbs of the knout bruised his tortured body. The thing to do was to bear it with dignity. He closed his eyes as if to conjure...who?

An olive-skinned woman appeared before him. Lovely. Miriam. Mary Magdalene. The Virgin Mary. Her hands were outstretched. Yes, he heard her whisper. Yes, my child. Go with God. Go with God and the pain will disappear. Go with God and I shall be waiting...Yes. Yes. Yes.

Bedorov shook him awake. "The coach is here, Alexei." He spoke as he would to a child. "Time to go."

"Wait, Peter. Please. I beg of you," he pleaded.

"What is it?"

"At least let me write to her. Be decent, old man. My honor..."

"Of course. But you'll write what I dictate, or I won't allow you to send anything at all." Bedorov withstood yet another round of weeping rage. He shrugged indifferently and added, "Suit yourself. We'll forget the letter. Let's go." He rang for an aide, for his brother-in-law was no longer in any condition to walk without help.

"All right. All right," the ghost of what was once Alexei mumbled. "I'll do it. What do you want me to write?"

FORTY-FIVE

He had promised to return no later than seven that evening. She had arranged a special dinner for them, a celebration in honor of their journey to America and a new life. She had ordered the table set in front of the open garden doors. Fragrant flowers. Flickering candles. Gleaming silver. Sparkling plates. The wine breathed in its crystal decanter while the champagne floated in a bucket of what had once been ice.

By eight that evening the food had grown cold.

By nine that evening she ordered it removed and had the servants prepare a cold supper instead.

By ten that evening she sent the servants to bed.

By eleven o'clock that evening she was frantic, convinced that harm had befallen him. Terrifying visions of her beloved Alexei's limbs mangled under the wheels of a carriage somewhere assaulted her. What if...what if he was dead? She wanted to run and search for him herself. Instead she woke one of the servants at midnight. She sent him in Alexei's carriage to see if he was still at the Winter Palace with Prince Bedorov, for that was where he had gone to meet his brother-in-law.

The servant returned two hours later. Miriam watched the bright glow of the summer solstice, but in her soul all was darkness. When her own *droshki* appeared in the courtyard, her heart leaped for joy. Alexei had taken her carriage to keep his appointment with Bedorov. It must be him, she thought, but her joy evaporated in the mist, for the servant was alone.

"What took you so long? Where is Count Razovsky?"

"Begging your pardon, Madame. I was made to wait all this time. Prince Bedorov and Count Razovsky are no longer in the palace. I was instructed to give you these." He offered her the note and a small box. When she recognized Alexei's hand on the note, a feeling of dread washed over her.

"What do you mean? Count Razovsky? Gone? Where?"

"The gentlemen departed two hours ago, Madame. The officer who gave me the box and the note for you said to tell you they were on their way to Kiev."

Miriam tore off the wax seal with trembling hands. Kiev? Why? Her eyes scanned the brief note, but her mind refused to believe the words.

Madame, By the time you read this, I shall be enroute to Kiev. I am to be married to Countess Marya Petrov there. It is my wish that we never see one another again. Count Alexei Nicholayevich Razovsky

Marriage? To Marya Petrov? I don't believe it! No! It's a lie, a...a trick of some kind. Yet it's written in his hand...no. He would never...she read and reread the note over and over again, but she didn't bother to open the familiar box. Miriam knew what was in it without having to inspect its contents. She was frantic. Must be Bedorov's doing. It can't be true. Not Alexei. But how did he...? Alexei would never agree willingly. He loves me. Doubt crept into her mind, but she rejected it. He loves me, not Marya! She told herself in desperation. Abduction! Yes, of course. That's it. Bedorov's abducted him against his will! Forcibly. Alexei would never leave me voluntarily. My God! He needs me! My darling needs me. I must go to him. Help him. But...what can I do? The diamonds! I'll...I'll offer the diamonds to someone. Pay them to steal him back. But...who? Must get him back. Do anything necessary. Anything. Be firm, Miriam, she told herself. Keep your wits about you! Think! Do whatever you must. He's in danger. He needs you. How? What? Who? Natasha! Of course! She'll know how to put a stop to this terrible...tragedy! She's so wise. Surely, Bedorov will listen to her.

"I must leave for Kiev at once! Pack my things quickly," she said to the astonished servant. "At once, do you hear? Wake the staff. Everyone! At once, I say! Hurry!"

FORTY-SIX

"Mines are highly profitable, Uncle Moses."

"A matter of opinion."

Dov did not respond to the provocation. "I expect your cooperation."

"Mining is full of risk."

"Why, sir?"

"Mines run dry, suffer natural disasters. Floods. Snowstorms. Mud slides."

"Then you give me no choice but to accept your resignation."

"I choose not to resign. I have that right."

"I've already replaced you. The new banker starts next week. I'm sorry."

Moses struggled for breath. "No you're not, Dov. You're not sorry in the least. Your grandfather may his soul rest in peace, would never have done such a thing."

⌘

"How is it with you, Alexei my dear," Natasha Gorov asked gently. It pained her to observe the hollow luster in his eyes, like the eerie glow of some nocturnal beast.

"Good of you to ask, Natasha. I am well. And how is it with you?" He clenched and unclenched his fists.

"Miriam's asked me to see you."

He raised his eyebrows in alarm. "You mustn't speak that name here. It is forbidden." He looked around furtively, then leaned forward and spoke in a low voice.

"I am fortune's fool, Natasha. Tell my lady I have a plan, good nurse. All is not lost though spies watch me."

"How can I help you, Alexei?"

"I cannot eat, you know. They're trying to poison me."

"Dear God! You're ill, Alexei."

"What wrong have I done, Natasha? They say they do this for my good."

"Nonsense. Peter and your sister serve only themselves. Tell me your plan and I will help you. Is it funds you need?"

"No. You must tell my sweet lady to sew her jewels back in her hem. We shan't need them after all. I cannot reveal my plan even to you, sweet nurse. Why does Marya Petrov marry me instead of God? Doesn't that pious good lady know that I am already betrothed?"

"Her father won't allow her to follow her calling. What is your plan?"

One eye twitched. "I cannot implicate you, or else they will destroy you, too. It's best to keep my own counsel."

Anya appeared and said, "Have you two had a nice chat? Shall you stay for tea, Natasha? I'm sure Peter would like that."

"No, I'll not stay." The old woman embraced Razovsky. "Courage, Alexei."

"I'll see you to your carriage. Be a good fellow and wait right here, dear brother."

Countess Gorov waited till they were out of earshot before she exploded. "He's ill, you fool. Can't you see how he's suffering? He thinks you're all trying to poison him."

"We've already had the doctor examine him. He's just a bit bewildered at the moment, but everything will be fine once he's wed."

"Why can't you see that he's deranged? Why force him into such a loveless match? For God's sake, let him go to America with Miriam."

"We're only thinking of him. Peter says he's humiliating us."

"You loved her once. What's changed your mind?"

"I've good reason. Peter says she's made us the laughing stock at court. I can't forgive her for that. Peter says I have my children to protect. Peter says..."

"You show lack of judgment when you talk such drivel. I'm warning you, this wedding will destroy him. Can you bear that sin? Alexei raised you after your parents died. How poorly you repay him for his love. Allow Miriam see Alexei. It's the least you can do."

"No. Peter does not wish it."

"You no longer possess a mind of your own, but mark me well. You will come to regret this terrible marriage."

FORTY-SEVEN

"A message, Madame."

"Thank you, Boris." The note was from Dov. She laid it aside.

"Are you well, Madame Zeklinski?" Boris asked, alarmed at her pallor.

"Yes, Boris. I'm glad to be home."

"Shall I bring tea?"

"No."

"Very well, Madame. The overseer wishes to see you."

She smiled. "Send him in."

"Welcome home," said her overseer.

"You can't know how good it is to see your friendly face, Josef." Her thoughts recalled the day she received Noah's letter.

⌘

"You sent for me?" asked Benjamin Moskowitz.

"I've received word that Sergeant Brodsky has been wounded in the siege of Ochakov. He is in the army hospital near the front. Have him brought here to recover."

"I'll see to it."

Brodsky arrived in late February. "I fear I cause you trouble, Madame," he said, too weak to protest further. Even so, in her company Josef found ease in spite of his shyness. She read to him every day. It gave her pleasure to fuss over him as though he were a child.

"I have a surprise for you, Josef," she said one day in mid-April. Some of the serfs in our carpentry shop made this for you. They were proud to do this for our war hero." Two servants helped him into a chair with wheels.

"As soft as the czarina's throne," he said.

She wheeled him around the room.

"You pamper me, Madame."

"You must call me Miriam, or I shall be cross with you, do you hear?" She feigned an angry look, but not for long. His smile lit up his face so much so, that he appeared to her to be handsome.

"It's a glorious day to be outdoors, my friend. We'll rest at the gazebo. You can admire the garden there."

Josef breathed in the fresh air. It was his first venture out of doors in months. When they reached their destination, she sat opposite him.

"I count my blessings that fate brought you back to me. You are like a brother to me." They sat silently, enjoying the gentle breezes that presaged a warm spring.

"Perhaps you'll find a wife here in Kiev."

"Perhaps," he answered, yet he was convinced he would never marry. Who would have me? He thought. I may be an invalid for the remainder of my life. Not such a prize for any woman.

"We'll make you a grand wedding," Miriam said. "We're your family now." She brushed one of his hairs back off his forehead, and the touch of her cool hand felt like a kiss. "May we be your family?"

"I've never really had a family. That would be nice."

His life revolved around his strolls with Miriam. When Miriam's father left the twins with her for a few weeks, the girls fought for the privilege of wheeling him about in his chair.

In time he began to ride horseback again. Thus he became acquainted with the length and the breadth of the Zeklinski estate. His shy, diffident nature endeared him to the serfs who had heard tales of his heroism in battle, thanks to Boris, who managed to embellish the saga with each telling.

He took to visiting the wood shop often, for Josef loved carpentry. Soon, he became a welcome presence everywhere.

The serfs had not forgotten his compassion when Borschov had so cruelly thrashed the young lad who left the hen door open. In fact, some of them were bold enough to confide their hatred of the overseer.

Miriam had her own reasons to hate the man. More than once she caught Borschov leering at her, as though daring her to question his authority. When Dov finally returned home in the fall, Borschov abruptly resigned.

"He's leaving?" Miriam asked.

"Yes. Petrov's hired him."

"I won't say I'm sorry to hear it, Dov."

"You've never liked him."

"I hesitate to mention this..."

"What's on your mind?"

"Josef Brodsky would make a fine overseer."

"Is he well enough?"

"He rides well, he's strong and he's honest. What's more, our serfs respect him."

"I've already made my choice."

"Oh?" Her heart sank at the news.

A curious smile played at the corners of his mouth. He rang. "Send the new overseer in, Boris."

"Reb Brodsky, sir." Boris said. A broad grin escaped from his usually somber countenance, for he and Josef had become fast friends.

⌘

"How is your leg, Josef?"

"When my leg aches, it's a sure sign we're bound for rainy weather," he smiled. "Kind of you to ask."

"You can't know how good it is to see you again." Miriam could not restrain her tears.

"Is there anything I can do? You nursed me back to health once. Let me try to repay your kindnesses."

"Oh, my friend." She said and began to sob, a merciful release from her anguish. "Please, Josef. Don't ask me to explain. I must ask you to keep silent. I don't wish to burden my husband with my personal sorrows just yet."

"Of course."

"Reb Zeklinski's carriage is at the door, Madame." Boris interrupted.

She took Josef's arm, not trusting herself to face Dov alone.

FORTY-EIGHT

Dov looked haggard. "Have dinner sent to our chambers, dear. You must excuse me, Josef. Arrange to see me in the morning."

Miriam followed him up after ordering dinner. He hasn't asked why I've returned to Kiev, she thought. "You don't look at all well, Dov. Is there something wrong?"

"I lost a million rubles in Sebastopol."

"But why?"

We've had problems with the workers. When we threatened to call in government troops, they set fire to two frigates that were ready to be launched. I have to find a way to cut our losses."

"By the way, I have some news. Alexei Razovsky's to be married next week." Her knees shook as she spoke the words.

"Who's the lucky bride?"

"Count Petrov's daughter Marya."

"We're invited, of course. He's been such a good friend all these years."

"No, Dov. Only the immediate family, according to Natasha."

"Petrov's doing, most likely. Alexei said he would never marry. When did you last see him?"

"Several weeks ago, shortly before he left Petersburg with his brother-in-law. He sent a note telling me of his intentions."

"I imagine he started gambling again and got himself into debt, and the Petrovs have a considerable fortune. Well, he always was a bit of a ne'er-do-well. Would you like some champagne?" He poured himself a glass without waiting for her answer.

"No, thank you."

"This has been a nightmare for me."

For me, too, Miriam thought. "I've never seen you like this before."

"I've never felt so vulnerable before." He set his glass down. "I'm sick of puzzling over this mess. In fact, I'd much rather make love to you. Come here, wife. I've missed you."

⌘

Alexei's disconnected thoughts were fixed on Miriam. My head on her breasts she cradles me in her arms her hands stroke my loins my thighs loves me never leave me yes always belong to me yes my love yes my own yes my life I know what I must do for her.

"Are you ready, brother dearest? We must go now."

"Sit by me. Take my hand. *Maman* and Papa used to call you Anyushka. I promised I would always care for you. I have, haven't I?"

"The carriage is waiting to take us to the church."

"Is Miriam ready for our wedding?"

"Now, now Alexei. Your bride is Marya. In time, you'll grow to love one another. Put Miriam out of your mind."

His eyes glistened with stinging tears. "I cannot. If you love me you will allow me to see her one last time."

She ignored his plea. "Here, let me button your cravat. Don't tug so at the lace on your cuffs, darling. Let me smooth your hair. You must stop pulling at it. Stop fidgeting, Alexei." Peter's right, she thought as she tried to calm her brother. That Jewess bewitches him.

"Don't weep so. It's your wedding day."

"Come, little sister. Mustn't keep my bride waiting. Marya, did you say? That's odd. When did she change her name?"

⌘

"*Count Alexei Nicholayevich Razovsky is to wed Countess Marya Gregorevna Petrov on Sunday afternoon at four o'clock. The wedding will take place at the Holy Church of Our Savior where the banns were posted. Both bride and groom were baptized there as infants. Immediately following the church ceremony, the distinguished guests will proceed to the Petrov estate for the grand wedding supper.*"—*The Kiev Weekly Sentinel.*

Alexei attempted to take his bride in his arms in their chambers, but she recoiled.

"Don't touch me." She began to sob piteously.

"Why do you weep so? Have I offended you, Miriam?"

"My name is Marya. I was destined to serve Our Lord, Alexei Nicholayevich. My parents forced you to marry me, may God forgive them. No man has ever touched me..."

"Are you a virgin, sweet Mary? I did not mean to frighten you. Come to bed, my bride. I shall be most gentle with you."

"In God's name, don't touch me." She stifled a scream with her fist. "Give me time to pray for His guidance to do what I must."

"Shall we pray? I, too, have need of His solace." He took his swollen-faced, red-eyed bride by the hand and led her before an icon resting in a small niche. Together they knelt before the holy portrait of Jesus and prayed until exhaustion overtook her. She fell across the bridal bed.

"I want to sleep now."

"I'll not disturb you, my love. I shall sleep in my study tonight."

Alexei searched the bookshelves in his study until he found the volume of Shakespeare and took it to his desk where he wrote the letter he'd been planning for weeks.

My love, I married you today, my Miriam. They say your name is Marya, but I know they lie. You are my bride. God alone knows how much I love you. No longer will the world doubt it after today. No one can part us now.

"See what a scourge is laid upon your hate
that heav'n finds means to kill your joys with love."

God revealed himself to me, my bride. Come to me. I wait for you. Thus with a kiss I die,
Your Alexei

The hot sealing wax scalded the back of his hand yet he felt no pain. He opened the gun cabinet and removed his father's embossed leather pistol case. He chose one and loaded it's chamber. He stroked the pearl-handled pistol as though it were the soft skin of the woman he loved. He placed its nozzle inside his mouth, savoring its taste, very like Miriam's warm tongue.

"Adieu, sweet bride. Come to me soon." Alexei squeezed the trigger.

⌘

"Count Alexei Nicholayevich Razovsky's death was ruled an accident by the authorities. The bridegroom attempted to clean his pistol and the gun discharged. His bride, Countess Marya Petrovna Razovsky, wishes to thank the many Christian souls who have expressed their sympathy. The bereaved widow plans to devote the rest of her life to prayer."—The Kiev Weekly Sentinel.

⌘

A determined Countess Razovsky announced to her parents that she would live in the Kiev Nunnery for the rest of her natural days praying for the soul of her dear, departed husband.

"Don't weep so, Anya dear. You were right to want Alexei to marry and to have a family, like any good Christian." Bedorov fumed as he tried to soothe his hysterical wife. What possessed him to kill himself? Thank God I found the note he wrote to that Jewish whore before anyone else read it. Man was insane! No question. Does it run in the family? My God, I hope not, for the sake of my children.

"Alexei is dead. Did we drive him to it? Did we, Peter? Whose fault is it, if not ours", asked Anya?

"Let me tell you where the fault lies, dear wife. That Jewess destroyed him."

"No, Peter. She loved him. I shouldn't have listened to you. I should have let him run away to America with her. At least he'd be alive now."

"She used you for her own selfish ends. She bewitched him. They say Jews can do that. No decent Christian in his right mind would want to marry a Jewess. She drove him to gamble again. You know so little of the ways of the world, my pet. You have one more unpleasant duty. You must write to the Jewess."

"Tell me what to write, Peter. You always know the right words."

"Tell her you wish never to see her again."

FORTY-NINE

Dov left for St. Petersburg before Alexei's wedding. He had received an urgent summons to return at once for the reconvening of the czar's, "Committee for the Amelioration of the Jews."

Natasha was unable to pry Miriam loose from the living hell in which she had buried herself.

"He's taken my soul with him, Natasha. There's no life for me without him, yet I haven't the courage to take my own." She despised herself for her cowardice. Time and again, she had tried to drive the knife she had stolen through her heart, yet she lacked the courage. Wasn't she already dead without him?

"Courage? Alexei had no courage. His suicide was an act of defiance." The dowager did not add that insanity led Alexei Razovsky to kill himself. No need to brutalize Miriam with the stark truth.

"Please, Natasha. I want to see his grave. Will you help me say goodbye to him?"

"I'll try to arrange it, but we'll have to slip in at night. His tomb's guarded. Now take some of this soup, for heaven's sake. You haven't eaten anything all day." Miriam gagged, but forced herself to swallow.

"If only I hadn't let him go to meet Bedorov that day. If only we'd run away that morning instead. We would be on our way to America right now."

"Stop torturing yourself, Miriam. Hold on to his love for you instead, for he loved no other. It will help you in your grief."

"Easier said than done, Natasha. The pain I feel is unbearable."

"Perhaps you ought to see his grave and say goodbye to ease it, then. I'll come back with some news for you as soon as I can arrange a visit."

⌘

Miriam knelt before her lover's crypt and wept until her tears were spent. "Forgive me, my beloved. Your Juliet hasn't the courage to plunge the knife into her heart. Every part of me will always cherish you, my dearest Romeo. The world puts so little stock in love, though they say otherwise. I love you, Alexei. Goodbye, my sweet, sweet Romeo. The house of Montague never mourned its son as deeply as I do." She started at a rustling noise behind her.

"Who's there?" She stiffened at the sound. Was someone watching? Miriam pressed her lips to the cold marble of the vault in which her lover had finally found peace and fled back to the waiting carriage.

⌘

"I sent for my cousin Dov. He should be here shortly. I'm so afraid for her." Sophie said to Josef.

"Excuse me," Boris interrupted. "Countess Gorov is here to see Madame Zeklinski."

"Send her in, please. She's a good friend," Josef said to Sophie by way of explanation.

Brodsky introduced them and retired to the window to wait for word from the doctor while Miriam's two friends appraised one another, each wondering why they had never met before today. As the afternoon wore on the two women talked, taking the measure of one another, cementing the beginnings of a strong bond borne of their mutual love for Miriam.

"What a pity we've not met before," Natasha said.

"Perhaps we can become good friends, Countess. That is if you'll allow it."

"Of course I'll allow it. Miriam should have introduced us years ago."

At dusk, Boris hastened to announce, "Reb Zeklinski," but Dov was hard on his heels. Without a word, Sophie hugged him, and the countess allowed him to kiss her hand, and Josef shook his hand.

"How is my wife?" He looked from one to the other for answer to his grim question. The tension in the air was palpable.

"The doctor has been with her all day."

"What's wrong with her?"

"We don't know, Dov. It began weeks ago, but she refused to let us summon the doctor until today. She cannot keep her food down. She retches every morning."

"Tell me what you know of this business, Natasha."

"I won't lie to you, Dov. She was terribly upset when Alexei Razovsky shot himself."

"I heard the news when I reached St. Petersburg. He was a good friend to her, but I can't see why that should make her so ill." He paused at a knock.

"Yes?"

"The physician wishes to see you, sir. Shall I show him to your study?"

"No. Send him in here. We're all concerned."

172

The physician glanced at Josef. "Reb Zeklinski.?"

"No, sir. I am Reb Zeklinski. How is my wife?"

"There's nothing I'm able to do for her."

"Nothing? Is there no hope? With all due respect sir, I insist you summon other physicians for a consultation. Send for them at once."

"That won't be necessary. None of us can help her in her present condition."

His sober words were met with stunned silence. Sophie stifled a sob, Countess Gorov's eyes widened in recognition of impending disaster, and Josef stared at his feet, his emotions in turmoil.

"How long has she to live?"

The physician managed a dour smile. "You misunderstand my meaning entirely. Your wife is nearing the end of the trimester."

"What does that mean?"

"Madame Zeklinski will require the services of someone other than myself."

"But why? Explain yourself, doctor."

"Allow me to be the first to offer you congratulations, sir."

"Congratulations? But I don't understand..."

"Your wife is with child. She'll feel much better in a few more days. "

Book Three
Kiev 1812

Pearl Wolf

FIFTY

"How many times do I have to tell you I cannot feed all the starving Jews in Russia? I do my best, don't I? What more do you want?"

"Use your influence with the czar, Dov. Is that too much to ask?"

"If I agree, will you agree to stop badgering me?"

"All right."

"Where's Kalman?"

"In the carpentry shop. The men made something special for him for his birthday. Josef's managed to keep it a secret from Kalman until today, though I can't imagine how. That child's curiosity knows no bounds." Dov laughed, as much with relief that their argument had ended as at their son's boyish inquisitiveness.

"At least we agree on one thing. Our love for Kalman."

"I suppose so." She hesitated, trying to subdue the fire of resentment within her. "Josef's such a treasure. I'm glad we have him. He's very kind to our son."

"Best thing I ever did was to hire Josef. Shows a handsome yearly profit."

"He doesn't steal the way Borschov stole, but you refused to see that at the time, didn't you?"

"Can't you let bygones be bygones?"

"I'd forgotten that you prefer to speak only of your successes. I'm sorry I brought it up. I'm tired of our quarrels as well." It's me, I suppose. I thought he'd change when Kalman was born, but business still comes before his son and me. Yet he was so overjoyed then.

⌘

Chaim Kalman Zeklinski was born on April 15, 1805. It was a difficult pregnancy yet an easy birth. He was a placid infant who renewed his father's dreams of a bright future in Russia for his heir. Kalman would tell his children about the historic role their grandfather Dov played in the Jewish legislation that became law in 1804.

The statute decreed that Jews could attend *gymnasia* as well as their own schools. They were encouraged to purchase unoccupied land, but only for farming in the Pale of Settlement.

At the same time, the Crown issued repressive edicts. Jewish families were forced to abandon their homes and face starvation. Village landowners lost revenue from Jewish tenants even as Jews were driven out by bands of peasants.

Czar Alexander was informed that Napoleon convened a *Sanhedrin* in Paris—a supreme council of Jewish leaders from all over Western Europe—to develop policy. Napoleon's purpose was to create laws so Jews would become citizens with full rights in the European country in which they lived.

Under the circumstances, the czar's advisors suggested, it would be wiser to postpone the edict and Alexander agreed in order to maintain his posture as an enlightened monarch in the eyes of the west.

⌘

Kalman ran from one parent to the other. "Come see the new *droshki* Josef made for me. The woodworkers helped him make it."

"Whose pony is that, son?"

"I can keep it for today because it's my birthday, but then I have to give it back."

"Do you like the pony?" Dov persisted.

"Isn't he beautiful? Josef says he's a Shetland. Josef says they're the best kind. They come all the way from Scotland."

"Let me ask you another question, since you're so clever. What would you do if you had your own pony?"

"Oh Poppa! I'd do anything in the world!"

"Would you study harder?"

"Leave him be, Dov. Kalman does his best."

Dov glared at his wife. "So long as you see to it that he pays more attention to his studies. The pony's a birthday present from your mother and me."

"For me? Thank you both." He wrapped his scrawny arms first around his mother and then his father.

"You can ride by yourself, but only when the stable boy supervises. Not too long today, darling. Aunt Sophie and Uncle Benjamin and all your cousins will be here soon. Aunt Natasha, too." Josef led the pony, instructing the boy as they walked.

"Kalman spends too much time with Brodsky, Miriam. I've been meaning to talk to you about that. I want him to work harder at his studies. That's more important."

"You expect too much. He's only seven years old."

The air between them crackled with anger. "When I was his age I spoke five languages with fluency. Kalman will be the head of Zeklinski Enterprises one day, won't he? It's my duty to prepare him for it. He spends too much time with Josef, time he might better use to study. Limit his leisure time and increase his study time, or is that too much to ask of you?"

"If you spent more time here at home, you could encourage him yourself. Why can't you see that?"

"I long for the peace and quiet of travel just to get away from your criticisms. You're just like your mother."

"My mother has nothing to do with us and you know it."

What an acid tongue she has. She should be content now that we have a son. "See that the boy studies harder."

"We go round in circles and end up nowhere when we argue."

"Then stop your bickering."

⌘

After their luncheon, all the children retired to play while the adults conversed.

"What do you think of Napoleon's chances?" Asked Dov. "They say Czar Alexander has two hundred thousand men camped on the Dvina and the Dniepr Rivers."

Natasha said, "We'll win, of course."

"Josef sent a full battalion from among our own serfs. They marched off in a blaze of patriotism, eager to defend their country. They rode out of here like the conquerors of ancient times. The women and children lined the road and cheered as their men marched off to war."

"Everyone talks of victory over the enemy," said Sophie Moskowitz.

Dov added, "I hear Napoleon had trouble raising troops. Last year there was a devastating economic crisis in France and he's pressed for funds. No one but Benjamin knows what I am about to reveal. Isn't that so?"

"I know only what you tell me, Dov," his mild-mannered aide answered.

"What the secret?" Miriam asked.

"Czar Alexander has asked me to help finance the war. I'm leaving for St. Petersburg tomorrow morning to discuss the details with Speransky."

"Bravo Dov. That's very patriotic," said the Countess.

"Why didn't you tell me you were leaving tomorrow?"

"I didn't want to spoil Kalman's birthday celebration, dear," he answered, taking pleasure in her annoyance at the news.

"I'm proud of you, cousin, for helping our country win the war," said Sophie.

"When shall you return?" Miriam's brittle tone did not escape the notice of Natasha.

179

"That's up to the czar. I have an idea. Why don't you and Kalman come with me? He's never seen our St. Petersburg, has he? We can show him the Capitol before I have to travel west again."

"No!" Miriam's vehemence startled her guests. Her intense response was clear only to Natasha. "The children at the orphanage need me. Besides, you've said you want Kalman to attend more to his studies. Wait a few more years until the child's old enough to appreciate the beauty of Petersburg."

"If you prefer," Dov answered, surprised at her sharp reaction. "Ah, here's the birthday cake. Thank the baker for us, Boris. And send the children in."

Natasha knows what I'm thinking, Miriam thought as she lit the candles on the cake. I'll never return to St. Petersburg. Seven years without Alexei. I lie down at night and I feel him beside me. I wake each morning and I see his face. It was never Dov's home. It was our home, Alexei's and mine.

"Happy birthday, son. Make a wish and blow out the candles."

FIFTY-ONE

Dov was punctual for his appointment with Count Speransky. He paid scant attention to the long wait in the anteroom, a fact of government life.

"This way sir," said an aide at last.

"Sit, Zeklinski."

Dov was stunned. "Prince Bedorov? I had an appointment with..."

"It's clear you haven't heard the news."

Dov was instantly on his guard. "No Sire, I haven't."

"Speransky was reassigned three weeks ago, by order of Czar Alexander."

"What is his new assignment??"

He has been appointed Governor General of Siberia. You shall conduct your business with me, sir, by order of His Majesty."

"Of course, Sire," Dov said hastily. "My congratulations, Your Majesty."

So Speransky's out, Dov thought, his head spinning. Means the diehard reactionaries have won. He was a good friend to me. He must have turned his back once too often, poor soul. Now he'll spend the rest of his life counting the birches as they say.

"The czar's to be congratulated on his choice, if I may say so. I shall send him a note to that effect."

"Don't bother. He left this morning for Vilna, to wait for Napoleon's army. How much money can you raise for the war?"

"How much has Czar Alexander requested?"

"We must have thirty million rubles."

"I shall proceed with the new bond issue at once, Sire. You shall have it within a week, two at the most."

"One week. Napoleon must be stopped at all costs. He means to march on Moscow. My wife and my family live there. I believe you know my wife."

"Yes, Sire. She and her brother befriended my wife and me, many years ago."

Bedorov frowned. "See to it that you people support our country in this campaign."

Dov seethed at the remark. "You have no reason to question Jewish loyalty to the Crown, Sire. His Highness is well aware of our patriotism."

"Napoleon has Jewish support from Warsaw. I refer to the adherents of the *Sanhedrin*."

"I fail to see what the *Sanhedrin* and Napoleon's ambitions have to do with me or my people. My allegiance has always been to the leader of my country. With all due respect, you have no reason to doubt it, nor do you have reason to doubt my loyalty to the Crown."

"No need to be testy Zeklinski. I have information that there are a number of Jews in Russia who support Napoleon's cause. No matter." He changed the subject so swiftly Dov was startled. "You have a shipyard in Sebastopol?"

"It does not belong to me. A Russian born widow owns the company. I see to her interests."

"Glad to hear she's Russian. Otherwise, I would be forced to seize her assets under the War Act."

"What is it you require, sir?"

"King Frederick of Prussia is providing supplies as well as twenty thousand men for the invasion of Russia. We need more frigates and war ships."

"How many?"

"Begin building five. Draw the funds from the bond issues. You will be notified of any further needs." The prince turned his attention to some papers.

⌘

The French army marched from Vilna to Vitebsk, a distance of 375 *versts,* but Napoleon's enemies were already on the road to Smolensk. His aides pleaded with him to encamp for the winter, but the Frenchman was determined to conquer Moscow. His men were reduced by death and defection to 160,000 soldiers who were exhausted from the long marches from their homeland. At Smolensk, the Russians took their stand, but both sides lost many men in battle.

General Kutuzov held to his strategy of retreat. By mid-September, he ordered the evacuation of Moscow, one day before Napoleon's entry into the city.

But fires set by Muscovites destroyed two thirds of Moscow. Napoleon wrote to Alexander complaining bitterly of the perfidy, but the czar did not deign to answer.

"A wise decision in the appointment of General Kutuzov after all," Prince Bedorov told the czar. "It is said, Sire, that the future is his who knows how to wait."

The chill winds of October began to dishearten the French conqueror. Napoleon was heard to complain that he bested the Russians in battle time and time again, yet it got him nowhere.

In Kiev, Miriam gave Josef permission to release another five hundred serfs to defend Mother Russia. Countess Gorov also sent five hundred, while Princess Bedorov, having fled Moscow for the safety of Kiev, sent one thousand serfs.

Men from all over the country poured into Kaluga, 135 *versts* south of Moscow, to join General Kutuzov. By October, Napoleon and fifty thousand soldiers retraced their summer route, while General Kutuzov marched parallel to them, taking every opportunity to harass the retreating French.

By the time the French retraced their steps to Smolensk, snow and ice had turned the countryside into treacherous terrain and then General Kutuzov was ready to fight the hungry French soldiers with a Russian army of eighty thousand well-fed, rested men well accustomed to Russian winter. Less than thirty thousand Frenchmen struggled across the Niemen River, the site of their entry six months earlier when they numbered four hundred thousand.

In victory, Czar Alexander took command of his forces and hounded the enemy all the way to Paris. As he rode triumphantly through liberated Prussia, he was greeted with shouts of, "Long live Alexander! Long live the Cossacks!"

FIFTY-TWO

Church bells pealed to signal the New Year in Wilhelmstadt, signaling the end of 1812. "Happy New Year, dear," Dov said to his mistress.

"The same to you, precious," she said. "Let us hope Hans returns unharmed."

"Come, come Lori. It's so unlike you to worry. Where's the cheerful woman I love? The war's as good as over. Prussia's again a Russian ally and Napoleon is finished. Hans will come home to us soon, I'm sure."

"I find myself dwelling on our children's future of late."

"What do you mean?"

"We nearly didn't succeed in getting Hans a commission as an officer because he's illegitimate. I'm forced to confess to you that it hurt me deeply."

"Your dedication to the children is one of your charms. Couldn't the prince arrange it?"

"You know his answer. If you convert to Christianity and we marry in church, he would record our children as legitimate subjects of the principality of Wilhelmstadt. He would also bestow a title upon you." She hesitated for a moment.

"What is it, my love?"

"Young Prince Wilhelm II has an eye for our Maria."

"What's wrong with Maria sharing an innocent romance with the prince?"

"The same old story, David. Wilhelm will not allow his son and heir to marry an untitled, illegitimate woman. I suspect he regrets that the two ever met in the first place."

He frowned. "You're not the only one pressing me to convert."

"The czar?"

"Who else but the czar?"

"Can Speransky help?"

He shook his head. "Czar Alexander consigned Speransky to Siberia where he languishes among false prophets, priests and prisoners. I suspect that Bedorov's behind it." Dov's thoughts assaulted him like the raging waters of a swollen spring. Convert to Christianity? Impossible! What have I been fighting for all these years? It's my destiny to lead the Jews in Russia."I was born a Jew and I'll die a Jew, Lori."

"Is that what you told Czar Alexander?"

"Of course not."

"What did you say?"

"I told him I'd give his suggestion some serious thought."

"Very diplomatic."

"The czar is threatening to embark on a campaign of Russification."

"Russification? Does that mean what I think it means?"

"Conversion. Mass conversion. No choice. 'Convert or die,' said Ivan the Terrible. What Alexander has in mind may be 'convert or quit Russian soil.' He wants me to set the example."

"If he succeeds, I shan't be sorry."

"I reminded the czar that Napoleon, our enemy, has enormous support from Jews in France and in Poland. The Jews might choose to quit Russia if given such a hard choice, but they would certainly leave a devastated economy in their wake."

"Did he agree?"

"No, but it made him thoughtful. I said, 'The Jews respect you, Sire. They think of you as their protector. Now is not the time to make such drastic changes,' or words to that effect."

"Bravo, David! You played the game well."

Dov laughed good-naturedly. "How can I lose? I've had the most wonderful tutor in the world." He hesitated.

"What is it?"

"I'll never convert, I promise you that."

FIFTY-THREE

Lieutenant von Hals policed Paris under orders from the King of Prussia to prevent plunder at war's end. More than once he faced the dangers of his own allies, especially drunken Russian Cossacks who chose to decamp on the Champs-Elysees.

One year later, when Napoleon escaped from exile in Elba, he battled Wellington's army at Waterloo.

Hans von Hals once again led his men in battle. When the fierce fighting ended, more than twenty-five thousand Frenchmen were dead. Wellington lost fifteen thousand Englishmen and the Prussian corps lost seven thousand in their final defeat of Napoleon. Among the dead was Lieutenant von Hals from Wilhelmstadt, aged twenty-three.

Princess Bedorov returned to Moscow to help rebuild her adopted city after the war, while St. Petersburg reopened the doors of its mansions and palaces along the Millionaya to gambling and to gaiety. Russian Royalty was so eager to celebrate the sweet taste of victory they took little note of the reactionary winds blowing throughout the land.

Czar Alexander's closest advisor, champion of tradition, Prince Bedorov, became even more indispensable to him. With his monarch's blessing, he set up military colonies in Mogilev, Kherson, Ekaterinoslav, and Slobodsko-Ukrainski.

Soldiers discharged after the war moved into each designated district, automatically turning all inhabitants back into soldiers in the army reserve. They worked in the fields alongside the *muzhiks*, their conscripted brethren, and spent the rest of their time teaching townsmen the art of war.

Marriages were arranged by lottery and fines were imposed on barren wives; cottages replaced centuries-old villages, one exactly like another, inspected regularly for their condition. Private life ceased for those unfortunate enough to be caught in the web of these experimental colonies.

Minister of the Army Prince Bedorov reported to the czar that the experiments were a great success in spite of a few minor uprisings.

When a military tribunal sentenced nearly three hundred *muzhiks* to death, Bedorov wrote to the czar that he had first asked God's counsel. He decided to allow the men to live, but they would be punished for flouting the law. The rebels had to run the gauntlet of a full battalion of one thousand men, who beat them with iron rods. After the punishment, Prince Bedorov, guided by his humanitarian spirit, chose forty ringleaders for severe torture and forgave the rest.

The czar ordered Bedorov to continue to apply the law to the offenders. The edict suited the prince well, for Bedorov detested the thieving, boasting, cheating habits of some Russian subjects. It was his mission in life to champion honor and loyalty and decency. An additional one hundred and sixty men were put to death.

On Sundays following church services, Prince Bedorov sang for family and friends who heaped praise upon him for his selfless devotion to Mother Russia.

FIFTY-FOUR

Dov's repeated requests to see Prince Bedorov were pointedly ignored. It made him uneasy. The government's notes to Dov were due and he needed funds to meet his own obligations. Curiously, he was having difficulty selling the notes even at a favorable discount. There were few buyers, which seemed very odd to him. That had never happened before, even in the worst of times.

"What do you make of it, Benjamin?" Sophie's husband had come to St. Petersburg to help in the current crisis, for Zeklinski Enterprises was in danger of collapse for the first time in its history.

"I just can't fathom it. Golanov writes he's having problems as well. He asked for a few more weeks to try to resolve them on his own. To make matters worse our factories report that orders have slowed to a trickle. They've had to let go hundreds of workers."

"When it rains, it pours, they say," said Dov.

"Lenders are threatening to seize assets if we don't meet our payments on time," added Benjamin.

"On time? If I had a kopek for every loan I let slide past the due date I'd be richer than Midas. Nobody pays loans on time in Russia. Isn't there any good news?"

"Kalman is fine and Miriam is well, but she grieves over Countess Gorov's death."

"Natasha dead? I didn't know. Tell Miriam how sorry I am. How old was she, do you know?"

"She was eighty-five. Sophie and I grew very fond of her. She died on New Year's Day. Miriam had invited us all to dinner to welcome in the New Year and she seemed fine. She never woke the next morning."

"Natasha gave me hope, you know. I always used to think that if there was one Russian as splendid as Natasha, there must be more out there somewhere, though I've yet to meet them. I'm glad she didn't suffer a painful death." Dov shook his head sadly. "Start back for Kiev in the morning. Stall our creditors one way or another. Tell them you saw me and I'm coming home with barrels full of rubles."

"What are you going to do?"

"I'll stay here and try to see Bedorov, but I won't wait all day. If he refuses to see me by ten, I'll go to Sebastopol. Maybe I can help Misha."

⌘

"What have you to report?"

"The shipyards are destroyed beyond repair, Your Majesty.

"What about Zeklinski's factories?"

"Closed. The workers have been sacked."

"Go on."

"Many of our own people lost their jobs as well. Be a cruel winter for Jew and Christian alike."

"We'll arrange for the Crown's factories to hire back our people." But not the Jews, Bedorov thought to himself. Not until they agree to convert.

"Our people will be glad to hear it."

"What else have you to report?"

"Zeklinski's creditors are closing in."

"And Zeklinski? Where is he?"

"He re-entered the country three weeks ago, Sire."

"Where does he go when he leaves Russia?"

"He crosses the border at the Niemen River, about twenty *versts* below Memel. He lives in a little principality called Wilhelmstadt. Has a mistress and children there. Prince Wilhelm is his patron."

So, Bedorov thought, Zeklinski leads a double life. No wonder Alexei took up with the Jew's wife. What a fool my brother-in-law was. He could have had so much. Now the picture's complete. I'll tighten the net until Zeklinski is ruined.

"Keep a close watch on the Jew and report back to me."

FIFTY-FIVE

Dov's shoulders sagged as though under a tremendous weight. His clothes were in disarray, his brow knotted in pain. He rubbed his hands as if washing them.

"What's wrong, Dov? Are you ill?" Miriam had never seen him so despondent.

"I'm finished. Done. The Russian bear has eaten me alive." He rubbed his eyes. "Sit beside me, Miriam. Would you do that for me?"

"Of course."

A tear trickled down his cheek as he held her hand to his lips. "I've lost everything. Zeklinski Enterprises no longer exists."

"How can that be?"

"There's nothing left. Nothing."

She tried to sort out the meaning of his words. "What are we to do? Have we lost the estate, too? How are we to live?"

"May I have some brandy?"

"Of course." She rose to fetch it.

"Hear me out first. Then I'll answer all your questions. All right?"

"Take your time."

"Things were fine at the beginning of the year. I hadn't a clue then, but I wasn't paying close enough attention to the warning signs. When I returned to Petersburg at the end of January, Benjamin was waiting for me."

"Yes. He left right after Natasha died. Go on."

"He traveled with heavy baggage. All at once our factory orders were off, he wasn't able to collect our debts, and our creditors began to snap at our heels like so many bears sniffing carrion." He rose to refill his glass. "Do you recall our first spring here? So nice then."

"Yes. Go on, Dov."

"Lately my mind seems to wander. Forgive me. I sent Benjamin back to Kiev to try to stall our creditors, and I went to Sebastopol to transfer funds from the shipyards, to tide the business over, something I'd done many times before."

"Is that old widow still alive? If she is, she must be ancient by now."

"Yes." Dov drained his glass. "Do you remember Misha Golanov?"

"The shipbuilder. I met him only once, on the day Czarina Catherine sailed."

"Misha ran the shipyards very well for me. He and Natasha were the only two decent Russians I've ever met. I was grieved to hear of her death."

"I'm sure of it. Do go on, Dov."

"By the time I reached Sebastopol, it was already too late. The von Hals shipyards were a field of ashes. Nothing left but a few charred timbers."

"But who would do such a thing?"

"Sebastopol's a city full of unruly thugs given to drinking and to fighting. We needed them during the war to help us build frigates for the Crown, but we had to sack them because there was no work. "In the middle of the night they murdered our guards, stole whatever tools they could carry and set fire to the rest."

"Didn't you tell me the shipyards weren't yours?" A sense of foreboding began to fill her with uneasiness. "Or were they? I'm confused."

"I purchased half the yards years ago. It's too complicated to explain. Suffice it to say that I'd frequently been able to borrow from the one to tide the other business over in bad times. Now all of a sudden, bad times hit everywhere all at once."

"I see," she said, wondering why he'd never mentioned this half-ownership before.

"It all happened so fast. For one, I was left holding government bonds— money I'd lent the Crown to finance the war. They're worthless now. For another, orders fell off at our factories. We had to let hundreds of workers go because we couldn't pay their wages."

"What are we to do now?"

He ignored her question as if he hadn't even heard it. "Have you not felt the effects of the recession here in Kiev? Hasn't Brodsky said anything? No matter. It will trickle down soon enough. Prices are falling because no one has the money to buy any more."

"We wouldn't have felt the pinch here in Kiev until harvest time, would we?"

"Most likely. Let me have some water, dear. My throat's parched."

"Of course."

"After the fire in Sebastopol, it dawned on me that there were far too many coincidences. I kept asking myself, why? Why Zeklinski Enterprises? Why von Hals Shipyards? Why me? Why everything we own? Forgive me."

"Forgive you? For what?"

"I lost your father's house. I'm sorry about that, but I couldn't save it."

Her thoughts returned to her days there with Alexei, but she pushed them from her mind. "What about this estate? Did we lose that, too?"

"I'm getting to that. By the time I reached St. Petersburg, it became clear to me. It wasn't the recession that was to blame."

"What do you mean?"

"It was a conspiracy." Dov barked a laugh. "I never even saw it coming. The clever Dov Zeklinski. Financial advisor to the Czar."

"But who is behind it? Do you know?"

"It was obvious, once I thought it all through. Prince Peter Bedorov, close advisor to our beloved Czar Alexander."

"Are you sure?" Miriam was stunned. Her insides twisted taut, like a sail fighting the wind in a storm. *Bedorov punished Dov for my affair with Alexei.*

"He did it because we're Jewish."

"No, Dov. That's not the reason." She steeled herself to tell him the truth.

"There are hundreds of thousands of Jews in this country, but only one Dov Zeklinski. My destiny was to bring enlightenment to the Russian empire, eh? You haven't heard the half of it."

"Tell me all of it," she said uneasily.

"I thought it was odd that I wasn't allowed to see Bedorov in January before I left for Sebastopol, but I didn't connect it then. When I returned last month, he finally agreed to see me."

Dov doesn't know it's me Bedorov's punishing, she thought, recalling the letter from Anya accusing her of Alexei's death. *I'll have to tell him. Can't let him think that Judaism's to blame. I'm to blame for this.*

"My audience with Bedorov was brief," he began, as though he were about to recite a familiar litany. "He denied knowledge of my financial problems. Waved it away as if it were of no importance. Instead, he discussed the Czar's hopes and dreams for a unified Russia."

"Go on."

"He said the czar had a divine revelation—a way to resolve the Jewish question once and for all."

"What is it?"

"Russification. We're expected to convert to Christianity. Renounce Judaism. Accept Jesus as the messiah. Only then will the czar consider us loyal subjects."

"Convert? We'd never do such a thing. How could we? And if we refuse?"

"Let me finish. I demanded to see the Czar but Bedorov informed me that Czar Alexander would see me only after I set an example for all Russian Jews and agree to convert."

"Oh, Dov. After all you've done for Russia. Ships. War funds. Army supplies. Does that count for nothing, then?"

"I'm afraid so."

"Where shall we go? We can't stay here, can we?" Dov paused in thought, his life parading savagely before him.

"Dov? Are you all right? Dov?"

He sighed and bent his head. "You can stay in Russia, Miriam."

"But if we're not going to convert, how is it possible to stay?"

"I've already made my choice," he said quietly.

"Choice? What choice?"

"I've had my audience with the czar."

The meaning of his words struck her with unremitting force. Her head reeled with the clear implication of his words, but her heart refused to accept it.

"You can't be serious."

"I was never more serious. I'm taking instruction."

"You'll renounce Judaism? *Shtadlan* Kalman Zeklinski's grandson? How can you even think of doing such a thing?"

"What do you expect me to do?" he exploded. "Live like a poor *shtetl* Jew after all these years? I'm too old for piety and I've no taste for poverty. I've done what I had to do because I know when I'm beaten. You ought to convert, too. For your own protection."

"I'd rather die than convert." Miriam felt as though she were sinking, sinking into hell, sinking into a world of darkness.

"We must all do what we must." He shrugged.

"I'm sorry for you, Dov, though strangely enough, I'm not as shocked as I should be. I suppose you've been Christian in many ways for years now. You don't observe the Sabbath, you stopped using your prayer shawl years ago, and I can't recall the last time you put on your phylacteries and said your morning prayers." She lapsed into silence, to gather strength for what she knew she must tell him, but he spoke before she could begin.

"I know you won't believe this, but I'm converting for your sake."

"No, Dov. You're doing it for yourself."

"I knew you wouldn't understand."

"Perhaps I don't. Tell me what it is you think you're doing for my sake."

"I'm converting to save your home for you."

"I've always thought it our home. You only do things to suit yourself. I won't let you blame me."

"It's true just the same. Czar Alexander is bestowing this estate, as a gift for my conversion. You can stay here for the rest of your life. I'm a man of honor in spite of what you think."

"Is there some reason that you said I can stay, and not, 'we' can stay?"

"I'm leaving Russia, Miriam. As soon as I can." He took a deep breath. "And I'm taking Kalman with me."

"What? Is this some kind of jest?"

"We weren't a good match from the beginning, were we? No matter. Water under the bridge as they say. There's another woman in my life, Hannelore von Hals."

"Who is she?"

Dov told her about his life in Wilhelmstadt. He told her about his three children. He told her about the tragic death of his son Hans at Waterloo. He told her about his castle in Wilhelmstadt and he told her what awaited him.

"Prince Wilhelm's agreed to bestow a baronetcy on me. I plan to marry the woman I love and legitimize my children. My daughter Maria will marry the prince she loves and rule by his side one day." He paused for breath. "I'm taking Kalman with me. He'll convert and be titled as well when he comes of age. Don't begrudge him the opportunity."

"You've thought of everything, have you? I should have expected as much. And what are your plans for me? Have you made those, too?"

"I'm not such a beast as you think. Try to remember that. Of course I've thought of you. Did you expect any less of me?"

"Shall I convert and become a baroness and live in your castle alongside your mistress? How cozy. Have you told her the good news yet?"

"You can continue to live here. The estate will provide handsomely for you for the rest of your days."

"All our problems tied in a pretty package. You and Kalman are to leave and I'm to stay. No loose ends."

"You've a right to be bitter. No. That's not all. I'm going to give you a divorce before I leave. The rabbi will be here first thing in the morning. I want you to be free to marry again. You can hate me all you like," he said listlessly, "but it won't change anything. It's all arranged. It's done. I've said everything I have to say."

"You will never take my son from me."

"Don't be stubborn about this, Miriam. It's all decided."

"No it isn't. Not by any means."

"What do you mean?" he asked, wary of the venom in her tone.

"My son isn't going with you."

"I have a right to take him, Miriam. I'm his father. That gives me the right in any court of law."

"No, Dov. You have no right to him at all."

"Don't be stubborn. There's no way you can stop me."

"Oh yes there is. You are not Kalman's father."

"Of course I'm his father. He looks like me. He even has blue eyes like me."

"Alexei had blue eyes," she said in a lethal tone, her eyes unwavering.

"Alexei?"

"Kalman is Alexei's son. We were lovers."

He stared at her, stunned.

"You never thought I'd be capable of a love affair, did you? Bedorov ruined you because he blamed me for Alexei's suicide."

"You're lying to me." She heard fear in his voice.

"I have a tale to tell as well," she said without emotion. Dov listened first in disbelief, and then in amazement.

"So you see, Kalman couldn't possibly have been your son."

"You're sure?"

"Without a doubt. Natasha knew it, too. She'd certainly verify what I'm telling you if she were alive. I've even saved her notes to us, the ones she wrote when we spent the summer in her cottage on Krestovski Island. Would you like to see them?"

"Kalman not my son? Yet I recall coming home the day before Razovsky's wedding. We made love that day."

"I'd already missed my time of the month by then."

"But Alexei wed Marya Petrov."

"We were planning to run off to America to start a new life. Bedorov forced him to marry Petrov's daughter. My love shot himself as a result. I had a vicious note from Anya right after he killed himself, accusing me of her brother's death and renouncing our former friendship. Odd. I didn't destroy that note either. Perhaps I knew I'd need it one day." She extracted a key from her locket and retrieved the note from a tiny locked drawer in the escritoire. She handed it to Dov without a word.

Dov looked up when he finished reading. "She believed you bewitched her brother."

"Anya is like one of those tiny little lizards that live in the tropics. When she hides in the greenery, she turns green, and when she wallows in the mud, she turns brown. Can't you see Bedorov's hand in this?"

"I'm stunned."

"I would gladly have run off with him if Bedorov hadn't stopped us."

"Somehow, that hurts me, even though I betrayed you, too."

She ignored his remark. "If Bedorov did you in, he did it for revenge, but he was wrong to stop us. Alexei and I would have been so happy in America. I'm sure of it."

Dov paced back and forth as Miriam spoke, thinking about his course of action. "Where were you going to get the money?"

"My father gave me some diamonds when my mother died. I still have them."

"Then why didn't you go?"

"Bedorov bought Alexei's gambling note. He refused to accept the diamonds in payment. He threatened to arrest him and send Alexei to Siberia if he didn't marry Petrov's daughter. Natasha said Alexei's mind snapped. All I have left of my love is his son Kalman."

"I've heard enough. I won't take Kalman from you since he isn't my son."

They fell silent, each wrapped in their own crippling wounds, until at last, she spoke.

"How ironic. Bedorov hates us both, doesn't he? Wants a pure Russia full of military colonies and obedient subjects. A Russia free of Jews. He's the true patriot, Dov. Not you."

"I suppose you're right."

"You were always too blind to see the hate. We fought about it all the time. It all boils down to a matter of state. Anti-Semitism is a State decision. Can you really believe that peasants and serfs would accept us into their churches? What a foolish notion. But they need us just the same. They need us to blame their failures on. The peasants, the serfs, the merchants, the nobility."

"You never tried to be a good wife to me. Do you want to know something? Hannelore loves me. She never criticizes me. Never. She's always glad to see me. I tried to love you, you know. I really tried."

She shrugged. "Ours was not a match made in heaven, was it?"

"I never meant to hurt you. I'm a decent man. I don't want to hurt you even now. I wish you and Kalman well. Really I do. I'm sorry about you and Razovsky. Sorry you couldn't live out your dream, as I am about to do. Perhaps one day you'll find someone who loves you the way I love Hannelore. I wish that for you."

"It doesn't matter."

"I forgive you your sins, Miriam. Can you forgive me mine?"

"Yes, I forgive you."

"I'd like to leave believing that."

"Go ahead then, for I mean it. We cannot help who we are. I'm sorry you have to renounce your heritage. It may come back to haunt you. Makes me think the hungry Russian bear hasn't so much defeated you as devoured you whole."

"We've been married almost thirty-one years. Damn few were happy ones, were they? We weren't good for each other, were we?"

"No, I suppose we weren't. For my part, I'm sorry that my love for Alexei had anything to do with your downfall."

"Maybe it did and maybe it didn't. Bedorov would have found a reason to destroy me anyway even if he didn't hold you responsible for Alexei's death. I'm inclined to believe it was just a convenient excuse. At any rate, what's done is done and there's no going back."

"When do you plan to leave?"

"I'll stay long enough to give you a *get*."

"I don't need a divorce. You're free to leave right now."

"Don't protest. It's for your own good. You know that you can never remarry without a *get*. One day you may have occasion to thank me for it. It's the least I can do."

The next few days seemed to Miriam like a scene from some preposterous drama. She allowed Dov and the rabbi to lead her through the ritual of a Jewish divorce, guessing why Dov found it so necessary.

"This relieves you of all responsibility toward me, doesn't it?" she asked calmly after the rabbi had gone.

"That's not true. I could have left without a word, but that's not my way. In spite of what you think, I'm an honorable man."

"May God forgive you for converting."

"Let's not part with bitterness."

"All right, Dov. I don't hate you for what you're doing. Does that surprise you?"

"I don't hate you, Miriam. I'm sorry about Kalman. I love him, you know." A discreet knock startled them both.

"Your carriage is here, sir."

"Yes, Boris. In a minute." He waited until the butler withdrew. "Well, it's time for me to go, Miriam. If you should ever need anything, write to me. I left the necessary information on your desk."

"Goodbye, Dov."

"Say goodbye to Kalman for me, will you?"

"Of course," she said.

"May I kiss you goodbye?"

"Yes, of course."

He took her in his arms and kissed her with a tenderness that caught her by surprise. She tasted the bitter salt of his tears upon her lips as she held him to her for the last time.

FIFTY-SIX

The recession brought ripples of discontent throughout the empire. Serfs and peasants chafed under the yoke of oppression, the more so since the enlightened policies of other European countries came to light. As if this weren't enough, thousands were out of work, due to the collapse of the economy.

Czar Alexander sought escape in religious mysticism. It relieved his melancholy, he told his confidante, Prince Bedorov. With Bedorov so firmly in charge, he said he had the utmost confidence in the proper discharge of affairs of state.

The prince disapproved of the czar's current choice of religious mystics, an obvious fraud. It bespoke change and that was not to his liking, not at all. And what of Mother Russia? Was she to be served by such charlatanism? Bedorov's reaction was to ally himself with the Russian clergy against the foul influences of mystical hysteria.

He managed to enlist the aid of the monk Photius, who successfully persuaded the Czar to abandon the mystic and return to the fold. Once again, the country began to feel the sting of repressive edicts against any religion other than the powerful Russian Orthodox Church.

⌘

"Kalman can stay with us for awhile. You need some time alone, to think things out. You've been so melancholy ever since Dov left."

"Perhaps you're right, Sophie. Kalman's happy when he's with his cousins. I haven't been able to climb out of this dejected state. I keep wondering how I'm meant to live out the rest of my life, a life that seems without purpose now."

"You have Kalman to think about. He's your purpose."

"It's odd, Sophie. When I wake up every morning, it takes me a moment to remember that Dov is gone for good. That brief moment is my only happy one. Do you understand?"

"Yes, dear. It was a monstrous thing for Dov to do. Now you must think of your son."

"All right. I'll have Boris pack a few things. Take him with you now." Miriam looked around Sophie's parlor. "Where's Benjamin? How is he taking the collapse of the business?"

"I think he's relieved, in a way. Now he can study Torah to his heart's content. We've more than enough money to last all our lives and then some. Benjamin never believed in spending too freely and now I have to admit that he was right, though I fought with him about it often enough. He's at the office preparing the deeds for the Zeklinski office buildings. He has to surrender them to the new owner in a few days."

⌘

Benjamin wasn't the only one concerned with the former offices of Zeklinski Enterprises. Others hidden from his view bore witness to the removal of the huge sign with the once-proud family name.

Igor Potowski exulted as he watched. Once he had been a respected barge builder, member of the Guild, a fine upstanding citizen. But Dov Zeklinski drove him into bankruptcy. Done in, he thought. *Parschivi Zhid!* Got what he deserved. They say the czar drove him out of the country.

Two other people had reason to remember Dov Zeklinski with hatred. Henriette and Rene DuBois never forgave Zeklinski for forcing them out of business years ago. They would have paid him back if only he'd given them a few more months' time. Their joy in watching the sign come down was dampened only by the despair they felt in their own hopelessness, for they never seemed to be able to save enough to return to their beloved France.

Misha Golanov watched with a heavy heart as the sign came down. He had returned to Kiev a wealthy man, thanks to Dov Zeklinski. His three married daughters had blessed him with ten grandchildren. He would grow old with dignity and with love surrounded by his fine family and his loving wife. He sorrowed for his friend Dov who would never know such peace.

He was startled out of his reveries by Igor Potowski, who slapped him heartily on the back. "So you're back, Misha. I hear you made a lot of rubles in Sebastopol."

"Didn't do badly, but now I'm retired."

"You didn't work for the Jew down there by any chance, did you?" Potowski asked suspiciously. "They say he had a shipyard there, but he lost it in the crash."

"I worked for von Hals Shipyards, Igor."

"Glad to hear it wasn't Zeklinski. Good Christians shouldn't be made to work for Jews. By the way, I don't blame you for buying me out when I went bankrupt. No hard feelings. Would have done the same to you. Business, eh? It was that Jew who done me in."

"You can't be sure of that, Igor."

"I'm sure all right. I wish I could spit on that sign, that's how sure I am. Zeklinski deserved what he got. I hear he converted. That true?"

"What of it?"

"Once a Jew always a Jew. He may be a Christian among his own people, but he'll never be a Christian among true believers."

"All water under the bridge, eh? Anyway, he no longer lives here."

Potowski shrugged. "You're right. How about a drink for old times' sake? I'll buy to celebrate Zeklinski's downfall."

"No thanks. I've no stomach for it just now."

Potowski wondered at the remark as he watched Dov's old friend walk slowly away. Then he shrugged and swaggered off to the tavern to tell all his friends a thing or two about that dirty Jew.

FIFTY-SEVEN

Count Petrov shook his head, in sadness. "Burned to the ground? The Razovsky estate? How could such a terrible thing happen?"

"The overseer beat one of the serfs to death and the others rebelled and took their revenge. They murdered him."

"Murdered the...what's this country coming to, Borschov? Serfs don't know their place anymore, I tell you!"

"The mob's still on a rampage, I'm afraid."

"How many of them are there?"

"There were twenty four hundred serfs on the estate, last I heard. At least half must be men."

"Are we in any danger here?"

"Not likely, sir. I have our own serfs well under control."

"Good! Send a messenger to warn the others nearby. If they're not in residence, warn their overseers. We'll need to stand together to stop the rabble. And hurry!"

Vassily Borschov did as he was told, and within two hours, seven estate owners and town officials were assembled in Petrov's study.

"This is a grave situation, gentlemen," Petrov began. "If we let the mob run wild, any one of us is liable to be next in line. It's my duty as Governor-General of Kiev to nip this conflagration in the bud. Any suggestions?"

"They're already running wild and that's not the worst of it. Looks like some of the townsfolk have joined them. There have been windows smashed and considerable looting already. They seem to want blood this time. Serfs out of control are dangerous enough, but when you add peasants out of work..." said one merchant.

"May I offer a suggestion?"

"My overseer, gentlemen. He may be able to help. He understands these people. Go ahead, Borschov. What do you suggest?"

"Why not try to divert the mob? The family hasn't occupied the Razovsky estate for years. Except for the overseer, poor man, no one was hurt. Perhaps we can get word to the ringleaders that the governor-general's office is prepared to forget the whole thing—no retaliation—if they cease right now."

"How do you propose to reach them?" one of the men asked.

"I have someone waiting outside. He has many friends. You know...other peasants. They trust him. He's willing to see what he can do. You know him, Count Petrov. He lives on your estate."

"Bring him in, then."

"Gentlemen, this is Igor Potowski. Tell them what you told me."

"Well, Your Highnesses...begging your pardon, Your Eminences. I think I can speak for the people, you understand. The men are angry because there's no work. And just before Easter. They blame the Jews, you see."

"The Jews? How's that, Potowski?"

He shuffled his feet and clutched his cap in his hand as he spoke. "Zeklinski Enterprises, Your Royal Highnesses. They say at the tavern that the Jew Zeklinski's responsible for the recession."

"Zeklinski? He's no longer here."

"Maybe not, but he started it, for sure! I have an idea that may put an end to it, before our whole city goes up in smoke."

"What do you propose?" asked Petrov.

"Zeklinski has an estate not far from the Razovsky property. Maybe we can satisfy the crowd's anger with just that one."

"That's a very dangerous game, Potowski. Who's to say we won't all lose our property if we agree to let them destroy one more?"

"Leave that to me, sir. I've known these people all my life, both serf and peasant. I know where the ringleaders are hiding. They'll listen to me because I'm one of them. I'm sure of it. Besides, I'll tell them that they have to stop after that one. Once they get it out of their system it will all be over and they'll go back to their homes if I give my word that they won't be punished."

"Is there anyone living at Zeklinski mansion other than the servants?"

"Zeklinski's wife and his son, I believe," answered Borschov.

"Madame Zeklinski? I know her. She and her son are not to be harmed, do you hear? Send someone to warn them to leave if we decide on this course of action, though it's a bad business, I must say. Not at all to my liking. I've no wish to hurt an innocent woman and her child. A little mischief's bad enough but we don't want dishonor by smearing the blood of innocent victims on our hands. Do you understand?"

"Of course, sir," answered Borschov. "I'll personally see to it at that the boy and his mother receive safe conduct."

"Good! In that case, wait outside, Potowski. We need to discuss this among ourselves first and then we'll let you know our decision."

⌘

The heated argument among the town fathers lasted till late in the afternoon. The men feared that a raging, out-of-control mob might not be willing to listen to reason. They weighed the idea of calling in government troops, but it was decided that the city might burn before such a rescue could be achieved.

"Let's not turn innocent serfs and peasants into brigands and murderers, gentlemen," said Count Petrov wearily. "I've no interest in seeing my property go up in smoke either. Let's give Potowski leave to tell the offenders we're prepared to forgive them, no questions asked, if they disperse peacefully after they have their bit of fun. I don't like it any more than you do, but what choice do we have? They're like naughty little children having a fit of temper."

In due time, the respected members of the town council agreed to follow Potowski's advice, because each man feared the loss of his own property, not to mention the loss of valuable runaway souls. As an added precaution, Count Petrov empowered Vassily Borschov to accompany Potowski to ensure that the rampage ended with the Jew's estate.

Thus, in the name of law, order and Mother Russia, the die was cast. Odd. Among the distinguished group of town fathers in the room that afternoon there were a number of men who were secretly relieved at the decision, for those noblemen still owed Dov Zeklinski money.

In fact, Benjamin Moskowitz had been after them to pay their debts—long overdue and with interest—to Zeklinski's wife. He'd even gone so far as to threaten to petition the chief magistrate. But when the Jews were driven out, who would dare recall such an insignificant fact?

⌘

Rumors raced through Kiev haphazardly, like random fallen leaves tumbling before gusty winds. When Misha Golanov heard that the rabble was heading toward the Zeklinski estate, he sent his son-in-law to warn Josef. By the time the young man reached him with the news, it was after noon.

"Thank your father-in-law for his warning," Josef said as he mounted his horse and sped toward the house.

"God be with you," said the man to Josef's receding form. He shook his head in remorse.

"Where's Madame Zeklinski, Boris?"

"I believe she's with the gardener in the potting shed. You look worried...what's wrong, Josef? Is there...?"

"And Kalman? Where is he?"

"He's staying with his aunt and uncle. What is it?" The old butler could not help but sense danger in Josef's urgency.

"Bad news. No time to talk. Get everyone out of the house. You too, Boris. Save yourselves. Take your things. Whatever you can carry. Send someone to spread the word. We've very little time left. There's a mob...serfs and peasants. They've already destroyed the Razovsky estate. They're coming this way."

"Sweet Jesus protect us! I'd...I heard something this morning, but I thought it was only a rumor. You know how the servants gossip. It's true then. They burned the Razovsky estate?" Josef nodded. "Then it's the end of this one, I'm afraid. Goodbye Josef. You've been good to us all. Go quickly! Find Madame Zeklinski and hide her. And tell her I am...deeply sorry. She's a decent woman and I will never forget her. Tell her my prayers go with her. Tell her I said that. May God go with you, too. Hurry!" Josef grasped the old man in a final embrace and raced off to find Miriam.

⌘

"What a surprise to see you here, Josef." Miriam smiled pleasantly when Josef found her in the greenhouse. "Let me just wash the soil off my hands."

"No time for that. Give me your hand. Quickly." He reached down and lifted her onto his horse. She sat behind him as he rode off to an abandoned tool shed far away from the main house. Then he told her what had happened at the Razovsky estate.

"We treat our serfs well, but a mob has its own rules. Golanov's son-in-law says they're bent on looting and destroying this estate. It no longer matters what the reason is, Miriam. I must get you away from here."

"What about my son? We must save Kalman. I can't lose him, Josef. What about Sophie and Benjamin and their children? What about the other Jews? Is it a *pogrom?*"

"I don't think so. I think everyone else will be fine. But you're in danger. You must hide under this canvas and stay hidden, do you hear? There's no telling what a wild mob will do. You mustn't show your face under any circumstances, all right? I'm going to get Kalman. I'll hide him at Misha Golanov's house. He'll be safe there. Then I'll come back for you." He hesitated for a moment.

"There's one more thing. I wouldn't ask if I didn't think it necessary, but..."

"What is it?"

"You can't remain in Kiev. Not safe. No telling what will happen. You and your son must leave the city, do you understand? I'll need some money for your passage. Do you have any? If it's in the house, tell me where I can find it."

"There's precious little money there. The harvest isn't in. Wait. I do have something." Miriam reached down to her hem and drew out the thin roll of muslin in which her diamonds were concealed.

"Here, Josef. Use these. There are five of them."

He removed one large diamond and returned the cloth that held the rest. "One should be more than enough. I'll ask Golanov to sell it for you. Put the others away and listen carefully. I've sent word to Golanov to try to arrange secret transport on a barge. You and your son may be able to leave late tonight if all goes according to plan."

Her heart pounded with fright. "And you, Josef? What will you do? After tonight, I mean."

"Don't worry. I'm safe enough here." He paused briefly. "Unless...would you like me to come with you?"

"Oh yes, Josef. Please come with us! I'm so afraid! I don't care about myself, but Kalman...what can a mere woman and a little boy do all alone? You love Kalman, don't you? Please. For his sake. Come with us. Protect us." The tears streamed down her face as she pleaded with him.

"I was hoping you'd ask, for I'd like nothing better. You saved my life once. You nursed me back to health." She wiped her tears with the back of a hand covered with soil and streaked her face.

"Go now, Josef. Hurry. You must save my son."

"Hide under this canvas and don't dare come out until I come back for you."

He arranged the filthy tarpaulin over her so it would look natural to the casual eye, then he raced off for the boy.

She lay still for what seemed like hours. When she heard the thundering sound of hoof-beats, coarse shouts and trampling feet pass dangerously close to the abandoned shed, her heart beat rapidly. She held her breath as they passed by, but no one entered the abandoned shed, to her great relief. She prayed that Josef would hurry back. What was taking him so long? Yet she knew it might be hours more before he would complete his desperate journey.

Her mind began to play cruel tricks, for she couldn't help but conclude that she was being punished anew for her sinful affair with Alexei Razovsky, for not being a good wife to Dov, for any wrong she could summon to mind. She prayed that her innocent little Kalman would not also be made to suffer for her terrible deeds. The intensity of her anguish wore her out after awhile, and she dozed fitfully.

Suddenly, the acrid smell of smoke roused her from sleep. She crept out from under the canvas fearing that the shed was on fire. The window in the unused shed was black with dirt and grime and she could see nothing through it. She pushed the door open carefully, for the smell of smoke seemed to be dangerously near. Satisfied that the shed was not on fire, she closed the door again.

They're probably burning the mansion down, she thought dully. Well, let them. Means nothing to me. Nothing. Brought me...brought Dov, brought us all...only misery. Might have been better off living in a poor Jewish *shtetl*. Won't miss this life at all, she thought defiantly as she crawled back under the canvas. Thank heaven no one saw me. Dear God, Josef. Hurry. Hurry.

Yet someone did see Miriam open the door of the shed after all. Unseen eyes. Perhaps the squeak of the rusty door made too much noise. Happenstance. If it had not been for those rusted hinges…

⌘

"Faster, Rene!" urged Henriette DuBois. "Upstairs! We must locate her chambers." The two ran ahead of the mob, searching from room to room. "Here. I'm sure of it. This must be hers. Shut the door. Shhh! Don't make so much noise, you idiot!" She ran to the dressing room and flung open the wardrobe doors.

"See? I was right. I certainly was right." Her eyes glittered in the dark like the eyes of a cat. "I recognize this gown! Ha!" She laughed bitterly. "Too bad the gown lasted longer than our fine business did, eh? Never mind. Help me find her jewels." The two ransacked each drawer and shelf in Miriam's chambers in a frenzy, upending bureau drawers in their wake.

"Over here, Henriette. I've found them! Here they are." She hurried to her husband's side. The brooch and earrings Dov had given his wife years before shimmered with light. "So, my pet. Your idiot is good for something, eh?"

"Good work, *mon cher*! They'll fetch a great many rubles. A great many rubles."

"Enough, do you think, to get us home to France?"

"More than enough. I'm sure of it. Thank God we won't have to spend another freezing winter in this barbaric country." A noise startled them from their pleasant reveries.

"Barbaric? Barbaric? What are you doing in our country, then? Who's to stop you from going back to your heathen homeland?" asked Igor Potowski, closing the door behind him. "And what are you hiding behind your back? Let me see!"

"It's…it's nothing," said DuBois. "Go about your business! My wife just wants some gowns she made for the Jew. That's all."

"Open your hands, DuBois! You Frenchies think you're so very clever, don't you? And you think us stupid. Barbarians, eh? Napoleon thought we were barbarians too, but we drove him and his army out of Russia, didn't we?" Potowski lunged forward and yanked at Rene Dubois' arms.

"Leave him alone, you dirty…peasant," Henriette shouted, and yanked the enemy's hair. "Fight, Rene! Those jewels belong to us! Fight, damn you!" Potowski was strong, yet Henriette scratched and clawed his back and yanked his hair, preventing him from concentrating his strength on her husband. They grunted and groaned and struggled on the floor in a desperate battle for the jewels.

None of them noticed in the heat of the battle, that tiny wisps of smoke seeped lazily through the bottom of the closed door.

Despite her efforts, Potowski succeeded in overpowering her husband. In one last desperate thrust, the burly barge builder applied all his strength and threw the Frenchman against the wall, knocking him unconscious.

"Now it's your turn, Madame Frenchie," he snarled, breathing heavily from the exertion.

"You'll have to kill me first, you wretch!" Henriette Dubois stuffed the jewels in the bosom of her dress with one hand and grasped heavy candelabra with the other.

"Kill you first? Suit yourself, mamoselle. You'll go the way of Napoleon's brave soldiers then." He stalked her menacingly around the room, panting and sweating. "Don't be foolish. Give me those jewels and tend to your weakling husband!"

"Never! Don't you take a step nearer or..."

"Or? Now, now, mamoselle. I thought you Frenchies were ladies. That's not ladylike..." He lunged at her and caught her wrist just as she raised the weapon to strike him. The force of his body threw her to the floor where they struggled for the prized jewels.

At almost the same moment, the two smelled the smoke of the fire. Henriette stopped abruptly, understanding at last.

"Stop, you fool! Can't you smell it? We'll all burn to death if we don't get out. Here, you greedy monster...you can have the Jew's filthy jewels! May you rot in hell with them!" She threw the jewel-encrusted brooch to the ground and raced to her husband's side.

"Get up, Rene! Please, *mon cher*. There's a fire," she pleaded.

"One brooch? Do you think you can fool me into settling for just one measly brooch? Zeklinski was richer than that! Where are all the others?" Potowski yanked her hair, spun her around and reached into the bosom of her dress.

"Now that your breasts are baptized by Russian hands you'll never want any other," he grunted in frenzy. Again they struggled while the large licks of flames began to dine on the silk fringes of the Oriental rug beneath their battling forms.

"Those jewels are mine, do you hear? That Jewish bitch owed them to me! For my work. Let go of me, you filthy beast!" She sank her teeth into his arm and he yelled in pain, yet he persevered, for the prize was too great to give up without a struggle.

One persistent tongue of flame grew rapidly as it fed on itself. It snaked its way to the dressing table where the skirt caught fire. At once, the sinuous red and gold stripes of fire ruptured into a roaring flame, causing the heavy damask drapes to smolder.

Neither Potowski, who by now had shredded the bodice of Madame Henriette's shabby dress, nor the lady herself, who fought back with the strength of a wounded tiger, took any notice of the flames. All at once, the jewels came apart in the contest and the pieces rolled in a different directions. The sensuous flames began to caress the unconscious Rene's clothing as the heedless adversaries scrambled for the scattered stones, but it was too late. For all of them.

The charred jewels survived, but their glory was destined to be buried in the debris for centuries, well hidden from human eyes under the ashes of the once magnificent Zeklinski Estate.

⌘

Miriam heard the creak of the door and threw the canvas back. "Thank God you're back, Josef," she whispered with relief, but there was no answer. "Josef?" she asked the darkness, squinting to make out the figure.

"No, Madame," a familiar voice answered from the shadows. "Yet, like him, I was your overseer once." He reached for a discarded axe handle and smashed the window nearest him.

"Borschov? Dear God!" she screamed in terror.

"That's better. Now I can see you in the light of the moon. So romantic in the moonlight, eh? Stand up!" he ordered harshly, but she lay frozen in fear. "Stand, I said!" He reached down and yanked her to her feet.

"Where's all your haughtiness now, Madame Zeklinski? Eh? Answer me!" She said not a word. "So. You tremble in fear, do you? Good. I like that. Really I do. That's very good. Once you thought you were better than me, didn't you? Didn't you?" Her knees gave way, but his angry hands clasped her shoulders and forced her to stand erect.

"Please, Vassily..."

"Sir! You will address me as 'sir,' you Jewish whore! Say it!"

"Sir. Please...sir. I'm a...mother..." she begged. "For my son's sake...don't harm..."

"Harm? Harm? Why would I want to harm such a lovely little morsel? They call you Razovsky's whore. Did you know that? Razovsky had his way with you, didn't he? Well? Didn't he? Answer me, you slut!"

"Please, Va...sir. He's dead. What difference...?"

"I saw you once. Years ago. Right after your lover shot himself. You wept at his grave. How touching! Such devotion. You won't be able to do it again, I'm afraid. His tomb is no more. The mob tore it apart and scattered what was left of his bones to the winds." She tried to struggle.

"Keep still, whore!" he snarled. "How was it with the count? Did you like it? I'll wager you did. I'll wager you thought you had finally found a man, didn't you? Yet you were wrong. He wasn't a real man. He was a drunkard and a whoremaster and a gambler! Nor was your mealy mouthed husband a real man. I hear they cut a piece of his thing off. Happens to all Jews, they say. I guess that means he never managed to fill you with his little...no. How could he, with such a short...Jews cut a piece off, don't they? Answer me, you bitch! Don't they?"

"What...what do you...want me to say?"

"Say yes."

"Y...ye...yes."

"Louder."

"Yes."

"That's better. Once more. Say yes, sir. Say it loud."

"Yes, sir."

"Now Madame High and Mighty, I'll show you what a real man can do! Who knows? You might even like it. Even beg for more."

Miriam clutched his arms in a despairing burst of strength and pleaded with him. "Please, Vassily! Please, sir. Let me go. Don't do this terrible thing! I'll...I'll give you...everything I have. You'll be a rich..."

"What you think you have to give is already up in smoke, my dear. What would I be able to do with a few charred sticks? Your grand mansion is no more, I'm afraid. All you have left is the clothes on your back."

"No, Vassily. Sir. I have...something else. Of great value. Let me go and I'll...I'll give it all to you. Everything! Please. For my son's..."

"All right, Madame," he answered with a smirk. "A fair bargain, so long as you're not lying to me, that is. What have you to trade for your...doubtful honor?"

Miriam reached for her hem with fingers that trembled like leafless branches quivering in the wind. She ripped the thin roll from her hem and the diamonds fell loose on the canvas. "You can have these. They're worth a fortune."

He picked up the radiant stones and examined them in the moonlight, one by one. Then he stuffed them into the pocket of his trousers. "Very kind of you. Yes, indeed. Most generous. I thank you, Madame. For your thoughtfulness." In a sudden, swift movement that caught Miriam unawares, he pulled her to him and pressed his mouth cruelly against hers. She struggled in vain, for his strength was overpowering.

"That was to thank you for the pretty baubles, Madame. Did you like my kiss? I'll wager you did. A kiss of a real man, eh? Say you liked it. Say it." He yanked her hair and forced her to look at him.

"Yes."

Again his mouth came down hard and bruised her lips. "Say 'Yes, Vassily. I like your lovely kisses.'" She screamed in pain as he jerked her hair again.

"Dear God! You have the jewels. Let me go." For answer he slapped her hard across the face.

"Say it, or you'll have more of the same. But perhaps you like it? Did he slap you? Razovsky? Did it excite you? Say it, damn you. Say it."

"I...I..." She fell limp in his arms so that he had to hold her to keep her from falling.

"Ah. You play the game of fainting. So be it, Madame, but it won't change a thing. I'll have you anyway. My gift to you in return for your diamonds, eh?" He let her fall to the canvas where she lay in a heap while he removed his trousers.

"Wake up, Jew! I want you to enjoy your reward." He slapped her and shook her till she opened her eyes. They were filled with a skin-crawling fear. She lay there as if paralyzed, unable to move as his crude fingers ripped her bodice and exposed her breasts. "A pretty pair, Madame. Yes indeed. Perfect for a Jewish whore." He fondled one with his hand as his mouth slavered on the other. Miriam lay perfectly still, listening to his rapid breathing.

A curious serenity spread over her. She closed her eyes and began to recite the Lord's Prayer to herself. "The Lord is my...my shepherd; I shall not...want..."

His hands ripped at her skirts as she lay still, enveloped in peaceful equanimity.

"...I...I will fear no evil: for thou art with me..."

"How nice, Madame Zeklinski. You've given up the battle. You like it already. No more false modesty, eh? I knew it the first time I saw you. Men know when women want them. You lusted after me, didn't you? That's right. Enjoy it. At last you will have the pleasure of knowing how a real man feels inside your hot Jewish loins." Borschov ripped her undergarments away and bared her legs.

She couldn't remember when she began to scream. Was it when his body crushed hers? Or when he entered her? Or was it when she felt warm viscous blood bathing her face? Whose blood? Her blood no doubt, for surely, she was dying. Odd. She would have thought there would be more pain in dying.

Who was it covered her bare body? Someone...? Had Vassily consummated this union of hell? Had he covered her with his shirt and lifted her lifeless body in his arms? Was it all some sort of nightmare? Or perhaps...was she already dead?

"It's all right. Shhh," soothed Josef in a quiet voice meant to calm her. "You must stop your screaming, Miriam. Come. We can't stay here any longer. It's too dangerous. We have to go." Josef carried her to the door and opened it stealthily. He looked both ways to satisfy himself that they were alone before he carried her outside.

"It's Josef. You're all right now. But you must help me. Open your eyes." She opened her eyes and stared at him in a stupor. Unknowing. Uncaring. Listless.

"Listen to me. I'm going to put you on my horse now. You must help me by holding the reins tight. Don't be frightened. Please, Miriam. You mustn't fall off. There's not much time..." he pleaded. "Do you understand?" She nodded her head.

"Don't fall off! Please. I'll only be a moment. That's right. Sit up straight and hold the reins like this. I'll be right back."

Josef returned to the shed and doused the floor with a can of lamp oil his eyes had located earlier that day. He struck a match and threw it on the floor. When he raced back to Miriam, he was relieved to find her sitting erect and clutching the reins, but as he began to untie his horse, she began to scream once again.

"Shhh. We'll be discovered. You mustn't scream any..."

"The diamonds! I gave him the diamonds to try to stop him from...he has the other four diamonds."

"Where did he put them? Think hard! Try to remember! Exactly where did he put them?"

"I...I can't remember...yes! They're in his...his...trousers. That's where they are. He put them in his trousers."

"Don't let go of the reins," he ordered and ran back into the burning shed. He searched through the thickening smoke for the trousers. They had been discarded not far from the man whose skull he'd battered with the first object his eyes had fallen upon—the rusted blade of an abandoned axe. He glared at the dead man for a brief instant, noting with grim satisfaction that the flames had already begun to feed on him.

Josef Brodsky hissed the words through clenched teeth. "May you rot in Hell for your foul deed." He covered his head with Borschov's bloody trousers and ran through the rapidly spreading wall of flame to safety.

FIFTY-EIGHT

Misha Golanov embraced Miriam at the wharf. She was clad in a peasant's dress and a babushka to conceal her identity. His daughter had provided the coarse clothing. "God go with you, Madame Zeklinski. Accept a miserable peasant's apology for the shameful acts of his countrymen."

She swallowed hard. It was clear that her words took considerable effort. "Thank you, Misha. Goodbye. God keep you and yours."

Golanov signaled to the barge captain to help her aboard and when she was safely on, he turned to Josef. "See that no further harm comes to Madame and the boy. They didn't deserve this terrible tragedy, did they?" His unashamed tears flowed freely.

"Farewell, Misha. You're a decent man. God bless you." Josef hesitated and searched the older man's eyes. "We never had time for good fellowship, did we? Perhaps in another life, but your good deeds will never be forgotten." He embraced the man and stepped onto the barge.

Misha Golanov, his heart weighed down with sorrow, watched the ponderous craft disappear into the morning mist of dawn.

The barge captain hugged the shoreline to remain hidden from view as long as possible, yet Miriam refused to hide despite Josef's urging, preferring instead to view the landscape in grim silence.

She noted the gaping space on the grimy white waterfront office building where once the proud sign, **ZEKLINSKI ENTERPRISES**, proclaimed its triumphant dominion. The huge empty rectangle glared back at her in silent witness, like the mouth of some brutal gargoyle meant to swallow her.

Her eyes fell on the second story windows where she had witnessed Catherine II enter the city in triumphant splendor; where three months later, she had witnessed the czarina depart in a sumptuous galley built with pride by Misha Golanov for Zeklinski Enterprises.

She reflected on the irony of her life in Kiev. *I was full of wonder then, like a...a princess in some ancient tale. The riches of empire come to pay homage to their sovereign. Persians, Turks, Uhlans, Cossacks—they colored the streets of*

Kiev in their jewels and their turbans and their sabers. Did I really suppose it was meant for me?

In the dawn light, the parade marched with brutal clarity before her eyes once again. What? She thought. No orchestras for my departure? No archbishops to bless my safe journey to the southern provinces? No fancy escorts? No cheering peasants? How odd. The taste of acid befouled her mouth. The more fool I for thinking I belonged. A harsh laugh, more like the sound of a frog's croak, escaped her lips.

"What is it? What's wrong?" Josef asked.

"I just thought of something...too funny. Imagine that. I too, had an escort out of Kiev, so to speak. Just like Czarina Catherine." She tried to laugh again, but a sob strangled her.

"Don't torture yourself. You're upsetting Kalman. He doesn't understand. Don't let him hear you say such terrible things. Not now. Time enough for that later."

"Whatever you say, Josef," she answered, the vision at once gone. She leaned her head on his shoulder, exhausted, but something caught her attention.

"Those billows of black smoke. It's the Zeklinski estate, isn't it?"

"Yes, but you have more important things to think about now," he hesitated.

"What is it?"

"The captain says he can only take us as far as Kaidak. That's the first of the Dniepr estuaries. No barge can manage the treacherous falls beyond that point. We'll have to decide what our final destination will be. Have you given any thought to it?"

"Oh yes."

"Where do you want to go?"

"To Odessa. I want to live near my sisters. They're all I have left now." She covered he face and began to sob.

"Shhh. It's all right. You're safe." He held her to him and rocked her in his arms as though she were a child, yet his own heart was near to shattering at her piteous grief.

When he'd quieted her down, he said, "Sophie and Benjamin Moskowitz told me they thought you'd would want to go to Odessa. I think it's a good idea, but we'll have to continue to travel on foot as peasants, Miriam. I can get by with my army papers, but..."

"What is it?" she asked in agitation.

"Benjamin had the foresight to have false papers drawn up for you and for Kalman. We used your maiden name, just in case..."

She looked at him quizzically. "Why?"

"You won't be questioned that way. The papers say you already live in Odessa, do you see? And I am going there because I own a plot of land the government awarded me when I was discharged from the army."

⌘

They reached her sisters in Odessa in the sweltering heat of August. During their inland journey, Miriam grew more and more despondent as the days went by, barely responding to Josef's or to Kalman's questions.

When they arrived in Odessa, Josef said, "I can't tell you what a relief it is to be here at last." Bela, the older twin, had made room for Miriam and Kalman, while Josef slept at Bluma's house just across the road.

"Your sister's ill. She's been through...hell." He told them what had happened, to spare Miriam the pain of reopening old wounds later. He told them everything, that is, but the details of her ordeal in the abandoned shed.

"Dov a...a...convert? His grandfather would spin in his grave if he knew. So would his father. So would my parents, may they rest in peace. Hard to believe," said Bela.

"You were wise to bring her here, Josef. We'll take care of her," added Bluma. "And you're welcome to live with Aaron and me for as long as you like. We're very grateful to you. You're one of the family now."

"That's kind of you, Bluma." What a terrible way to gain a family, he thought unhappily.

"Bela dear," said her husband Moses, "...why don't you ask your cousin Malke to seek Samuel's advice to help your sister?"

"All right. First thing tomorrow." She turned to Josef. "We've had a letter from Sophie and Benjamin. It came just yesterday. They're planning to move here as well."

"I'm not surprised," Josef answered. "I had a feeling this terrible business would hurt the other Jews in Kiev."

"She writes that the governor general of the Mogilev oblast is threatening to double the taxes, but only for Jews. Those who can afford it are leaving."

"The governor general? That would be Count Petrov. He was once an acquaintance of the Zeklinskis." He shook his head in sadness. "What else does she say?"

"She writes that Kiev has only bitter memories for them now and they're determined to come live near all of us."

"Miriam will be pleased to hear it, I'm sure."

Yet nothing roused Miriam, not even the news of Sophie and Benjamin's decision. She spent her days in bed, staring at the ceiling. Samuel gave her powders to sleep, powders to stimulate her appetite, powders reputed to cure her malaise. Yet none of them helped. Even the sight of Kalman brought no response.

She languished through empty days and nights, losing weight, not caring whether she lived or died. Her sisters pleaded with her to eat. They begged her to get up and dress. They implored her, if only for Kalman's sake, to renew her interest in life.

The doctor visited and prescribed bleeding to cure her. The rabbi visited and said a prayer. Her sisters heated cups to draw the sickness from her emaciated body. Wizened men and women with reputations as magical healers visited, not a few with ointments and healing salves, but she did not respond.

Josef managed to find employment at a shipyard on the Odessa waterfront and rented a room nearby, so as not to be a burden to Bluma and her husband Aaron. Every evening after dinner he came to see Kalman and Miriam. He'd play with the boy a bit and tell him a bedtime story. Then he'd sit by Miriam's bedside.

Fall leaves turned bright red. Pale yellow. Deep gold. But Miriam took no notice. Kalman brought home excellent reports from school, which brought a wan smile to her face. Then she sent him off to play with his cousins.

November chilled the air and her condition worsened. When the weather permitted, Josef took to carrying her outside to feel the sun on her face, if only to stimulate her appetite. She did as she was told without complaint, yet she grew alarmingly thin, for she managed to swallow only the barest amount of food, no matter how hard they all begged.

On the surface, Miriam appeared to cooperate with Josef and her family. Yet there was one thing she did not have the courage to tell her loved ones. She was waiting to die. Retribution for her sins. Now that Kalman was safe with her sisters, there was no reason to go on with the charade called life. She made her way through listless days, one exactly like the other, without energy, without complaint, fervently praying the pain within her would end and that she would not wake the next morning.

The skeletal form of her friend horrified Sophie when she and her family arrived shortly after the New Year. "My God, Miriam. What have you done to yourself? Why aren't you eating? The twins are frantic. Don't you dare turn your head to the wall! Look at me. Well? Answer me."

"I suppose I can tell you, Sophie, but you mustn't tell my sisters. I'm dying."

"What on earth are you talking about? You're a fool. You'll do no such thing if I have anything to say about it! Not on your...never mind! What you will do now that I'm here is get busy and start living again, do you hear? Sit up," she ordered.

"I can't. I'm too weak."

"Sit up, I said. Let me comb your hair. You're a fright."

"Don't, Sophie dear. Don't trouble yourself. Leave me be, if you love me. Just leave me be. It doesn't matter. Can't you see that?" Sophie had to strain to hear her frail voice.

"Dying? Leave you be? Why you foolish, self-indulgent, ungrateful...is that how you repay the people who love you? By starving yourself to death right before their very eyes? And what of your son? Don't you see how selfish you're being?"

"My sisters will care for him when I am gone. They're so good to him."

"Your sisters are frantic with worry, you miserable, heartless creature. Look at you. Even a skeleton looks healthier. I didn't give up my home in Kiev just to come down here to watch you waste away. Not on your life. The misery party's over, Miriam. You're not going to die if I have anything to say about it. Just you wait and see." She stalked out of Miriam's room in a fury and made straight for the drawing room, where the twins were waiting.

"See to it that everyone's here tonight after dinner." Sophie demanded. "We'll all have to help Miriam snap out of this...this sickness. She's preparing to die. She told me so just now. But we're not going to let her wish come true. Not if I have any say in the matter."

Sophie took charge like a general on the battlefield that night. "Well? Do any of you have a better solution, or do we just sit and watch her die? How about you, Samuel? Any more magic powders in your bag of tricks?"

"I resent that, Sophie," Malke said hotly. "Samuel's tried his very best to help her. He's the finest apothecary in Odessa."

"Oh be quiet, Malke! Stop jumping to Samuel's aid. I'm not faulting him. I'm not faulting anybody. But we have to do something." Sophie glared at each one in turn.

"We try, Sophie. Bluma holds her and I try to feed her, but she gags and she doesn't swallow. Only a little soup, maybe."

"I know she's been through hell. We all know that. But that's beside the point. Stop begging her to eat. You too, Josef. You must all stop treating her like a helpless child. Let her learn to want to live again." The silence was thunderous.

"It's worth a try," said Bela's husband Moses.

"Why not?" added his cousin Aaron, for the two men were very close and tended to think alike, just as their wives did. "Nothing else seems to work."

"What do you think, Samuel?" asked Malke. "After all, Samuel knows more about these things than anyone in this room, including you, Sophie." She sniffed to signal her disapproval.

"It can't do any harm," he answered.

Sophie glared at Malke in triumph. "What about you, Josef?"

He took what seemed an eternity to frame his answer. "Two weeks, Sophie. Try it for two weeks. No more than that."

"Two weeks should be long enough. If we can't pull her out of it by then, we'll have to leave her fate in God's hands, come what may. Here's what we'll do."

Battle plan in place, Sophie sent Kalman to live across the road with his Aunt Bluma. She ordered Bela to bring Miriam a tray and leave it in her room, but she had to remove it precisely one hour later, regardless of whether or not Miriam had eaten.

Miriam would have to ask for food if she grew hungry between meals. Her sisters were admonished not to go near her—not even to visit. The tactic Sophie counted on to pry her friend loose from her death-like malaise was to force Miriam to abandon her wish to die.

"I warn you, Sophie," said Josef. "Only two weeks. Miriam isn't strong enough to endure more than that."

FIFTY-NINE

Every night the family gathered to discuss Miriam's progress, rejoicing at the description of each new morsel she'd helped herself to, and despairing when she refused to eat. On the evening the first day, Bela reported that Miriam had eaten a few bites of bread and sipped a little sweet tea.

"That's all?"

"It's only the first day. Don't worry so much, Josef. We won't let her starve," Sophie asserted with a certainty she did not feel, praying all the while that she would be proven right.

On the eve of the third day, Bela reported that Miriam had helped herself to a few spoonfuls of soup, half a slice of bread, and a morsel of chicken. "She asked about Kalman today. I told her he was studying at Bluma's house."

On the fifth day, Bela reported that Miriam asked where Josef had gone to, and on the sixth day she asked after Sophie.

"She's breaking my heart," said Bela. "My poor sister looks worse than a scarecrow. She's lost so much weight and she's so weak. She hasn't washed or combed her hair...I don't know how much more of this I can stand, Sophie."

"Bluma, why don't you serve her this week? Let's give your sister a rest," said Sophie, relenting a bit.

"Of course. Don't cry, Bela."

On the thirteenth day of her scheme meant to shake Miriam from her dangerous torpor, Sophie asked, "What have you to report, Bluma?"

"She ate everything tonight. There wasn't a crumb left on her dinner tray."

"Did she ask for more?"

"No, but..." Bluma hesitated.

"What?"

"She asked to see Josef. Four times she asked where he was and why he didn't come to see her any more."

"She did?"

"Yes. When I brought her a dinner tray..."

"You didn't give her anything special, did you?"

"Well, a little extra soup..."

"Bluma! You promised."

"What could it hurt, Sophie? Just a little clear chicken soup, that's all."

"All right. Tell me everything she said."

"She just asked, `Where's Josef?' That's all."

"She didn't ask for Kalman?" Bluma shook her head. "All right. Prepare her breakfast tray tomorrow morning, but don't you dare bring it to her. Let's see if we can force her out of bed." The twins exchanged doubtful glances.

"She's ready, don't you see? Besides, tomorrow's our last day. Send your husband and children to Bluma's house for the day. I'll be here first thing in the morning. All right?"

When Miriam woke, she scratched her unwashed head furiously. She lay there for a time, staring at the ceiling, but she was forced to use the chamber pot. Hunger pangs gnawed at her. As usual, she ignored the washbasin. She searched for her breakfast tray in vain.

Too early for breakfast, she thought, shuddering in the bitter February cold. Doesn't matter. Even Josef doesn't bother to come to see me any more. He knows I'm being punished for my sins. The twins probably know, too. Won't even bring my son here to see his worthless mother. Just as well. They'll take good care of Kalman. No food today. They must want me to die now. Get rid of me. I'm such a nuisance.

Yet hunger assailed her until she could no longer focus on her familiar litany of self-flagellation. Her mouth dried as she waited.

Is this the day I die? Most likely. So quiet in the house today. They all went away so I could die. She folded her hands on her chest and assumed the position of the dead, as if in a coffin. But her hunger pangs would not subside.

Better go down and see if anyone's here. Just to be sure. She rose unsteadily and struggled into her robe. She had to hold on to the wall for support because she felt light-headed. The latch gave her trouble, but at last she managed to open it. She walked to the head of the stairs and held on to the railing to keep from falling. She heard no noise, which confirmed her notion that she'd been left to die. Hunger raged within her as she almost crawled, step by step, down the stairs.

"Hear that noise? Must be Miriam. Don't make a sound." Sophie's eyes gleamed with hope. "Remember what I said. Let her be the first to speak."

Miriam leaned against the open parlor door and smiled wanly. "I...I didn't think anyone was home..."

"Hello, Miriam," said Sophie. Her warning glance kept the twins silent, but she was just as appalled at the sight before her as they were.

"I...I couldn't..find..."

"Come sit next to me." Sophie's tone gentled. Her friend's wretchedness nearly destroyed her resolve, for Miriam's face was like a death mask in its pallor.

It was smudged with dirt and her lackluster eyes were piteous to behold. Dull, unkempt black hair fell in wild disarray. Like a child, she obeyed Sophie and sat next to her. No one spoke, yet tension filled the air.

"I'm hungry," Miriam admitted.

"What would you like to eat?" asked Sophie.

"Oh...anything."

"You'll have to decide, Miriam. What is it you want to eat?"

Her dry mouth and complaining stomach forced her to speak.

"A...a little...tea?" She paused. "And...and bread? Do you have any fruit? Is that all right? Is it...allowed?"

Sophie's eyes blazed in triumph as Bela raced to the kitchen.

The three watched in silence as Miriam devoured every crumb. She ate with her hands, as though she were a starving animal who hadn't eaten in weeks. By the time she finished, her face was covered with preserves.

Sophie handed her a napkin. "Feel better?"

"It was...tasty." She looked from one to the other. "Where's...?"

"Where is who?" prodded Bela.

"Are you...is he...Kalman?" she mumbled, casting her eyes downward.

"Would you like to see your son?"

"Is it allowed?" Miriam's mind spun in confusion.

"Yes, dear," Sophie answered. "Kalman's at Bluma's house. Just across the way. But you don't want him to see you looking the way you do. You'll frighten him. You'll have to wash yourself and you'll have to dress...what is it?" Sophie asked in alarm, for tears had begun to streak Miriam's grimy face.

"Sophie?" Miriam leaned her head back and squeezed her eyes shut, but the tears stung just the same.

"What?"

"Sophie?" She looked around her. "Bela? Bluma?"

"What is it, Mirele?" asked the twins in one voice.

"I...I...I don't want to...to die," she wailed.

"Say it again, Miriam. We can't hear you. Go ahead, darling. Say it," urged Sophie.

"I...don't...want...to...d...die," she cried, rampant tears rolling down her unwashed cheeks.

SIXTY

Her ordeal was over. The sweetness of life flowed back into her veins. Miriam had regained the will to live, bathed in loving family waters. Slowly, to be sure, but it was there, that primal need to endure. It was there just the same. It wasn't easy at first, yet her admission that she wanted to live, once voiced, had a life force of its own.

Kalman once again filled her with his love and his boyhood curiosity. Josef steadied her with his serenity. Sophie helped her to fathom the monstrous malaise within her soul that nearly destroyed her.

Weeks later, Sophie said, "You made life hell for yourself, didn't you? No, no. Don't protest. You did it. No one else, do you see? But now that's all in the past. You must keep it there."

"I don't know, Sophie. Sometimes, I wake in the middle of the night...and I'm drenched to the skin. I sweat with fear when I remember..."

"No one expects you to forget the horror. How can you? But those terrible memories will lose their sting as time wears on. I promise you that, but you've got to help them to disappear."

"But...how? God must have sent you to help me want to live, Sophie dearest, for I'd forgotten how. Help me. What must I do?"

"For one, you must learn to take care of yourself. I'm a good cook. They say I make the best *challah* and honey cake in all of Russia. Let me teach you how."

Miriam laughed. "I've never cooked a day in my life. Do you really think I can learn?"

"Of course. And you must let your sisters teach you how to sew. They're both wonderful with a needle, you know."

"Sew? Cook? Bake? Is that what you mean? Keep busy? Yes, of course! Why didn't I think of that myself?"

"That's the idea. The business of life, as they say, is made up of small things. Take up playing the piano again."

"Good idea." She frowned.

"What?"

"There's something else I want to do."

"What's that?"

"I want to learn to be a good Jew all over again. I've forgotten how, it's been so long, but I want that more than anything. I want to go to synagogue. I want to observe the *Shabbos*. I want to light candles again every Friday night. I want to go to the ritual bath—*mikveh*—every month and have my head shaved, my nails trimmed. I never allowed it, you know. I never allowed them to shave my head because I didn't believe it was necessary for a modern Jewish woman to shave her head. *Haskalah* was only an excuse for my vanity. But now, I owe it to God to follow His law. He must have had some...some higher purpose in mind for me, don't you think? I was so close to death, wasn't I? I felt it, you know. I really felt death upon me."

"No matter, Miriam. So long as you're well now. All right. We'll join the sisterhood together, God help us. Your twin sisters will, too. We'll all become the holiest of *rebbitzens*," she laughed, and paused for thought. "There's one more thing you need to do."

"What's that?"

"It's...Josef."

"Josef? What about him? I don't understand."

"Are you blind?"

"Blind? What on earth are you driving at? Of course I notice Josef. He's here every night, isn't he? I owe him my life. I owe him my son's life, too. I'll never forget what he did. You know that. He's a dear friend to me."

"What makes you think he wants to remain just a...friend?"

"What are you trying to say? Out with it, Sophie, for heaven's sake. It's not like you to hold back your thoughts."

"Don't you know? Open your eyes, Miriam. We all see it. Me. Benjamin. The twins. Moses and Aaron. Even Malke, when she can tear her mind away from promoting her husband's very important position as 'Holy Apothecary' for the city of Odessa," she said with scorn. Miriam laughed at the barb.

"What is it you all see that I don't see? What am I missing?"

"Search your soul and you'll find the answer."

"Stop playing games," Miriam pleaded in exasperation. "If I knew what you were driving at I wouldn't be asking, would I?"

"All right. Let me tell you what's clear to all of us. He loves you, Miriam. I suspect he's loved you for a long time. And it's more than just the love of a friend, I'd say, from the way he looks at you. He's smitten. You didn't see his face during the two weeks it took to shock you out of your misery. If ever a man..."

"How can that be? Why, we're just good friends, Sophie. He's like a...a brother to me."

"Brother? Brother, indeed. You really are blind, if that's what you think. But perhaps you don't love him the way he loves you. More's the pity, my friend. There's a man for you. And his only ambition is to make you happy, from the look of things."

Miriam pictured Josef in her mind. Josef? Loves me? Impossible. Why? Doesn't he know? How...how unworthy I am? He's so...fine. Decent. Kind. Dare I think of him like that? As a...a lover?

Visions of that cruel night in the shed caused her to shiver. Could she ever love that way again after that night? The idea made her skin crawl. Yet if it were...Josef? Gentle Josef, whose strong hands had rescued her?

"No, Sophie. I've burdened him enough. He deserves better than me. Please don't ask me to explain. Not now. Maybe someday I'll be able to tell you..."

Sophie erupted in anger. "Why tell me? Tell Josef Brodsky. Tell that wonderful man you don't want his attentions. Tell him to stop loving you. You're such a fool, Miriam. Why can't you see that he doesn't want anyone but you? Why else would he spend every night here? You were so intent on destroying yourself, you never thought to ask how the rest of us felt. Josef suffered the most let me tell you. Benjamin and I have suspected it for years. Your sisters see it. Their husbands see it. Even high and mighty Malke sees it."

Miriam sighed. "I seem to have a knack for destroying everything I touch. What if I destroy him, too? Like...Dov? Look what I did to Dov." And look what I did to Alexei, she thought, but she kept that pain to herself.

"Destroy Dov? You have it all wrong. He destroyed himself, so you'd better stop taking all the blame. Let it go. Dov Zeklinski or whatever he calls himself now, will have to answer to God when his time comes."

"You're wrong, Sophie. I helped in Dov's destruction just the same. I was vain and arrogant, just like him, and it led to our undoing. How can you ask me to burden Josef with my sins? That...saintly man? Besides, I...I don't know if I have it in me to love again. I'm not sure I have anything left to give. I'm empty, don't you see?"

Sophie changed her tack and asked her next question with tenderness, for Miriam was growing agitated. "Will you promise me something?"

"If...if I can, Sophie. What is it?"

"Think about what I said. Don't run away from Josef's love. You need him more than you know, but he needs you, too. Promise me you'll open your eyes and try to let go of the past."

"Is that possible? I wake up in the middle of the night and relive the nightmare. Every night! The...the terror. The burning. The smell of ashes still stings my nostrils. I can still smell the fire...and the..." Borschov's brutality leaped at her. "I can still remember...our flight. I can still remember the fear. I want desperately to let go of the horror, but it doesn't seem to want to let go of me."

"You're like a tired old horse pulling a cart, seeing neither left nor right, afraid to look at anything but your next step lest you fall again. So what if you fall? Everyone falls. Life's full of falls. Take off the blinders, my friend." She paused, then added, "You're being selfish, you know."

"What do you mean?"

"What about Kalman? The boy needs a father."

SIXTY-ONE

The melting snows of winter turned the roads of Odessa into oozing, slippery mud. The city—in transition from a Turkish stronghold to a thriving Russian port—had not yet found time to pave its streets. March, that bragging, blustery month full of arrogant winds, brought with it moments of the gentle promise of spring.

In many ways, Odessa was a city more European in flavor than Russian. Greeks, Frenchmen, Englishmen, peasants and Jews were all drawn to its pioneering rusticity. The sought their fortunes in industry. Buildings rose overnight. Hotels. Theaters. Opera houses. Brothels. Gambling houses. The Russian Crown gave land away to all who promised development. Serfdom did not exist in Odessa, which pulsated with the lively spirit of a new frontier.

Despite the mud and the treacherous roads, Josef took Miriam riding whenever the weather permitted. He carried her over planks of wood to sidewalk cafes where they sipped hot chocolate and ate French pastries. They talked for hours on end.

He told her the brief details of his early life in the orphanage. His parents had died in a severe epidemic that swept away their little village in 1770. He told her of his days in the army and the purpose it had given to his life. He'd found a home among the men. They cared about him, his soldiers. It was the first time anyone ever took notice of him, he said.

She told him about the early days with Dov and of their quest to become part of the social fabric of Kiev. She confessed that she had doubts as to whether they would succeed on their course—*Haskalah*—but Dov held firm, and she had assumed that he was right.

They talked about everything under the sun, discovering one another, unraveling their lives bit by precious bit, as though each piece, each tale were part of some grand design. She came alive when he called upon her and was content when he left. There were even nights without nightmares.

And during the day when he was at work, she learned to cook and to bake under Sophie's skilled tutelage. She learned to sew from her sisters. She practiced the piano. She exulted in the thrill of creating something with her own hands. Something useful. Something necessary.

And always, there was Josef, gentle Josef, whose strong arms lifted her without effort in and out of the carriage, whose shy smile lit up his face as well as her heart, and whose touching devotion helped restore her near-shattered faith in herself.

Young Kalman responded well to his mother's recovery. She greeted him when he returned from school every day with some small surprise often made with her own hands. And in return, he showered her with pleasure. He was a joyous lad, full of energy, full of lively curiosity, and full of love.

As March gave way to April, Miriam busied herself with preparations for Kalman's twelfth birthday celebration. Bela and Bluma supervised the cooking for the family gathering, but she insisted upon baking the cake herself, with a little help from Sophie. The empty pit within her, which lay for so long like some abandoned mineshaft, began to fill with love and rejuvenate her spirit. It was good to be alive after all.

On the day of Kalman's birthday, the family swore that Miriam's cake was delicious. Josef's gift to Kalman was a tree house he had built in Bela and Moses Teitelbaum's yard, to the delight not only of the boy, but also of his many young cousins. Aaron Teitelbaum produced the sweet wine he had made in his cellar with malaga grapes, and they celebrated all day long. Everyone except Malke, who felt put out at the family's lack of attention to her, though Samuel murmured his approval when he was sure that his wife was out of earshot.

"Malke may not agree, but I've always suspected that love is good medicine for some ailments," Samuel said to Sophie, to her great satisfaction.

"You're right Sophie. My mother would have called you a witch," Miriam laughed some weeks after the party.

"Of course I'm right. I'm always right, but you'll have to refresh my memory. What am I right about this time?"

"About Josef."

"I wish Benjamin would look at me the way Josef looks at you," Sophie laughed. "He loves you. It's written all over him. And why not? You're a good woman. This is your second chance. God-given, perhaps. Make the most of it."

"I'm going to, Sophie. I've made up my mind to do just that."

⌘

They strolled along the waterfront on the Black Sea. "Are you happy, Josef?"

"When I'm with you I'm happy. It pleases me to see you well again."

"I've never thanked you, have I? No, don't protest. Let me say what I feel in my heart. You saved my life. I wanted to die that night in the tool shed. In fact, I yearned for death. It was awful. I felt so...profaned...so violated...when that monster touched me. I thought my life was over. I felt as though God meant to punish me...for all my sins."

"Sins? What sins? You're too good a person. I can't believe..."

"You don't know me well, Josef. I'm touched by your faith, but I've sinned mightily. Yet it all seems so far away now. Another lifetime." They walked quietly for a time. The wind was still and for once, the black dust, blanketing the city with grime, did not sting the eyes. "Something plagues me, Josef."

"What is it?"

"Borschov. You killed him to save my life. Will the authorities ever find out and punish you for it? It frightens me to think his death will come back to haunt you one day."

"No, Miriam."

"How can you be so sure?"

"Golanov and his sons took care of it for me."

"How?"

He hesitated. "I don't think you need to know that."

"Tell me, Josef. I'm strong enough now."

"When I told them what I did to save you, they risked their lives by moving his charred body to the main house. When the authorities found his remains, they ruled that Borschov was murdered by one of the rampaging serfs. They never did find out who did it. Golanov sent me the clipping from the *Kiev Sentinel*. So you see, there's no need to worry."

For a time, they watched the sea in silence. "I love the smell of the sea air. Somehow, it renews me," she said at last. "Makes me feel...alive. God's design. Odd. That He permits me to enjoy it again."

"He forgives our transgressions. Perhaps it's time for you to forgive yourself."

"Forgive...myself?"

"Yes. Throw the weight of your sins in the Black Sea on *Rosh Hashonah*," he said, referring to the Jewish New Year. "Begin the year with a clean slate."

"Josef?" She hesitated. "Do you really think God forgives? Everything? Even the most horrid...?"

"Of course." He smiled at the hope he heard in her voice. "It is written in the scriptures."

She sat in the Odessa Synagogue in the place set aside for women. Her sisters, her cousin Malke, and Sophie sat with her, while Josef and Kalman prayed with the other men. A curious peace descended upon her as she listened to the ancient liturgy. The cantor's haunting voice raised her flesh when he sang the Hebrew refrains of the *Rosh Hashonah* services. Her heart was full at the sound of the *shofar*, the ram's horn, which signaled the beginning of the Jewish New Year. *Rosh Hashonah* was followed by the eight Days of Repentance, a ritual celebrated by Jews everywhere.

227

Josef's words did not leave her mind. She walked to the water's edge with the rabbi and the congregation and repeated the ancient prayers, full of hope, full of faith. And then she threw her sins into the sea.

On Yom Kippur eve, she listened to the beautiful chants of *Kol Nidre*. The plaintive melody filled her with serenity, its ancient Hebrew words holding new meaning for her. It purified her soul.

> *"For the sin we have committed before thee by unchastity;*
> *And for the sin we have committed before thee in presumption...*
> *For the sin we have committed before thee by evil inclination;*
> *For all these, O God of forgiveness, forgive us, pardon us, grant us remission."*

At the conclusion of the High Holy Days when the sun went down, the ram's horn sounded its mournful, bleating wail.

"Happy..."

"...New Year," the twins said in unison.

"*L'shana Tova*! May you be written in the Book of Life, for a year of peace and prosperity," said Sophie.

"Happy New Year, son," Miriam said. "Next year when you pray with Josef and your uncles, you'll be a man. You'll be thirteen in April and we'll celebrate your *Bar Mitzvah*."

After they broke the fast with the entire family, Josef asked, "Would you like to go out riding? I want to show you something, but if you're too tired, it can wait..."

"I'd love to ride out tonight." The two slipped away, not unnoticed, as Sophie and her two sisters exchanged conspiratorial nods.

"Where are we going?"

"You'll see." He stopped in front of a weed-filled, empty field, well lit by a full moon and a clear sky. There were houses scattered here and there, but open space abounded.

"What is this place?"

"It's my land. The government gave it to me when I was discharged from the army."

"Oh yes. I remember. You told me that you had land in the southern provinces. I didn't know that it was right here in Odessa. What are you planning to do with it?"

"I'm planning to build a house on it."

"That's nice."

"Not just for myself, I hope."

Her heart quickened as she guessed his meaning. "Who else are you building it for?"

"For you, too. I...I love you, Miriam. I want you to...to be my wife. I'm not a rich man, but I can take care of you and Kalman. I wish I had more, but all I have to offer you is myself."

"All? All? Look at me, Josef Brodsky," she chided, "...don't ever say `all!' You're a prince of a man, do you hear? One of God's finest creations. You're a splendid man. Will I marry you? God help you, for when I get my hands on you, I'll never let you go. Never! Marry you? What a foolish question. Of course, I'll marry you. I love you. I was beginning to wonder just how long it would take for you to get around to asking."

She put her arms around his neck and kissed him long and hard, her searching tongue probing his. She clung to him, unwilling to separate from the warmth of his embrace.

Finally, she pushed him away from her and said, "But first, you must hear me out, my darling. I want you to know everything about me. The bad as well as the good. All right?"

"What's done is done, Miriam. It doesn't matter to me. Your past is not important..."

"It matters to me, Josef. I won't live any more lies, do you see? You must know the truth. Please? It won't eradicate my sins, but if you still want me after...we'll start fresh."

She told him then about Razovsky and their year of passion. She told him all, from beginning to end. She left nothing out.

"I suspected about Razovsky. You were so devastated when he killed himself," he said when she had finished. "But it doesn't matter to me. I'm delirious with my own good fortune because you've agreed to marry me. That's what matters. Not your past. Besides, we all have our...sins."

"Surely not you?"

"Did you think I was a saint? I had a mistress in Kiev. A widow. She lived on your estate, in fact. Her children were already grown and married, so it was just the two of us. Her name is Katya. She moved in with me when I became your overseer."

"I'm glad for you, Josef, but if that was your only sin," her laughter interrupted her words, "...I happily forgive you. What happened to her? Did you have time to say goodbye?"

"Yes, of course, though I regretted the time it took when I found you with that...never mind. That's behind us now. I gave her every kopek I had in the world. She wished me Godspeed, fully understanding that it was meant to happen some day. A Jew and a Christian. It can't be permanent. Not in Russia. She said she'd go to live with her son and his wife. The money I gave her would go a long way toward easing their wretched lives."

"I feel sad for her, Josef, for losing you."

"Will you marry me in spite of it?"

"Name the day, my darling. I want to be your wife more than anything else in the world." It was his turn to kiss her. She drank his love as though she were a thirsty wanderer in an arid desert.

"You're a beautiful man, you are, my darling," she said at last.

"No. I'm as ugly as a scarecrow, as any fool can see."

"Oh, no! You're beautiful inside, where it counts. Your soldiers knew it. Kalman knows it. I know it. My family knows it and we all love you for it, but I love you most of all."

"I used to dream about you when I was in the army, and the dreams kept me warm during the bitter cold of winter."

"And my...sinful past?"

"Your past doesn't matter to me. Nothing matters except that you said yes tonight. I promise to try to make you happy. And I promise that, so long as I live, no one will ever hurt you again."

Her delighted laughter bubbled over until she had to gasp for breath. "I'm not making fun of you, Josef. It's just...I never thought...it's Dov. I'm very grateful to him."

"Grateful? For what?"

"For insisting on giving me a *get*—a divorce. I didn't care at the time, but to him it was a point of honor. If he hadn't, I never could have said yes to your proposal of marriage, could I?"

"He hurt you a great deal, didn't he?"

"We hurt each other. I was as much to blame as he was. Let's leave that story for another night, if you want me to bore you with it, that is."

⌘

By early December Josef completed the outside shell of the house with the help of hired hands. He worked evenings and Sundays to finish, for they had decided to marry in February. The plot of land lay mid-way between the homes of her twin sisters and Sophie's newly built home. Miriam's cousin Malke and her family lived above Samuel's apothecary in town.

Miriam wanted a simple home, one she could take care of herself, without servants. There were to be two chambers and a water closet upstairs, a tiny vestibule inside the front door just large enough to shed their winter clothing and a parlor and a dining room facing front on either side of the central hall. Behind the parlor and the dining room was to be a huge kitchen and a small library with room for a piano. Both the kitchen and the library faced the garden, with doors opening out to it. And tucked away in a corner of the garden, Josef had built himself a tool shed for his woodwork, for he was a gifted craftsman.

Every afternoon, Miriam visited her new home with either one or both of her sisters, and sometimes with Sophie or Malke. When the windows were finally in place, the twins helped her measure and sew the curtains herself. She marveled at her good fortune, half expecting to wake and find it all a dream. She felt so much richer now, though she couldn't help contrasting her elation now to the way she felt when she was Dov's wife.

Farewell to that foolish young girl I once was, she thought, full of joy. Another world. Better this time. We have only each other to please. Not all of Russia. She felt as though a veil had been lifted from her eyes. How could she have been so blind? How is it that she had never noticed the love in Josef's eyes? Sophie said it had always been there. Had it? No matter. Better to know it now than never to know it at all.

SIXTY-TWO

They were married on a Sunday morning in the middle of February, under the canopy of the Odessa Synagogue. The bride wore a pale blue velvet gown and the groom wore a new brown suit. It was a brief, simple ceremony after which the family repaired to Bela's house to celebrate.

"Call me Sophie the matchmaker," her friend beamed. "Be happy, Miriam. You've had enough sadness in your lifetime."

"I will, Sophie. God in His infinite wisdom helps you forget, doesn't he? I'll spend my life loving Josef and thanking Him for this gift."

The boisterous festivities lasted well into evening, and shortly after ten o'clock, Miriam and Josef sent a sleepy but protesting Kalman off to bed. He would remain with his cousins tonight, while the bride and groom spent their wedding night alone in their new home.

"I love you, Reb Brodsky. With all my heart."

"Are you really my bride? Or am I dreaming?"

"If it's a dream, don't wake me. You can put me down now," she said, for he had carried her over the threshold of their new home. They shed their heavy cloaks in the vestibule, and walked into the parlor.

"Brrr!" Miriam hugged herself. "It's freezing in here."

"I'll make a fire."

"No. Let's go upstairs and make a fire. Then we'll make our own fire."

He grinned at her. "All right, but I want to carry you upstairs to our wedding bed."

"Of course, dear husband. Only I've gained some weight. Be careful not to drop me."

They were like two children at play. He nuzzled her and she complained that his nose was as cold and as wet as a puppy's. She kissed him so hard, he begged her to stop bruising his lips. Soon, it was no longer freezing.

Miriam examined every part of him, kissing each crevice. She let her hands trail down his thighs only to tease up again to his chest. She murmured his name over and over again, inflaming his desire for her all the more.

"No, no. Let me, darling. Wait a bit longer, Josef," she urged. "We have a lifetime ahead of us but I want tonight to be perfect. Lie back, my love. Close your eyes. There, there," she crooned softly. She sang her song lovingly. With her voice. With her lips. With her hands. With her body. She fashioned a fire within him he had not thought possible. No. Not she. Their love. Strong. Gentle. Fervent.

"My Josef, my darling," she whispered, as her fingers undid the fasteners on his shirt.

"Let me do it," he said.

"No, sweet angel. I want to do it. My gift to you," she brushed his lips lightly with her fingers. "My symphony, Josef. I wrote it just for you. *Andante* first." Her mouth grazed his nipples and he gasped with pleasure. She explored his leanness. Her fingers undid his trousers and slipped them off. "Am I too...brazen do you think?"

"Of course, but I love you all the more for it." He caressed her already disheveled hair.

"Then I'll continue. *Andante* is *finito*. Now for *Allegro*." Her own cravings intensified as she heard his breath quicken.

"Wonderful instrument, husband," she murmured, as she played on it with her mouth, pleasuring in his gasps of delight. *Allegro* lingered until he could not bear the tantalizing intensity of his passion. He pulled her to him at last.

"My turn," he said. His hands caressed her breasts. He began his own urgent strokes. His lips burned her body with intense heat.

"Go on, my love. My angel. My Josef," she gasped. "Oh do, darling. Do. Do," she moaned in luxurious pleasure.

He gave her that bliss only love provides. More than connubial. More than passion. Oh yes. So much more than that. There were no longer any words to describe their giving, their yearning, their ache for one another. Were they two? No. They rose and fell in rhythm. *Andante. Allegro. Fortissimo.* The hunger of her rhythm matched his own. They were as one.

"Your face is like a painting framed by the firelight, my angel."

"I'm freezing again, darling." She jumped out of bed before he could protest and put more logs in the fireplace. "Come, Josef. Let's lie here in front of the fire. My sweet husband. Builder of my mansion. I propose to add a coda to our symphony. *Staccato. Fortissimo. Crescendo.*"

It was different this time. She moaned with joy at the pleasure of his touch, and when they reached the height of their fervor again, it was incredible. Miriam shouted with exultant laughter, in which Josef joined in soon after. They laughed for the sheer pleasure of the splendid symphony they had created together for the second time as husband and wife.

Their days were filled with goodness. It was springtime in their spirits, though winter was far from over. Kalman was eager to return home from school every day, for their love engulfed him as well. In fact, Miriam had never seen her son so happy.

Josef taught him how to carve and how to build with wood inside their tool shed. And the first time Kalman came home crying and bloodied, the result of a schoolboy's tussle with a bully, Josef took him behind the shed and taught him how to defend himself. It never happened again.

Miriam spent her mornings cleaning and washing and preparing dinner. In the afternoon, she found time to visit her sisters or Sophie or Malke. She was active in the synagogue sisterhood as well, doing charitable works in the growing *shtetl* full of pious, but poor Jews.

She had a talent, she discovered, for the simple diversion of cooking and baking. Every night she prepared another surprise for her husband and her son for dinner. In fact, it was a constant source of good-natured teasing.

They began to plan Kalman's *Bar Mitzvah* in April, on the boy's thirteenth birthday. It was his rite of manhood in the eyes of Judaic law. The rabbi helped the boy study the ancient Hebrew words he would read from the *Torah* so he would perform flawlessly on that auspicious morn.

⌘

"Would you like some tea and cookies, darling? I baked them this morning with raisins, the way you like them. Very sweet."

"No thanks. You're sweet enough for me. Last night's dinner forced me to make a pig of myself and I'm still stuffed. You're turning me into a fat man, you know."

"Fat?" She laughed. "You? Not your nature. I'm the one that's fat," she said in mock disgust. "I'm almost as fat as my mother was, poor dear. I've even had to let the waist of my gown out twice since we were married."

"One year ago. Doesn't seem that long, does it?" He rose and took her in his arms and held her to him. "Sometimes...sometimes, I rush home from work afraid that I might not find you here."

She returned his embrace. "You'll never get rid of me, my love. Don't you dare run off, Reb Brodsky, or I'll have the authorities hunt you down and bring you right back to me."

"You won't have to. And you don't have to worry about getting fat, either. You're beautiful just the way you are. You'll always be the most beautiful woman in the world to me. Don't you know that?" Don't you know, he thought, that you've filled my life with love? Me? Ugly Josef Brodsky? Tongue-tied orphan who could never say more than one word at a time? But not to you. Not to you, my love...

"Even with my thick waist? Even with my gray hair? Even though I can no longer see without my spectacles? Face the truth, Reb Brodsky," she teased. "You're married to a fat old lady."

"People dream all their lives. The pray to God for one thing or another. How sad for them. I dreamed of you all my life and my dream came true. God favored me after all. With you."

"With a blind, fat, gray-haired old woman, you mean. Aren't you afraid I'll bankrupt you with all the food I eat?"

"Eat all you want, wife. That's not why I married you."

"Why did you marry me, you wretch?"

"I like the music you make. Keep on playing those extravagant symphonies in bed for the rest of our days. Is that too much too ask?"

"Come home to me every night for the rest of our days and I promise I'll be ready and willing to play for you."

SIXTY-THREE

"I don't want you to have anything to do with those...those radicals at school!" Miriam pleaded, fearful for Kalman's safety.

"I'm just telling you what I heard, Momma. No need to make a fuss."

"Well and good, but mind your own business, hear? You'd best concentrate on your studies."

Newly enrolled in the *gymnasia*, he had been reporting rumors about the severe censorship of poets, historians and journalists. Josef sided with Kalman, insisting that these things were simply hearsay, and, even if true, the trouble would pass, as indeed, it had before. But Miriam was wary of the growing signs of repression in Czar Alexander's regime.

In spite of her misgivings over the Crown's unsettling edicts, the rhythm of Miriam's life flowed peacefully within their small circle of relatives. Her husband had been made foreman at the Karamanlis Grain Company, and her son continued to be an outstanding student. Thus, Miriam basked in the warmth of love and affection, within the confines of her close-knit family.

"Sometimes, when I wake in the morning I pinch myself, Sophie, just to make sure my life with Josef isn't a dream."

"Thank God it's a pleasant one, Miriam. But tell me," Sophie asked, bent on mischief, "...don't you miss the excitement of your other life? Don't you miss having all those servants?"

"Not in the least. Our life in Kiev brought Dov and me nothing but pain."

"Who asked him to convert? He went too far. You said he destroyed himself, Miriam, didn't you?"

"Who knows? We'll just have to leave his judgment to God. What about you, Sophie? Do you miss that other life in Kiev?"

"Only the servants, my friend. Only the servants."

⌘

In spite of the ominous clouds of repression, the royal court in St. Petersburg continued to play their gay, sophisticated games. The wealthy danced, ate caviar and drank imported French champagne. They played whist and they flocked to the theater in order to see and to be seen. Fans fluttered, eyebrows raised above lorgnettes, and handsome young officers lounged in boxes in studied poses of indifference, though everyone understood that these gentlemen were in amorous pursuit of secret assignations.

Who knows which came first? Was it a new order of poets and playwrights and philosophers who made sport of the nobility's stubborn resistance to progress, or was it the Czar's mystical belief in tradition?

Artists and writers—Pushkin, Karamzin, Glinka, Krylov—were all the rage both in the capital and in Moscow. Philosophy flourished. Ideas ripened. Thought prospered. In spite of the ban on both the printing and the circulation of forbidden works, secret societies grew steadily among the literati. One group devoted itself to new ideas in modern language, while its opposite championed tradition. Another, calling itself, "The Green Lamp," discoursed on literature and politics.

Still another chose to call themselves, "The Young Men of the Archives." They engaged in passionate dialogues devoted to the improvement in the quality of life.

All these clandestine activities were dutifully reported to Prince Bedorov, who received the information from the elaborate network of spies in the Ministry of Information, the secret service he had created. He saw in their rebellion an affront to the Crown. It was, therefore, his duty to enlighten His Imperial Highness concerning such perversities.

"Have you a recommendation, Bedorov?"

"Yes, Sire. These treacheries must be eliminated. With your permission, I shall reinforce supervision of the conduct and morals of our subjects, for the good of Mother Russia, of course."

By 1818, the czar created a committee in the Ministry of Education whose ambition was to suppress any Russian literature which opposed Christianity. Bedorov had won his argument that such works amounted to sedition.

Aristotle's works were forbidden, Pushkin was expelled from St. Petersburg, and the Czar's mission to maintain a centuries-old way of life grew stronger.

Ironically, His Imperial Majesty managed to maintain the fiction of his early liberal posture. Secretly, he endorsed all the oppressive measures proposed by Bedorov. Openly, he agreed with the court commission who recommended the abolition of serfdom. The czar thanked the distinguished commission for their fine recommendations before consigning their report to oblivion, buried deep within the State archives.

He welcomed British missionary Lewis Way who recommended that Jews should be given full rights as Russian subjects in an effort to improve their economic plight. The purpose of such largesse would reveal to them the benefits of Christianity. Encouraged by Alexander's stance as a humanitarian, Way submitted his proposals to the assembled heads of European States for their consideration at the Congress of Aix-Chappele in 1818. The program granted Jews access to public office, encouraged them to farm and to resettle in barren dominions, and pressed them to point their sons toward more productive occupations.

The Congress hailed Way's model solutions to the ever-vexatious Jewish problem as a landmark blueprint, especially for the most destitute, the eastern European Jews. But once the European Heads of State went home, the plan was forgotten.

Prince Bedorov did not approve of Lewis Way or of his plan, but he kept it to himself when the czar returned to the Winter Palace. He chose instead, to encourage the czar's belief in the Russification of the Jews.

"A wise position, Sire," he said when they discussed the plan. "Your Christian mission, I believe."

"To convert the Jews? Yes, God surely put me here for His grand purpose. Too bad Zeklinski chose not to remain in Russia after his conversion. He would have been a fine example for all Russian Jews to follow, eh? Whatever became of him?"

"He resides in Wilhelmstadt, a small principality in the Prussian provinces. He married a Russian woman who bore him some children. Changed his name. Baron von Secklin now."

"He succeeded in securing a title, eh?" The czar chuckled. "I suspected he had such designs, you know. Such an arrogant, pompous little man."

"Your majesty's knowledge of human nature is uncanny."

"You think so? Whatever happened to his Jewish wife?"

"He divorced her, Sire."

"Do Jews do that? She was most attractive. Black hair, dark eyes. Exquisite. Very like a sultan's daughter. Intelligent. What was it she said when Speransky presented her to me? Oh yes. I recall. Something like, 'The question of conversion is not a Jewish problem, Sire. Rather it is a Christian one, for throughout history, when Christians pressed for conversion, my people were sure to die.'"

"I knew her, Sire," Bedorov remarked.

"Did you? Speransky said she was someone's mistress. Who...?"

"Count Razovsky, Your Majesty. My brother-in-law."

"Oh yes. I recall, he died...So sad. Sorry."

"An...accident while cleaning his pistol."

"What became of Madame Zeklinski?"

"She remarried."

"Does she still reside in Kiev? I deeded the estate to her when Zeklinski converted."

"Most generous of you, Sire. Unfortunately, it burned to the ground in a serf uprising that also destroyed my wife's ancestral home, a great loss, Your Majesty. Zeklinski's wife lives in Odessa now."

"Was anything done to punish the serfs who were responsible for such wanton destruction?"

"Count Petrov, whom your Highness had the wisdom to select as governor-general, punished the rebels severely when he learned that the mob also murdered his own valued overseer."

"That was appropriate. Bad examples are set if serfs go unpunished for their crimes."

"I agree, Sire."

"I wonder, Bedorov. What do the Jews think of their Czar?"

"I have it on good authority that they think of you as their protector."

"Do they really?"

"No doubt of it, Your Majesty," Bedorov answered adroitly, leading his sovereign closer to a personal vision of a pure Russia, unsullied by heathens, Jews or otherwise.

In fact, it bothered the prince not at all to hear Alexander talk generously of freeing the serfs, or of alleviating the misery of the starving Jews living in small villages. He knew these things would never come to pass. He knew that once said, the czar was sure to forget his words, for his sovereign was opposed to change of any kind. By and large, Bedorov's despotic rule prevailed throughout the land.

When the czar leaned toward mysticism once again, Bedorov took pains to point out that pietist hysteria might easily destroy the values of the traditional Russian Orthodox Church among the populace. He received the czar's blessings to crush all opposition to the church, and thus felt free to arrange for Baroness von Krudener's swift departure from Petersburg, thwarting for all time her influence over the monarch.

In May of 1820, Alexander issued a decree that doubled the taxes of all Jews and forbade them to employ Christian servants. Bedorov praised his stand, stating that the decree was a firm step toward Russification of the Jews. For their own good, of course.

SIXTY-FOUR

"Josef, you're demented! Stop it," Miriam protested, flushed from the heat of the kitchen.

"Why? Don't you like it anymore?" he teased, for he'd stolen up behind her, in order to kiss her neck and fondle her breasts. Let's go upstairs. Before Kalman gets home."

"What am I going to do with you, my sweet husband? Can't you see I'm baking? The bread will burn." She turned to hug him. "There! Now you have flour all over your blouse, too."

"We'll have to eat burnt *challah* then." He grasped her bottom to pull her closer. "I'm hungry, but not for bread."

"Save it for tonight, my love," she said trying to sound stern even as her hands caressed him and her lips sought his. "Shh, Josef. Is that the door?"

"Must be Kalman. There goes my wonderful plan." He made a face and she laughed. "Call us when your're ready to leave for synagogue. I promised him we'd finish his new desk today."

She completed preparations for their Sabbath dinner, which the three would eat when they returned from services.

"How are you faring in school, son?" Asked Josef after dinner.

"My professor expects me to score the highest when I take my examinations in June."

"And why not? You certainly study hard enough," said Miriam.

"He says he can help me earn a government post in the Engineering Corps after university. Thinks I'm very smart even though I'm Jewish."

Josef chuckled at the irony. "Probably thinks he's doing you the greatest of favors. Is that what you want to do? Build roads and bridges?"

"I thought I might try it for awhile, just to see if it suits me. Besides, it pays very well."

Miriam beamed at her son. "It's hard for me to believe that my baby's old enough to graduate from *gymnasia*."

"I'm not a baby any more, Momma. I'll be sixteen in April."

"Dear me. I'd forgotten," she said with wry good humor. "And after that, I suppose, Josef and I will be forced to choose a bride for you."

"Can't that wait?" he asked, reddening at the thought.

"Why? Don't you want to marry?"

"Of course he does, Miriam. What a question. He just wants a chance to finish his studies first." Josef exchanged a sympathetic glance meant to relieve the young man's discomfort. He tactfully changed the subject. "I heard some interesting news this morning."

"What's that?"

"Three Jewish families from the congregation are planning to emigrate. To Rumania."

"Why would they do such a thing?" Miriam asked.

"They're unhappy about the double taxation imposed on Jews by Czar Alexander. They say that the rise in taxes is only the beginning, and more trouble for the Jews is sure to follow."

"Nonsense, Josef. Besides, what makes them think things are better in Rumania?"

"They say that the Rumanian *voivods* are promising freedom from taxation, among other things, but it's ironic just the same."

"What do you mean?" asked Kalman.

"Not very long ago, those same *voivods* greedily oppressed not only Jews, but also peasants and serfs. The poor souls chose to flee the country rather than starve to death. Now Rumania's desperate for tradesmen, farmers, merchants and skilled professionals. Right now, Kalman, you could probably earn more money as an engineer in Rumania than in Russia."

"Don't talk nonsense, Josef. Kalman isn't going anywhere. You'll stay right here with us, won't you dear?" Miriam could not hide the alarm in her voice.

"Of course I will, Momma. I'm not planning to go anywhere. Besides, Josef didn't mean to frighten you. He was only repeating what he heard," her son answered gently.

"I'm sorry, Miriam. I didn't mean..."

"I know you didn't mean it, Josef. It's my fault for getting upset over such a silly notion. Go on with your story, dear."

"There isn't much more to tell. The families were assured that, in addition to not having to pay any taxes, they could own their own land. They were also promised free land for a synagogue, a *mikveh* and burial grounds."

"I still think those people are foolish," said Miriam. "Why leave the life they're sure of in Odessa for some unknown promise in a far-off country they know nothing about? And besides, who can be sure the Rumanians will keep their promise?"

"They've signed a contract with the Rumanian government."

"Contract? Contracts are made to be broken. Not worth the paper they're written on, sometimes. Besides, even a good contract is no reason to emigrate. Odessa hasn't suffered any Jewish persecution since Russia won it from the Turks. It isn't altogether a question of bigotry, is it? The Russians ask for double taxes because they're greedy, that's all. I would not be in favor of pulling up our roots just to save a few measly rubles."

"Nothing to get upset about, Miriam," Josef said mildly. "We're not moving anywhere."

"Upset? I'm not...yes. I suppose you're right. It's just that I...I don't like to hear such talk. We have a fine life here in Odessa, don't we?"

"Who's suggesting otherwise?" Josef answered.

Miriam rose from the table. "All right, my loves, we've chatted long enough. Help me clear the table."

SIXTY-FIVE

Nikos Karamanlis listened soberly to the questions put to him by local officials, but he had already made his decision. He was a tall, well-dressed man in his fifties. His office faced the Odessa harbor, a busy seaport on the Black Sea situated between the Bug and the Dniepr Rivers.

"Is it true, sir, that you plan to let many workers go?"

Karamanlis assumed a mournful expression and answered, "I'm sorry, gentlemen, but I have no choice. The recession..."

"Yes, yes. Times are bad, but we're here today to ask you..."

"To beg you..."

"The port of Odessa has made you wealthy..."

"Just a minute, gentlemen. Perhaps one of you can speak for the rest. I cannot hear any of your arguments when you all talk at once," Karamanlis protested. The members of the town council exchanged glances and nodded to the highest official, the town magistrate.

"How many workers must you sack?"

"Three hundred, more or less."

"Three...?"

"Impossible!"

"This will cause chaos."

"...riots!"

"Enough!" exclaimed their leader. He waited until the others were quiet. "With all due respect sir, that is an unusually large number. Is there any way we can persuade you to reconsider your decision?" The grain magnate shook his head.

"But Easter is three weeks away, sir. One of Christendom's most sacred holidays, is it not? These men have families. If you could manage to keep them working for just three more weeks, until after..."

"I can't even consider it, gentlemen. You must realize how badly business has fallen off. I can't sell the grain already stored in my warehouses. Of course, I'm mindful of my civic responsibilities. Odessa, as you point out, has been a fine port for a business like mine. But a recession causes hardships for everyone, does it not? How can I possibly pay wages if I can't sell grain at a reasonable price?"

"Could you sell at cost, perhaps? Just this once?"

"Lord knows there are unscrupulous profiteers in this city, gentlemen, who would be only too willing to take the grain off my hands...at a severe loss to me. It would bankrupt me. Then there would be no chance of my ever hiring back these men, would there?"

The magistrate, a short stocky man with melancholy brown eyes, continued to plead with Karamanlis, who listened to his arguments without further comment. The Greek had been putting off meeting with the delegation for weeks, for he knew they would not like what he had to tell them. He also knew that the workers were restless. Rumors of imminent dismissals had been rife for weeks, and discontentment bred talk of riots in the city. The town commandant had already written to the governor for military reinforcements in the event of riots.

"May I speak?" a voice from the back of the crowded office asked.

"Go ahead, Rabbi Goldman."

The old rabbi wore the traditional black dress of caftan and wide-brimmed hat. He had a face which usually shone kindly through dark beard and ear locks streaked with gray, but today he looked somber. The rabbi strode forward through the opening the men made for him.

"We fear your decision will lead not only to riots, but to *pogrom*," he said bluntly. "Such a catastrophe might destroy our city and that would certainly damage your business, perhaps for all time, sir. Postpone your dismissals till after Easter. It will make all the difference."

At the same time that the delegation was imploring his employer to reconsider drastic terminations of employment, Josef Brodsky, Karamanlis' foreman, tried to find work enough for idle hands, for he had also heard the rumblings of discontent. Most of the men who worked under his supervision respected him, yet there were a few troublemakers among them.

He rotated his grain loaders every day. He had the others clean the grain bins—over and over again. He designated some laborers to repair broken chutes and bins and others to check the idle carts that hauled the grain to and from waiting ships.

One fourth of all shipping passed through Odessa in normal times, but these were not normal times. The recession had halted activity to a trickle. Each ship entering port was greeted with cheers and huzzahs, in the vain hope that, somehow, those shouts would magically bring more commerce to feed them all.

"What did you say?" asked Josef sharply. "Did I hear you call me a `stinking Jew?'" He grabbed the offending longshoreman by the collar. "Answer me!"

"I...I...didn't say...anything," the man muttered, mindful of the legend of Josef's extraordinary strength.

"Make sure you think twice before you speak such words in front of me again or you're out of work for good!" Josef let the transgressor go, but the encounter made him uneasy. No one had ever dared to slander him to his face before.

Under his breath, the embittered peasant repeated the vile curse he had muttered aloud a moment before. *"Parshchivi Zhid!"*

SIXTY-SIX

Miriam hummed as she purified the house in preparation for the Passover holidays. She threw the windows open to air the house, part of the prescribed ritual of cleansing. And just as Jewish wives had done for centuries, she removed all traces of *hametz*—leavened bread made with wheat, rye, barley, oats or spelt. For the eight days of Passover, the family would eat only *matzoh*, unleavened bread, to commemorate the exodus from Egypt.

At Jewish tables all over the world the youngest child would ask the Four Questions on the night of the first *seder*. The answer was the retelling of the Pharaoh's cruelty to their brethren, the magical parting of the Red Sea to aid their escape, and their wanderings in the desert for forty years. They would sing *Had Gadya* and *Day-Enu*, the traditional songs that would gladden their hearts.

The children would scramble to steal the hidden matzoh—the *afikomen*—for the privilege of a sweet reward. The adults would eat too much food and drink too much wine, but the end result would be that special feeling of joy in each person's heart as they performed the ancient rituals in the company of their loved ones.

This year the first *seder* would be at the Brodsky home. On that special night, a riot of children and adults would happily invade them. Miriam had insisted upon doing all the cooking and baking herself, without any help from the other women. She'd argued that she had never prepared an entire Passover *seder* by herself before. It was her turn to repay their years of generosity.

Josef made the wine for the ritual, with Kalman's help. They hid their homemade winepress in the cellar below Josef's workshop, for it was against all regulations. Yet it was common enough not only in every Jewish home with room to hide the illegal equipment, but also in every Christian home, since taxes on distilled spirits were high all over the country.

Miriam hummed the melodies of the Passover songs as she moved each piece of furniture to chase the dirt behind it. She hummed as she scrubbed the floors. She hummed as she washed the curtains. She hummed as she took the oven apart, piece-by-piece, subjecting each part to an unmerciful scouring.

"Who's there?" she sang out when she heard an unexpected noise at the front door. Who can it be? She wondered. Too early in the day for Kalman or Josef to be coming home. The twins? Malke? Probably Sophie. She wiped her wet hands on her apron and hurried to the door, only to freeze at the terrifying sight before her.

"Kalman," she screamed, putting her fist to her mouth, for her son's head was wrapped in a bloody bandage. The lad's clothes were covered with blood. He wore dark trousers tucked into his boots, over which his blouse was belted in the Russian fashion. He might have been taken for any *gymnasia* schoolboy, for he chose not to wear the traditional garb of the Orthodox Jew. He had grown into a tall, appealing young man, whose lively blue eyes defined his warmth. Today those eyes were bloodshot.

For support, he leaned against Josef who put his finger to his lips to silence Miriam as they led the boy into the parlor. She trembled with fear, but she managed to help Josef settle Kalman on the divan.

Are you in pain? What happened?" she asked at last.

"There was a fight. At the *gymnasia*," Josef said grimly. "Kalman came to me at the grain yards already bloodied. He didn't come here first because he didn't want to frighten you."

"It was a band of ruffians, Momma. They came crashing into the courtyard during recess. I was minding my own business. Just talking to my friends. You know who I mean..."

"Of course," she said, understanding all at once the reason for his bloodied head, for though he did not dress that way, the orthodox students' mode of dress, black caftans, *shtremels*, ear locks, clearly marked them as Jews.

"They were armed with clubs and shouted things like, `Death to the Christ-killers,' and `Zhids get out!' Some of us fought back, but they swung clubs and threw rocks at us." He closed his eyes in weariness.

"Whatever possessed you to fight? You don't dress like the orthodox students. You could have run away. Why didn't you? You might have been killed. Then what would I have done," she asked, on the edge of hysteria. "You should have tried to save yourself..."

"Miriam," Josef warned. "Control yourself. Leave the boy alone. He did the right thing. He had to fight back. Don't ask him to give up his honor."

Miriam began to sob, and Josef relented. He put his arm around her and let her weep.

"There were just too many of them, Momma. They took us by surprise. Don't cry. Please. It's not a bad wound. I'll be all right. Really I will. Tell her Josef. Tell her I'm fine."

"He's telling you the truth, dear. We went at once to the doctor who wrapped his head. It's just an ugly gash." Josef reached into his blouse pocket, and handed her some powders. "Samuel prepared these, to help Kalman sleep it off. I know he looks terrible with that bandage, but it isn't serious. He'll be as good as new in the morning. That's what the doctor said. Please, Miriam. You must get hold of yourself."

"All right, Josef." She made an effort to compose herself. "What else must we do for him? Tell me everything that Samuel told you." Why couldn't it be me? Punish me, dear God. Punish me for my sins, not my innocent son.

"You'll have to bathe the wound and change the bandages every few hours." Josef took her hand. "Don't be alarmed when you take them off. It's a nasty looking gash. Kalman had to have a few stitches...no, no. Don't cry again. Not that many. You'll see when you take the bandages off. Get him a glass of water and give him one of the powders so he can sleep." He rose to leave.

"Josef? Where...where are you going? You can't leave us alone at a time like this. Please," she begged. Dark visions of...Kiev...Borschov...the flames...her fears...assaulted her.

"I'm...needed. Please try to understand. There are riots in every Jewish quarter. You and Kalman will be fine here. There aren't enough Jews in this area to make it worth their while, but they're creating havoc in the ghettoes. Those poor Jews are defenseless. Let go of my arm, dear. I must go," he declared firmly.

"Please, Josef," she implored, still clinging to him. "I beg of you. You love us, don't you? We need you more than they do! Don't leave us alone! What if they come here...like the last time? You can't have forgotten Kiev..."

"Shhh, darling. I love you and Kalman with all my heart. Would I let anyone hurt either of you? The troublemakers are nowhere near here. Didn't Kalman and I come home safely? But they're destroying the *shtetl*." He held her and let her sob.

"You're not alone. Kalman is here with you," he soothed, conscious of the justification for her fears. Had he not killed to save her life once? He raised his eyes to Kalman, pleading silently for his support.

"Come here, Momma. Sit with me. Josef has no choice. He must go, can't you see? They need him. We'll both be fine here. No harm will come to us, I promise you."

"Wh...where...? Where are you going?" she persisted, in a desperate attempt to postpone his departure.

"The men are meeting at the synagogue. Everyone. Moses. Aaron. Benjamin. Samuel. Their sons. We must try to put a stop this. We can't let the senseless destruction go on without at least doing everything we can to stop it."

"*Pogrom?*"

"I'm afraid so. Hard to bear, but there it is." Josef Brodsky kissed his wife and hurried away.

"Momma? Come here," ordered Kalman firmly. "Bring me a glass of water for that powder Uncle Samuel gave me, won't you? My head throbs terribly.

Then sit with me. All right?" Without a word, she left the room to fetch the water. She flinched when she heard the front door close.

"Why do they do these...terrible things to us, Kalman?"

"It's their...ignorance, Momma. They blame Jews for the recession, they blame us for sacrificing their children, they blame us for desecrating their churches...all foolish nonsense."

"Foolish? No. Not foolish. Deadly. They call us the Chosen People. That's what we are, aren't we? Is this what God chose us for? To be persecuted, to suffer needlessly? For crimes we did not commit? What kind of God is that?" she asked with bitterness. "What a way to repay us for our devotion to Him!"

"Neither God nor Judaism is at fault, Momma. It isn't our doing. No. Not at all. You've always told me that the real criminal is ignorance, isn't that so? They preach against us from every pulpit in Russia. We're denounced as the killers of Christ. We're denounced for our clever ways with money. We're denounced for unheard of imaginary crimes. We're scapegoats, Momma. Just like you've always said."

"But...why, Kalman? Why us?"

"Because we're here. We're a target to strike out at, with blind hatred and repressive edicts. Takes the pressure off the people in power. They make the mistakes and we pay. Yet I wouldn't give up my devotion to Judaism for that. Quite the contrary. It makes me even more determined to practice Judaism. My father was wrong to convert. I wonder if he knows that? Someday, maybe I'll ask him if he knows what a terrible mistake he made." He closed his eyes in exhaustion, for the soothing powder had begun to take effect.

"Rest now, my son," she whispered, but the boy was already asleep. She covered him to keep him warm, but she was too restless to sit still. Not knowing what else to do, she returned to the task from which she'd been interrupted. She put the gleaming pieces of the oven back together again.

She tiptoed back to the parlor every few minutes to see if Kalman was still asleep, but she needn't have bothered. Samuel's potion was effective. Miriam ground the squares of matzoh she'd purchased at the Jewish market that very morning—was it only a few scant hours ago? She pulverized the thin boards into fine meal and busied herself by baking with it. She measured the spices and mixed it with the meal. Then she set the dry ingredients aside. She broke the eggs and separated the whites from the yolks carefully, beating each in turn and then together. She poured the batter into the waiting tins and put them into the oven.

It was soothing to bake. It calmed her uneasy spirit and helped to pass the time until Josef...but she forced him from her mind. Don't think about it, she scolded herself. Not now, Miriam. Work. Keep busy. A *pogrom*? How odd. Jews die and I bake.

She scoured the vegetables and salted the ritually slaughtered chickens. She set the pot of water to boil and prepared some more meal for matzoh balls for the soup. Her hands flew through their repetitive tasks, yet her soul trembled with fear for Josef's safety.

When Kalman woke she fed him supper, but Josef was still not home. She bathed the wound and placed a fresh bandage on it. She gave Kalman another powder to ease the throbbing pain. She did it quietly. Efficiently. Soothingly. Without tears.

When her son finally fell back to sleep, Miriam Brodsky sat by the window in the parlor to begin her vigil. No more baking. No more cooking. No more cleaning. Nothing left to do but to wait for Josef to return.

Midnight. The chimes of the clock struck twelve times. Where is he? Something terrible has happened to him. Yes. I see it all clearly now. He's not coming back. Even he isn't strong enough to overcome a wild mob. They'll come soon, to tell me he's dead. Maybe we'll all be dead by morning.

God of Abraham and Isaac and Sarah...why didn't You give me the courage to plunge the knife in my breast when Alexei died? Why didn't You let Borschov murder me? Why weren't You merciful? Why torture me with the gift of...of Josef's love, just to rob me of it and punish me once again? Is that Your plan? My retribution? For my vanity? For Alexei? Silent tears trickled down her cheeks, but she took no notice. Instead, she rose to fetch her bible. She wanted to pray. For Josef.

She wondered if she should say *kaddish*, the Hebrew prayer for the dead, but thought better of it. She wiped her tears and blew her nose. Then she found her spectacles. She searched idly for a suitable passage in the bible, but she had difficulty focusing on the words at first. She wanted to read something that would calm her taut nerves and subdue her shattered spirit.

At length her eyes focused on the Song of Songs. She scanned the words, searching for some meaning to explain the madness, the senselessness of *pogrom* to her. There had to be a reason, she thought in anguish. There had to be a reason to warrant her dread sense of impending loss.

> *Every man hath his sword upon his thigh,*
> *Because of dread in the night.*

She read the words over and over again as the clock struck one. If I can just find the words to explain this terrible mystery...

> *How fair is thy love, my sister, my bride;*
> *How much better is thy love than wine!*

Josef, my darling, please come back to me. You've always loved the Song of Songs.

The grandfather clock in the hallway chimed just twice. It woke Kalman and she fussed over him, but he needed nothing more than a bit of water before he fell back to sleep.

Josef must be dead by now, she thought. My final retribution. A life sentence. Worse than any punishment for my past transgressions. Now my life is truly over. Miriam clutched the bible to her breast and stared out into the melting darkness.

Dawn emerged, yet the glow of light failed to illuminate the blackness within her soul. She turned the wick down. No need of light now. Again she opened the bible. Her finger lay resting on the words she sought and she read them softly.

Then was I in his eyes
As one that found peace.

Peace. Josef is my peace. Shall I engrave it on his tombstone? 'He gave me peace.' He's dead. It's clear to me that he's dead. Payment to a wrathful God. An eye for an eye. Where's his body? I must go and find him. Yes! I must find him and bring his body here to prepare for the burial. She rose from her seat and wandered in a daze to the door.

"Where are you going?" Kalman asked in alarm, for her movements had stirred him awake. "I'm thirsty. Bring me a little more water, will you?"

"Water? I'll bring you a pitcher. Do you want anything else?"

"Answer me, Momma. Where are you going?"

"I...I must go out and look for Josef."

"No. You mustn't go out there. Not yet. He'll come back. It isn't safe for you to..."

"He's dead, Kalman. I'm sure of it. I must go and find his body..."

"Don't you dare go out." Kalman stood up, but dizziness forced him to sway.

"What's wrong?" Miriam cried in alarm. "Dear God! Don't take my son, too!"

"Be quiet, Mother," Kalman ordered. "You're not going anywhere, do you hear? You're hysterical. Come over here and sit next to me. Now! Do you hear me? Now!"

Miriam hesitated at the open door, but her son's urgent cry forced her to close it and return to his side. Her face was twisted with grief as she spoke. "My God, Kalman! What shall I do without Josef?"

"Everything will be all right," he murmured. "Take my hand. There. Go ahead and cry. Have faith, Momma. I promise you. Nothing has happened to our Josef. My head hurts. Will you hold it on your lap? The way you used to do when I was a little boy?" She did as he asked while he continued to talk, trying to soothe her anguish until, at last she fell into an exhausted, but fitful sleep of her own, only to wake at a sound she had never again expected to hear.

"I'm home," Josef said.

SIXTY-SEVEN

"It was a horror," he began, staring at the burns on his hands. "The things I saw tonight..."

"Your hands, Josef...let me put some ointment on them. Can't the story wait till later? You must be exhausted..."

"No. I never want to forget this night as long as I live. It was worse than war. Much worse." Miriam and Kalman listened intently as he began his somber account.

A vicious rumor had run rampant through the shacks and shanties of the poorest quarters in Odessa. No one knew how or where it began, but by noon, every man in every tavern in the city was convinced that the Jews had desecrated the holy cross in the church.

"Which church?"

"What does it matter, Kalman? It never happened. It never happened!" Josef shouted. "Do you want to hear something funny? I'd laugh, but it hurts too much. The man who deserves most of the blame is Nikos Karamanlis."

"Karamanlis? Your employer?"

"Yes. He turned his back on us. He knew what was bound to happen. The magistrate told him. Rabbi Goldman told him. He had ample warning, you see. He might have waited, but he chose to sack three hundred men as soon as the riots began, right in the middle of all this." He laughed. A short bark.

"But why?"

"Everyone was too busy maiming Jews and looting and burning to cover the evidence of their treachery. Who would bother to notice that three hundred men were put out of work in all the excitement? His news would take a back seat, do you see? I can just hear the tavern talk now," Josef continued in bitterness.

"'It's the Jews! Their fault we lost our jobs. They did it to us. Let's get them!' What difference does the truth make anyway? We're just the scapegoats."

"What happened when you reached the synagogue?" asked Kalman.

"Rabbi Goldman told us that the town fathers turned their backs on us. They used the extra troops sent by the governor to protect Christian property, the very churches where we were supposed to have burned a cross. The Christian homes of the town officials were also guarded. Our rabbi pleaded for some protection in the poor Jewish ghettoes, but they said they were short of soldiers.

"Two hundred Jews dead, I tell you! And for what? They were just...poor defenseless Jews! Such Christian bravery! Do you know who they chose to murder, those brave defenders of the cross? Those holy keepers of the Christian faith?" Hot tears of anger stung his cheeks as he shook with rage.

"Don't, Josef. Don't torture yourself."

"I cannot forgive them, Kalman. Those good Christians murdered helpless old men in gray beards and black caftans. They murdered little boys with *paess*. Those sweet curls will never bounce again for the little *Hassidic* lads who lay dead in the streets. Women and children and old men were slaughtered." He took a sip of the water Miriam held for him.

"When we gathered at the synagogue," he continued, "...we armed ourselves with sticks and chased them, but it was too late. The damage had already been done. The *synagogue* is littered with the wounded. We tried to put out the fires, but it was no use. The *hassidic* ghetto has burned to the ground. Not a stick left standing. We left Samuel behind to care for the wounded in the synagogue because he was most needed there. Moses and Aaron and Benjamin and I joined the other men, and when we could do no more, we returned to the synagogue. That's when we heard about the wharves."

"The wharves?"

"Yes, son. The mob was very selective, you see. They set fire only to Jewish businesses. Makes you wonder whether they had official help, doesn't it? How does a mob know which grain houses belong to Jews and which to Christians? Karamanlis must be jumping for joy. He's one of the few left standing. Now, I suppose he'll be a hero and rehire the men he fired yesterday."

"How...dreadful," murmured Miriam.

"There isn't a Jewish grain house or business left on the wharf. I saw the headline this morning, just before I left the synagogue. Someone came rushing in with a one-page special edition of *The Odessa Journal*, as if it mattered. The editors must have been up all night printing it. Do you know what it said?" His face was streaked with fury.

"Josef, please," Miriam pleaded, "Don't upset yourself so."

He ignored her plea, needing to rid himself of the poisonous hatred within.

"I would have brought it home, but we only had one copy. The synagogue ought to frame it, as an eternal reminder of the regard of our countrymen. The country I fought for. That single page is a silent witness to my years of devotion to my country, and to the lameness in my leg. What a reward for my bravery at Ochakov." He spat out each word as though it were venom.

"Tell us what it said," implored Kalman.

"Something about the masses rising up, rightfully—rightfully—mind you, against Jewish exploiters. It said that men made destitute by Jews—by Jews— the unemployed, the starving, good Christians all, rose up against the injustice of 'the exploitation of Christians at the hands of heretics and foreigners.'"

The clock chimed eight times, yet no one stirred.

"What shall we do now, Josef?" Miriam's voice shook.

"There's only one thing we can do. It's already decided."

"Decided? What do you mean...decided?"

"We're going to leave Russia. All of us."

"Leave Russia? Where are we going to go? Won't it be the same all over?" Miriam bit her lip.

"I don't know. I only know that we can't stay here. I must get some sleep now. Why don't you both rest, too? We're out of danger. The party's over. Our pious 'executioners'are getting drunk in the taverns to celebrate. The liquor's free, I hear, most likely paid for by all the Christian merchants who are well satisfied that there won't be any more Jewish competition. The family has all agreed to meet here tonight after dinner to decide where we'll go. All right?"

That night, the argument was loud and long. Their small circle didn't begin to gather till well past ten in the evening. Now, after midnight, they had come to a decision.

"Then we're going to resettle in Rumania. Agreed?" Josef looked from one person to the other. Moses nodded. Aaron nodded. The twins nodded. Benjamin and Sophie nodded. He didn't need to look at his wife. They had already made their decision.

Malke glanced at her husband Samuel and spoke with quiet determination. "We've decided to stay, Josef. We're not going to leave Odessa."

"Stay here? Stay here?" Sophie repeated angrily as though she couldn't believe what she had just heard. "What for? Haven't you had enough?" She turned to Benjamin for support.

"Say something, Benjamin! You always complain I never let you say a word! Now's your chance. Say something!"

"Well," he began, "...maybe you should go with us...but then again, if you must, I suppose, then do what you think is best for you and your family..."

Sophie glared reprovingly at her husband. "Do...? Best...? Is that all you have to say? Oh, be quiet, Benjamin! You don't know what you're talking about!"

"Our minds are made up," said Malke. "The pogrom is over, isn't it?"

"For now, you mean."

"For now, Sophie. But...Samuel makes a good living here. And not only from Jews. We've established a name for ourselves in Odessa. Silverman Apothecary counts for something. Can't you see that?"

"We all make...or rather, made a good living, Malke."

"You don't understand. It's our...our life, Josef. Samuel is fifty-four and I'm fifty-three. We don't want to start all over again somewhere else. It won't be so bad here now that the worst is over. What's done is done. It can't happen again. Lightning never strikes twice, they say."

"Doesn't it? What's to stop them next Easter, or the one after that? They didn't smash your pharmacy this time, Samuel. But who's to say what will happen the next time?"

"Josef's right, Samuel. Our offices were burned to the ground," added Moses.

"All we lost was the furniture, thanks to Josef," said his cousin Aaron. They had all heard the daring tale of Josef's entry into the smoldering building to empty the safe of precious stones and cash. "You're wrong to stay, Malke. It's foolhardy."

"That may well be, Aaron," answered Malke, "...but Samuel's a...a professional man. The Jews who remain still need us. Even the gentiles...we have very important gentile friends, you know."

"You're fooling yourself, cousin. Open your eyes. It might have been any one of us lying dead or wounded or homeless. There are too many families inside the synagogue without a roof over their heads tonight. We were just fortunate."

Samuel answered for his wife this time, for Malke had begun to weep. "Do you think it's been an easy decision for us? We've talked about nothing else all day today. Our daughters and their families have decided to stay also. Not every Christian is bad. There are good people in Odessa. With God's help, we'll be fine."

Miriam relented. "Of course, Samuel. Come, Malke dear. Don't cry. We mustn't let this terrible thing tear us apart. We all love you very much." She hugged her. "You must do what you think best. It's all right, Malke. No one here thinks the worse of you for wanting to stay." The twins followed Miriam's lead and embraced their older cousin. Sophie consoled her too, though her anger at what she considered to be Samuel and Malke's blindness to the truth would not fade.

Miriam insisted upon the observance of Passover and the *seder* rituals in spite of the *pogrom*. Thus, the family gathered at her home for the first *seder*, their last in Russia.

Josef led them all in the poignant tale of the exodus of the Jews into the desert. They sang *Had-gad-ya*. They sang *Day-enu*. They sang with tears in their eyes, as though the lively tunes were a dirge. The children scrambled for the *afikomen*, the hidden *matzoh*, receiving gifts for it as was the custom, but there was no joy in the game. Not this year. No, not this year. But there was always next year. In Rumania.

⌘

The weeks passed with dizzying speed. The four families were among those who booked passage on a ship that would take them and whatever possessions they could carry from the Black Sea to the Danube River and to their final destination, Bucharest, Rumania.

A few days before they were due to sail, Kalman came home with the sober news that he'd passed the special examinations given him at the *gymnasia*.

"Congratulations, darling. I'm proud of you."

"Congratulate my professor, Momma, not me. If it weren't for his help, the special examination just for those of us who are leaving Odessa would not have been possible."

"He's a decent man. I hope Aunt Malke and Uncle Samuel meet others like him, if there are any more, that is. One good apple in a whole barrelful of rotten ones."

"Be thankful, Kalman," said Josef. "That's one more decent Christian than a Jew has any right to expect in this country."

"Do you think my degree will have any meaning in Rumania? I want to be able to go to the university and study engineering."

"Let's hope so, darling. But for now, you must put it all out of your mind and help us pack."

By the time they were ready to set sail, each family had sold their home and their larger possessions and had received the necessary papers from the Rumanian Embassy, giving them permission to resettle in Rumania.

Josef refused Miriam's offer of her remaining four diamonds for their passage. It wasn't necessary, he explained. There was enough from his wages as well as from the sale of the deed to their house. To spare her further misery, he neglected to tell her how little he had received—only half its true worth. Had she known, it would have broken her heart.

"Goodbye, house. I won't miss you one bit," Miriam said.

"You won't? I thought you loved this house."

"Only the people in it, darling. Only the people in it."

"The carriage is waiting, Momma. Ready?" interrupted Kalman.

"Come here, Kalman," Miriam ordered. She hugged them both.

"Never believe, for one moment, that a house has any importance by itself. We were this house. You and Josef and me. God alone, in his mercy, allowed me to keep both of you. I'll spend the rest of my life giving thanks to Him for this treasure. Don't be bitter about leaving. So long as you come home to me every night, that's where home will be, even if we live like wild gypsies under the Rumanian stars."

Josef and Kalman laughed, caught up in her infectious good humor. Her chin jutted defiantly, as she slammed the front door for the last time and linked her arms through theirs. Thus, they left their home in far better spirits than they had felt since the terrible night of the *pogrom*.

Malke and Samuel came to see them off at the pier. It was a wrenching, tearful farewell. Miriam felt sad for her cousins. To herself, she had to admit that Sophie was right, though she wouldn't dare say so to her friend. Malke and Samuel refuse to see the dangers before them.

It's their life, after all, Miriam thought, Aloud she said, "Goodbye, dear cousins. Take care of yourselves. I'll write when we're settled in Bucharest."

"Don't be angry with us, Miriam. We're doing what we think is right. God be with you."

"Of course I'm not angry. God be with you, too, Malke dearest. And with all your family."

As the days on board ship wore on, dejected family members came to depend upon Miriam. She led the children in song and games. She insisted that the adults look to the future with joy and talk only of their new life, without so much as a backward glance.

"You're like the Miriam of the bible, my darling wife," Josef remarked as they stood at the rails together looking out at the sea one evening.

"What do you mean?"

"There's a fire in you I've never seen before. You're like Moses and Aaron's sister Miriam, who led her people across the parted Red Sea."

"The prophetess?"

"Yes. Your fierce determination gives us all hope. You exhort us day and night to stand tall. You wipe away our grimy tears and our pitiful sorrows. Miriam undaunted. Miriam proud. Miriam determined. Miriam standing tall, head unbowed. Miriam allowing no tears. Miriam waving her timbrel and leading her brethren out of bondage. My own, my dearest, my remarkable dark-eyed beauty."

BOOK FOUR
Bucharest, Rumania 1839

SIXTY-EIGHT

Kalman? What a surprise. I didn't expect you tonight. I thought you were coming home tomorrow. How was your meeting?"

"Hello, Mother. I finished my business sooner than planned. Am I interrupting anything?"

"No, dear, of course not. I was just about to finish reading a novel, but that can certainly wait. Much nicer to have a bit of company, especially when it's you."

"How are you feeling?"

"Well enough, though I'm not as nimble as I used to be. What can you expect from a woman of seventy? Still, my mind's active and I'm not too forgetful. That's something, isn't it?"

"My wife says Rachel plays the piano very well due to your excellent instruction."

"Your daughter's very clever for a five-year-old. She's a bit more musical than her brothers. My life is full, with you and Anna and the five delightful grandchildren you've blessed me with. I'm afraid I've become an insufferable grandma who bores every woman in the sisterhood to tears, with boasts of my grandchildren's exploits. They're the pride of my life, but you know that, don't you?"

He smiled. "Yes, though it never hurts to hear your repeated praises of my children. However, I didn't walk over here to visit tonight to talk about my wonderful brood. I came by to bring you some...news."

"News? What news?"

"I've news of...my father."

Her heart thundered. "You can't mean Dov?"

"Yes. His name is Baron David von Secklin now."

"How odd. I haven't thought about Dov for years. How on earth did you...?"

"He's here, Mother."

"Here? Where?" She peered over Kalman's shoulder, half expecting to see Dov.

261

"In Bucharest."

"But...why?"

"I arranged it. He's known for years that I'm his son."

"But, how does he...did you...?" She folded her arms to hide her trembling hands.

"Do you recall when Anna and I went to an engineer's convocation in Danzig ten years ago? I presented a paper to my European colleagues. It was in 1829, just after Hershl was born."

"Yes, I remember. Josef and I took care of...let me see," she knit her brows, "...Joshua was five, Leon was...three, and Hershl was only three months old. Before Daniel and Rachel were born, right? How could I forget? Josef teased that he'd refuse to give his grandsons back to you and Anna. He was such a doting grandfather, wasn't he? He thought of himself as your father. He never thought of himself as anything else, you know."

"I can't argue with that. Josef was my father in every real sense of the word. The best any son could have. Still, I harbored a nagging desire to know my real father. Does that surprise you? Yes. I see that it does. Oh, it wasn't anything like a...an obsession. It was just that my curiosity about my natural father was always there do you see? And when the opportunity presented itself, I arranged to meet him."

"How did you find him? Why didn't you ever tell me?"

"Anna and I went to visit him in Wilhelmstadt. Josef told me where he lived."

She frowned and then she laughed. "Why, that scoundrel! He never said a word to me! Must have thought it would hurt my feelings. Just like him to try to protect me. His love was like that. Even now he brings a smile to my lips, though I grieved so when he died. He's still alive, you see, in my heart." She hesitated. "How did Dov...receive you?"

"He was cordial. Asked a lot of questions, mostly about you. Then he said something that astonished me and made me feel sorry I'd made the visit after all. He denied that he was my father." Kalman's eyes pierced his mother and her heart sank.

"Yes. It's true. I told Dov that, Kalman. Were you angry with me when he denied he was your father?"

"I was enraged. I wanted to make you suffer for lying to me." His anger clouded his vision for a moment. "On the night we came home, I waited outside your door for Josef to leave, so I could confront you alone. 'Ask your mother who your real father was,' the baron had said, and I meant to do just that.

"Why didn't you?"

"Josef spied me hiding outside when he left the house and demanded to know what was the matter. When I told him, he insisted it wasn't true and pleaded with me not to upset you. When he told me what he swore was the truth, he made such a convincing case of it, I agreed to let the matter drop."

"What did he say?"

"You lied to my father so you could keep me with you."

"That's the truth," but only part of it, she thought to herself, wondering whether now was the time to tell him what had really happened so long ago. But her curiosity about Dov was overwhelming and she postponed the decision.

"Why do you suppose Dov agreed to see you?"

"He wanted to know about you. When I told him you had married Josef Brodsky, he seemed pleased.

"'Then I was right to grant her a divorce. Wish them well for me,' he said that day, '...for I bear no ill will toward your mother. It wasn't entirely her fault.'"

She laughed in spite of herself. "Dov said that? Not 'entirely' my fault? Meaning, of course, that it was at least 'partly' my fault? Just like him. Sorry Kalman, but you can't know just how funny that is. Please. Go on."

"The odd thing was, though he kept denying he was my father—he must have repeated it dozens of times during our visit—he insisted upon telling us the story of his life. He had three children, but his eldest son Hans died during the battle of Waterloo. His daughter, Princess Maria, is married to the regent of Wilhelmstadt, Prince Wilhelm II. His youngest son Johann is a prosperous banker who lives in Berlin with his wife and his family."

"And Dov's wife?"

"His wife Hannelore died three years earlier." Kalman rose and helped himself to a brandy.

"Dov lives well?"

"Magnificent is more like it. In a beautiful castle. Anna and I were impressed."

"Doesn't surprise me. I wouldn't expect any less of him."

"He's confined to a wheelchair now."

"Really? Why? An accident of some sort?"

"No. He has a...a rare blood disease."

"Sorry to hear it. Truly I am, for I harbor no ill will toward him."

"He seemed loath to let us go that first time. He insisted we stay for dinner and spend the night. My wife guessed that he was lonely. I had the feeling that he wanted you to know. He kept telling us little stories just to keep us a bit longer."

"Did you stay overnight?"

"No. Anna wanted to," he smiled. "She'd never slept in a castle before. But I was still nursing my fury at you for lying to me about the identity of my real father. We started for home at once.

"All the way home my wife kept insisting that I looked like the Baron. Same color eyes, light brown hair, though his was mingled with gray by then. Even our facial expressions were similar, she said. She also thought that our own little Joshua resembled the portrait of his son. That painting astonished me. It also confused me."

"Which son? You said that he had two."

"The portrait hung over the mantle in the drawing room. It was a likeness of his oldest son Hans, in the uniform of a Prussian officer, the one who died at Waterloo. When I saw it, I didn't know what to think."

"But why?"

"He looked like just like me when I was his age, except for the color and the texture of his hair, which according to the portrait, was a very pale blonde and very straight."

"I see," she said quietly. So many years, she thought, yet my past persists in coming back to haunt me.

Visions of Dov and happier days danced before her eyes briefly, but then the man became Alexei, laughing blue eyes, rakish grin, blonde wisps of hair falling on his brow, eternally youthful Alexei, never grown old.

"Did Josef tell you...everything?"

"Everything? I don't know what you mean, Mother. He said that you deliberately lied to keep me with you. He said you concocted some sort of tale that convinced him. Is there something more I should know?"

Something more? She asked herself. Oh Kalman! More? A lifetime. Shall I tell you? Yes, I must. Will it hurt you to know of your mother's betrayal? Miriam took a deep breath.

"Yes, dear, there's a great deal more that you should know. I owe it to you. I always have, though I've tried all these years to hide it, for it was very painful to me. It may be very painful for you. Do you want me to tell you in spite of the sorrow it may cause?"

"I'm not a child any longer."

"Then it's time you knew the truth about your parents' betrayal of one another. Of course I lied to your father. I waited so long to give birth to you. He could have taken you with him if he chose. The law was on his side, you see. He had Czar Alexander's blessing to convert you as well. Did you know that?"

"No. That hadn't occurred to me, though he mentioned something about the czar's influence on his decision to convert."

"Forgive my cowardice for not telling you sooner. I was afraid you'd hate me and I couldn't bear to face that. Now I can see that the sad tale needs to be told, if only to remember the treachery and the anguish, the misguided notions we harbored. Your family's pitiful legacy, if you will."

"Pitiful? I don't think so. We came through it, didn't we? Besides, it's my heritage."

"Yes, I suppose so, though that's a curious word. We were so idealistic when we first married. We were going to conquer Russia. I was a silly, romantic, fifteen-year-old and he was a brash and arrogant sixteen. We really believed that our destiny was meant to serve Judaism, but we were wrong. We were terribly wrong."

It was well past midnight by the time Miriam had finished. She told him of Dov's ambition. She told him of their betrayal of one another and she told him of her passionate love for Alexei Razovsky.

"It was so easy to fool your father, you see. He thought of Alexei as someone who would help us enter into royal society. I don't imagine that Dov ever let go of that idea, in all the years we were married. I could lie to you and say that he forced me into another man's arms in his eagerness to belong to Russian nobility, but I was an adult. I knew better.

"I loved Alexei Razovsky with all my heart. We were planning to run away to America, but his brother-in-law had other ideas. Prince Bedorov was a close advisor to Czar Alexander. His interference led to Alexei's destruction."

"What happened to Alexei?"

"He shot himself."

"How terrible."

"At the time, I thought so, too. Water under the bridge now, as they say, yet I couldn't help wishing for the courage to join him in my misery. He thought we were like Romeo and Juliet. I tried to kill myself, but I couldn't. I'm glad now that I didn't, for soon after, I had a compelling reason to live."

"Which was...?"

"I became pregnant with you."

"And you were sure who...?"

"There is no doubt in my mind. You are Dov Zeklinski's legitimate son. I hadn't been with Alexei...that way for at least four months before he died."

"And my father didn't realize that?"

"Only God knows why he chose to believe my lie. At the time, I suspected he was relieved to hear it."

"Did Josef know? About Count Razovsky, I mean?"

"Yes. I refused to marry him until he knew all about me. He said it didn't matter to him."

"That portrait I saw of my father's dead son...that was proof enough, but I was too angry with you to see it then."

"There's one more thing." she sighed.

"What is it?"

"Do you recall our journey to Odessa?"

"How can I forget? I was terrified when I saw our home in flames. I can still recall your illness, when the family wouldn't even let me visit you. I thought you were going to die."

"I didn't want to live. I was so ashamed."

"Of your affair?"

"No. Something else happened the day before we fled Kiev. I took it as punishment for my infidelity."

"You mean the destruction of our estate?"

"No. I was brutally molested the night of the fire."

Kalman turned pale. "What?"

"Vassily Borschov, our former overseer, raped me. He found me hiding in an abandoned shed where Josef had left me while he went to get you and make arrangements for our flight to Odessa.

"When Josef came back for me, he murdered the man and set fire to the shed. A friend covered up the deed. The authorities thought it was the rampaging mob that murdered Borschov. Thank heaven no one ever discovered the truth."

"My God, how terrible for you." He hugged her to him as if to erase the pain. "I'm sorry for making you relive such horrid memories. I'm proud that you had the courage to fight to keep me with you."

"I wanted Josef to adopt you, but he couldn't because Dov was alive and Josef wouldn't allow me to contact him for approval. He said it didn't matter. In his heart he was your father."

"Josef, gentle Josef. Hard to believe he murdered that man, but you were brave, too."

"Brave? I never thought of it that way."

"It took courage for you to lie to save me."

"I did what any mother would. I fought like a tiger to keep you, even if it meant lying. Well worth it, I assure you, for my life has been full ever since. Josef taught us all to value life. I see evidence of it in how you and Anna raise your children. He taught me to forgive myself. Somehow, I feel close to him tonight, as if he's here helping me tell my son the truth at last." The two sat quietly for a time, in comfortable silence. At last Kalman spoke.

"My father wishes to see you."

"See me? Why?"

"You're one of the reasons he chose to come to Bucharest."

"And the other reason?"

"Only one. There's a famous clinic here. You've heard of it, I'm sure." She nodded. "It's his last hope. I went to Wilhelmstadt to bring him here for treatments, not to another engineering convocation as I led you to believe. My wife and I feel sorry for him."

"What about his other children?"

"They rarely see him."

"Why is that?"

"He says they're ungrateful, but I suspect it has something to do with his conversion, because he hinted that it hurts them in subtle ways that he once was a Jew. You don't have to see him if you don't want to, you know."

"Of course I'll see him. Go ahead and arrange it."

SIXTY-NINE

Miriam might never have recognized him had she not been aware of his identity. His hands shook with a constant tremor. His pale cheeks were hollowed, a bony, cavernous face, skin stretched taut. He smiled a skeletal smile—a death mask. His blue eyes, once so lively, were now faded and dull.

"Hello, Miriam. Been a long time."

"Hello, Dov."

He laughed an old man's cackle. "Dov? No one's called me that in years."

"How are you feeling?"

"Not well, as you can see." He shifted in his wheelchair.

"You wanted to see me?"

"Yes. I wanted to forgive you."

"Forgive me? I hadn't realized I needed to be forgiven. What is it I'm being forgiven for?"

"I forgive you for lying to me about Kalman. At the same time, I thank you for him as well. Kalman has been a great comfort to me, especially now. My other children are too busy with their own lives. You've done a fine job raising him, Miriam." He ran his fingers through his sparse hair.

Can this really be Dov? Miriam wondered in astonishment. This sickly old man? "Kind of you to say so. How are your treatments coming along? Feeling any better?"

"No. But I didn't expect much. My doctors tell me there's no cure for my ailment. Kalman suggested I try the clinic, so..." he shrugged, "...here I am. I didn't think you'd agree to see me."

"Why not?"

"Because I caused you such pain."

"If it's any comfort to you now, I bear you no ill will, Dov, or would you prefer that I call you Baron von...?"

"No, no. Call me Dov. Please. It comforts me to hear it."

"As you wish. Did you find peace when you left Russia?"

"At first, for I loved my Lori, you see. When I converted, we posted the banns and were married in church shortly afterwards. Prince Wilhelm bestowed royal titles upon us as a wedding gift. Cost me a small fortune." He smiled, pleased at having drawn a smile from her.

"Then you had to pay for the title."

He shrugged. "I'm accustomed to paying my way." He studied her carefully. "The years have been most kind to you, Miriam. You look well."

"I'm seventy years old. If you can call my gray hair, my spectacles and too much fat looking well, then I suppose I do."

"I didn't mean that. You look serene."

"I am happy with my life. What about you?"

"My wife arranged everything, our social life, the marriage of our children. I loved her dearly, but..."

"Were you not content, then?"

"I won't lie to you. I was never fully accepted. I wasn't a Jew anymore, but I wasn't a Christian either, at least among Christians. There you have it. The eternal outcast."

"Did that come as a surprise to you?"

"At first it did, but I grew used to it. All in all, I'd say it wasn't such a bad life. I had my Lori, and when the children were younger..." he shrugged. "And you? Do you still believe in *haskalah*?"

"Yes, I do. In spite of the Odessa *pogrom*, in spite of the destruction of our home in Kiev, in spite of double taxation for Jews here in Rumania, I still believe. We have to keep on trying. I don't really know if we'll ever be accepted here or anywhere else, but I believe in two things. I believe in Judaism and I believe in the basic goodness of the human spirit.

"Good people like Natasha and Misha and our butler Boris helped me hold on to my beliefs. There have to be more good people like them out there somewhere. We Jews can't keep our heads buried in the sand. We must keep on trying to become part of the world in spite of the bigotry, because we're all part of God's human design. I often wonder what Christianity would do without us. Who would they hate? Who would the poor vent their anger on while the authorities look the other way?"

"I used to be the optimist, and you used to be the doubter. Now it appears to be the other way around."

"I'm just older and clear-eyed. Josef and I talked about leaving Bucharest once we discovered there was little difference between Russia and Rumania. Anti-Semitism is official State policy in much of eastern Europe, it seems. It would be the same wherever we went. At least the local authorities here leave us alone so long as the bribes are suitably large. Funny, isn't it? The Christians make us fight back just to survive when all we want is to be loyal to their country and still be allowed to worship as we please."

"You persist in your devotion to Judaism."

"It's part of my soul, Dov, as much a part of me as breathing. My faith helps me to survive." She changed the subject, sensing Dov's unease. "Anna's lovely, isn't she?" Dov nodded. "I have five grandchildren. Four boys and my beautiful granddaughter Rachel."

"They're mine, too."

"Yes, of course. I'd forgotten. Has our Joshua tried to proselytize you?"
Dov smiled. "About what?"

"He's only fifteen, an ardent Palestinian nationalist. Believes Jews should fight to reclaim their holy land."

"Your influence, I suppose."

"No. Joshua has a mind of his own, though he loves to argue and defend his position with me," she laughed. "He belongs to a secret society, `Sons of Palestine', they call themselves."

"You used to love to argue, too, I recall."

She chose to ignore his barb. "I see the grandchildren almost every day."

"I envy you that, for I rarely see my other grandchildren. My son lives too far away, and my son-in-law's ashamed of me."

"Sorry to hear it."

"On State occasions, when my son-in-law feels he must invite me for appearance' sake, I visit my daughter and her children at the palace."

"Are you a believer?"

He smiled. "Only you would dare to ask me such an impertinent question, Miriam. The answer is no. It shouldn't surprise you that I never really believed. I haven't been to church since my wife's funeral. In fact, I've taken to worshipping as a Jew again. It's a great comfort to me. Does that surprise you? I kept my phylacteries and my prayer shawl all these years and now I put them on every morning and I pray. So you see, I'm still a Jew."

⌘

Six weeks after Dov left for Wilhelmstadt, Kalman received news of Dov's death. A formal State funeral led by Prince Wilhelm II and the grieving Princess Maria, daughter of the deceased, was followed by three days of mourning. Baron David von Secklin was interred in the family crypt, next to his beloved wife Hannelore and his son Hans.

SEVENTY

"Go on home, Rachel dearest. And don't forget to practice your scales. Give your Aunt Sophie a kiss good-bye." The diminutive youngster wrapped her arms around her great-aunt affectionately.

"Thank you, darling. Tell your momma that Aunt Sophie said hello."

"*Bon jour, Grandmere. Bon jour, Tante* Sophie," the child sang out before she skipped away.

"*Bon jour, mon ami*," Miriam called after her. She waited till the child was well out of sight. "Come, Sophie. Lunch is ready." Miriam served them both while the two old friends chatted easily of this and that.

"Delicious, Miriam. I'll suffer terrible heartburn, but who cares? Everything I eat gives me heartburn lately. No fun growing old, is it? Never mind. So? What was this terribly important news you had to tell me?"

"It's about Dov. He's dead."

"Dov? But how did you hear of it? I didn't know you were in touch with him."

"I wasn't. I saw him here in Bucharest a few months ago."

"He was here?" Sophie was unable to hide her shock.

"Kalman brought him here for treatment, but he was too far gone."

"Why didn't you tell me he was here?"

"He asked me not to."

"Why, that ungrateful...! He was my cousin."

"It's not what you're thinking, Sophie. He just didn't want you to see how badly he looked."

"What vanity. Still the same, self-centered Dov."

"Hush, Sophie. Don't speak ill of the dead."

"Where did he die? Here?"

"No, in his castle in Wilhelmstadt. He was buried with honors at a State funeral. That would have pleased him."

"I'm sure. So? Tell me the whole story. You know you're dying to tell me, am I right? Isn't that why you made me such a fattening lunch? What else is there left for two old hens but interesting stories?" Her laugh was so infectious—Miriam was forced to join her.

She spent the rest of the afternoon relating the remarkable tale of her final meeting with Dov.

"Imagine that! I've often wondered about him, but I was afraid to ask."

"It's all right, Sophie. I don't mind talking about him."

"My mother hated him. She blamed him for my father's death when Dov insisted he retire. My father had a stroke that same day."

"I'm so sorry, Sophie. You never told me."

"You needn't be sorry. It's Dov who'll have to answer to God now. I worshipped Dov when I was growing up, yet I ended up hating him for his treachery toward my father and toward you, especially when he left you."

"You're such a loyal friend. What would I have done without you all these years? Here we sit like two withered branches, twisted and gnarled, hanging by a thread, ready to fall off and feed the worms." Sophie laughed with her. "Don't blame Dov for everything. I wasn't such an angel either."

"What do you mean by that?"

"Would you like me to tell you the tale of a Jew named Miriam who strayed from the fold? I made a clean breast of it to my son. Why not to my best friend?"

"I don't believe it," said Sophie incredulously when Miriam had finished.

"It's true. Every word."

"And no one knew?"

"Natasha Gorov knew. She warned me it would lead to disaster. She was right, of course."

"Natasha was a remarkable woman."

"I loved her, Sophie. More than my own mother, God forgive me. She understood the human condition better than anyone I've ever met."

"I never thought to ask you before today, but I've always wondered..."

"What is it?"

"I met Natasha for the first time when we discovered you were pregnant with Kalman. Why didn't you introduce us before then?"

"Don't be angry with me, Sophie. The answer's simple, though you probably won't like hearing it. I didn't want to share her with anyone. I wanted Natasha to belong only to me. She was my own special treasure, better than any jewel I'd ever owned. Selfish of me, I know, but there it is. Can you forgive me?"

"At this late date? Who would I have left to gossip with if I didn't forgive you? No matter. She and I became good friends." Sophie paused for thought. "I never met Alexei Razovsky either. Did you really love him? Or was it just...you know?"

"I wanted to die when he killed himself."

"And the...other?" Miriam looked puzzled.

When Sophie's meaning dawned on her, she giggled like a schoolgirl. "Why you sly old lecher! Alexei was an artist in bed, if that's what you want to know."

"Better than Dov?"

"With Dov it was a business arrangement, soon over and done with."

"I thought it was the same for all women, the soon over and done with part. What about...? Never mind. None of my business."

"You want to know about Josef? He was the best. There was no pain in loving my Josef, just joy because he lived to please me both in and out of bed, just as I lived to please him. He loved me without reservation, and that made all the difference. Josef was my rock. When we made love, it was a new adventure each time."

"I used to envy you your fancy mansion, your fancy clothes, your fancy friends. All but Natasha, for she was dear to me as well."

"Alexei loved her, too. So did Dov, for that matter. Alexei and I loved her for her wise spirit, but Dov loved her largely for the fact that she was an influential countess."

"Was he really such a snob?"

"It was just his way. He measured the worth of people by what they could do for him."

"I thought you said he loved you when you were first married."

"In his fashion, I suppose, until it became clear to him that I couldn't bear him children. Then he lost interest. I don't want to be mean-spirited now that he's dead, but it was his downfall, this tendency to measure the worth of everyone he met by what they could do for him.

"He was flattered by the attentions of the nobility. He lent them money and they fawned over the 'Advisor to the Czar'. When he was forced into bankruptcy, he didn't even see it coming, but the signs were there. His eagerness to be accepted blinded him to the truth. Dov made lots of enemies, Sophie. Powerful men always do." Miriam fell silent for a moment.

"Doesn't sound as if he was accepted when he converted, either, so he was still an outcast."

"Aren't we all outcasts? Alexei felt that way, you know, in spite of his royal position. I did, too, much more than Dov did. He actually thought he was a part of Russian society. His bankruptcy wounded him. Feeling outside of life wounds us all, I suppose. The sense of not belonging hurts, but I belong now, Sophie. I belong to my family, to my religion and to my friends, but most important, I belong to myself."

The two sat in reflective silence, taking comfort in the peace. "Do the twins know? About you and Razovsky?"

"No. I'll tell them Dov is dead, but not the other. You'll keep my naughty secret, won't you?"

"Of course." Sophie chuckled.

"What's the joke?"

"Who would have thought it? Sweet, innocent Miriam had a love affair. With a Russian count no less. Was this the same young girl who was terrified of her wedding night, who begged me to tell her beforehand what went on between the sheets?" Their chuckles turned to laughter hearty enough to bring tears to their eyes.

They spent the afternoon reminiscing about their carefree childhood in Shklov. They recollected their friends and relatives. They shared tales about their grandchildren, giving Sophie cause to brag about her three great-grandchildren.

"If you think the grandchildren are wonderful, just wait till you're a great-grandmother. That's even more fun. Thank God my Benjamin lived to see his grandchildren. He loved them so."

"Do you miss him, Sophie?"

"Miss Benjamin? What a question! Of course I miss him."

"Don't be offended. I mean at night. In bed."

"You haven't changed a bit," Sophie teased. "All right. I'll tell you what I miss. I miss his body next to mine. Not the other, for I never cared for it as much as he did, but my feet are always cold nowadays. Even in summer. I miss his warm backside. He had such a wonderful tush. What a way to remember him, eh?"

"Did you love him?"

"Love him?" She thought for a moment. "What would my life have been without him? If that's what you call love, then I loved him. But knowing it now only makes me sad."

"Why? What can possibly make you sad now?"

"In all our years together, I never once told him I loved him."

SEVENTY-ONE

The song of life begins as a lullaby and ends as a dirge. It is a round, a folk-tune sung in ragged circles. Birth. Betrothal. Wedding. Children. Death. It is a triumph of the spirit in spite of the pain.

Miriam Brodsky grew frail with advancing age. In her declining years she cherished the warmth of her family, her sisters and their families, as well as her dear friend Sophie.

Through her flowed the seed of her son Kalman. Through her, five sturdy shoots blossomed. She nurtured her grandchildren as she nurtured the flowers in her garden.

In 1837, she mourned the death of her beloved husband Josef. Yet, barely two months later, she stood tall and proud in synagogue and listened to Joshua read the Hebrew words on the occasion of his *Bar Mitzvah*.

In 1839, it was Leon's turn to become a man according to Judaic law. By then, it was difficult for her to walk the steps of the synagogue where the women prayed, but she managed it without help nevertheless. She sat between her sisters Bela and Bluma. Sophie was there, too. So was her sweet daughter-in-law Anna.

In 1842, when Hershl celebrated his *Bar Mitzvah*, she could no longer manage the synagogue stairs. Instead, her sixteen-year-old grandson Joshua helped his father carry her upstairs to the women's section where she heard Hershl's voice sing out in ritual joy.

In 1845, after Daniel's coming of age at the synagogue, her son and his wife pleaded with her to live with them, but she refused to give up living in her own home. Kalman and Anna arranged instead for a woman to help her with the cooking and the cleaning every day, in spite of her protests.

She wept with her sisters when Malke wrote from Odessa that Samuel was dead. She wept again when her cousin Malke died barely a year later.

In time, she lived to hear the mournful wail of the railroad's whistle as the strange iron shapes rumbled through Bucharest. What was the world coming to

275

she wondered when Kalman explained the alien noises. Cars on wheels rushing crazily across steel tracks? A miracle.

Inexorably, the day came when Miriam had to admit to Kalman that she needed help to visit Josef's grave. First Joshua, then Leon, then Hershl in his turn, drove her there in the family carriage. They waited in the distance on Sunday mornings while she chatted with her Josef, telling him everything that had happened since the previous week's visit.

On one particular Sunday, she could barely wait to tell him news of great importance. Hershl helped her down and held her arm until she sat securely on the stone bench next to Josef's grave.

"Special news today, my love," she began. "Our Rachel is betrothed to a handsome young rabbi. His name is Mordecai Cohen. He's from such a fine family, darling. Aren't you proud? You carried her on your shoulders on her third birthday, before you left me. She's fifteen years old now, and she's getting married next year, in January. It would be nice, don't you think, if I could live long enough to see our only granddaughter married? I'll be eighty-one by then. Is it too much to ask of God? I dearly hope He will allow me this final pleasure.

"I grow wearier day by day, but I'll admit that only to you, my darling. I can hardly walk anymore. I'm such a burden to Kalman and his children. After the wedding, I'll be content if God will let me lay my head down next to yours. It won't be long before we're together again. I'm sure of it, my beloved."

⌘

"What? What did you say? Sorry Rachel. I wasn't paying attention," said Miriam. "Go ahead, dear. Read the last page over again."

"I wasn't reading to you, Grandma. I came here today because you asked to see me. Can you remember what it was you wanted to see me about?" Except for her mother's high forehead and fair skin, Rachel looked very like her grandmother at the same age, for her eyes and her hair were jet black.

"Wanted? What?" Rachel took Miriam's hand and stroked it in answer. Her grandmother's bouts of forgetfulness had grown more and more frequent.

"Oh yes, Rachel! I do remember now. Why didn't you remind me how important it was? Never mind, dear. What I want is to give you something, something very special. A wedding present." Miriam reached down to the hem of her dress. She felt for it with frail, spidery fingers, for she was blind. When she found what she wanted, she drew the thin roll out carefully, working each gem out of its hiding place.

"Give me your hands, Rachel dearest." She felt the young woman's outstretched hands, satisfied that they were open. "There you are. These are for you, a gift from your great-grandfather Chaim, my father. He gave these to me after my mother died. There were five beautiful, two-carat diamonds, but I used

one for Josef and your father and me. It saved our lives a long time ago."
Miriam again lapsed into forgetfulness.

"Grandma? Are you all right?"

"Of course, dear. I was just thinking about my father. Such a wonderful
man. He told me to keep the diamonds with me all the time. My secret
treasure. Now they're your secret, just as they were my secret for so many
years. Weave them through the hem of your petticoat. Here, let me show you
mine. My mother used to do it this way and so have I, every day of my life. Will
you do it, too?"

"Of course, Grandma," Rachel said and squeezed her hand to let her know
she understood, but by that time, Miriam's mind had wandered elsewhere.

SEVENTY-TWO

It is raining on this last day of April in the year 1850. Gentle rain droplets, like gentle tears feed the dormant buds, an awakening, a reminder of the seasons of life. In springtime life stirs, there is new hope—the silent earth prepares to bring forth and to receive.

Kalman's sons, grown tall and sturdy like their father, bear the coffin to the waiting earth. The gaping grave, newly pierced—a pinpoint in time—is ready to receive a Daughter of Zion, one of God's Chosen.

Kalman and his aunts Bela and Bluma, the chief mourners, walk arm in arm behind newly ordained Rabbi Mordecai Cohen. Sophie's daughters support their grieving mother, while the rest of her family follows.

Kalman weeps as he watches his mother return to the sodden earth from whence she came, buried in a grave next to Josef, the man who had taught her to believe in the affirmation of life.

At a signal from his son-in-law, Kalman Zeklinski chants the mourner's liturgy—*kaddish*—for his mother. "*Yisgadal v'yiskadash sh'may rabbo b'olmo...,*" he begins.

Oddly, the Aramaic and Hebrew litany is not a prayer that mourns death. It is instead a prayer in praise of the greatness of God. It asks for redemption. It is a celebration of life.

Miriam's granddaughter Rachel, bride of but a few scant months, bows her head as she listens to her father repeat the ancient words.

Suddenly, the wind turns mean, whipping Rachel's rain-soaked dress around her body. She feels two unfamiliar sensations at once. The first is a twinge, a ripple, a faint shudder of new life growing within her. The second is the weight of a diamond brushing her ankle.

The ritual prayers cease. Young Rachel bends to scoop a handful of earth and drops it on her grandmother's casket. Through blinding tears as soft as rain, she whispers her final farewell.

"*Bon nuit, grandmere*. Rest in peace. And thank you. Thank you for teaching me to speak French. Thank you for teaching me to play piano. Thank you for your love and your wisdom and your wedding gift."

Author's Note

As a result of the partitions of Poland beginning in 1772, the Russian Empire expanded its territories into Poland-Lithuania. Thus there was a large population of Jews who now found themselves under Russian dominion. Prince Potemkin persuaded Czarina Catherine that these new Jewish subjects would prove financially invaluable to the Crown. Potemkin formed a liaison with Shtadlan Joshua Zeitlin who grew enormously wealthy under the patronage of the prince as did his son-in-law, Abraham Peretz (1771-1833). Peretz was a leader in the Jewish community in Russia, and well known in Russian society for his financial prowess. He became advisor to Czar Paul and a member of Czar Alexander's famous committee for drafting Jewish legislation. Peretz lost his shipbuilding and commercial fortune during the Napoleonic invasion of Russia. He divorced Zeitlin's daughter, converted to Christianity and married a German woman.

This is a work of fiction. Except for actual historical events and noted historical figures, the characters are all my own invention

Pearl

Bibliography

Arendt, Hannah, *Antisemitism*, Part One of *The Origins of Totalitarianism*, Harcourt Brace Jovanovich, New York, 1951

Cronin, Vincent, *Catherine Empress of All the Russias*, An Intimate Biography, William Morrow and Company, Inc. 1978

Custine, Astolphe, Marquis de 1790-1857, *Empire of the Czar*, A journey through Eternal Russia, Doubleday, New York, 1989

De Maderiaga, Isabel, *Russia in the Age of Catherine the Great*, Yale University Press, New Haven and London, 1981

Donin, Rabbi Hayim Halevy, *To Be A Jew*, A Guide to Jewish Observance in Contemporary Life, Basic Books, New York, 1972

Durant, Will and Ariel, *The Age of Napoleon:* A history of European Civilization from 1789 to 1815, Part XI, The Story of Civilization, Simon and Schuster, 1975

Hazlip, Joan, *Catherine The Great:* A biography. G. P. Putnam's Sons, New York, 1977

Johnson, Paul, *A History of the Jews,* Harper & Row, New York, 1987

Massie, Suzanne, *Land of the Firebird,* The Beauty of Old Russia, Simon and Schuster, New York, 1980

Roth, Cecil. Editor, *Encyclopedia Judaica,* Volumes 1-16, Keter Publishing House Ltd. Jerusalem, Israel, 1972

Troyat, Henry, *Alexander of Russia,* (translated by Joan Pinkham) E. P. Dutton, Inc. New York 1982

Glossary

Afikomen—The middle *matzoh* of three is broken in half to be shared by everyone at the end of the meal. Today, the *afikomen* is hidden in many homes, so the children may seek it and receive a gift for their labors.

Bar Mitzvah—When a boy reaches the age of thirteen, he becomes a man in Judaic law. He is a *Bar Mitzvah* and is called upon to read from the *Torah*.

Blini—A Russian crepe filled with cook's choice of cheese, meat, jellies, etc. The Yiddish term for this delicacy is *blintz*.

Borscht—Beet soup

Boruch ato Adonai elohenu melech ha-olom Asher kidhsonu b'mitzvosov v'tzivonu l'hadlik ner shel shabbos—(prayer) Blessed art Thou, Lord our God, King of the universe who has sanctified us with His commandments and commanded us to kindle the Sabbath lights

Challah—Bread eaten at Friday evening meals by Jews

Dacha—Russian term for country house or summer cottage

Day-Enu—Song sung at the *seder*

Droshki—Russian term for a small open carriage

Get—A Jewish divorce

Gubernia—Province governed by a gubernator

Gymnasia—Russian term for school

Had Gadya—**Song sung at the** *seder*

Hametz—**Leavened bread, forbidden in Jewish homes for the week of Passover**

Haskelah—**Jewish enlightenment movement in the eighteenth century**

Hassidism—**Messianic movement in the eighteenth century**

Kaddish—**Aramaic prayer for the dead**

Kahal—**Eastern European Jewish community**

Kasha—**Groats**

Kashruth—**Jewish dietary laws**

Kol Nidre—**Asks God to forgive all transgressions**

L'chayim—**Hebrew toast to life**

L'shana Tova—**New Year's felicitations greeting given during Jewish New Year**

Matzoh—**Unleavened bread eaten during the week of Passover**

Mikveh—**Jewish rite of purification**

Muzhiks—**Russian peasants**

Nazdrov'ya—**Russian toast to life**

Parshchivi Zhid—**Russian for 'dirty Jew'**

Passover—**Celebrates deliverance of Jews from Egyptian bondage**

Pogrom—**Russian word meaning attack**

Rebbitzen—**Rabbi's wife**

Rosh Hashonah—**Hebrew term for New Year**

Sanhedrin—**Hebrew for court of justice. Napoleonic *Sanhedrin* examined secularism**

Seder—**Jewish ritual meal on the first two nights of Passover**

Shabbos—**A holy day meant for prayer and rest**

Shalom—**Hebrew greeting**

Shiva—**Seven days of mourning**

Shofar—**Ram's horn, blown during** *Rosh Hashonah* **and** *Yom Kippur*

Shtadlan—**Highly respected representative of the Jewish community**

Shtetl—**Yiddish word for small community**

Shtremel—**Wide-brimmed fur hat**

Torah—**Holy vessel containing tenets of Judaic law**

Tsarskoye-Selo—**Catherine's summer palace**

Tsitsis—**prayer vest with fringes**

Ukase—**Russian decree**

Verst—**One *verst*=0.663 miles**

Voivod—**Rumanian term for prince**

Yom Kippur—**Day of Atonement during which Jews fast**

Photo of Pearl Wolf by Duncan Ball

SONG OF MIRIAM is Pearl Wolf's first historical novel. She is also the author of three children's books published when she taught in the New York City Public School system. She divides her time between New York City and Southampton. Her family, especially her children and her fantastic grandchildren, are among her greatest pleasures.

She was elected to the YWCA's Academy of Women Achievers and honored as Woman of the Year by the New York City Coalition of Labor Union Women. Pearl is past president of Sisters in Crime NY/Tri-State Chapter, as well as a Mystery Writers of America mentor to new writers. When she finds the time, she is an avid bridge player. Currently, she is working on her next historical novel.

She lectures nationally on Women in the Eighteenth Century, and The Politics of Anti-Semitism in the Eighteenth Century, historical topics related to her novel, SONG OF MIRIAM. Visit her website: www.pearlwolf.com. She can be reached through her publisher: Hilliard & Harris or email her at pearl.wolf@verizon.net.

Printed in the United States
22361LVS00007B/27